MARVEL-VERSE
CAPTAIN AME

CAPTAIN AMERICA #255

WRITER: **ROGER STERN**
ARTIST: **JOHN BYRNE**
COLORIST: **BOB SHAREN**
LETTERER: **JOE ROSEN**
EDITOR: **JIM SALICRUP**
SPECIAL THANKS TO JOSEF RUBINSTEIN

THE FIGHTING AVENGER #1

WRITER: **BRIAN CLEVINGER**
ARTIST/COLORIST: **GURIHIRU**
LETTERER: **TOM ORZECHOWSKI**
COVER ART: **BARRY KITSON,
DAVE McCAIG & GURIHIRU**
EDITORS: **NATHAN COSBY,
MICHAEL HORWITZ & JOHN DENNING**

CAPTAIN AMERICA #100

WRITER: **STAN LEE**
PENCILER: **JACK KIRBY**
INKER: **SYD SHORES**
LETTERER: **ART SIMEK**
EDITOR: **STAN LEE**

MARVEL TEAM-UP #13

WRITER: **LEN WEIN**
PENCILER: **GIL KANE**
INKER: **FRANK GIACOIA**
COLORIST: **GLYNIS WEIN**
LETTERER: **JUNE BRAVERMAN**
EDITOR: **ROY THOMAS**

CAPTAIN AMERICA CREATED BY JOE SIMON & JACK KIRBY

COLLECTION EDITOR: **JENNIFER GRÜNWALD**
ASSISTANT MANAGING EDITOR: **MAIA LOY** ASSISTANT MANAGING EDITOR: **LISA MONTALBANO**
EDITOR, SPECIAL PROJECTS: **MARK D. BEAZLEY** VP PRODUCTION & SPECIAL PROJECTS: **JEFF YOUNGQUIST**
RESEARCH: **JESS HARROLD & JEPH YORK** BOOK DESIGNERS: **SALENA MAHINA** with **JAY BOWEN**

SVP PRINT, SALES & MARKETING: **DAVID GABRIEL** EDITOR IN CHIEF: **C.B. CEBULSKI**

MARVEL-VERSE: CAPTAIN AMERICA. Contains material originally published in magazine form as CAPTAIN AMERICA (1968) #100 and #255, CAPTAIN AMERICA: FIGHTING AVENGER (2011) #1, and MARVEL TEAM-UP (1972) #13. First printing 2020. ISBN 978-1-302-92513-0. Published by MARVEL WORLDWIDE, INC., a subsidiary of MARVEL ENTERTAINMENT, LLC. OFFICE OF PUBLICATION: 1290 Avenue of the Americas, New York, NY 10104. © 2020 MARVEL No similarity between any of the names, characters, persons, and/or institutions in this magazine with those of any living or dead person or institution is intended, and any such similarity which may exist is purely coincidental. **Printed in Canada.** KEVIN FEIGE, Chief Creative Officer; DAN BUCKLEY, President, Marvel Entertainment; JOHN NEE, Publisher; JOE QUESADA, EVP & Creative Director; TOM BREVOORT, SVP of Publishing; DAVID BOGART, Associate Publisher & SVP of Talent Affairs; Publishing & Partnership; DAVID GABRIEL, VP of Print & Digital Publishing; JEFF YOUNGQUIST, VP of Production & Special Projects; DAN CARR, Executive Director of Publishing Technology; ALEX MORALES, Director of Publishing Operations; DAN EDINGTON, Managing Editor; SUSAN CRESPI, Production Manager; STAN LEE, Chairman Emeritus. For information regarding advertising in Marvel Comics or on Marvel.com, please contact Vit DeBellis, Custom Solutions & Integrated Advertising Manager, at vdebellis@marvel.com. For Marvel subscription inquiries, please call 888-511-5480. **Manufactured between 6/5/2020 and 7/13/2020 by SOLISCO PRINTERS, SCOTT, QC, CANADA.**

10 9 8 7 6 5 4 3 2 1

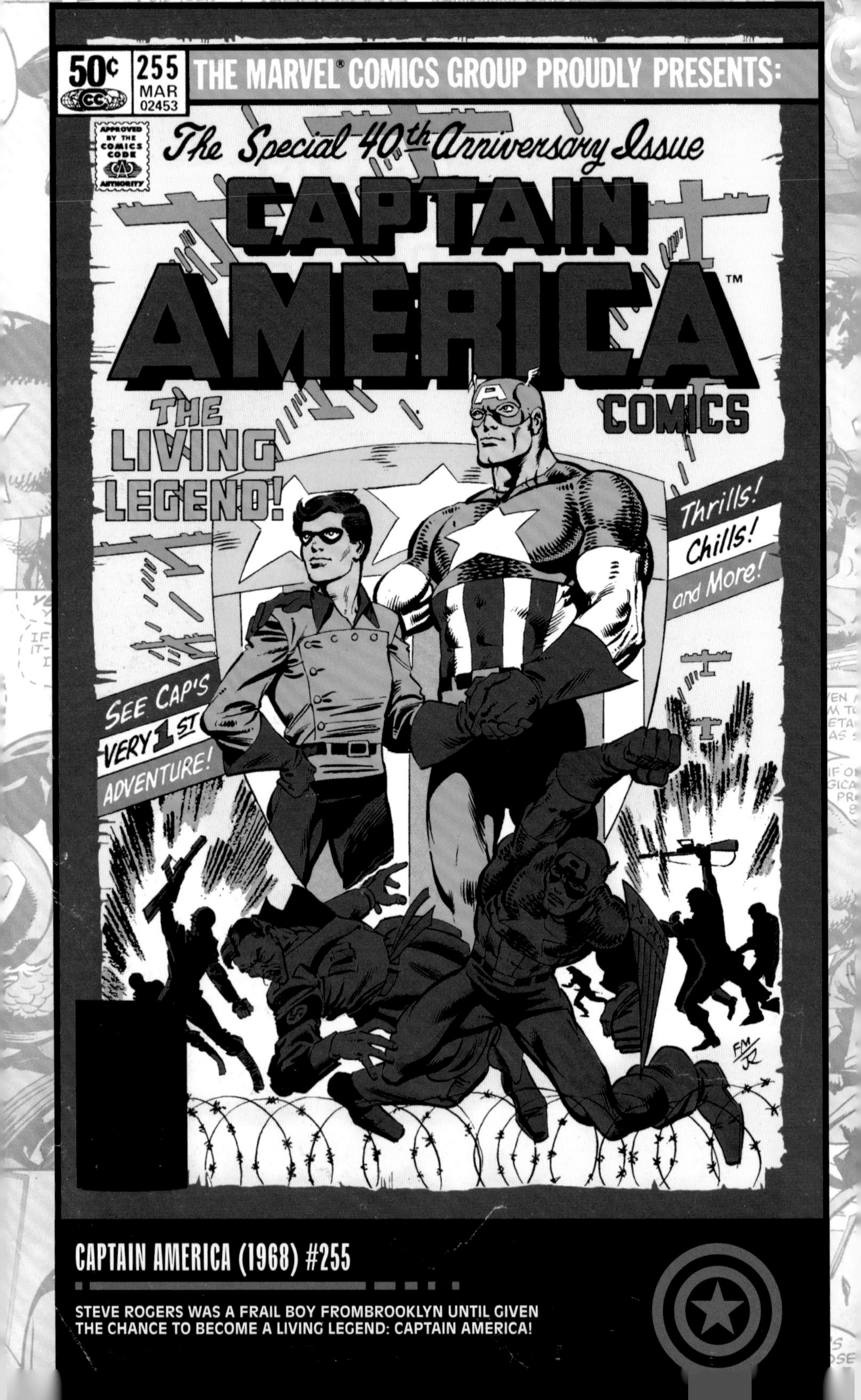

50¢
255
MAR
02453
THE MARVEL® COMICS GROUP PROUDLY PRESENTS:
APPROVED BY THE COMICS CODE AUTHORITY
The Special 40th Anniversary Issue
CAPTAIN AMERICA™ COMICS
THE LIVING LEGEND!
Thrills! Chills! and More!
SEE CAP'S VERY 1ST ADVENTURE!

CAPTAIN AMERICA (1968) #255

STEVE ROGERS WAS A FRAIL BOY FROMBROOKLYN UNTIL GIVEN THE CHANCE TO BECOME A LIVING LEGEND: CAPTAIN AMERICA!

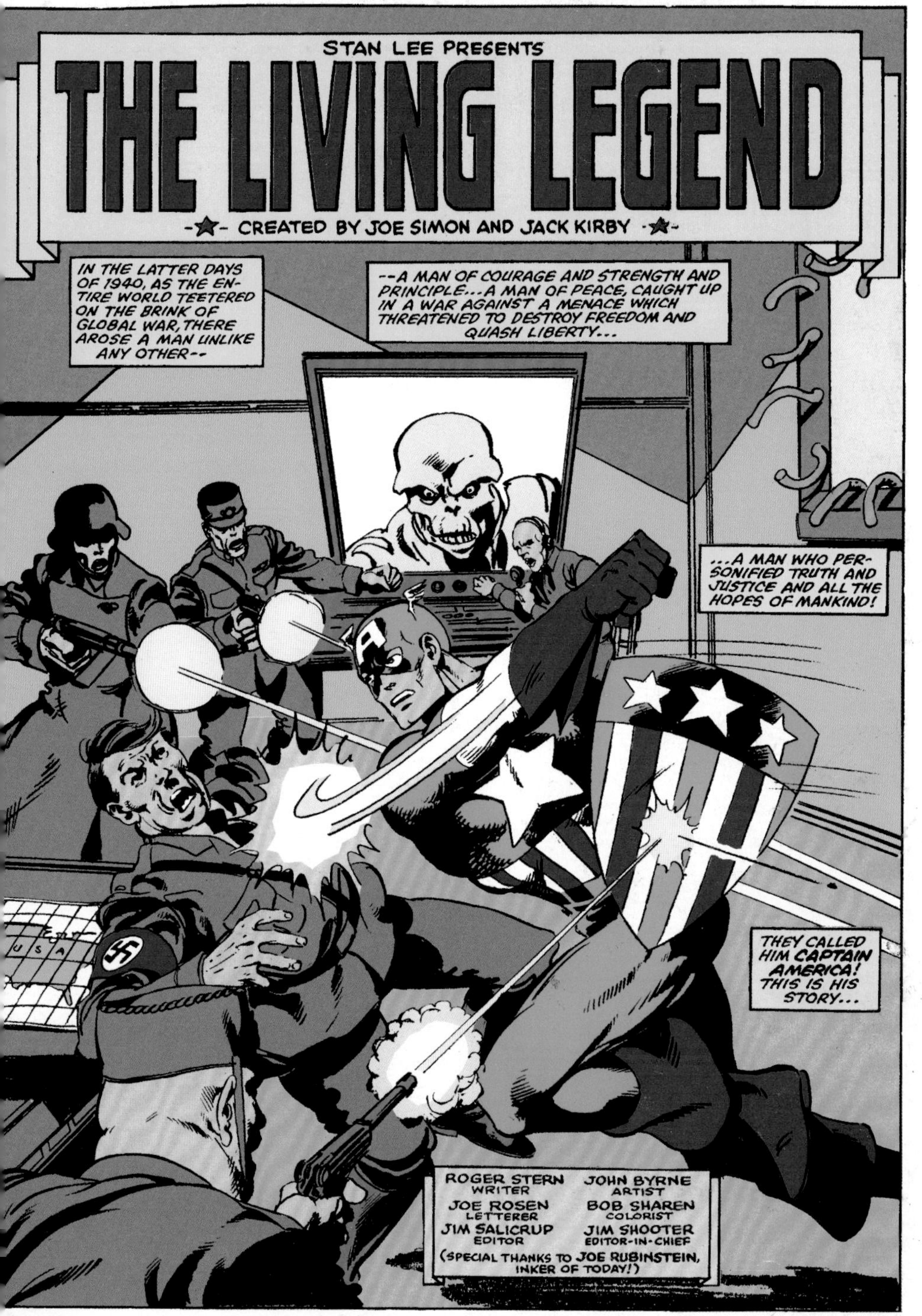
STAN LEE PRESENTS
THE LIVING LEGEND
CREATED BY JOE SIMON AND JACK KIRBY
IN THE LATTER DAYS OF 1940, AS THE ENTIRE WORLD TEETERED ON THE BRINK OF GLOBAL WAR, THERE AROSE A MAN UNLIKE ANY OTHER--
--A MAN OF COURAGE AND STRENGTH AND PRINCIPLE... A MAN OF PEACE, CAUGHT UP IN A WAR AGAINST A MENACE WHICH THREATENED TO DESTROY FREEDOM AND QUASH LIBERTY...
...A MAN WHO PERSONIFIED TRUTH AND JUSTICE AND ALL THE HOPES OF MANKIND!
THEY CALLED HIM CAPTAIN AMERICA! THIS IS HIS STORY...
U S A
ROGER STERN WRITER
JOHN BYRNE ARTIST
JOE ROSEN LETTERER
BOB SHAREN COLORIST
JIM SALICRUP EDITOR
JIM SHOOTER EDITOR-IN-CHIEF
(SPECIAL THANKS TO JOE RUBINSTEIN, INKER OF TODAY!)

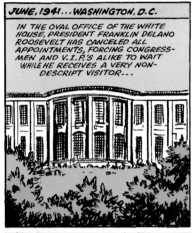

JUNE, 1941...WASHINGTON, D.C.

IN THE OVAL OFFICE OF THE WHITE HOUSE, PRESIDENT FRANKLIN DELANO ROOSEVELT HAS CANCELED ALL APPOINTMENTS, FORCING CONGRESSMEN AND V.I.P.'S ALIKE TO WAIT WHILE HE RECEIVES A VERY NON-DESCRIPT VISITOR...

...A YOUNG COURIER FROM G-2, THE INTELLIGENCE ARM OF THE DEPARTMENT OF THE ARMY.

WELL, SON, LET'S GET ON WITH IT! I HAVE THE EDITOR OF *THE WASHINGTON POST* COOLING HIS HEELS OUTSIDE-- AND I'M SURE I'LL HEAR ABOUT IT IN TOMORROW'S HEADLINES!

YES, SIR... I'M SORRY, SIR!

OH, THAT'S ALL RIGHT! I'VE DEVELOPED A FAIRLY THICK SKIN AS FAR AS BAD PRESS IS CONCERNED!

THIS IS IT?

YES, SIR. AS PER YOUR REQUEST, THIS IS THE FULL AND COMPLETE DOSSIER ON *OPERATION: REBIRTH!*

YOU KNOW, SON, SOMETIMES I DESPAIR. THIS WAS ONE OF THE MOST AMBITIOUS TOP-SECRET PROJECTS IN THE NATION'S HISTORY...

OPERATION: REBIRTH

...AND IT CAME TO SUCH A TRAGIC END! BUT, I WANTED TO LEARN MORE ABOUT *REBIRTH'S* TEST SUBJECT... THIS YOUNG LAD, STEVE ROGERS. HMM... I SEE HERE--

"-- THAT HE GREW UP ON THE LOWER EAST SIDE OF NEW YORK CITY! EVIDENTLY, MUCH OF HIS YOUTH WAS SPENT--

OPERATION: REBIRTH

"--TRYING TO HELP HIS FAMILY MAKE ENDS MEET DURING THE DEPTHS OF THE DEPRESSION. OH...I SEE...

"...HIS FATHER DIED WHEN HE WAS STILL A CHILD, AND HIS MOTHER HAD TO STRUGGLE JUST TO KEEP HER SON AND HERSELF FED.

"STILL, DESPITE THEIR DEPRIVATION, STEVE KEPT UP WITH HIS SCHOOLING, AND BECAME A VORACIOUS READER...*ESPECIALLY OF FANTASY!*

"GIVEN THE STATE OF HIS REALITY, I CAN WELL UNDERSTAND WHY!'"

"AH, IT SEEMS THAT THE BOY ALSO HAD A NATURAL TALENT FOR ART. BUT HE KEPT HIS LOVE OF ART, AND OF BOOKS, A SECRET TO AVOID TAUNTS AND BEATINGS AT THE HANDS OF HIS PEERS.

AS THE DEPRESSION WORE ON, TIMES BECAME INCREASINGLY DIFFICULT FOR THE ROGERS' HOUSEHOLD. SARAH ROGERS TOOK IN LAUNDRY...AND TAXED HERSELF TO THE LIMIT TO PROVIDE FOR HER SON.

"BUT TIME AND HARDSHIP EVENTUALLY TOOK ITS TOLL, AND AS STEVEN ENTERED HIS LATE TEENS, HIS MOTHER PASSED ON--

"--A VICTIM OF PNEUMONIA.

"OUT ON HIS OWN, YOUNG ROGERS MANAGED TO FIND A CHEAP BOARDING HOUSE AND TOOK A JOB AS A DELIVERY BOY. IT WAS NOT AN EASY LIFE, NOR A VERY GOOD ONE...

"...BUT SOMEHOW, HE SURVIVED.

AND THEN, ONE DAY, WHILE TRYING TO ESCAPE INTO THE FANTASY WORLD OF THE MOVIES, STEVE ROGERS ENCOUNTERED AN EVEN HARSHER REALITY--

"--IN NEWSREEL FOOTAGE OF THE NAZI WAR MACHINE IN ITS RELENTLESS MARCH ACROSS A WAR-TORN EUROPE!"

THE SEA HAWK
ERROL FLYNN

THOSE NEWSREELS...IT'S AWFUL...*AWFUL!* IT'S AS IF HALF THE WORLD HAS GONE MAD!

IF THE NAZIS AREN'T STOPPED SOON, THERE WON'T BE A FREE MAN LEFT ALIVE ANYWHERE! I HAVE TO DO SOMETHING...I *HAVE* TO!

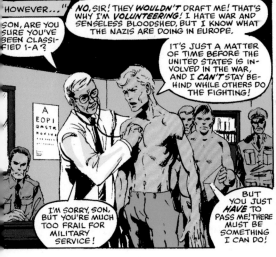

"HOWEVER..."

SON, ARE YOU SURE YOU'VE BEEN CLASSIFIED 1-A?

NO, SIR! THEY *WOULDN'T* DRAFT ME! THAT'S WHY I'M *VOLUNTEERING!* I HATE WAR AND SENSELESS BLOODSHED, BUT I KNOW WHAT THE NAZIS ARE DOING IN EUROPE.

IT'S JUST A MATTER OF TIME BEFORE THE UNITED STATES IS INVOLVED IN THE WAR, AND I *CAN'T* STAY BEHIND WHILE OTHERS DO THE FIGHTING!

I'M SORRY, SON, BUT YOU'RE MUCH TOO FRAIL FOR MILITARY SERVICE!

BUT YOU JUST *HAVE* TO PASS ME! THERE MUST BE SOMETHING I CAN DO!

I COULDN'T HELP OVERHEARING, SON, I'M GENERAL PHILLIPS...ARE YOU REALLY SERIOUS ABOUT WANTING TO TAKE PART IN THE BIG PICTURE?

I *AM*, SIR! I'LL DO ANYTHING--*ANYTHING!*

"IT MUST HAVE BEEN KISMET! IN STEVE ROGERS, GENERAL PHILLIPS HAD FOUND THE IDEAL TEST SUBJECT FOR OPERATION: REBIRTH.

"WITHIN MINUTES, ROGERS WAS ON A PLANE, SPEEDING TOWARDS WASHINGTON. AND, AS NIGHT FELL, HE WAS TAKEN TO A SMALL CURIO SHOP ON A LITTLE-KNOWN CAPITAL SIDE STREET.

ANTIQUES and COLLECTABLES

"I CAN WELL IMAGINE THE SURPRISE ROGERS FELT UPON ENTERING THAT MOLDERING OLD STOREFRONT..."

AGENTS L-7 AND X-9 REPORTING, AGENT R! THE PASSWORD IS "EAGLE."

WE HAVE "THE VISITOR" WITH US.

HALT! IDENTIFY YOURSELVES OR DIE!

ENTER AND LOCK THE DOOR BEHIND YOU!

I-I DON'T GET IT! HOW CAN SUCH AN IMPORTANT PROJECT BE HOUSED IN A SMALL SHOP LIKE THIS? NOTHING I'VE SEEN SO FAR SEEMS TO MAKE SENSE!

IN WORK SUCH AS OURS, THINGS ARE SELDOM WHAT THEY SEEM.

WHY...YOU... YOU'RE NOT--! THAT IS...I THOUGHT--!

FORGIVE THE THEATRICS. I ASSURE YOU, THEY ARE QUITE NECESSARY.

"IT MUST HAVE BEEN A NIGHT FULL OF SURPRISES FOR OUR YOUNG 'VISITOR.' AS AGENT R STOOD GUARD, ROGERS WAS CONDUCTED UP A NARROW FLIGHT OF STAIRS, THROUGH A HIDDEN DOORWAY, AND INTO ONE OF THE MOST ADVANCED BIOCHEMICAL LABORATORIES IN THE FREE WORLD."

IT...IT'S AMAZING! LIKE SOMETHING OUT OF H.G. WELLS!

GET USED TO IT, ROGERS. YOU'RE GOING TO BE SPENDING SOME TIME HERE.

"AND THEN..."

WELCOME TO OPERATION: REBIRTH, MR. ROGERS. I'M DR. ANDERSON, THE DIRECTOR OF PROJECTS... AND THIS IS OUR HEAD SCIENTIST, PROFESSOR REINSTEIN!

REINSTEIN? WHY, THAT'S DR. ABRAHAM ERSKINE, THE FAMOUS BIOCHEMIST!

BUT I THOUGHT HE'D DIED LAST SPRING IN AN AUTO CRASH!

THAT IS WHAT WE WANTED THE WORLD TO BELIEVE, MY BOY!

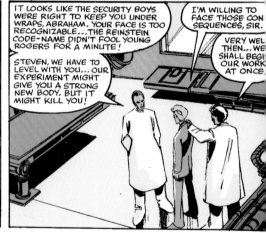

IT LOOKS LIKE THE SECURITY BOYS WERE RIGHT TO KEEP YOU UNDER WRAPS, ABRAHAM. YOUR FACE IS TOO RECOGNIZABLE...THE REINSTEIN CODE-NAME DIDN'T FOOL YOUNG ROGERS FOR A MINUTE!

STEVEN, WE HAVE TO LEVEL WITH YOU... OUR EXPERIMENT MIGHT GIVE YOU A STRONG NEW BODY. BUT IT MIGHT KILL YOU!

I'M WILLING TO FACE THOSE CONSEQUENCES, SIR.

VERY WELL THEN... WE SHALL BEGIN OUR WORK AT ONCE.

"OVER THE NEXT FEW WEEKS, ROGERS WAS PUT THROUGH A GRUELING SERIES OF TESTS TO DETERMINE THE EXACT LIMITS OF HIS PHYSICAL ABILITIES-- WHILE DR. ERSKINE WORKED ON HIS SECRET TISSUE-BUILDING SERUM!"

"AND THEN, THAT DAY ARRIVED WHEN ANDERSON BURST IN ON THE GENERAL AND MYSELF WITH THE NEWS..."

THE CHEMICAL IS PERFECTED, GENTLEMEN-- AND I SUGGEST THAT WE PROCEED AT ONCE!

THEN THE TIME HAS COME AT LAST!

THERE IS NOTHING MORE TO BE SAID. I WISH YOU ALL GOD-SPEED!

"CHANGING TO CIVILIAN CLOTHING, GENERAL PHILLIPS AND UNDER-SECRETARY SIMMS WERE CONDUCTED TO THE HIDDEN LABORATORY BY DR. ANDERSON HIMSELF.

"AND WHEN THEY ARRIVED, A MAN WHOSE CREDENTIALS IDENTIFIED HIM AS SPECIAL AGENT CLEMSON WAS ALREADY THERE...

"...WAITING!"

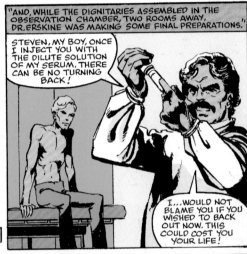

"AND, WHILE THE DIGNITARIES ASSEMBLED IN THE OBSERVATION CHAMBER, TWO ROOMS AWAY, DR. ERSKINE WAS MAKING SOME FINAL PREPARATIONS."

STEVEN, MY BOY, ONCE I INJECT YOU WITH THE DILUTE SOLUTION OF MY SERUM, THERE CAN BE NO TURNING BACK!

I...WOULD NOT BLAME YOU IF YOU WISHED TO BACK OUT NOW. THIS COULD COST YOU YOUR LIFE!

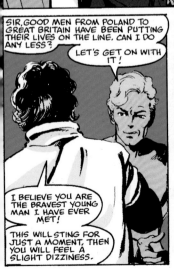

SIR, GOOD MEN FROM POLAND TO GREAT BRITAIN HAVE BEEN PUTTING THEIR LIVES ON THE LINE. CAN I DO ANY LESS?

LET'S GET ON WITH IT!

I BELIEVE YOU ARE THE BRAVEST YOUNG MAN I HAVE EVER MET!

THIS WILL STING FOR JUST A MOMENT, THEN YOU WILL FEEL A SLIGHT DIZZINESS.

"THEN, ERSKINE LED HIS SUBJECT INTO THE MAIN LABORATORY..."

GENTLEMEN, THIS DISTINGUISHED YOUNG VOLUNTEER HAS ALREADY BEEN INJECTED WITH MY SECRET SERUM--

--HE IS NOW READY TO TAKE THE ORAL FORM OF THE COMPOUND!

YOU MUST DRINK THIS QUICKLY, BEFORE THE CHEMICALS LOSE THEIR POTENCY. GOOD LUCK, MY BOY!

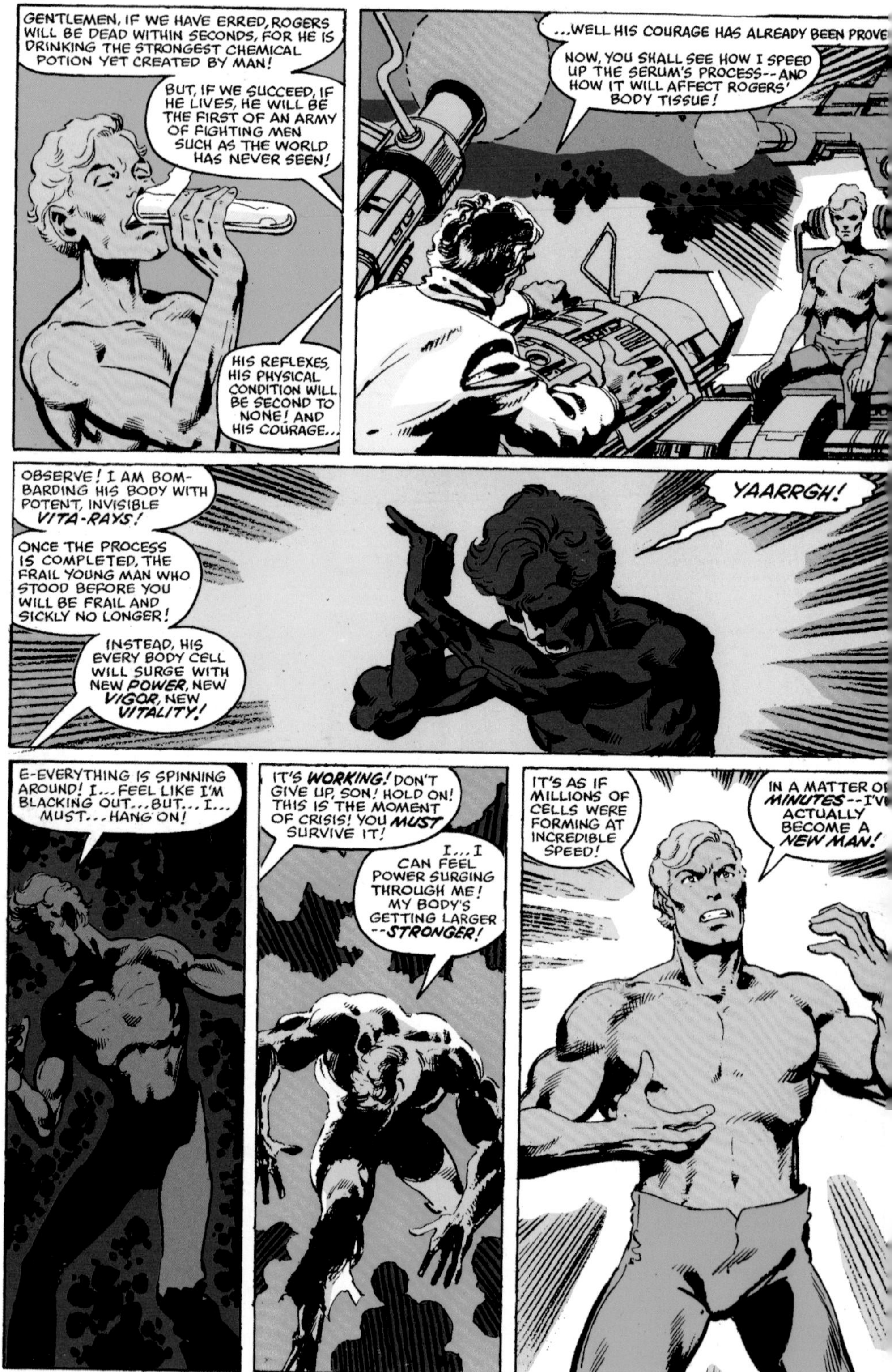

GENTLEMEN, IF WE HAVE ERRED, ROGERS WILL BE DEAD WITHIN SECONDS, FOR HE IS DRINKING THE STRONGEST CHEMICAL POTION YET CREATED BY MAN!
BUT, IF WE SUCCEED, IF HE LIVES, HE WILL BE THE FIRST OF AN ARMY OF FIGHTING MEN SUCH AS THE WORLD HAS NEVER SEEN!
HIS REFLEXES, HIS PHYSICAL CONDITION WILL BE SECOND TO NONE! AND HIS COURAGE...
...WELL HIS COURAGE HAS ALREADY BEEN PROVE
NOW, YOU SHALL SEE HOW I SPEED UP THE SERUM'S PROCESS--AND HOW IT WILL AFFECT ROGERS' BODY TISSUE!
OBSERVE! I AM BOMBARDING HIS BODY WITH POTENT, INVISIBLE VITA-RAYS!
ONCE THE PROCESS IS COMPLETED, THE FRAIL YOUNG MAN WHO STOOD BEFORE YOU WILL BE FRAIL AND SICKLY NO LONGER!
INSTEAD, HIS EVERY BODY CELL WILL SURGE WITH NEW POWER, NEW VIGOR, NEW VITALITY!
YAARRGH!
E-EVERYTHING IS SPINNING AROUND! I... FEEL LIKE I'M BLACKING OUT... BUT... I... MUST... HANG ON!
IT'S WORKING! DON'T GIVE UP, SON! HOLD ON! THIS IS THE MOMENT OF CRISIS! YOU MUST SURVIVE IT!
I... I CAN FEEL POWER SURGING THROUGH ME! MY BODY'S GETTING LARGER --STRONGER!
IT'S AS IF MILLIONS OF CELLS WERE FORMING AT INCREDIBLE SPEED!
IN A MATTER OF MINUTES--I'VE ACTUALLY BECOME A NEW MAN!

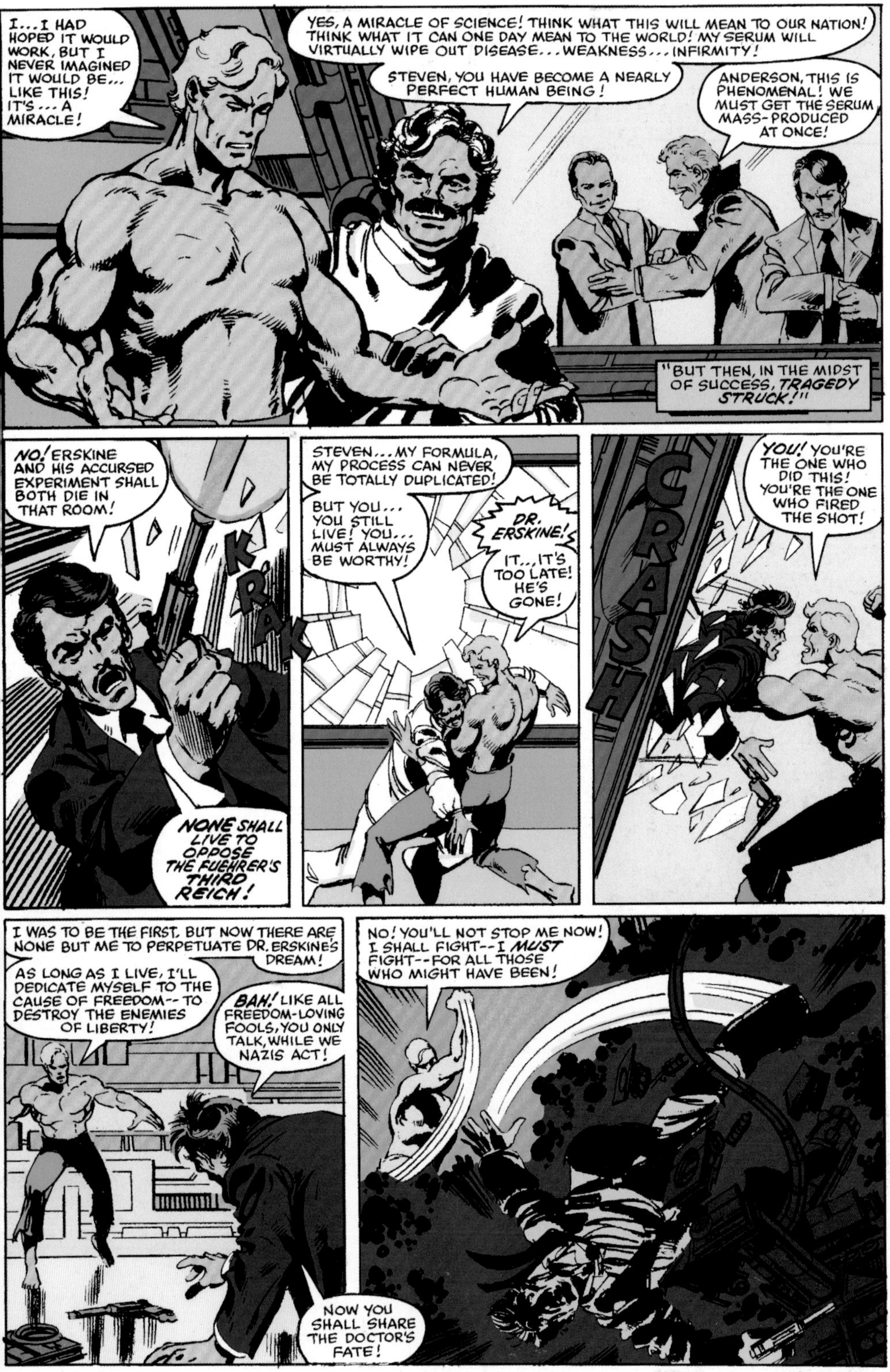
I... I HAD HOPED IT WOULD WORK, BUT I NEVER IMAGINED IT WOULD BE... LIKE THIS! IT'S... A MIRACLE!
YES, A MIRACLE OF SCIENCE! THINK WHAT THIS WILL MEAN TO OUR NATION! THINK WHAT IT CAN ONE DAY MEAN TO THE WORLD! MY SERUM WILL VIRTUALLY WIPE OUT DISEASE... WEAKNESS... INFIRMITY!
STEVEN, YOU HAVE BECOME A NEARLY PERFECT HUMAN BEING!
ANDERSON, THIS IS PHENOMENAL! WE MUST GET THE SERUM MASS-PRODUCED AT ONCE!
"BUT THEN, IN THE MIDST OF SUCCESS, TRAGEDY STRUCK!"
NO! ERSKINE AND HIS ACCURSED EXPERIMENT SHALL BOTH DIE IN THAT ROOM!
KRAK
NONE SHALL LIVE TO OPPOSE THE FUEHRER'S THIRD REICH!
STEVEN... MY FORMULA, MY PROCESS CAN NEVER BE TOTALLY DUPLICATED!
BUT YOU... YOU STILL LIVE! YOU... MUST ALWAYS BE WORTHY!
DR. ERSKINE!
IT... IT'S TOO LATE! HE'S GONE!
CRASH
YOU! YOU'RE THE ONE WHO DID THIS! YOU'RE THE ONE WHO FIRED THE SHOT!
I WAS TO BE THE FIRST, BUT NOW THERE ARE NONE BUT ME TO PERPETUATE DR. ERSKINE'S DREAM!
AS LONG AS I LIVE, I'LL DEDICATE MYSELF TO THE CAUSE OF FREEDOM-- TO DESTROY THE ENEMIES OF LIBERTY!
BAH! LIKE ALL FREEDOM-LOVING FOOLS, YOU ONLY TALK, WHILE WE NAZIS ACT!
NOW YOU SHALL SHARE THE DOCTOR'S FATE!
NO! YOU'LL NOT STOP ME NOW! I SHALL FIGHT-- I MUST FIGHT-- FOR ALL THOSE WHO MIGHT HAVE BEEN!

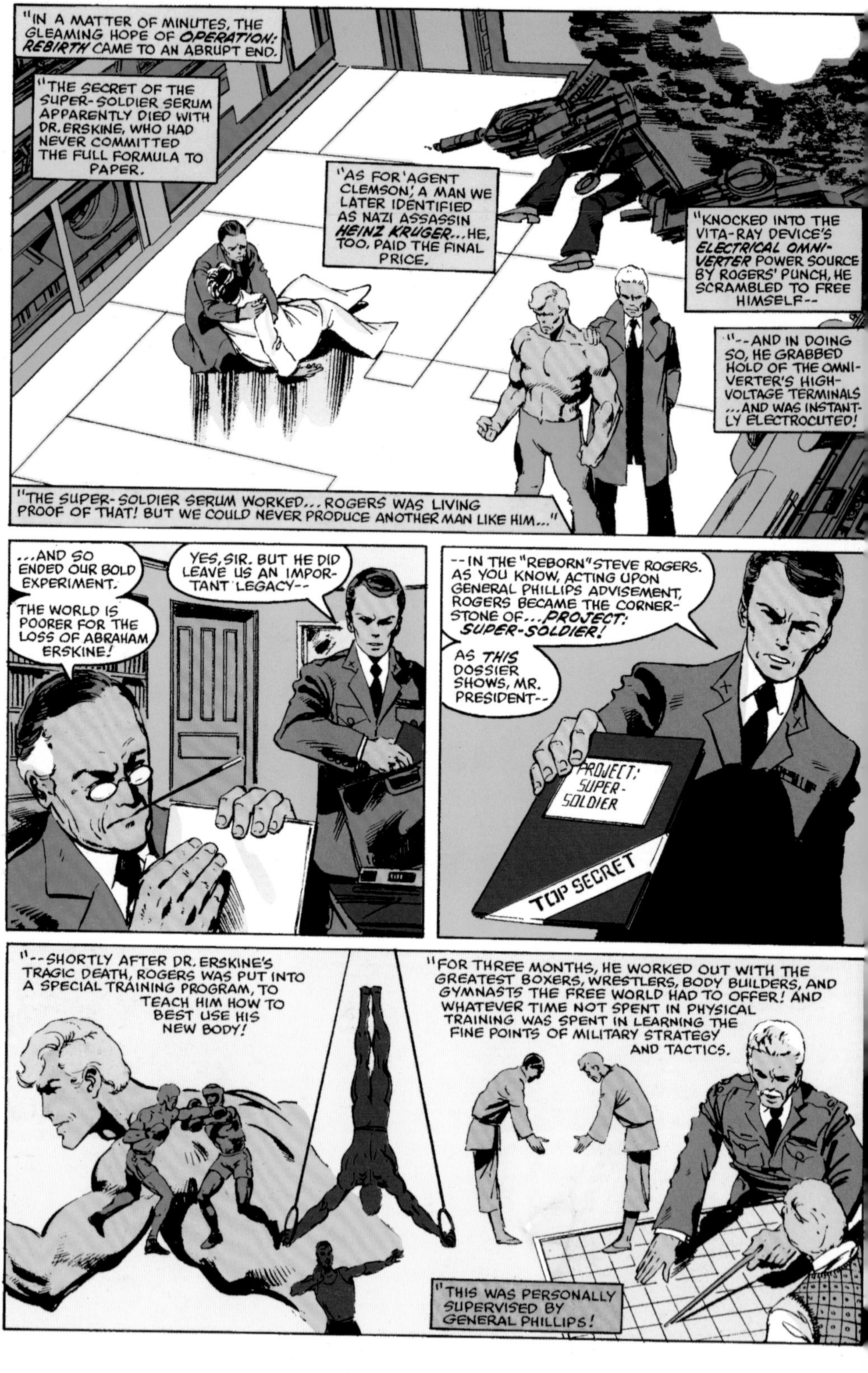
"IN A MATTER OF MINUTES, THE GLEAMING HOPE OF OPERATION: REBIRTH CAME TO AN ABRUPT END.
"THE SECRET OF THE SUPER-SOLDIER SERUM APPARENTLY DIED WITH DR. ERSKINE, WHO HAD NEVER COMMITTED THE FULL FORMULA TO PAPER.
"AS FOR 'AGENT CLEMSON,' A MAN WE LATER IDENTIFIED AS NAZI ASSASSIN HEINZ KRUGER... HE, TOO, PAID THE FINAL PRICE.
"KNOCKED INTO THE VITA-RAY DEVICE'S ELECTRICAL OMNIVERTER POWER SOURCE BY ROGERS' PUNCH, HE SCRAMBLED TO FREE HIMSELF--
"--AND IN DOING SO, HE GRABBED HOLD OF THE OMNIVERTER'S HIGH-VOLTAGE TERMINALS ...AND WAS INSTANTLY ELECTROCUTED!
"THE SUPER-SOLDIER SERUM WORKED... ROGERS WAS LIVING PROOF OF THAT! BUT WE COULD NEVER PRODUCE ANOTHER MAN LIKE HIM..."
...AND SO ENDED OUR BOLD EXPERIMENT.
THE WORLD IS POORER FOR THE LOSS OF ABRAHAM ERSKINE!
YES, SIR. BUT HE DID LEAVE US AN IMPORTANT LEGACY--
--IN THE "REBORN" STEVE ROGERS. AS YOU KNOW, ACTING UPON GENERAL PHILLIPS ADVISEMENT, ROGERS BECAME THE CORNERSTONE OF... PROJECT: SUPER-SOLDIER!
AS THIS DOSSIER SHOWS, MR. PRESIDENT--
PROJECT: SUPER-SOLDIER
TOP SECRET
"--SHORTLY AFTER DR. ERSKINE'S TRAGIC DEATH, ROGERS WAS PUT INTO A SPECIAL TRAINING PROGRAM, TO TEACH HIM HOW TO BEST USE HIS NEW BODY!
"FOR THREE MONTHS, HE WORKED OUT WITH THE GREATEST BOXERS, WRESTLERS, BODY BUILDERS, AND GYMNASTS THE FREE WORLD HAD TO OFFER! AND WHATEVER TIME NOT SPENT IN PHYSICAL TRAINING WAS SPENT IN LEARNING THE FINE POINTS OF MILITARY STRATEGY AND TACTICS.
"THIS WAS PERSONALLY SUPERVISED BY GENERAL PHILLIPS!

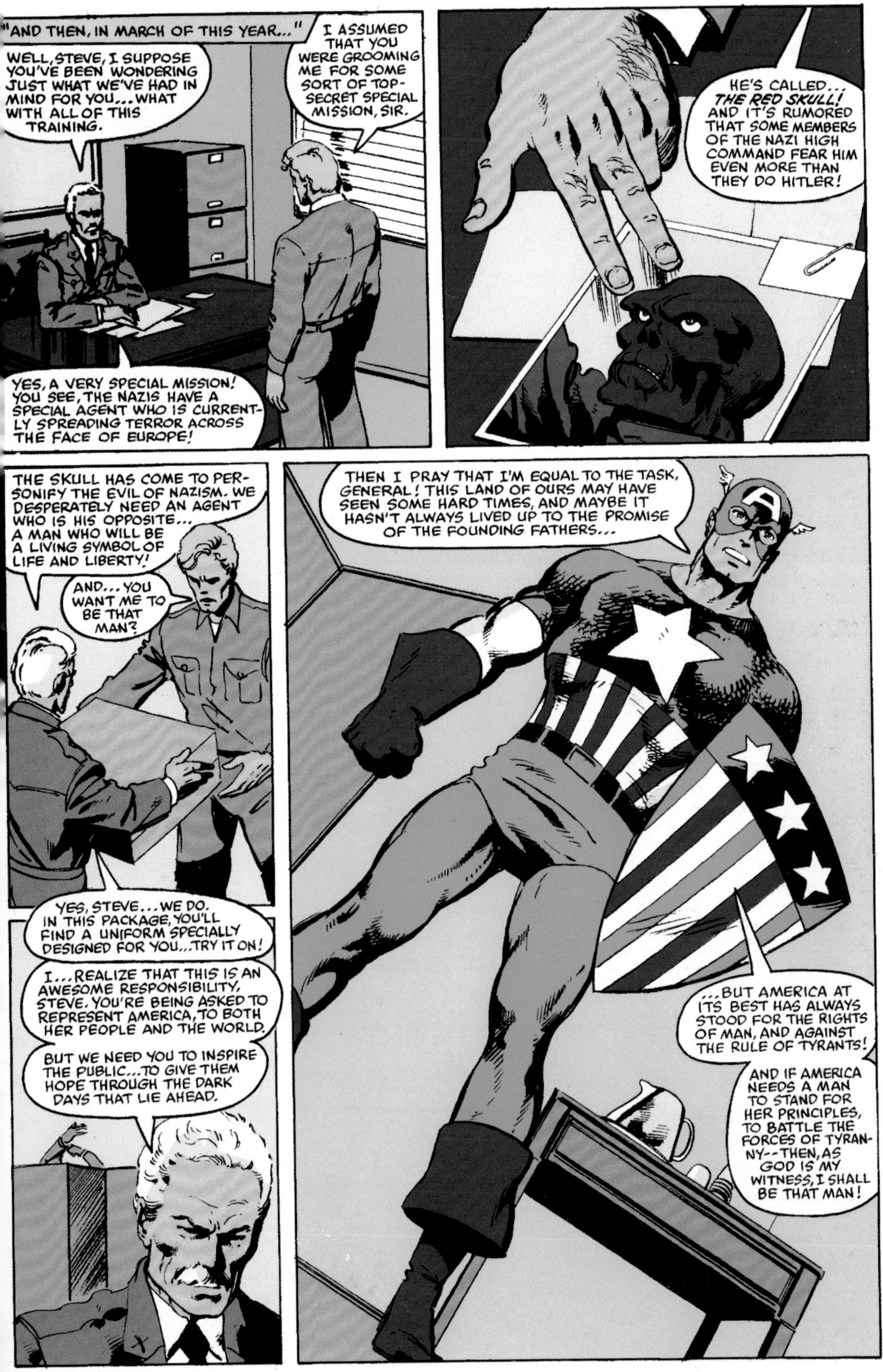
"AND THEN, IN MARCH OF THIS YEAR..."
WELL, STEVE, I SUPPOSE YOU'VE BEEN WONDERING JUST WHAT WE'VE HAD IN MIND FOR YOU... WHAT WITH ALL OF THIS TRAINING.
I ASSUMED THAT YOU WERE GROOMING ME FOR SOME SORT OF TOP-SECRET SPECIAL MISSION, SIR.
YES, A VERY SPECIAL MISSION! YOU SEE, THE NAZIS HAVE A SPECIAL AGENT WHO IS CURRENTLY SPREADING TERROR ACROSS THE FACE OF EUROPE!
HE'S CALLED... THE RED SKULL! AND IT'S RUMORED THAT SOME MEMBERS OF THE NAZI HIGH COMMAND FEAR HIM EVEN MORE THAN THEY DO HITLER!
THE SKULL HAS COME TO PERSONIFY THE EVIL OF NAZISM. WE DESPERATELY NEED AN AGENT WHO IS HIS OPPOSITE... A MAN WHO WILL BE A LIVING SYMBOL OF LIFE AND LIBERTY!
AND... YOU WANT ME TO BE THAT MAN?
YES, STEVE... WE DO. IN THIS PACKAGE, YOU'LL FIND A UNIFORM SPECIALLY DESIGNED FOR YOU... TRY IT ON!
I... REALIZE THAT THIS IS AN AWESOME RESPONSIBILITY, STEVE. YOU'RE BEING ASKED TO REPRESENT AMERICA, TO BOTH HER PEOPLE AND THE WORLD.
BUT WE NEED YOU TO INSPIRE THE PUBLIC... TO GIVE THEM HOPE THROUGH THE DARK DAYS THAT LIE AHEAD.
THEN I PRAY THAT I'M EQUAL TO THE TASK, GENERAL! THIS LAND OF OURS MAY HAVE SEEN SOME HARD TIMES, AND MAYBE IT HASN'T ALWAYS LIVED UP TO THE PROMISE OF THE FOUNDING FATHERS...
...BUT AMERICA AT ITS BEST HAS ALWAYS STOOD FOR THE RIGHTS OF MAN, AND AGAINST THE RULE OF TYRANTS!
AND IF AMERICA NEEDS A MAN TO STAND FOR HER PRINCIPLES, TO BATTLE THE FORCES OF TYRANNY--THEN, AS GOD IS MY WITNESS, I SHALL BE THAT MAN!

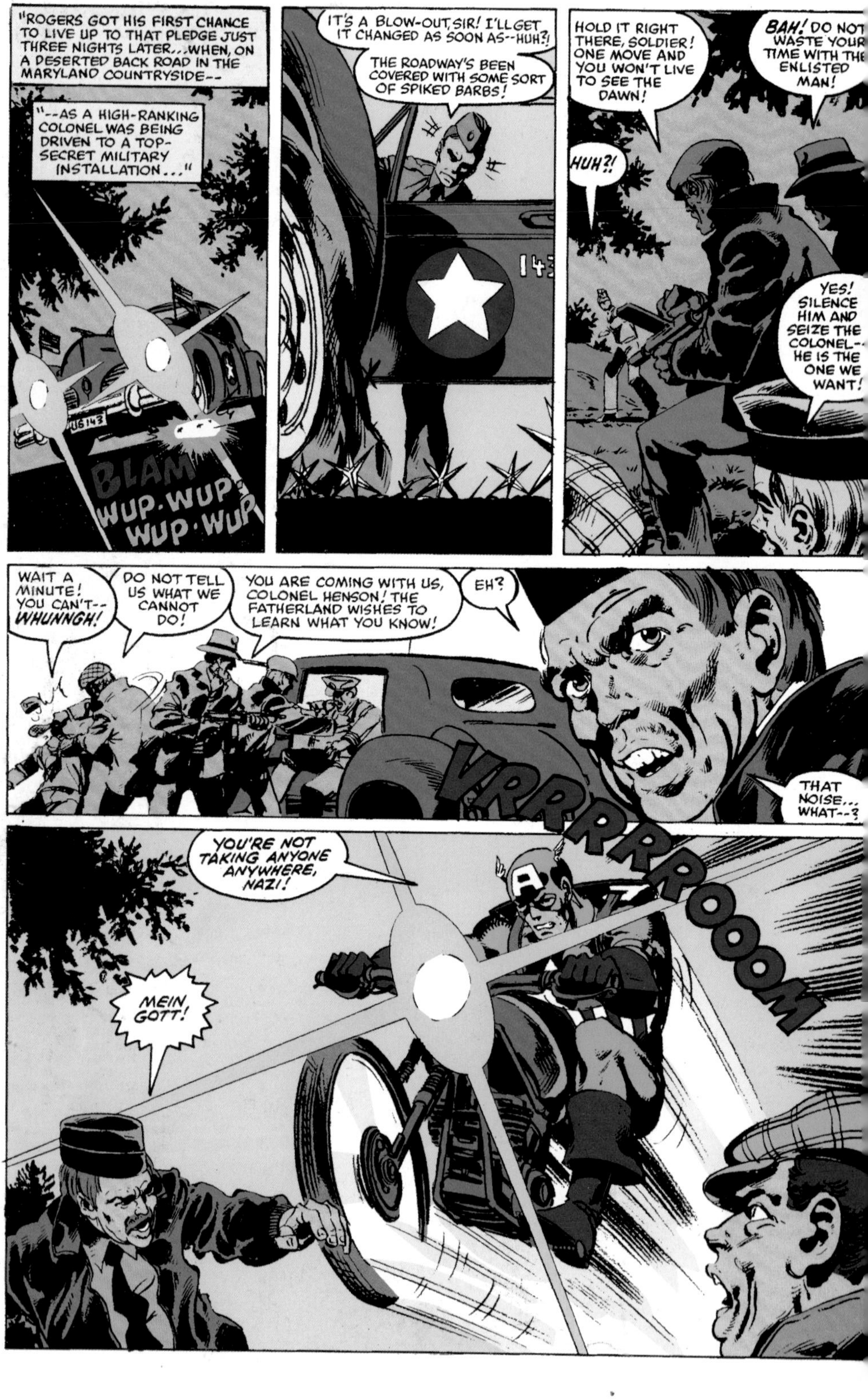
"ROGERS GOT HIS FIRST CHANCE TO LIVE UP TO THAT PLEDGE JUST THREE NIGHTS LATER... WHEN, ON A DESERTED BACK ROAD IN THE MARYLAND COUNTRYSIDE--
"--AS A HIGH-RANKING COLONEL WAS BEING DRIVEN TO A TOP-SECRET MILITARY INSTALLATION..."
BLAM
WUP·WUP WUP·WUP
IT'S A BLOW-OUT, SIR! I'LL GET IT CHANGED AS SOON AS--HUH?!
THE ROADWAY'S BEEN COVERED WITH SOME SORT OF SPIKED BARBS!
HOLD IT RIGHT THERE, SOLDIER! ONE MOVE AND YOU WON'T LIVE TO SEE THE DAWN!
BAH! DO NOT WASTE YOUR TIME WITH THE ENLISTED MAN!
HUH?!
YES! SILENCE HIM AND SEIZE THE COLONEL--HE IS THE ONE WE WANT!
WAIT A MINUTE! YOU CAN'T-- WHUNNGH!
DO NOT TELL US WHAT WE CANNOT DO!
YOU ARE COMING WITH US, COLONEL HENSON! THE FATHERLAND WISHES TO LEARN WHAT YOU KNOW!
EH?
THAT NOISE... WHAT--?
VRRRRRROOOM
YOU'RE NOT TAKING ANYONE ANYWHERE, NAZI!
MEIN GOTT!

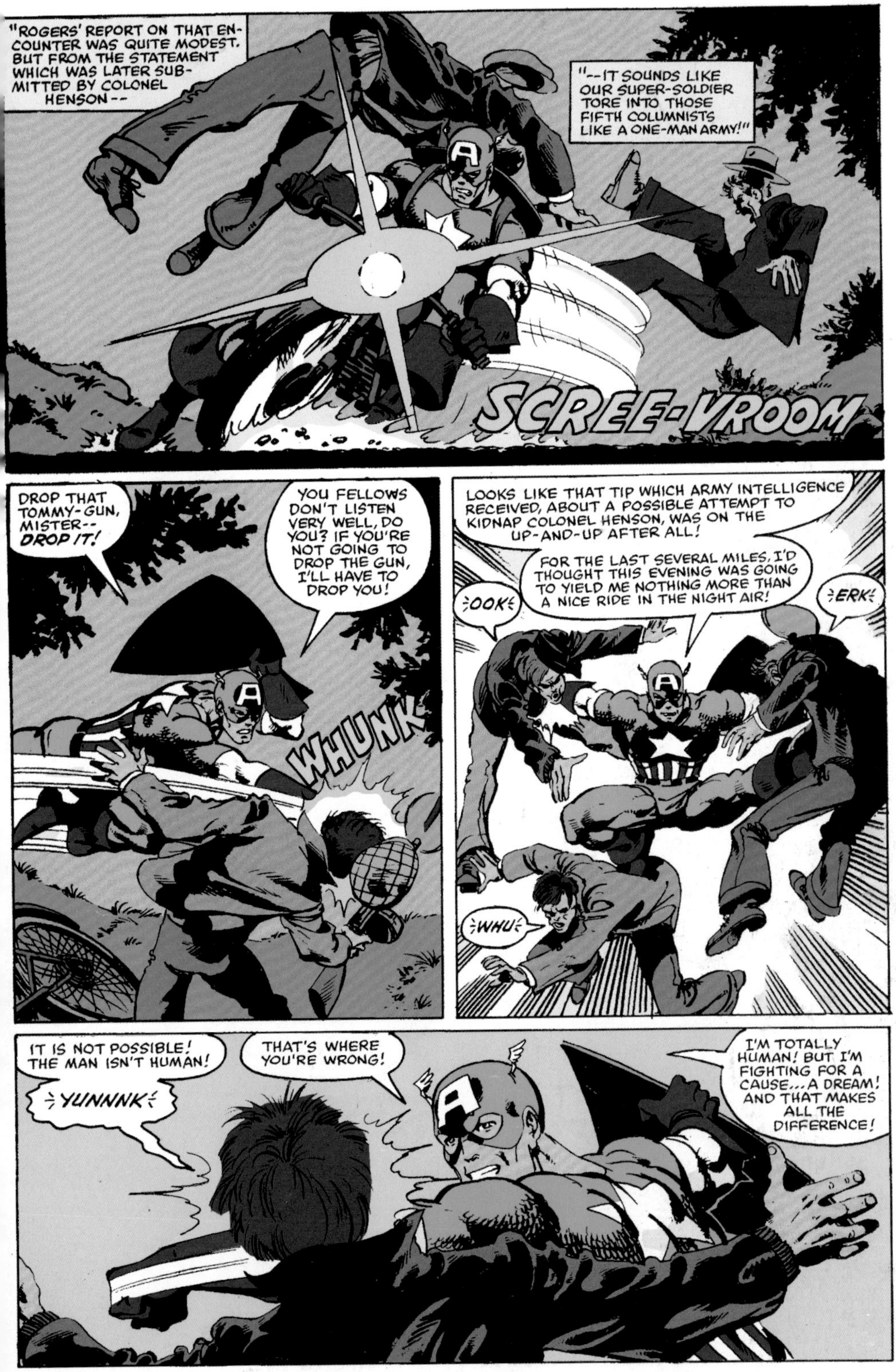
"ROGERS' REPORT ON THAT ENCOUNTER WAS QUITE MODEST. BUT FROM THE STATEMENT WHICH WAS LATER SUBMITTED BY COLONEL HENSON --
"--IT SOUNDS LIKE OUR SUPER-SOLDIER TORE INTO THOSE FIFTH COLUMNISTS LIKE A ONE-MAN ARMY!"
SCREE-VROOM
DROP THAT TOMMY-GUN, MISTER-- DROP IT!
YOU FELLOWS DON'T LISTEN VERY WELL, DO YOU? IF YOU'RE NOT GOING TO DROP THE GUN, I'LL HAVE TO DROP YOU!
WHUNK
LOOKS LIKE THAT TIP WHICH ARMY INTELLIGENCE RECEIVED, ABOUT A POSSIBLE ATTEMPT TO KIDNAP COLONEL HENSON, WAS ON THE UP-AND-UP AFTER ALL!
FOR THE LAST SEVERAL MILES, I'D THOUGHT THIS EVENING WAS GOING TO YIELD ME NOTHING MORE THAN A NICE RIDE IN THE NIGHT AIR!
OOK
ERK
WHU
IT IS NOT POSSIBLE! THE MAN ISN'T HUMAN!
YUNNNK
THAT'S WHERE YOU'RE WRONG!
I'M TOTALLY HUMAN! BUT I'M FIGHTING FOR A CAUSE... A DREAM! AND THAT MAKES ALL THE DIFFERENCE!

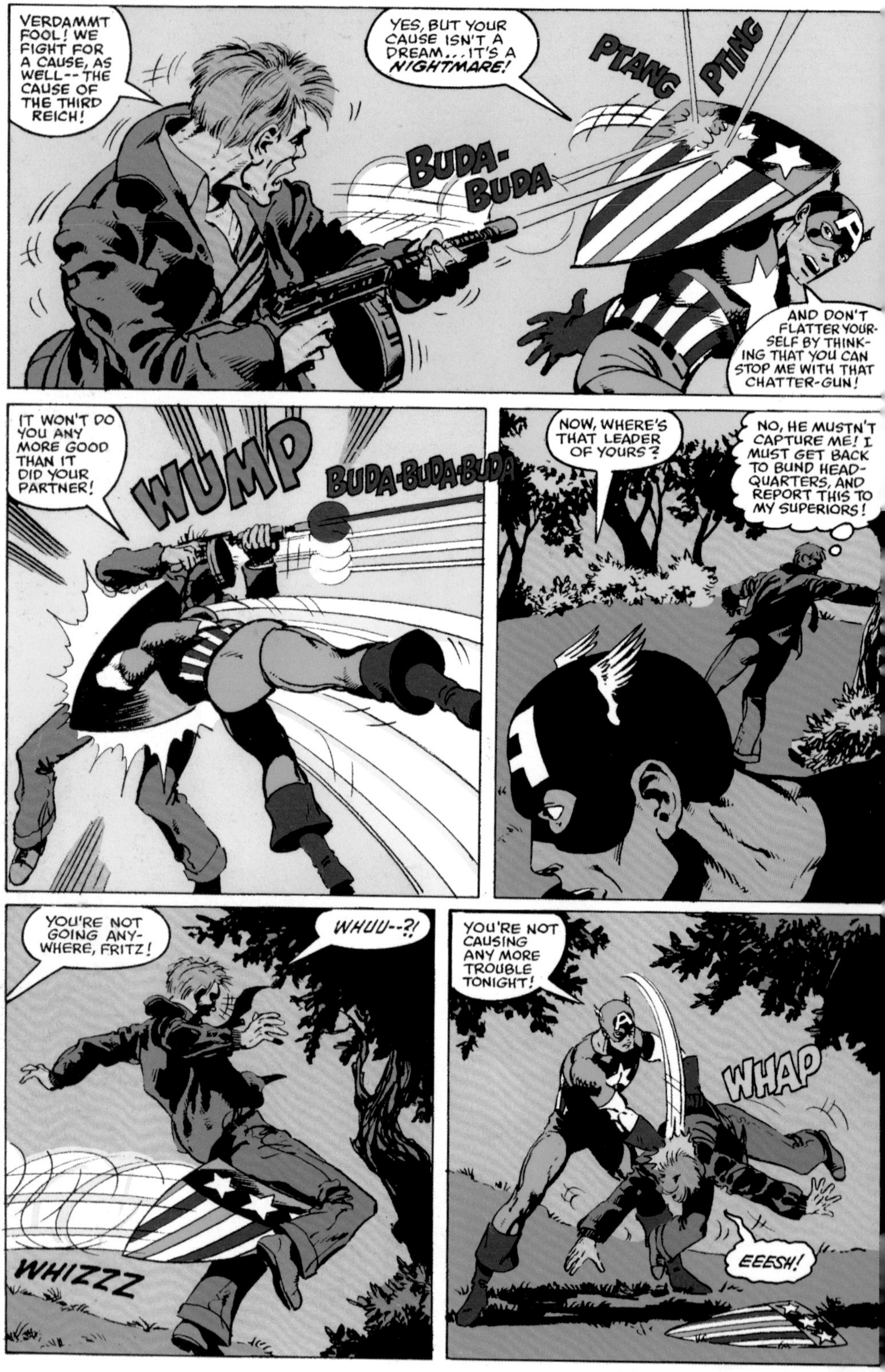
VERDAMMT FOOL! WE FIGHT FOR A CAUSE, AS WELL-- THE CAUSE OF THE THIRD REICH!
YES, BUT YOUR CAUSE ISN'T A DREAM... IT'S A NIGHTMARE!
PTANG
PTING
BUDA-BUDA
AND DON'T FLATTER YOURSELF BY THINKING THAT YOU CAN STOP ME WITH THAT CHATTER-GUN!
IT WON'T DO YOU ANY MORE GOOD THAN IT DID YOUR PARTNER!
WUMP
BUDA-BUDA-BUDA
NOW, WHERE'S THAT LEADER OF YOURS?
NO, HE MUSTN'T CAPTURE ME! I MUST GET BACK TO BUND HEAD-QUARTERS, AND REPORT THIS TO MY SUPERIORS!
YOU'RE NOT GOING ANYWHERE, FRITZ!
WHUU--?!
WHIZZZ
YOU'RE NOT CAUSING ANY MORE TROUBLE TONIGHT!
WHAP
EEESH!

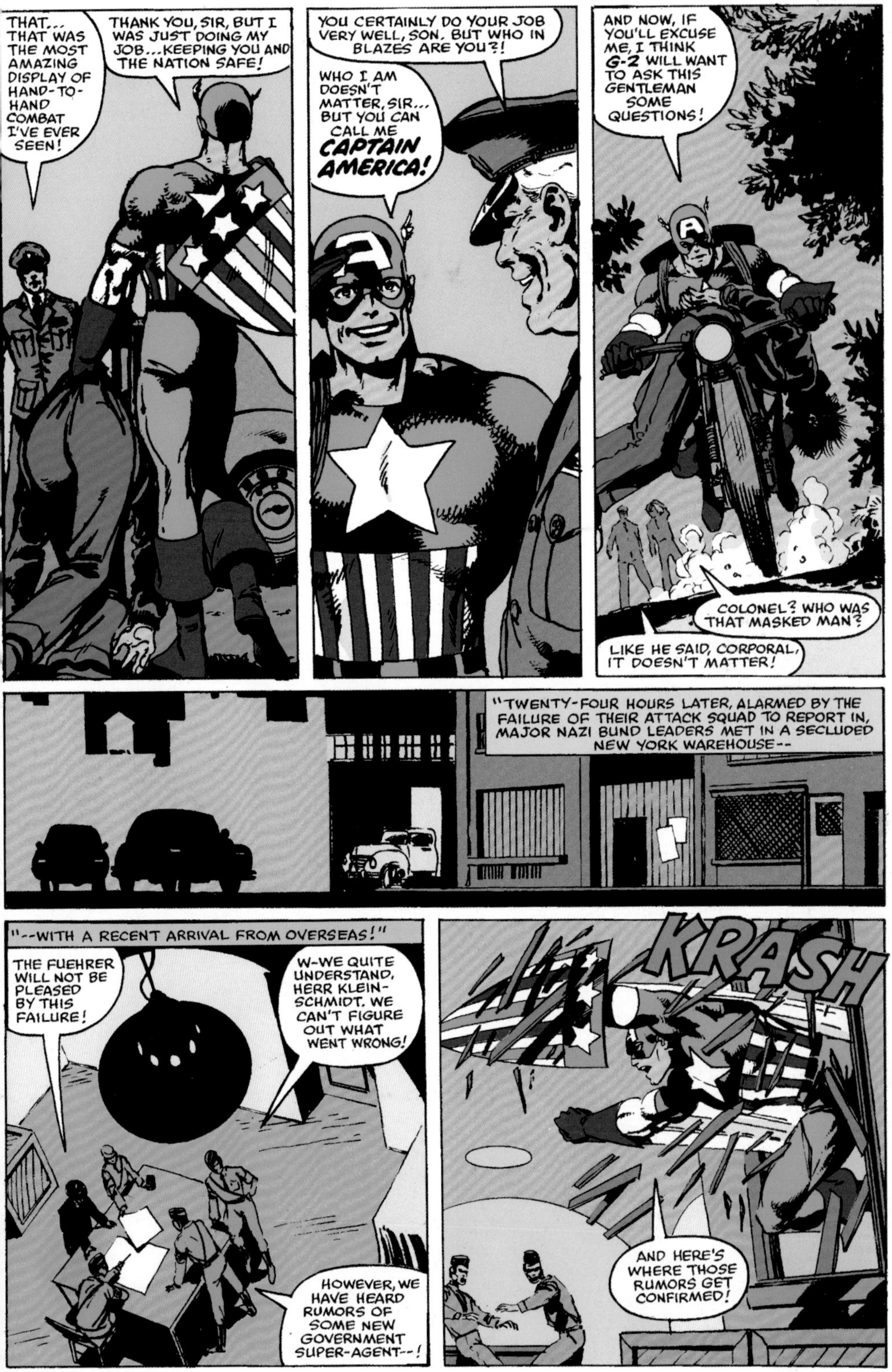

THAT... THAT WAS THE MOST AMAZING DISPLAY OF HAND-TO-HAND COMBAT I'VE EVER SEEN!
THANK YOU, SIR, BUT I WAS JUST DOING MY JOB...KEEPING YOU AND THE NATION SAFE!
YOU CERTAINLY DO YOUR JOB VERY WELL, SON. BUT WHO IN BLAZES ARE YOU?!
WHO I AM DOESN'T MATTER, SIR... BUT YOU CAN CALL ME CAPTAIN AMERICA!
AND NOW, IF YOU'LL EXCUSE ME, I THINK G-2 WILL WANT TO ASK THIS GENTLEMAN SOME QUESTIONS!
COLONEL? WHO WAS THAT MASKED MAN?
LIKE HE SAID, CORPORAL, IT DOESN'T MATTER!
"TWENTY-FOUR HOURS LATER, ALARMED BY THE FAILURE OF THEIR ATTACK SQUAD TO REPORT IN, MAJOR NAZI BUND LEADERS MET IN A SECLUDED NEW YORK WAREHOUSE--
"--WITH A RECENT ARRIVAL FROM OVERSEAS!"
THE FUEHRER WILL NOT BE PLEASED BY THIS FAILURE!
W-WE QUITE UNDERSTAND, HERR KLEIN-SCHMIDT. WE CAN'T FIGURE OUT WHAT WENT WRONG!
HOWEVER, WE HAVE HEARD RUMORS OF SOME NEW GOVERNMENT SUPER-AGENT--!
KRASH
AND HERE'S WHERE THOSE RUMORS GET CONFIRMED!

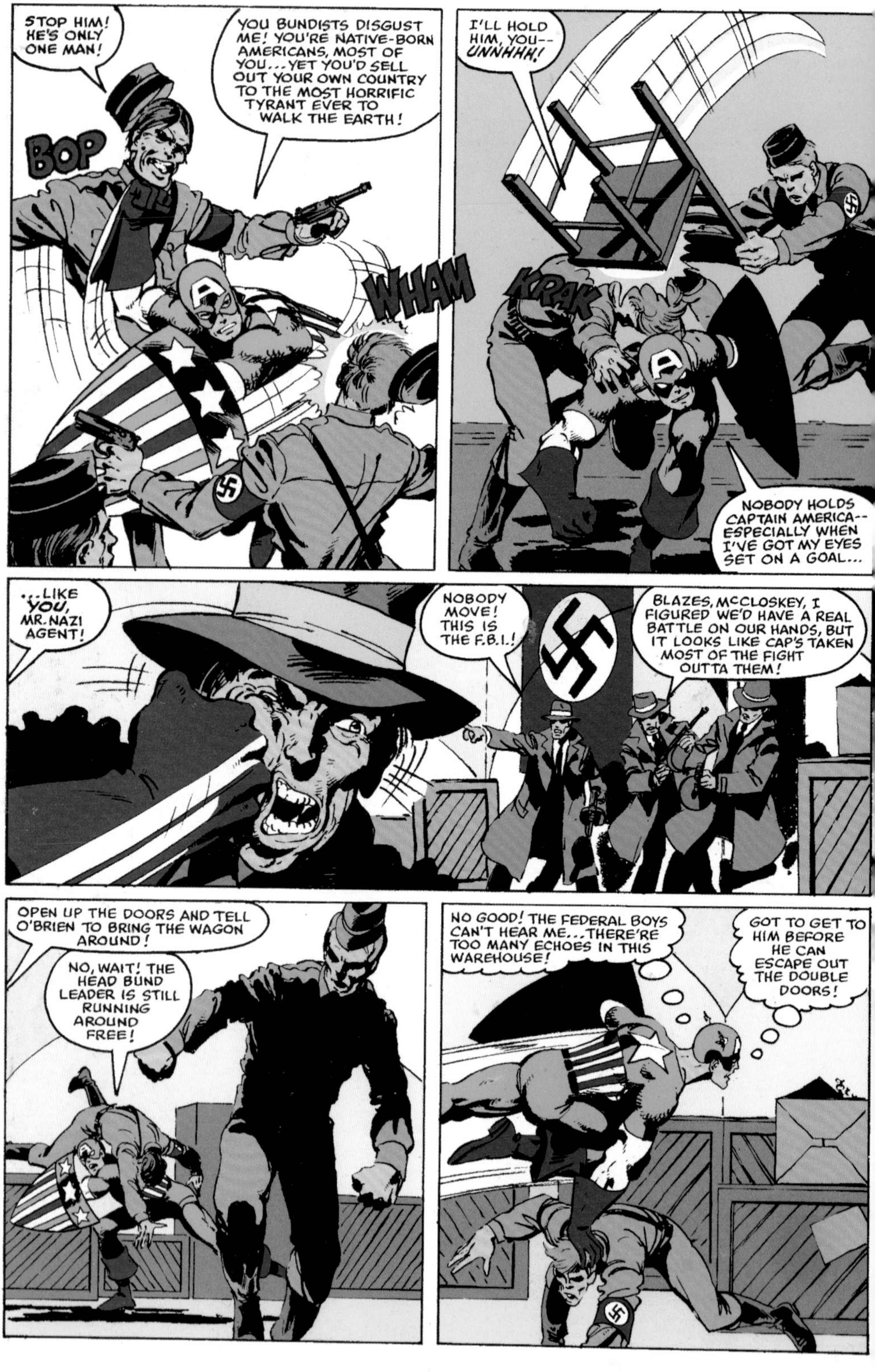
STOP HIM! HE'S ONLY ONE MAN!
YOU BUNDISTS DISGUST ME! YOU'RE NATIVE-BORN AMERICANS, MOST OF YOU... YET YOU'D SELL OUT YOUR OWN COUNTRY TO THE MOST HORRIFIC TYRANT EVER TO WALK THE EARTH!
BOP
WHAM
I'LL HOLD HIM, YOU-- UNNHHH!
KRAK
NOBODY HOLDS CAPTAIN AMERICA-- ESPECIALLY WHEN I'VE GOT MY EYES SET ON A GOAL...
...LIKE YOU, MR. NAZI AGENT!
NOBODY MOVE! THIS IS THE F.B.I.!
BLAZES, McCLOSKEY, I FIGURED WE'D HAVE A REAL BATTLE ON OUR HANDS, BUT IT LOOKS LIKE CAP'S TAKEN MOST OF THE FIGHT OUTTA THEM!
OPEN UP THE DOORS AND TELL O'BRIEN TO BRING THE WAGON AROUND!
NO, WAIT! THE HEAD BUND LEADER IS STILL RUNNING AROUND FREE!
NO GOOD! THE FEDERAL BOYS CAN'T HEAR ME... THERE'RE TOO MANY ECHOES IN THIS WAREHOUSE!
GOT TO GET TO HIM BEFORE HE CAN ESCAPE OUT THE DOUBLE DOORS!

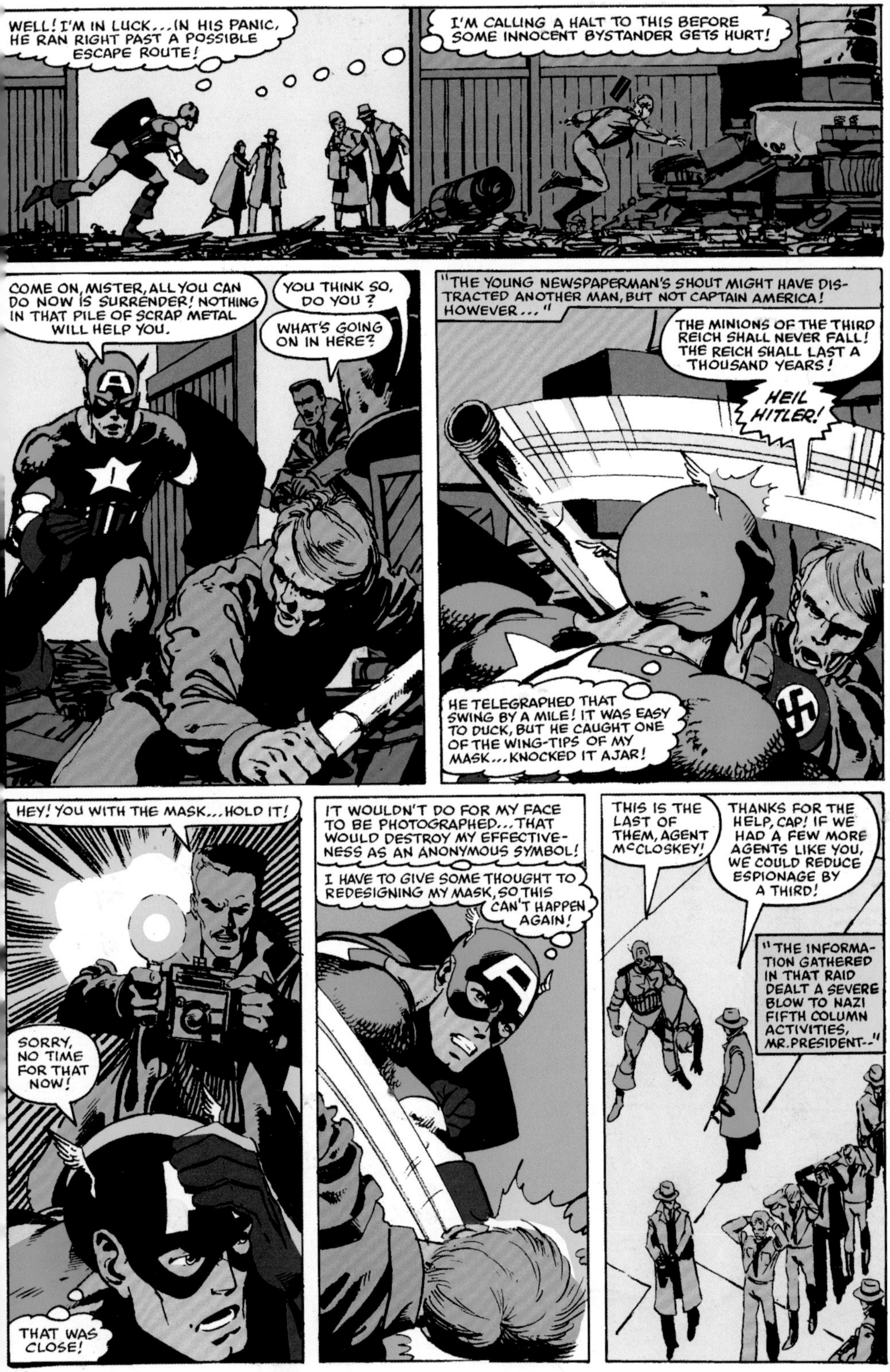
WELL! I'M IN LUCK...IN HIS PANIC, HE RAN RIGHT PAST A POSSIBLE ESCAPE ROUTE!
I'M CALLING A HALT TO THIS BEFORE SOME INNOCENT BYSTANDER GETS HURT!
COME ON, MISTER, ALL YOU CAN DO NOW IS SURRENDER! NOTHING IN THAT PILE OF SCRAP METAL WILL HELP YOU.
YOU THINK SO, DO YOU?
WHAT'S GOING ON IN HERE?
"THE YOUNG NEWSPAPERMAN'S SHOUT MIGHT HAVE DISTRACTED ANOTHER MAN, BUT NOT CAPTAIN AMERICA! HOWEVER..."
THE MINIONS OF THE THIRD REICH SHALL NEVER FALL! THE REICH SHALL LAST A THOUSAND YEARS!
HEIL HITLER!
HE TELEGRAPHED THAT SWING BY A MILE! IT WAS EASY TO DUCK, BUT HE CAUGHT ONE OF THE WING-TIPS OF MY MASK...KNOCKED IT AJAR!
HEY! YOU WITH THE MASK...HOLD IT!
SORRY, NO TIME FOR THAT NOW!
THAT WAS CLOSE!
IT WOULDN'T DO FOR MY FACE TO BE PHOTOGRAPHED...THAT WOULD DESTROY MY EFFECTIVENESS AS AN ANONYMOUS SYMBOL!
I HAVE TO GIVE SOME THOUGHT TO REDESIGNING MY MASK, SO THIS CAN'T HAPPEN AGAIN!
THIS IS THE LAST OF THEM, AGENT McCLOSKEY!
THANKS FOR THE HELP, CAP! IF WE HAD A FEW MORE AGENTS LIKE YOU, WE COULD REDUCE ESPIONAGE BY A THIRD!
"THE INFORMATION GATHERED IN THAT RAID DEALT A SEVERE BLOW TO NAZI FIFTH COLUMN ACTIVITIES, MR. PRESIDENT--"

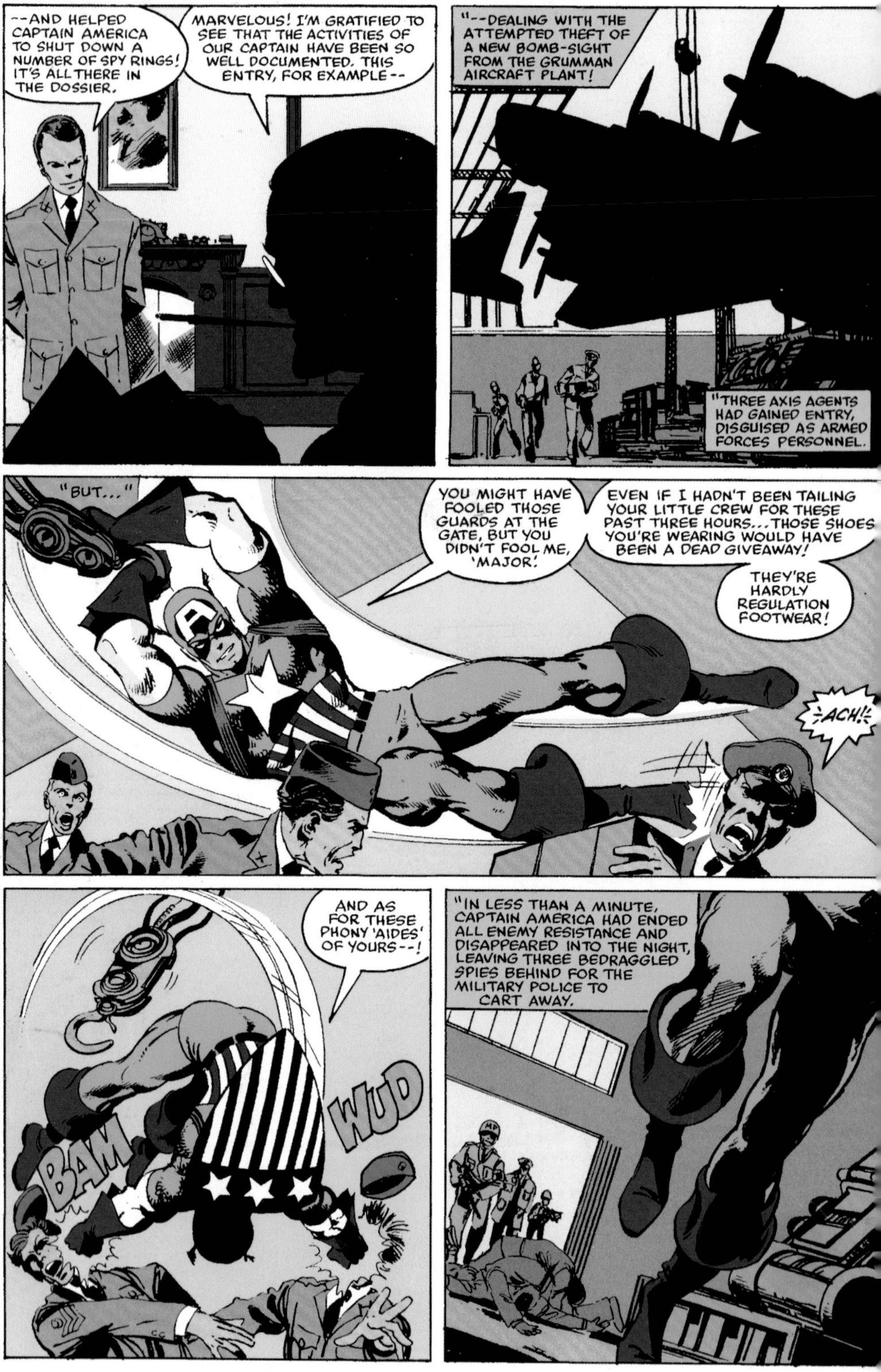
--AND HELPED CAPTAIN AMERICA TO SHUT DOWN A NUMBER OF SPY RINGS! IT'S ALL THERE IN THE DOSSIER.
MARVELOUS! I'M GRATIFIED TO SEE THAT THE ACTIVITIES OF OUR CAPTAIN HAVE BEEN SO WELL DOCUMENTED. THIS ENTRY, FOR EXAMPLE--
"--DEALING WITH THE ATTEMPTED THEFT OF A NEW BOMB-SIGHT FROM THE GRUMMAN AIRCRAFT PLANT!
"THREE AXIS AGENTS HAD GAINED ENTRY, DISGUISED AS ARMED FORCES PERSONNEL.
"BUT..."
YOU MIGHT HAVE FOOLED THOSE GUARDS AT THE GATE, BUT YOU DIDN'T FOOL ME, 'MAJOR'!
EVEN IF I HADN'T BEEN TAILING YOUR LITTLE CREW FOR THESE PAST THREE HOURS... THOSE SHOES YOU'RE WEARING WOULD HAVE BEEN A DEAD GIVEAWAY!
THEY'RE HARDLY REGULATION FOOTWEAR!
ACH!!
AND AS FOR THESE PHONY 'AIDES' OF YOURS--!
WUD
BAM
"IN LESS THAN A MINUTE, CAPTAIN AMERICA HAD ENDED ALL ENEMY RESISTANCE AND DISAPPEARED INTO THE NIGHT, LEAVING THREE BEDRAGGLED SPIES BEHIND FOR THE MILITARY POLICE TO CART AWAY.

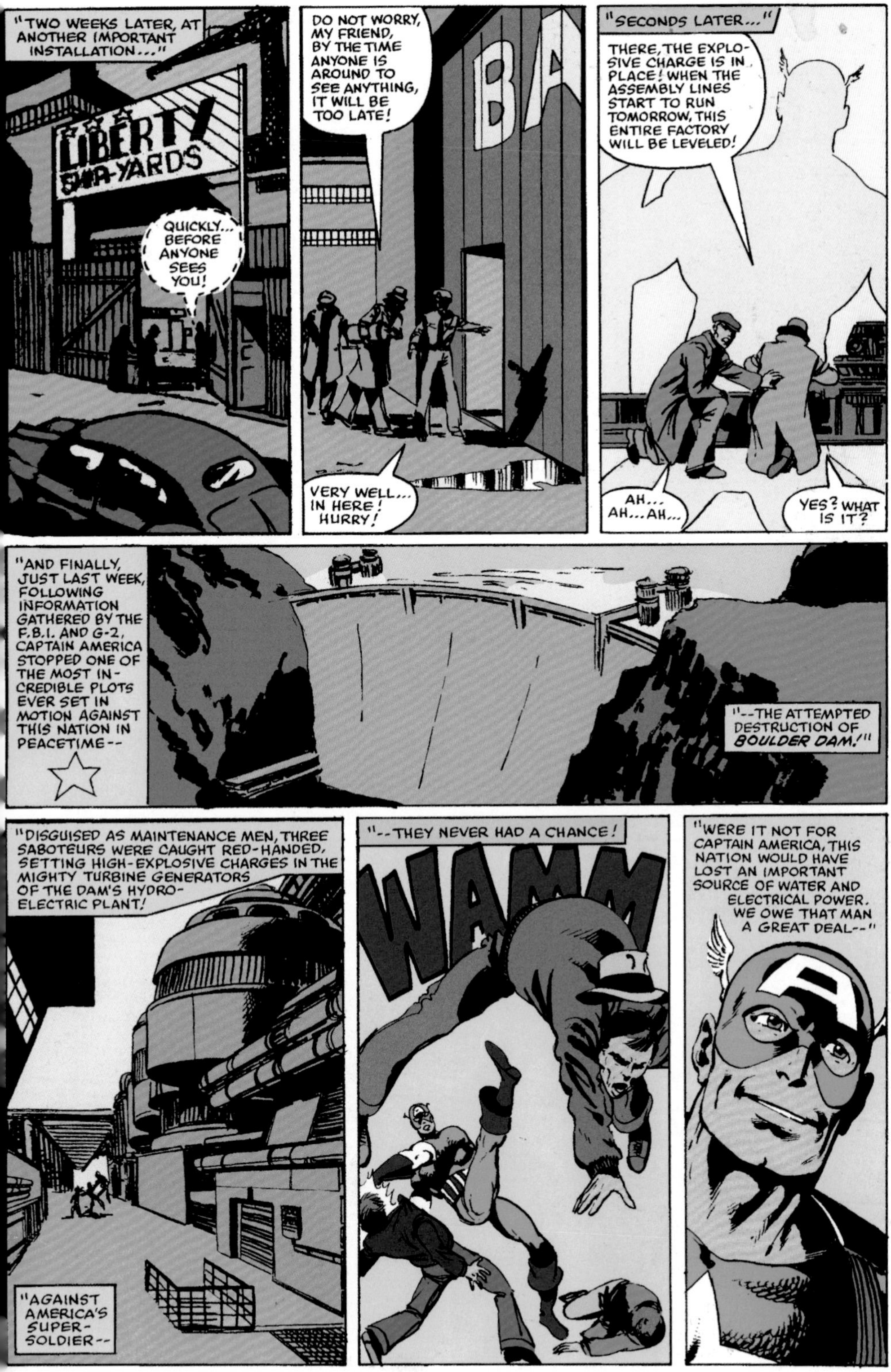
"TWO WEEKS LATER, AT ANOTHER IMPORTANT INSTALLATION..."
LIBERTY! SHIP-YARDS
QUICKLY... BEFORE ANYONE SEES YOU!
DO NOT WORRY, MY FRIEND, BY THE TIME ANYONE IS AROUND TO SEE ANYTHING, IT WILL BE TOO LATE!
VERY WELL... IN HERE! HURRY!
"SECONDS LATER..."
THERE, THE EXPLOSIVE CHARGE IS IN PLACE! WHEN THE ASSEMBLY LINES START TO RUN TOMORROW, THIS ENTIRE FACTORY WILL BE LEVELED!
AH... AH... AH...
YES? WHAT IS IT?
"AND FINALLY, JUST LAST WEEK, FOLLOWING INFORMATION GATHERED BY THE F.B.I. AND G-2, CAPTAIN AMERICA STOPPED ONE OF THE MOST INCREDIBLE PLOTS EVER SET IN MOTION AGAINST THIS NATION IN PEACETIME--
"--THE ATTEMPTED DESTRUCTION OF BOULDER DAM!"
"DISGUISED AS MAINTENANCE MEN, THREE SABOTEURS WERE CAUGHT RED-HANDED, SETTING HIGH-EXPLOSIVE CHARGES IN THE MIGHTY TURBINE GENERATORS OF THE DAM'S HYDRO-ELECTRIC PLANT!
"AGAINST AMERICA'S SUPER-SOLDIER--
"--THEY NEVER HAD A CHANCE!
WAMM
"WERE IT NOT FOR CAPTAIN AMERICA, THIS NATION WOULD HAVE LOST AN IMPORTANT SOURCE OF WATER AND ELECTRICAL POWER. WE OWE THAT MAN A GREAT DEAL--"

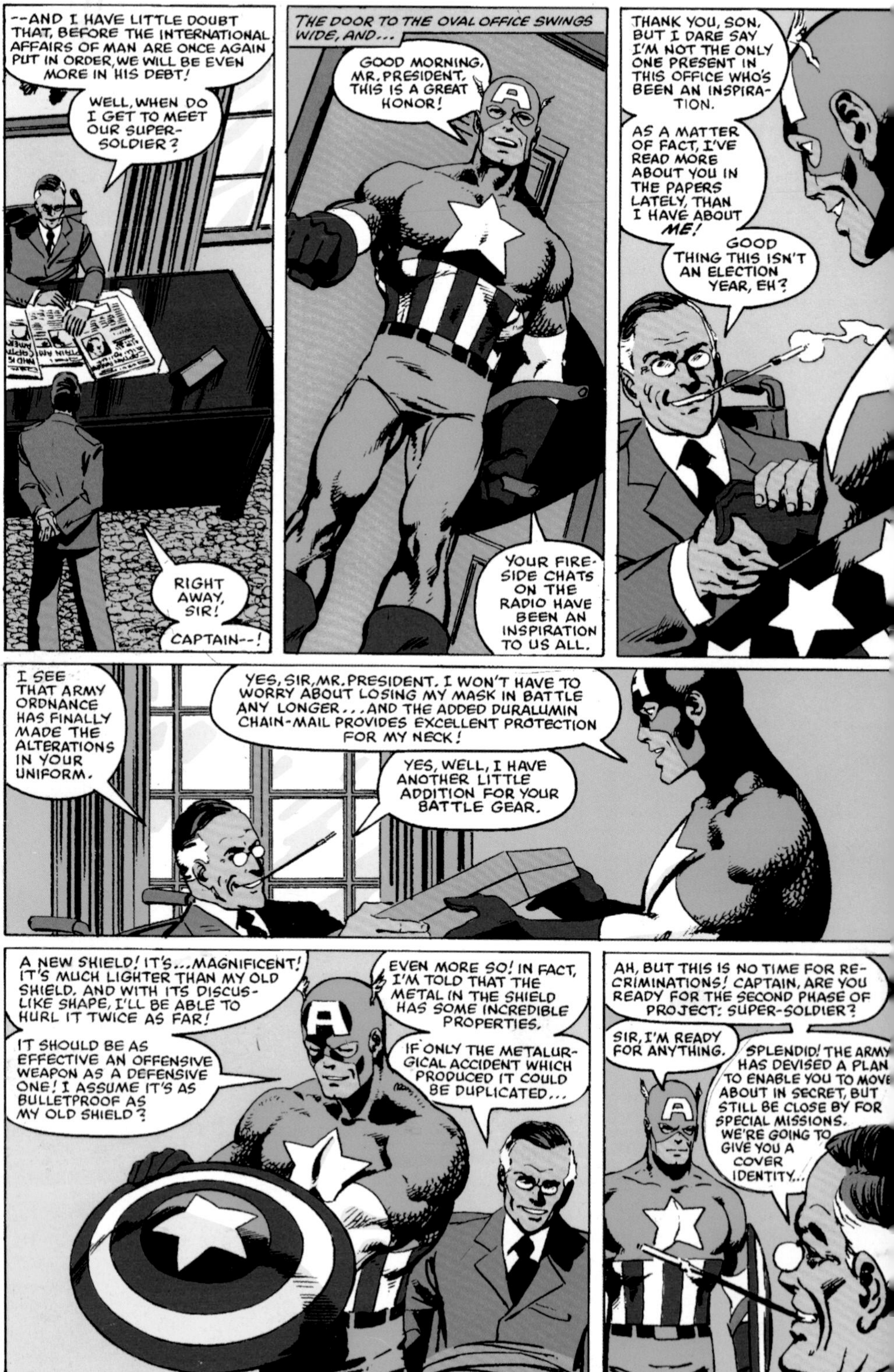
--AND I HAVE LITTLE DOUBT THAT, BEFORE THE INTERNATIONAL AFFAIRS OF MAN ARE ONCE AGAIN PUT IN ORDER, WE WILL BE EVEN MORE IN HIS DEBT!
WELL, WHEN DO I GET TO MEET OUR SUPER-SOLDIER?
RIGHT AWAY, SIR!
CAPTAIN--!
THE DOOR TO THE OVAL OFFICE SWINGS WIDE, AND...
GOOD MORNING, MR. PRESIDENT. THIS IS A GREAT HONOR!
YOUR FIRE-SIDE CHATS ON THE RADIO HAVE BEEN AN INSPIRATION TO US ALL.
THANK YOU, SON, BUT I DARE SAY I'M NOT THE ONLY ONE PRESENT IN THIS OFFICE WHO'S BEEN AN INSPIRATION.
AS A MATTER OF FACT, I'VE READ MORE ABOUT YOU IN THE PAPERS LATELY, THAN I HAVE ABOUT ME!
GOOD THING THIS ISN'T AN ELECTION YEAR, EH?
I SEE THAT ARMY ORDNANCE HAS FINALLY MADE THE ALTERATIONS IN YOUR UNIFORM.
YES, SIR, MR. PRESIDENT. I WON'T HAVE TO WORRY ABOUT LOSING MY MASK IN BATTLE ANY LONGER...AND THE ADDED DURALUMIN CHAIN-MAIL PROVIDES EXCELLENT PROTECTION FOR MY NECK!
YES, WELL, I HAVE ANOTHER LITTLE ADDITION FOR YOUR BATTLE GEAR.
A NEW SHIELD! IT'S...MAGNIFICENT! IT'S MUCH LIGHTER THAN MY OLD SHIELD, AND WITH ITS DISCUS-LIKE SHAPE, I'LL BE ABLE TO HURL IT TWICE AS FAR!
IT SHOULD BE AS EFFECTIVE AN OFFENSIVE WEAPON AS A DEFENSIVE ONE! I ASSUME IT'S AS BULLETPROOF AS MY OLD SHIELD?
EVEN MORE SO! IN FACT, I'M TOLD THAT THE METAL IN THE SHIELD HAS SOME INCREDIBLE PROPERTIES.
IF ONLY THE METALURGICAL ACCIDENT WHICH PRODUCED IT COULD BE DUPLICATED...
AH, BUT THIS IS NO TIME FOR RECRIMINATIONS! CAPTAIN, ARE YOU READY FOR THE SECOND PHASE OF PROJECT: SUPER-SOLDIER?
SIR, I'M READY FOR ANYTHING.
SPLENDID! THE ARMY HAS DEVISED A PLAN TO ENABLE YOU TO MOVE ABOUT IN SECRET, BUT STILL BE CLOSE BY FOR SPECIAL MISSIONS. WE'RE GOING TO GIVE YOU A COVER IDENTITY...

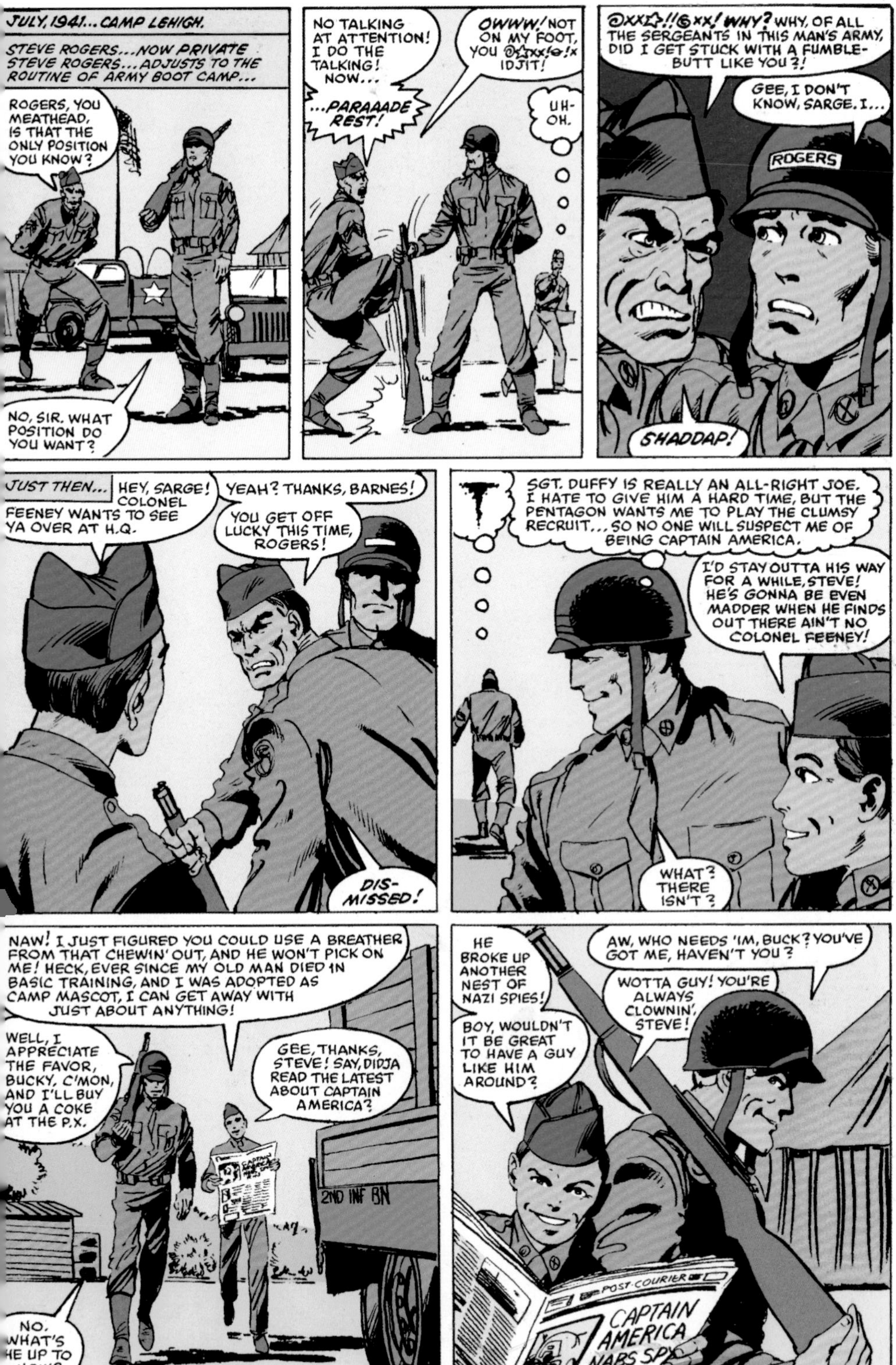

JULY, 1941... CAMP LEHIGH.
STEVE ROGERS... NOW PRIVATE STEVE ROGERS... ADJUSTS TO THE ROUTINE OF ARMY BOOT CAMP...
ROGERS, YOU MEATHEAD, IS THAT THE ONLY POSITION YOU KNOW?
NO, SIR. WHAT POSITION DO YOU WANT?
NO TALKING AT ATTENTION! I DO THE TALKING! NOW...
...PARAAADE REST!
OWWW! NOT ON MY FOOT, YOU @☆xx!⊛!x IDJIT!
UH-OH.
@XX☆!!⑤XX! WHY? WHY, OF ALL THE SERGEANTS IN THIS MAN'S ARMY, DID I GET STUCK WITH A FUMBLE-BUTT LIKE YOU?!
GEE, I DON'T KNOW, SARGE. I...
ROGERS
SHADDAP!
JUST THEN...
HEY, SARGE! COLONEL FEENEY WANTS TO SEE YA OVER AT H.Q.
YEAH? THANKS, BARNES!
YOU GET OFF LUCKY THIS TIME, ROGERS!
DIS-MISSED!
SGT. DUFFY IS REALLY AN ALL-RIGHT JOE. I HATE TO GIVE HIM A HARD TIME, BUT THE PENTAGON WANTS ME TO PLAY THE CLUMSY RECRUIT... SO NO ONE WILL SUSPECT ME OF BEING CAPTAIN AMERICA.
I'D STAY OUTTA HIS WAY FOR A WHILE, STEVE! HE'S GONNA BE EVEN MADDER WHEN HE FINDS OUT THERE AIN'T NO COLONEL FEENEY!
WHAT? THERE ISN'T?
NAW! I JUST FIGURED YOU COULD USE A BREATHER FROM THAT CHEWIN' OUT, AND HE WON'T PICK ON ME! HECK, EVER SINCE MY OLD MAN DIED IN BASIC TRAINING, AND I WAS ADOPTED AS CAMP MASCOT, I CAN GET AWAY WITH JUST ABOUT ANYTHING!
WELL, I APPRECIATE THE FAVOR, BUCKY. C'MON, AND I'LL BUY YOU A COKE AT THE P.X.
GEE, THANKS, STEVE! SAY, DIDJA READ THE LATEST ABOUT CAPTAIN AMERICA?
2ND INF BN
NO. WHAT'S HE UP TO NOW?
HE BROKE UP ANOTHER NEST OF NAZI SPIES!
BOY, WOULDN'T IT BE GREAT TO HAVE A GUY LIKE HIM AROUND?
AW, WHO NEEDS 'IM, BUCK? YOU'VE GOT ME, HAVEN'T YOU?
WOTTA GUY! YOU'RE ALWAYS CLOWNIN', STEVE!
POST-COURIER
CAPTAIN AMERICA NABS SPY

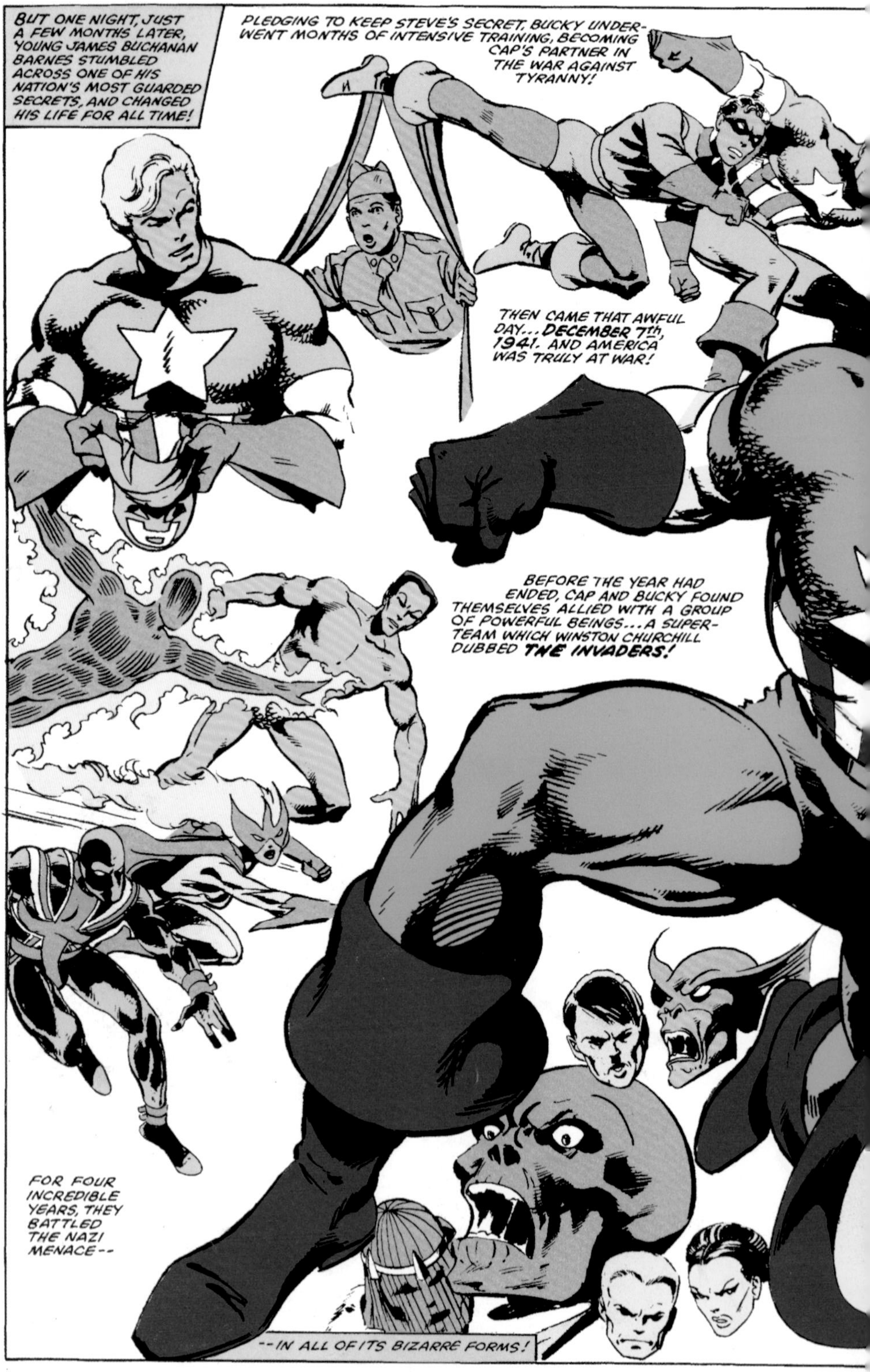
BUT ONE NIGHT, JUST A FEW MONTHS LATER, YOUNG JAMES BUCHANAN BARNES STUMBLED ACROSS ONE OF HIS NATION'S MOST GUARDED SECRETS, AND CHANGED HIS LIFE FOR ALL TIME!
PLEDGING TO KEEP STEVE'S SECRET, BUCKY UNDERWENT MONTHS OF INTENSIVE TRAINING, BECOMING CAP'S PARTNER IN THE WAR AGAINST TYRANNY!
THEN CAME THAT AWFUL DAY... DECEMBER 7th, 1941. AND AMERICA WAS TRULY AT WAR!
BEFORE THE YEAR HAD ENDED, CAP AND BUCKY FOUND THEMSELVES ALLIED WITH A GROUP OF POWERFUL BEINGS... A SUPER-TEAM WHICH WINSTON CHURCHILL DUBBED THE INVADERS!
FOR FOUR INCREDIBLE YEARS, THEY BATTLED THE NAZI MENACE--
--IN ALL OF ITS BIZARRE FORMS!

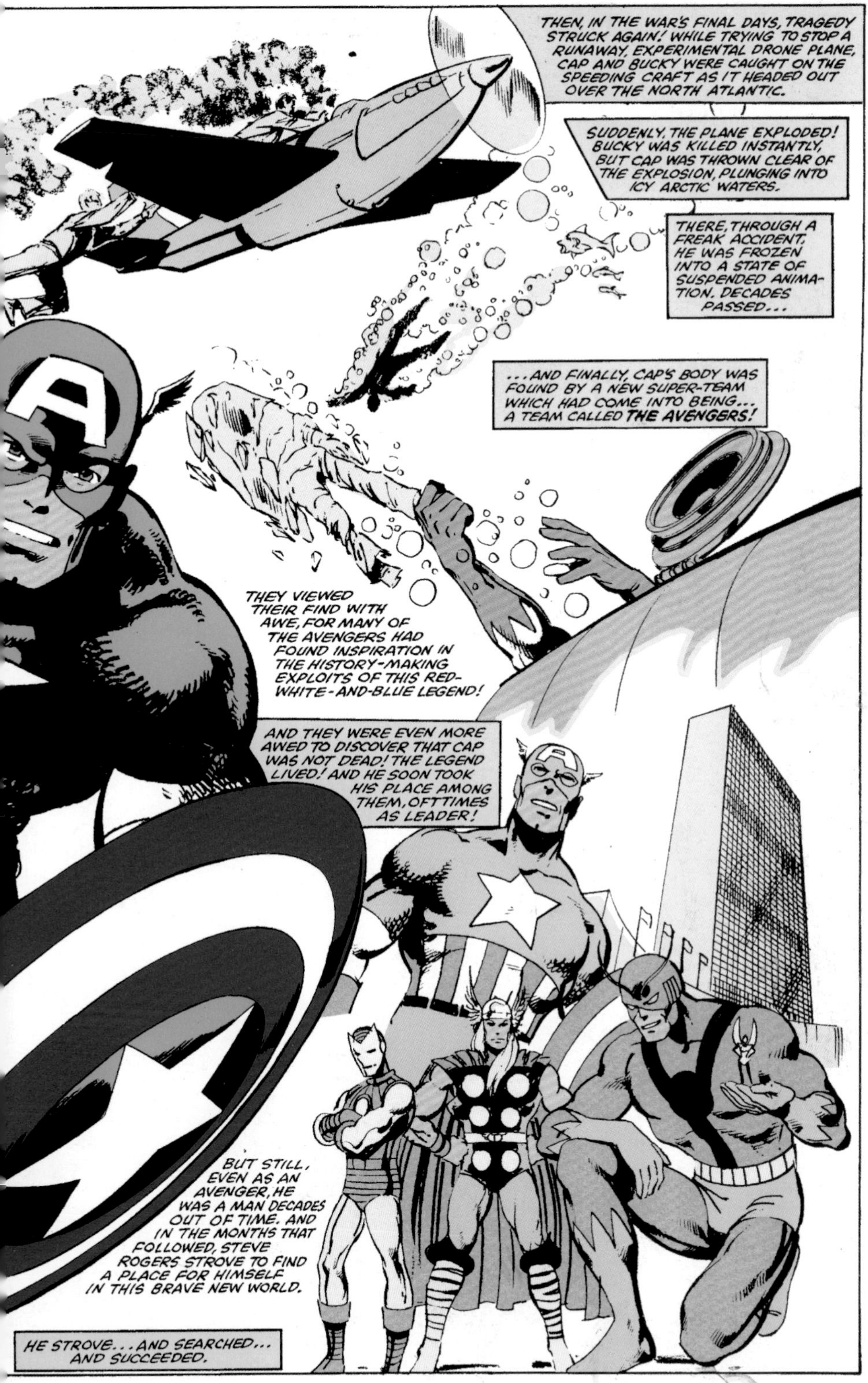
THEN, IN THE WAR'S FINAL DAYS, TRAGEDY STRUCK AGAIN! WHILE TRYING TO STOP A RUNAWAY, EXPERIMENTAL DRONE PLANE, CAP AND BUCKY WERE CAUGHT ON THE SPEEDING CRAFT AS IT HEADED OUT OVER THE NORTH ATLANTIC.
SUDDENLY, THE PLANE EXPLODED! BUCKY WAS KILLED INSTANTLY, BUT CAP WAS THROWN CLEAR OF THE EXPLOSION, PLUNGING INTO ICY ARCTIC WATERS.
THERE, THROUGH A FREAK ACCIDENT, HE WAS FROZEN INTO A STATE OF SUSPENDED ANIMATION. DECADES PASSED...
...AND FINALLY, CAP'S BODY WAS FOUND BY A NEW SUPER-TEAM WHICH HAD COME INTO BEING... A TEAM CALLED THE AVENGERS!
THEY VIEWED THEIR FIND WITH AWE, FOR MANY OF THE AVENGERS HAD FOUND INSPIRATION IN THE HISTORY-MAKING EXPLOITS OF THIS RED-WHITE-AND-BLUE LEGEND!
AND THEY WERE EVEN MORE AWED TO DISCOVER THAT CAP WAS NOT DEAD! THE LEGEND LIVED! AND HE SOON TOOK HIS PLACE AMONG THEM, OFTTIMES AS LEADER!
BUT STILL, EVEN AS AN AVENGER, HE WAS A MAN DECADES OUT OF TIME. AND IN THE MONTHS THAT FOLLOWED, STEVE ROGERS STROVE TO FIND A PLACE FOR HIMSELF IN THIS BRAVE NEW WORLD.
HE STROVE... AND SEARCHED... AND SUCCEEDED.

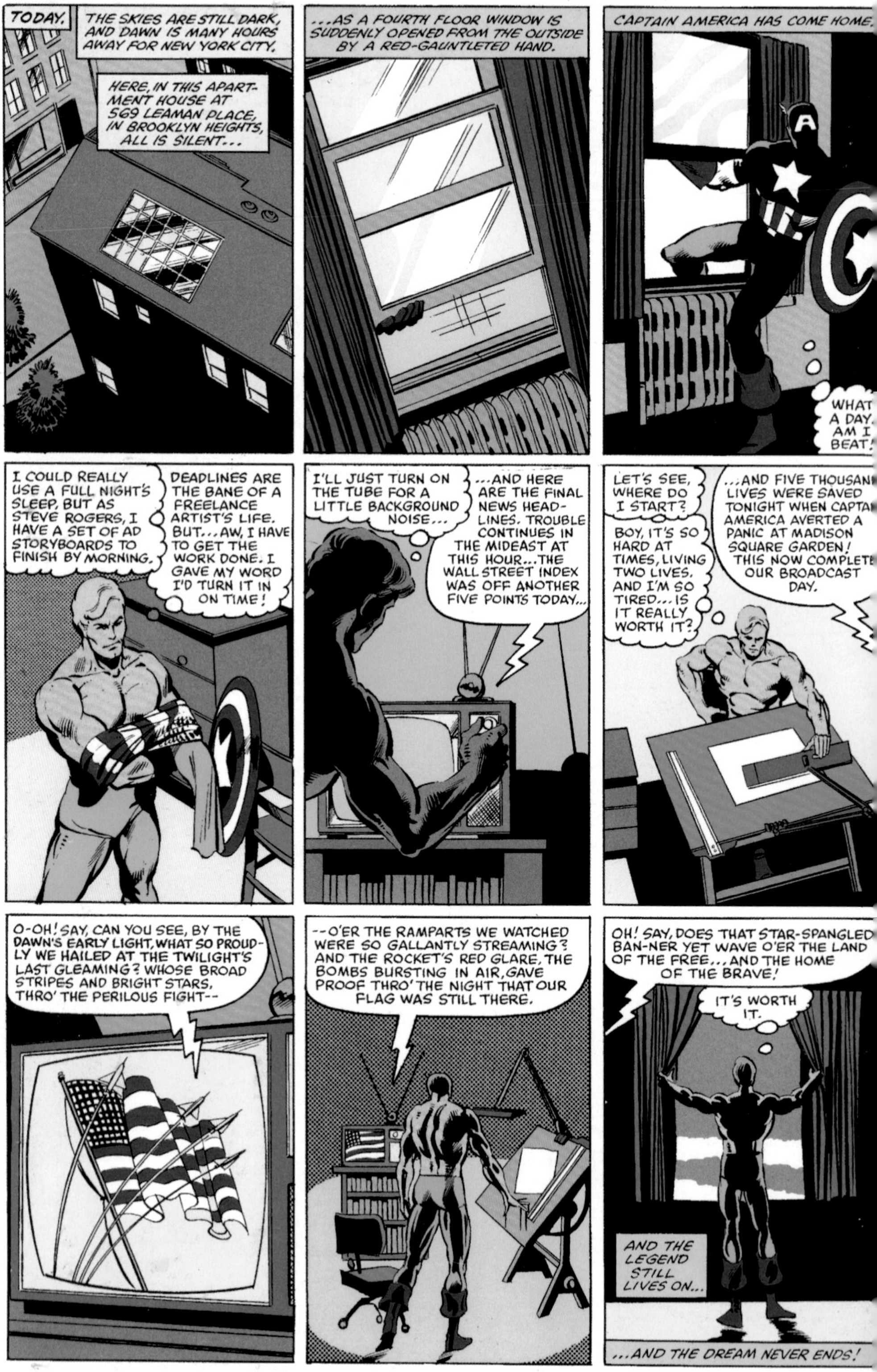
TODAY.
THE SKIES ARE STILL DARK, AND DAWN IS MANY HOURS AWAY FOR NEW YORK CITY.
HERE, IN THIS APARTMENT HOUSE AT 569 LEAMAN PLACE, IN BROOKLYN HEIGHTS, ALL IS SILENT...
...AS A FOURTH FLOOR WINDOW IS SUDDENLY OPENED FROM THE OUTSIDE BY A RED-GAUNTLETED HAND.
CAPTAIN AMERICA HAS COME HOME.
WHAT A DAY. AM I BEAT!
I COULD REALLY USE A FULL NIGHT'S SLEEP, BUT AS STEVE ROGERS, I HAVE A SET OF AD STORYBOARDS TO FINISH BY MORNING.
DEADLINES ARE THE BANE OF A FREELANCE ARTIST'S LIFE. BUT... AW, I HAVE TO GET THE WORK DONE. I GAVE MY WORD I'D TURN IT IN ON TIME!
I'LL JUST TURN ON THE TUBE FOR A LITTLE BACKGROUND NOISE...
...AND HERE ARE THE FINAL NEWS HEADLINES. TROUBLE CONTINUES IN THE MIDEAST AT THIS HOUR... THE WALL STREET INDEX WAS OFF ANOTHER FIVE POINTS TODAY...
LET'S SEE, WHERE DO I START?
BOY, IT'S SO HARD AT TIMES, LIVING TWO LIVES. AND I'M SO TIRED... IS IT REALLY WORTH IT?
...AND FIVE THOUSAN LIVES WERE SAVED TONIGHT WHEN CAPTAI AMERICA AVERTED A PANIC AT MADISON SQUARE GARDEN! THIS NOW COMPLETE OUR BROADCAST DAY.
O-OH! SAY, CAN YOU SEE, BY THE DAWN'S EARLY LIGHT, WHAT SO PROUDLY WE HAILED AT THE TWILIGHT'S LAST GLEAMING? WHOSE BROAD STRIPES AND BRIGHT STARS, THRO' THE PERILOUS FIGHT--
--O'ER THE RAMPARTS WE WATCHED WERE SO GALLANTLY STREAMING? AND THE ROCKET'S RED GLARE, THE BOMBS BURSTING IN AIR, GAVE PROOF THRO' THE NIGHT THAT OUR FLAG WAS STILL THERE.
OH! SAY, DOES THAT STAR-SPANGLED BAN-NER YET WAVE O'ER THE LAND OF THE FREE... AND THE HOME OF THE BRAVE!
IT'S WORTH IT.
AND THE LEGEND STILL LIVES ON...
...AND THE DREAM NEVER ENDS!

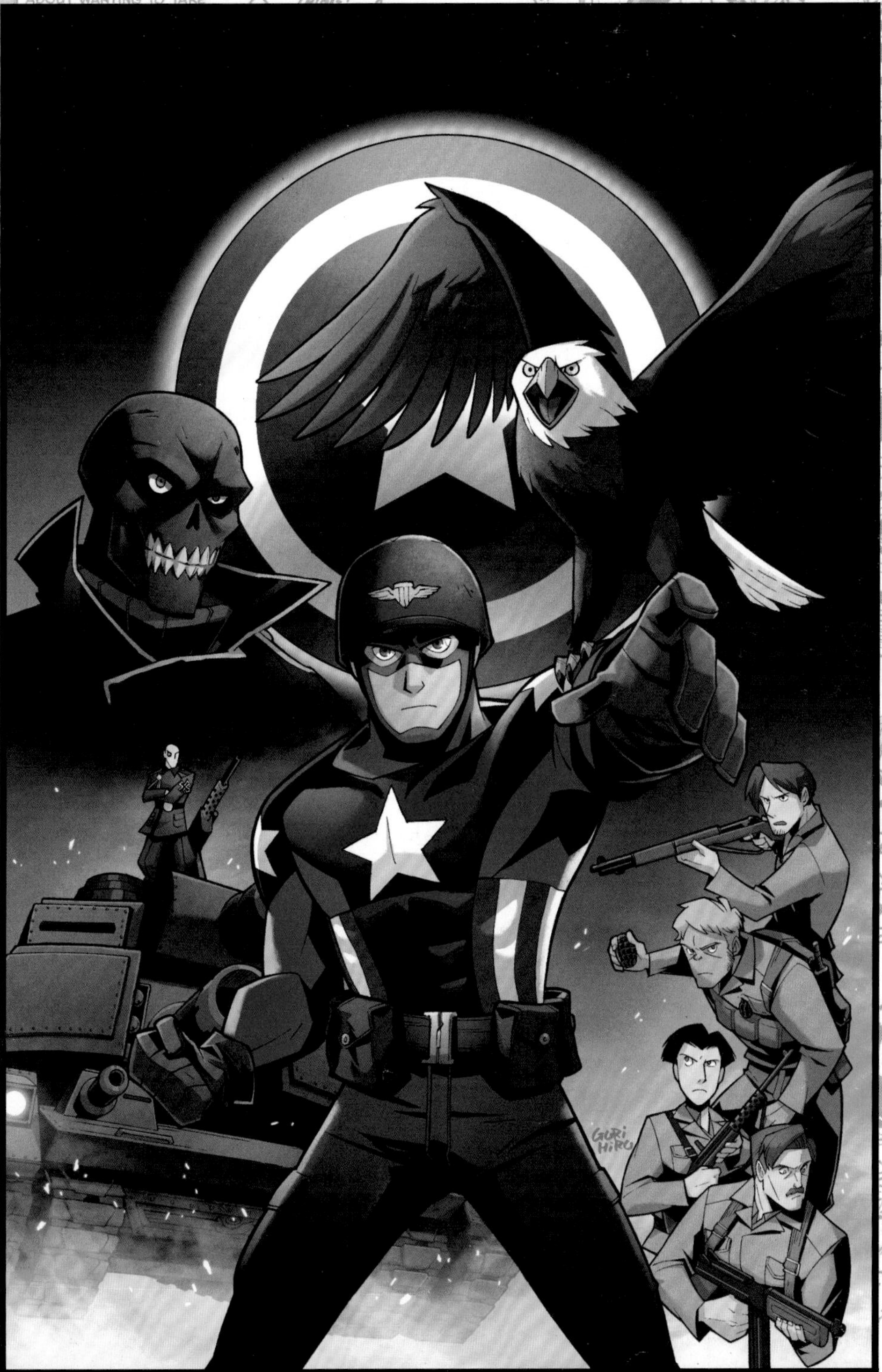
GURI HIRU

CAPTAIN AMERICA: THE FIGHTING AVENGER #1

ON HIS FIRST MISSION AS CAPTAIN AMERICA, STEVE ROGERS WILL HAVE TO CONTEND WITH BARON VON STRUCKER AND THE RED SKULL.

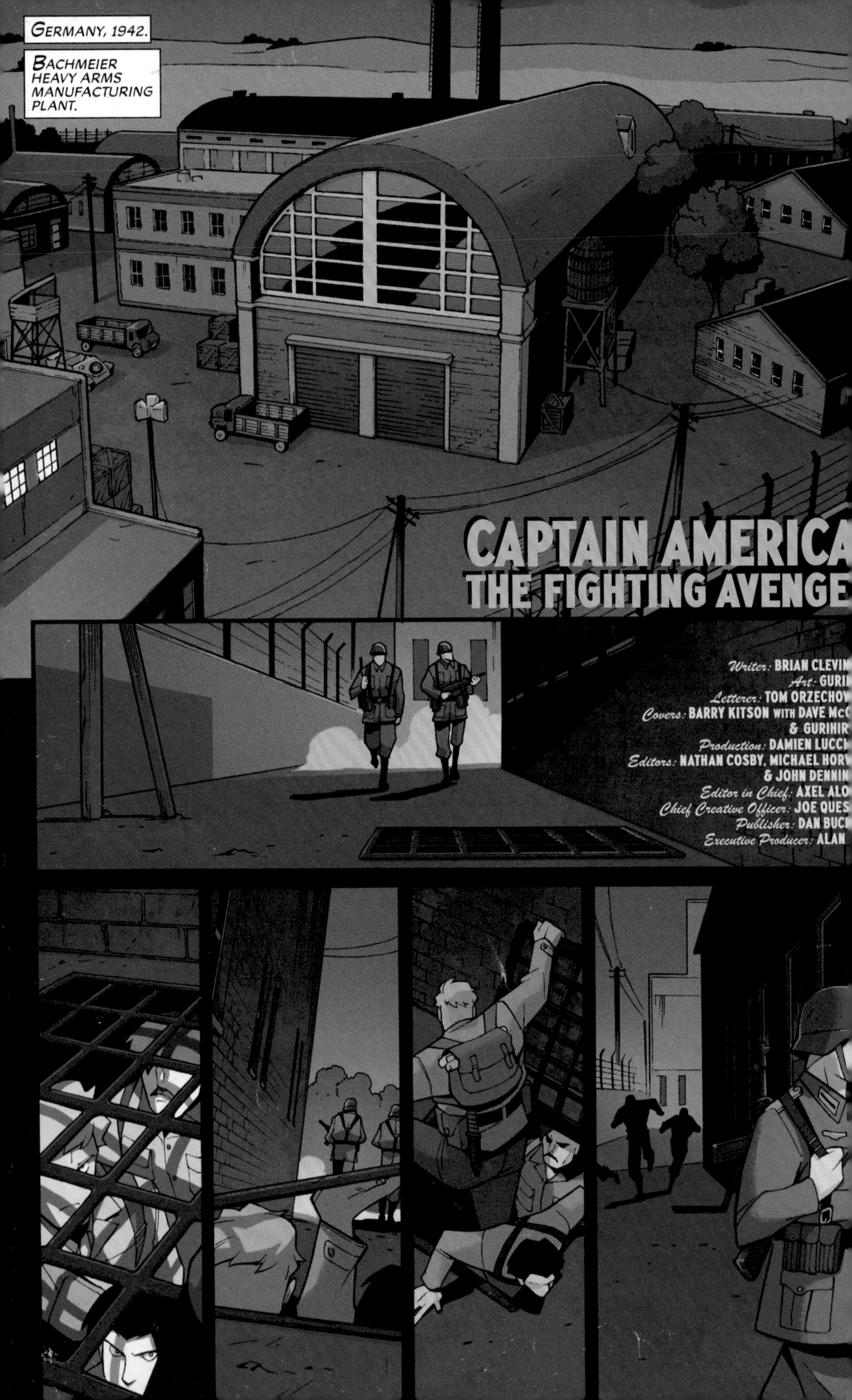
GERMANY, 1942.
BACHMEIER HEAVY ARMS MANUFACTURING PLANT.
CAPTAIN AMERICA
THE FIGHTING AVENGE
Writer: BRIAN CLEVIN
Art: GURI
Letterer: TOM ORZECHOW
Covers: BARRY KITSON WITH DAVE McC
& GURIHIR
Production: DAMIEN LUCCH
Editors: NATHAN COSBY, MICHAEL HORW
& JOHN DENNIN
Editor in Chief: AXEL ALO
Chief Creative Officer: JOE QUES
Publisher: DAN BUCK
Executive Producer: ALAN

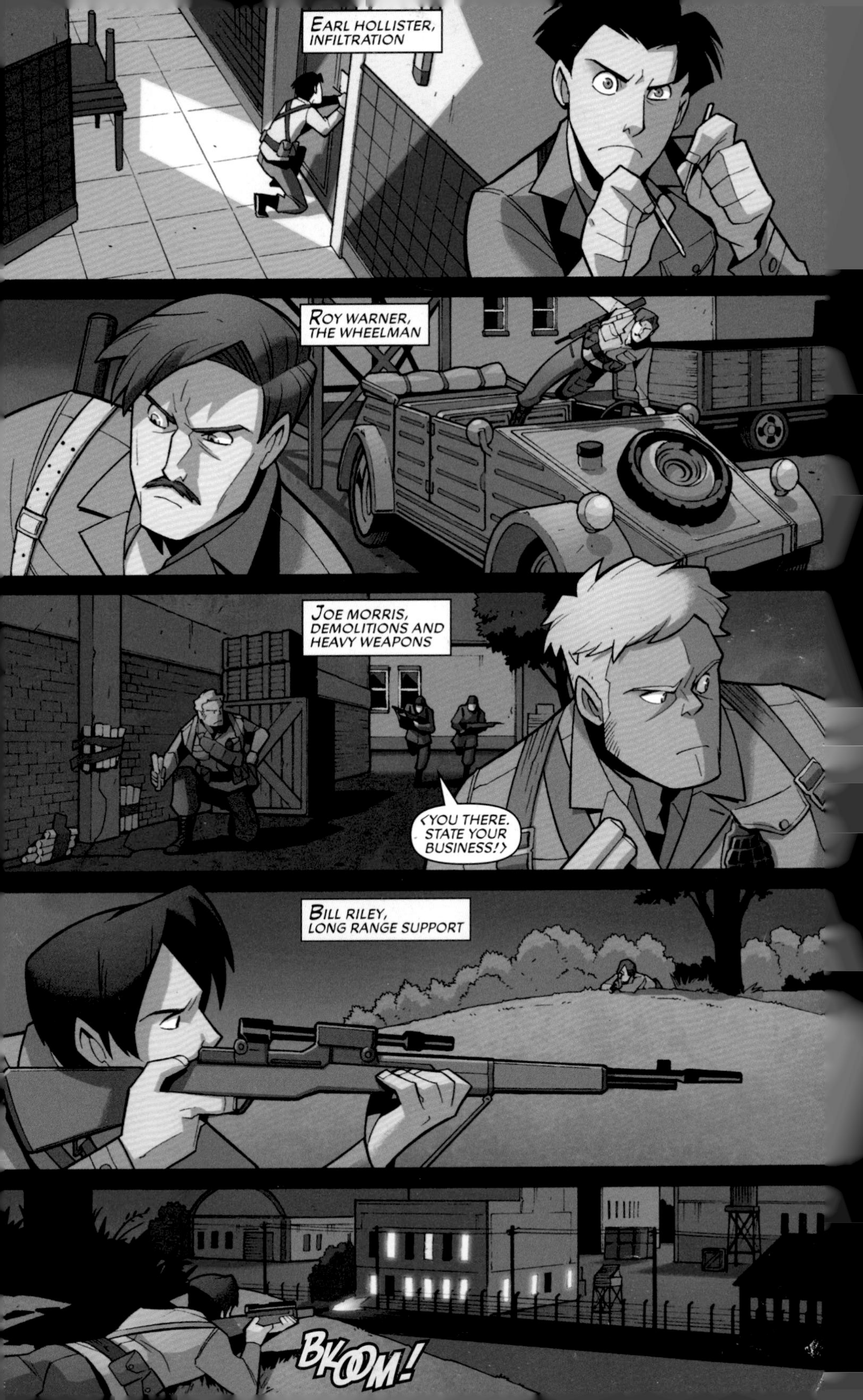
EARL HOLLISTER, INFILTRATION
ROY WARNER, THE WHEELMAN
JOE MORRIS, DEMOLITIONS AND HEAVY WEAPONS
<YOU THERE. STATE YOUR BUSINESS!>
BILL RILEY, LONG RANGE SUPPORT
BKOOM!

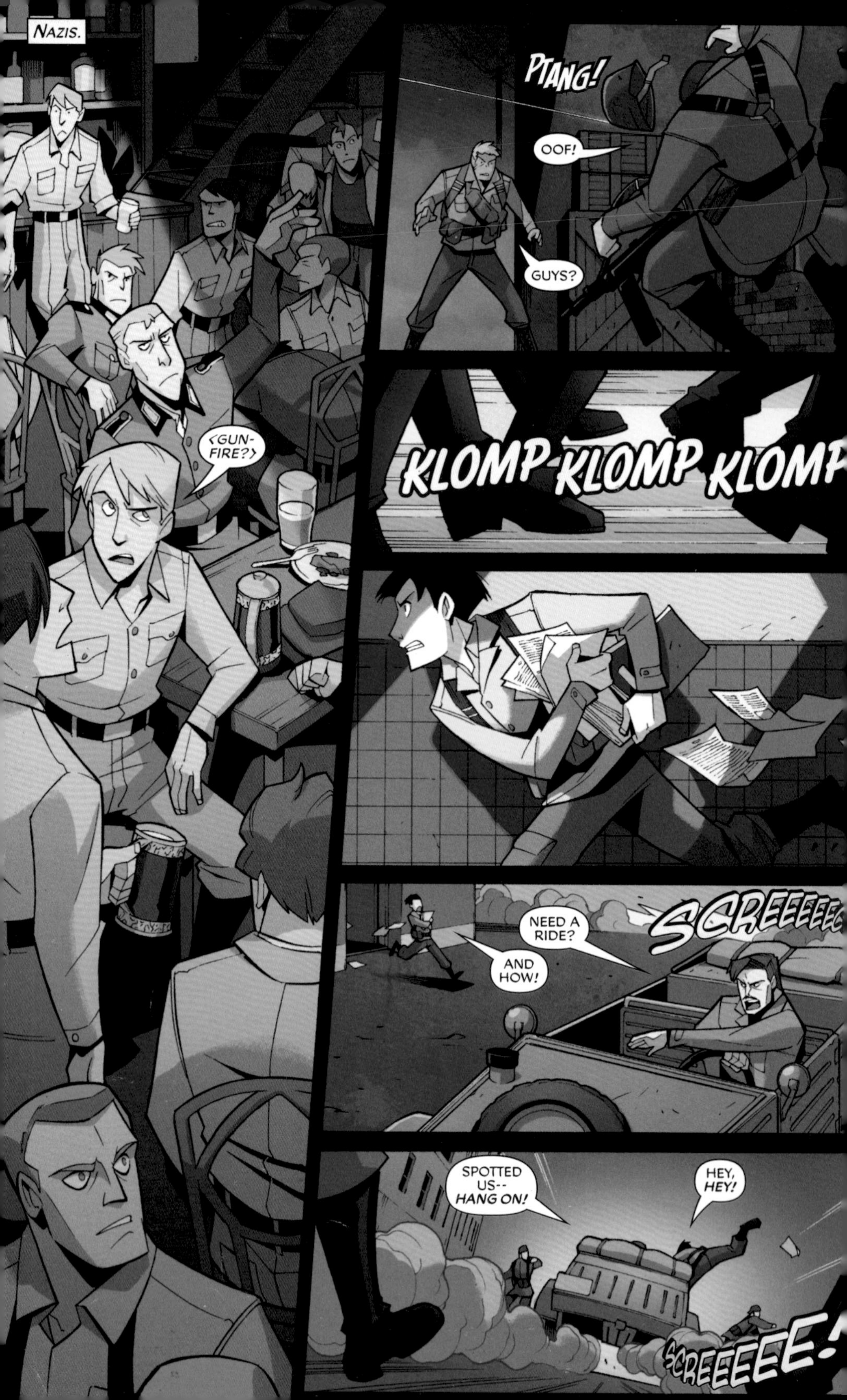
NAZIS.
<GUN-FIRE?>
PTANG!
OOF!
GUYS?
KLOMP KLOMP KLOMP
NEED A RIDE?
AND HOW!
SCREEEEEC
SPOTTED US-- HANG ON!
HEY, HEY!
SCREEEEEE!

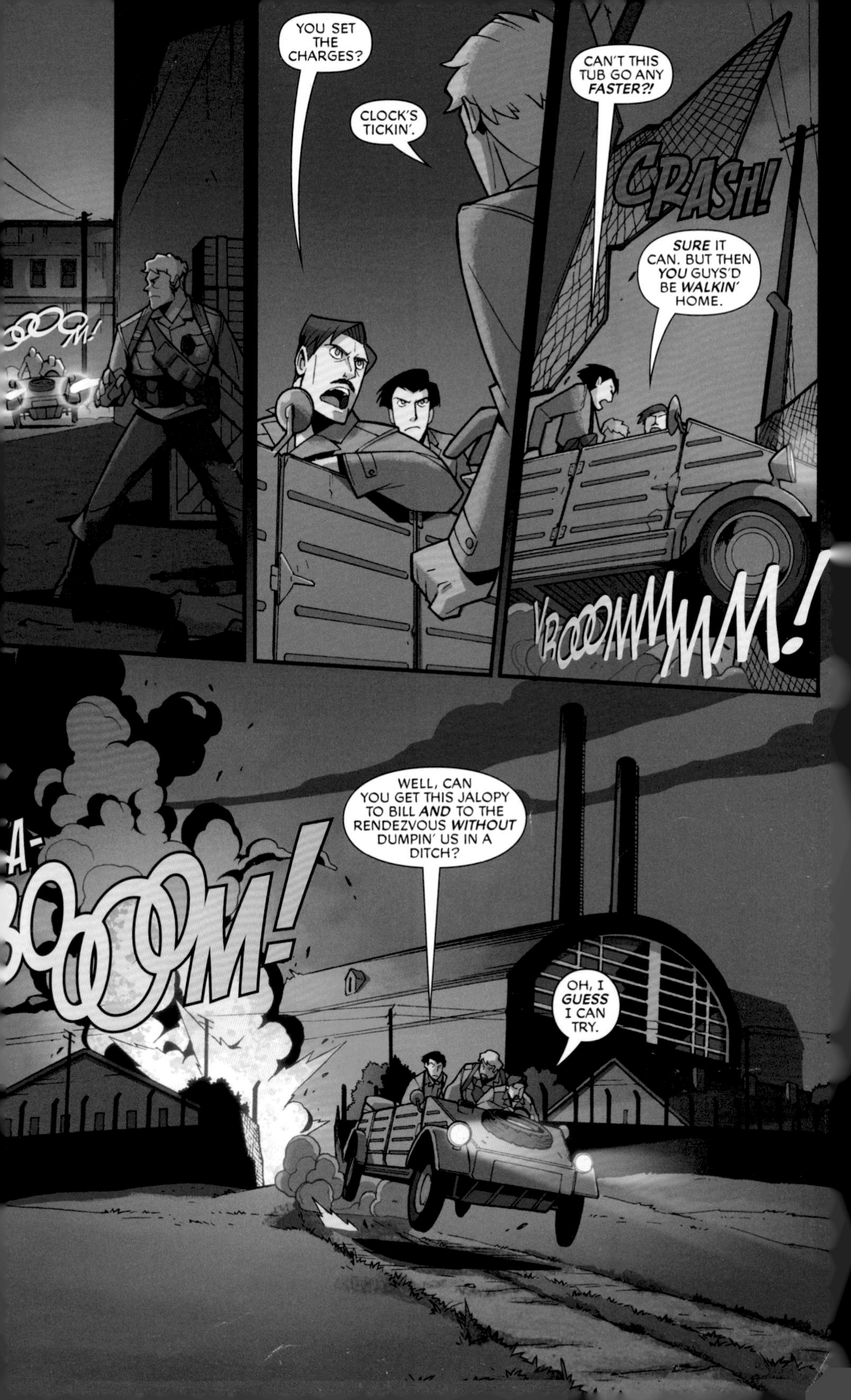
YOU SET THE CHARGES?
CLOCK'S TICKIN'.
CAN'T THIS TUB GO ANY *FASTER?!*
CRASH!
SURE IT CAN. BUT THEN *YOU* GUYS'D BE *WALKIN'* HOME.
VROOMMMMM!
A-BOOOM!
WELL, CAN YOU GET THIS JALOPY TO BILL *AND* TO THE RENDEZVOUS *WITHOUT* DUMPIN' US IN A DITCH?
OH, I *GUESS* I CAN TRY.

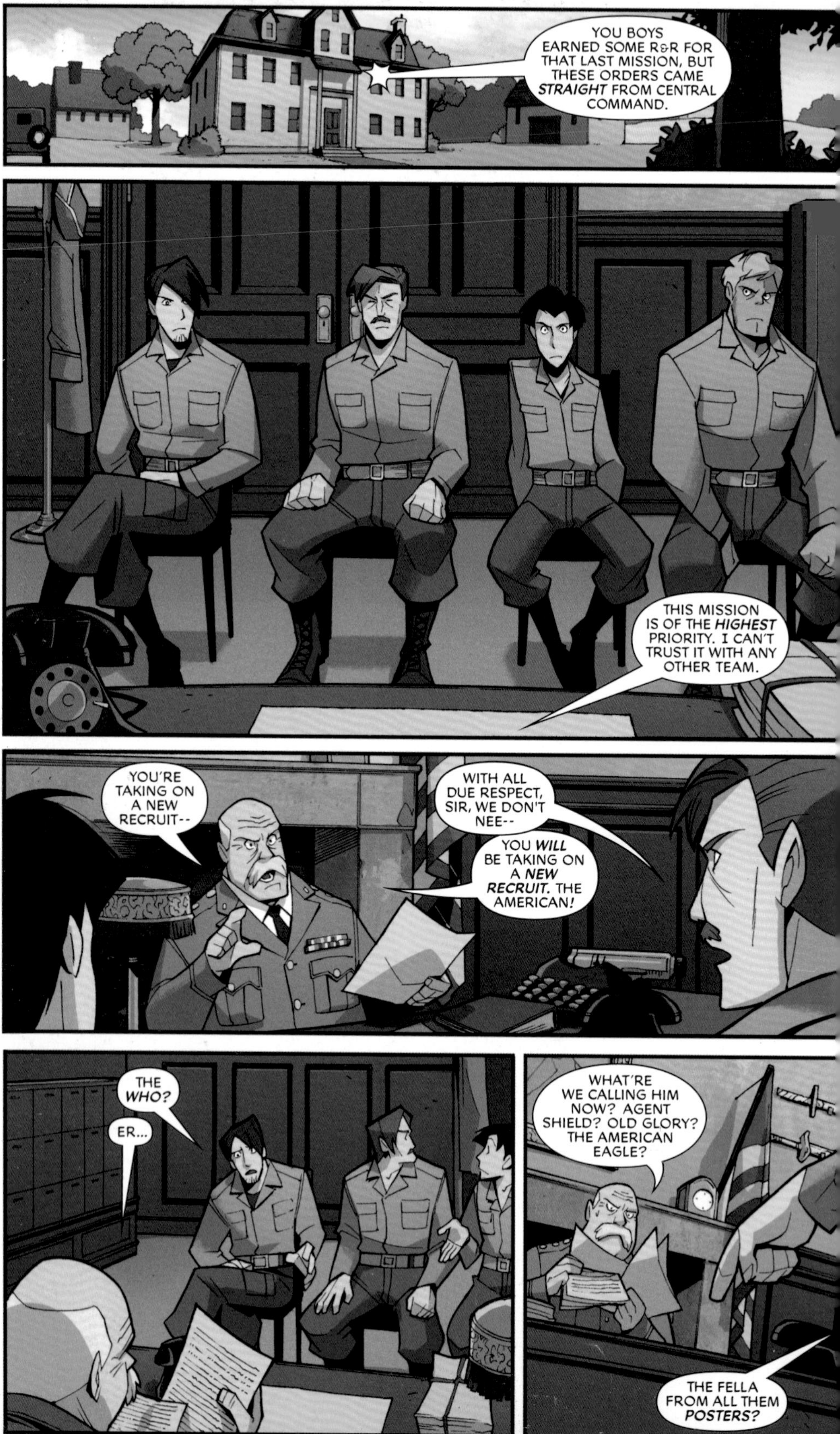
YOU BOYS EARNED SOME R&R FOR THAT LAST MISSION, BUT THESE ORDERS CAME STRAIGHT FROM CENTRAL COMMAND.
THIS MISSION IS OF THE HIGHEST PRIORITY. I CAN'T TRUST IT WITH ANY OTHER TEAM.
YOU'RE TAKING ON A NEW RECRUIT--
WITH ALL DUE RESPECT, SIR, WE DON'T NEE--
YOU WILL BE TAKING ON A NEW RECRUIT. THE AMERICAN!
THE WHO?
ER...
WHAT'RE WE CALLING HIM NOW? AGENT SHIELD? OLD GLORY? THE AMERICAN EAGLE?
THE FELLA FROM ALL THEM POSTERS?

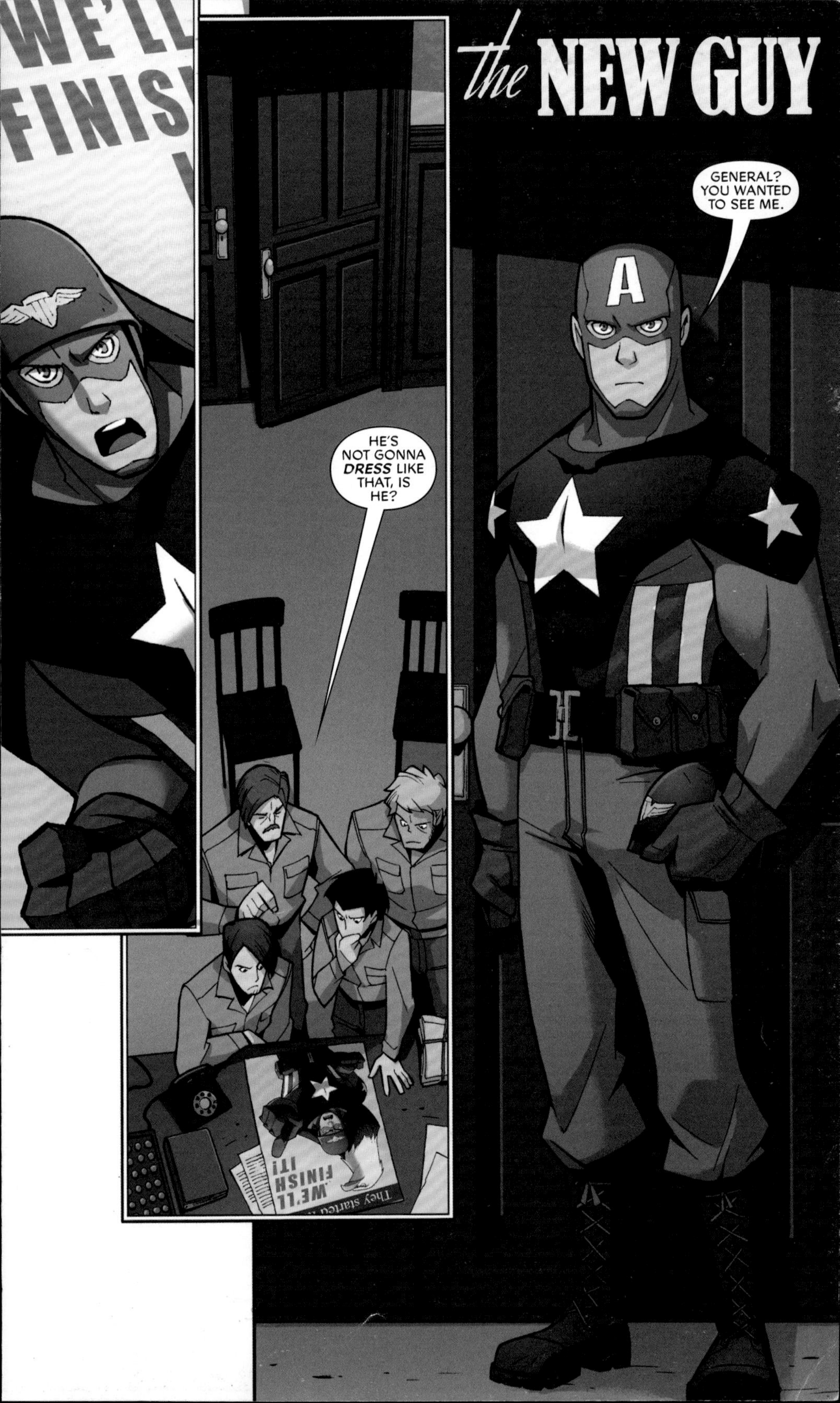
the NEW GUY
HE'S NOT GONNA *DRESS* LIKE THAT, IS HE?
GENERAL? YOU WANTED TO SEE ME.

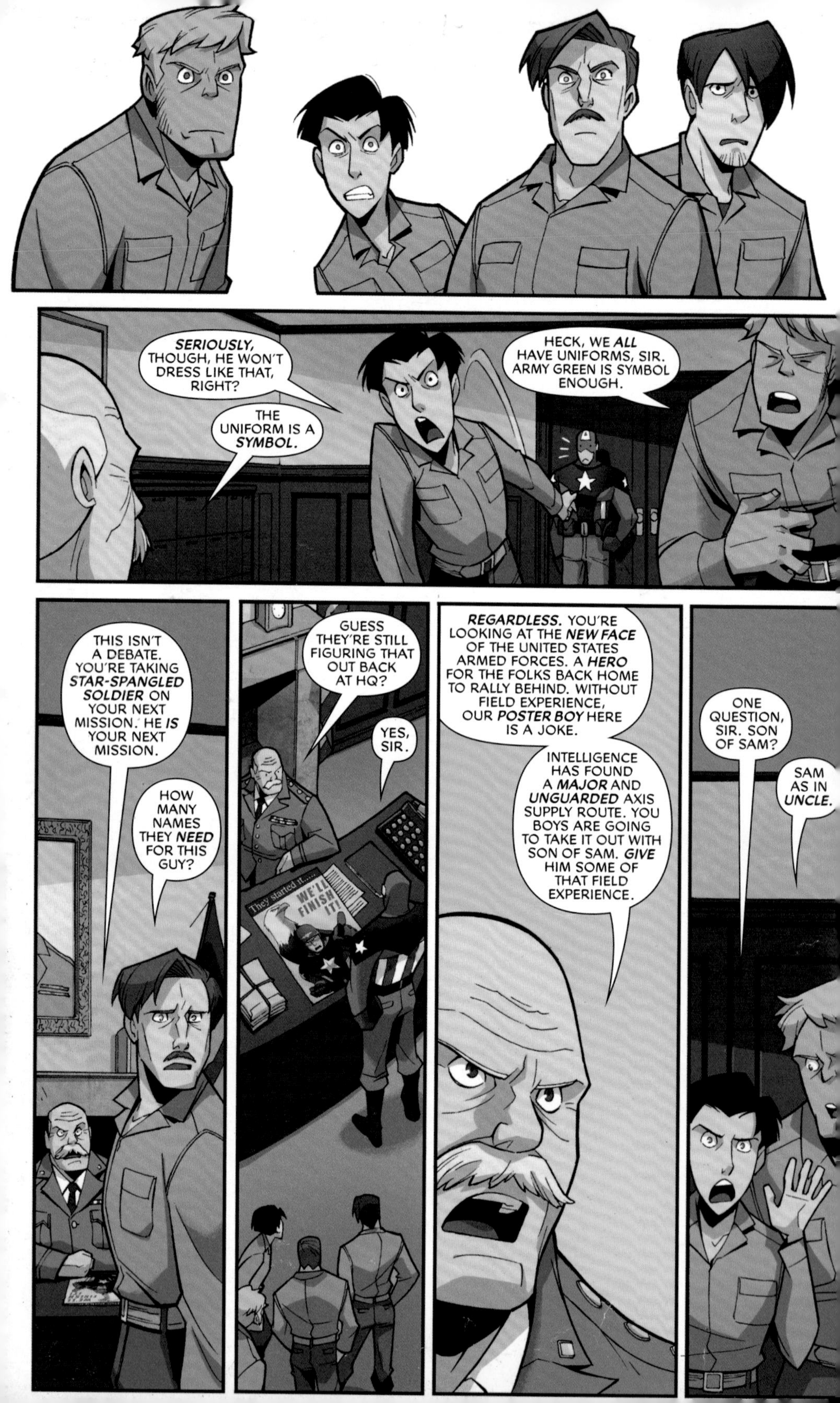

SERIOUSLY, THOUGH, HE WON'T DRESS LIKE THAT, RIGHT?
THE UNIFORM IS A SYMBOL.
HECK, WE ALL HAVE UNIFORMS, SIR. ARMY GREEN IS SYMBOL ENOUGH.
THIS ISN'T A DEBATE. YOU'RE TAKING STAR-SPANGLED SOLDIER ON YOUR NEXT MISSION. HE IS YOUR NEXT MISSION.
HOW MANY NAMES THEY NEED FOR THIS GUY?
GUESS THEY'RE STILL FIGURING THAT OUT BACK AT HQ?
YES, SIR.
They started it.....
WE'LL FINISH IT!
REGARDLESS. YOU'RE LOOKING AT THE NEW FACE OF THE UNITED STATES ARMED FORCES. A HERO FOR THE FOLKS BACK HOME TO RALLY BEHIND. WITHOUT FIELD EXPERIENCE, OUR POSTER BOY HERE IS A JOKE.
INTELLIGENCE HAS FOUND A MAJOR AND UNGUARDED AXIS SUPPLY ROUTE. YOU BOYS ARE GOING TO TAKE IT OUT WITH SON OF SAM. GIVE HIM SOME OF THAT FIELD EXPERIENCE.
ONE QUESTION, SIR. SON OF SAM?
SAM AS IN UNCLE.

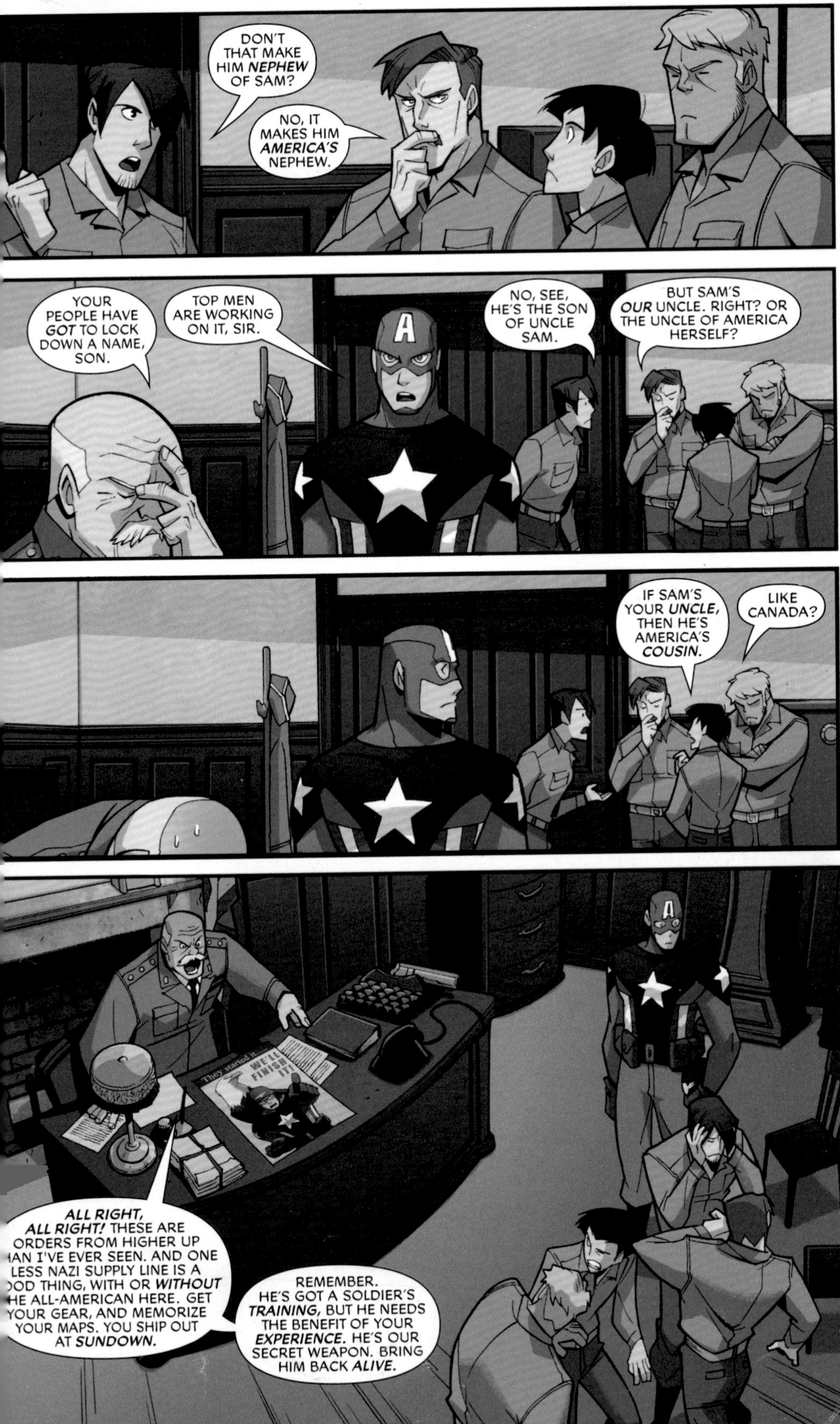
DON'T THAT MAKE HIM NEPHEW OF SAM?
NO, IT MAKES HIM AMERICA'S NEPHEW.
YOUR PEOPLE HAVE GOT TO LOCK DOWN A NAME, SON.
TOP MEN ARE WORKING ON IT, SIR.
NO, SEE, HE'S THE SON OF UNCLE SAM.
BUT SAM'S OUR UNCLE. RIGHT? OR THE UNCLE OF AMERICA HERSELF?
IF SAM'S YOUR UNCLE, THEN HE'S AMERICA'S COUSIN.
LIKE CANADA?
ALL RIGHT, ALL RIGHT! THESE ARE ORDERS FROM HIGHER UP HAN I'VE EVER SEEN. AND ONE LESS NAZI SUPPLY LINE IS A OOD THING, WITH OR WITHOUT HE ALL-AMERICAN HERE. GET YOUR GEAR, AND MEMORIZE YOUR MAPS. YOU SHIP OUT AT SUNDOWN.
REMEMBER. HE'S GOT A SOLDIER'S TRAINING, BUT HE NEEDS THE BENEFIT OF YOUR EXPERIENCE. HE'S OUR SECRET WEAPON. BRING HIM BACK ALIVE.

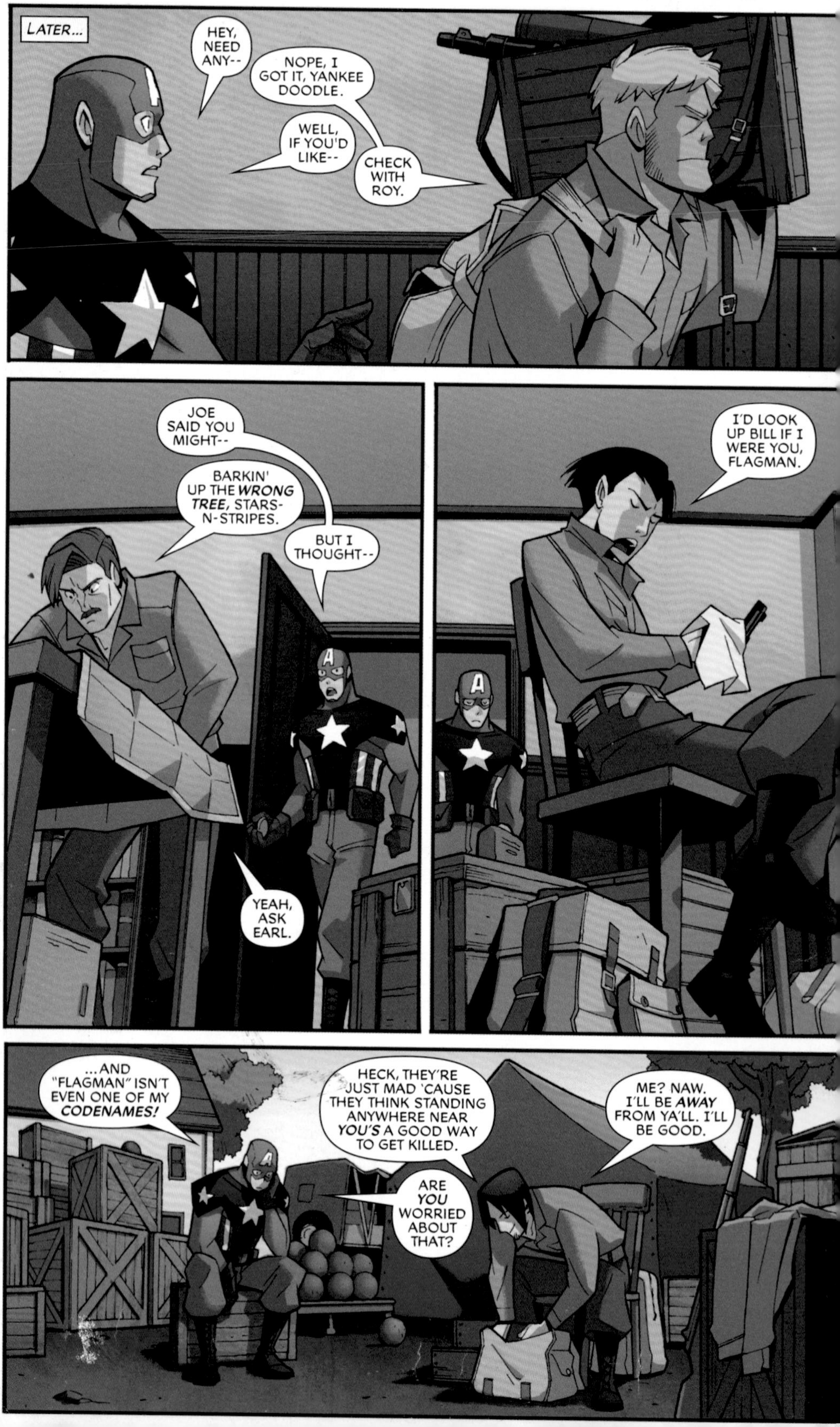
LATER...
HEY, NEED ANY--
NOPE, I GOT IT, YANKEE DOODLE.
WELL, IF YOU'D LIKE--
CHECK WITH ROY.
JOE SAID YOU MIGHT--
BARKIN' UP THE *WRONG TREE,* STARS-N-STRIPES.
BUT I THOUGHT--
YEAH, ASK EARL.
I'D LOOK UP BILL IF I WERE YOU, FLAGMAN.
...AND "FLAGMAN" ISN'T EVEN ONE OF MY *CODENAMES!*
HECK, THEY'RE JUST MAD 'CAUSE THEY THINK STANDING ANYWHERE NEAR *YOU'S* A GOOD WAY TO GET KILLED.
ARE *YOU* WORRIED ABOUT THAT?
ME? NAW. I'LL BE *AWAY* FROM YA'LL. I'LL BE GOOD.

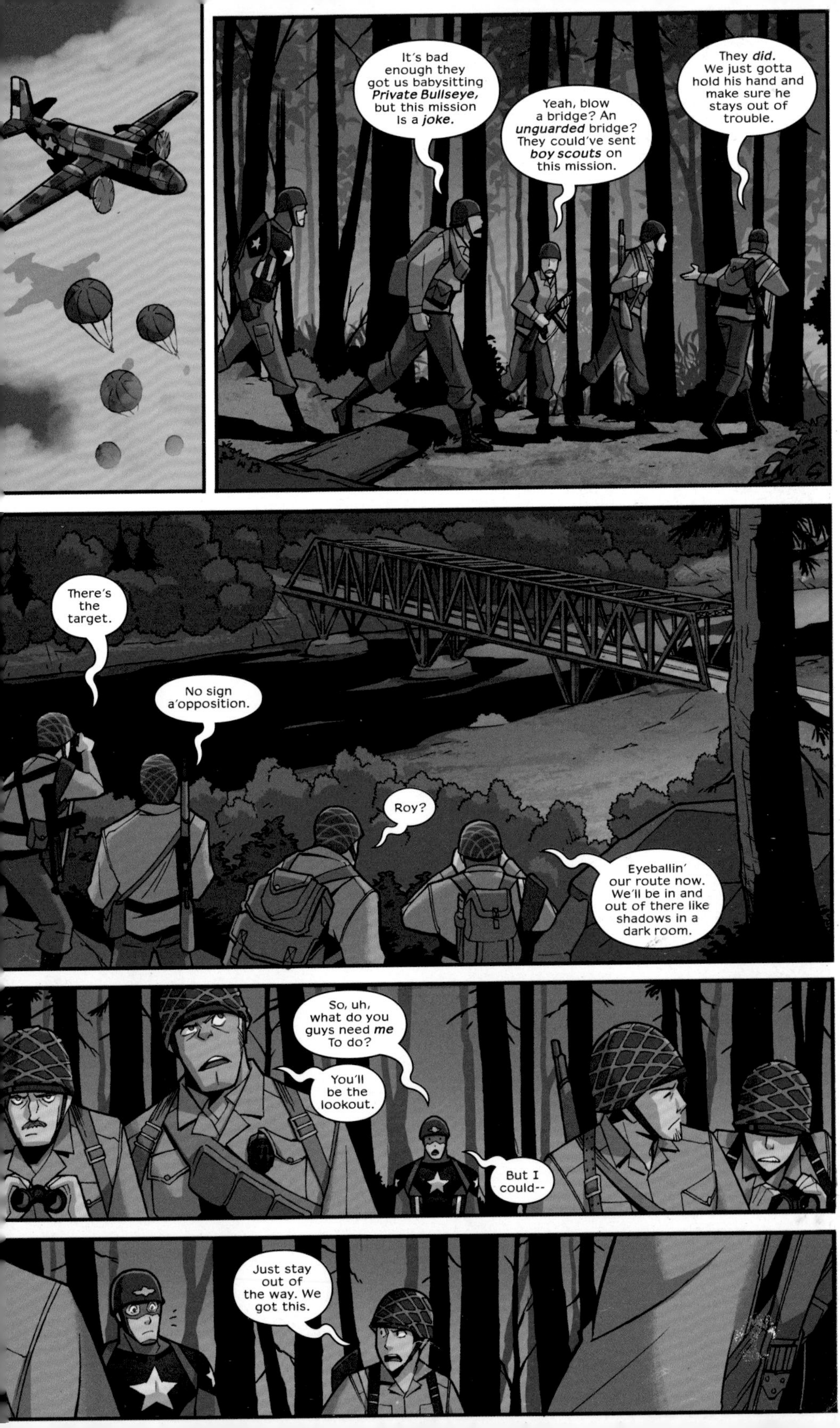
It's bad enough they got us babysitting *Private Bullseye,* but this mission Is a *joke.*
Yeah, blow a bridge? An *unguarded* bridge? They could've sent *boy scouts* on this mission.
They *did.* We just gotta hold his hand and make sure he stays out of trouble.
There's the target.
No sign a'opposition.
Roy?
Eyeballin' our route now. We'll be in and out of there like shadows in a dark room.
So, uh, what do you guys need *me* To do?
You'll be the lookout.
But I could--
Just stay out of the way. We got this.

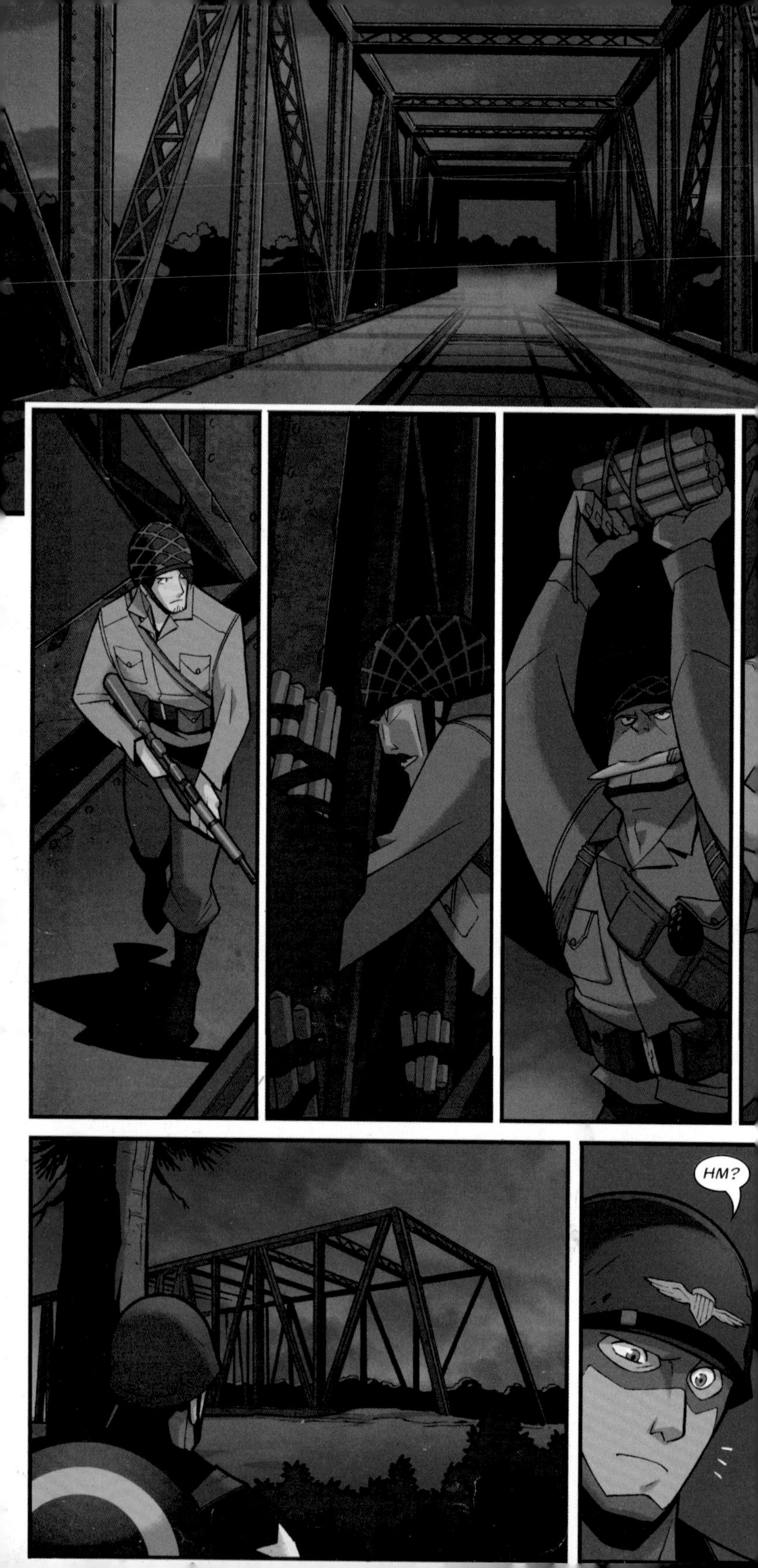
HM?

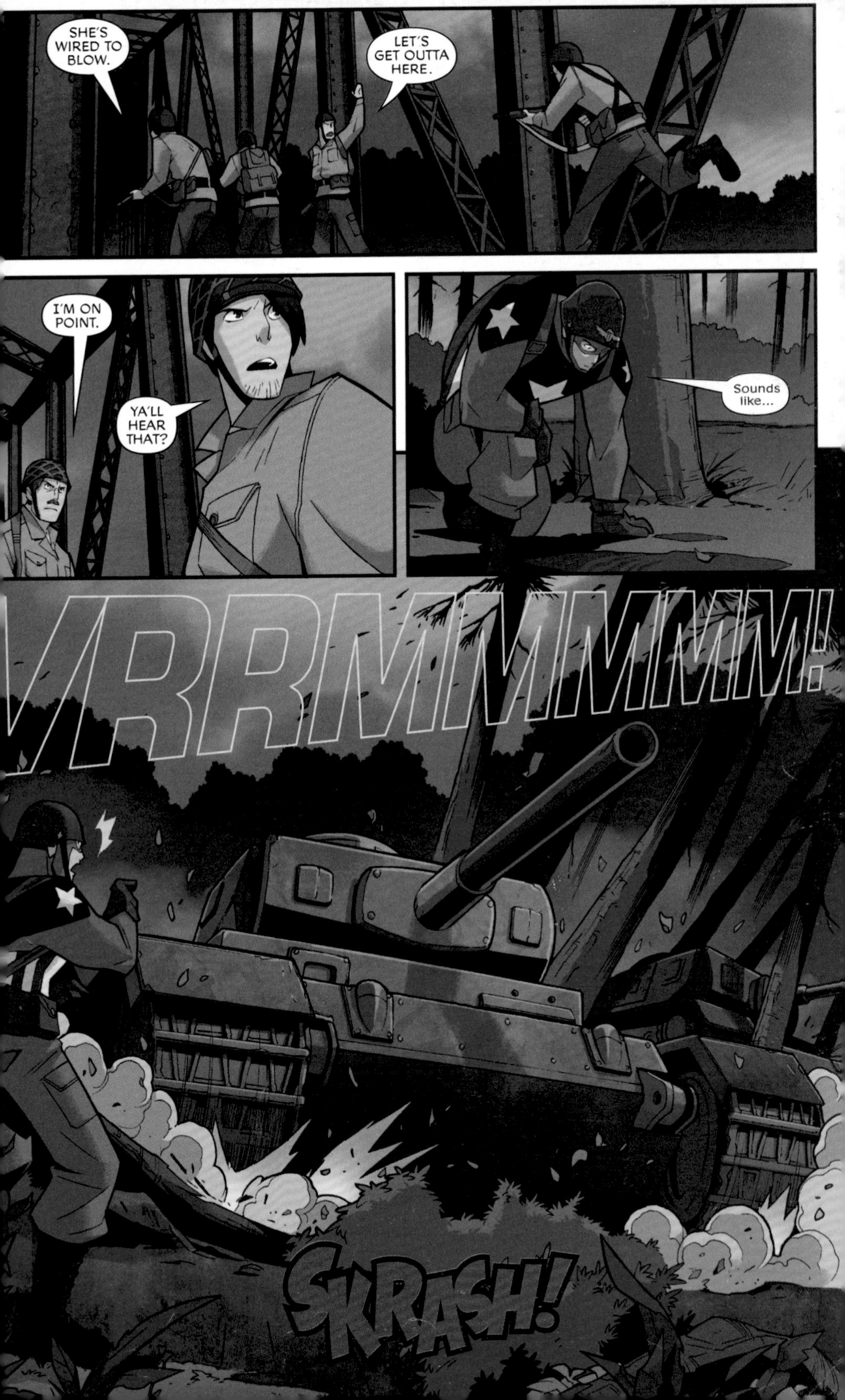
SHE'S WIRED TO BLOW.
LET'S GET OUTTA HERE.
I'M ON POINT.
YA'LL HEAR THAT?
Sounds like...
VRRMMMMM!
SKRASH!

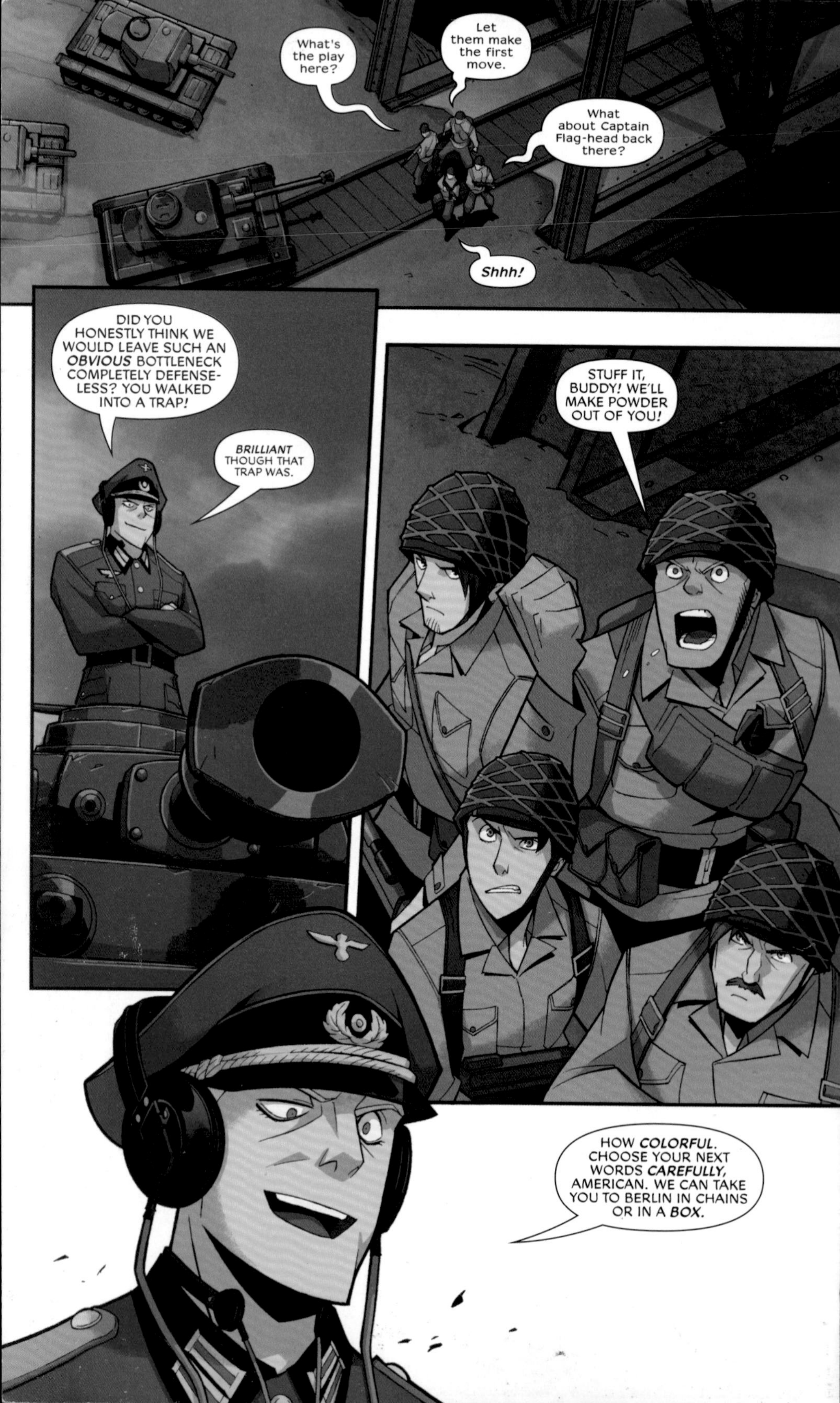
What's the play here?
Let them make the first move.
What about Captain Flag-head back there?
Shhh!
DID YOU HONESTLY THINK WE WOULD LEAVE SUCH AN OBVIOUS BOTTLENECK COMPLETELY DEFENSE-LESS? YOU WALKED INTO A TRAP!
BRILLIANT THOUGH THAT TRAP WAS.
STUFF IT, BUDDY! WE'LL MAKE POWDER OUT OF YOU!
HOW COLORFUL. CHOOSE YOUR NEXT WORDS CAREFULLY, AMERICAN. WE CAN TAKE YOU TO BERLIN IN CHAINS OR IN A BOX.

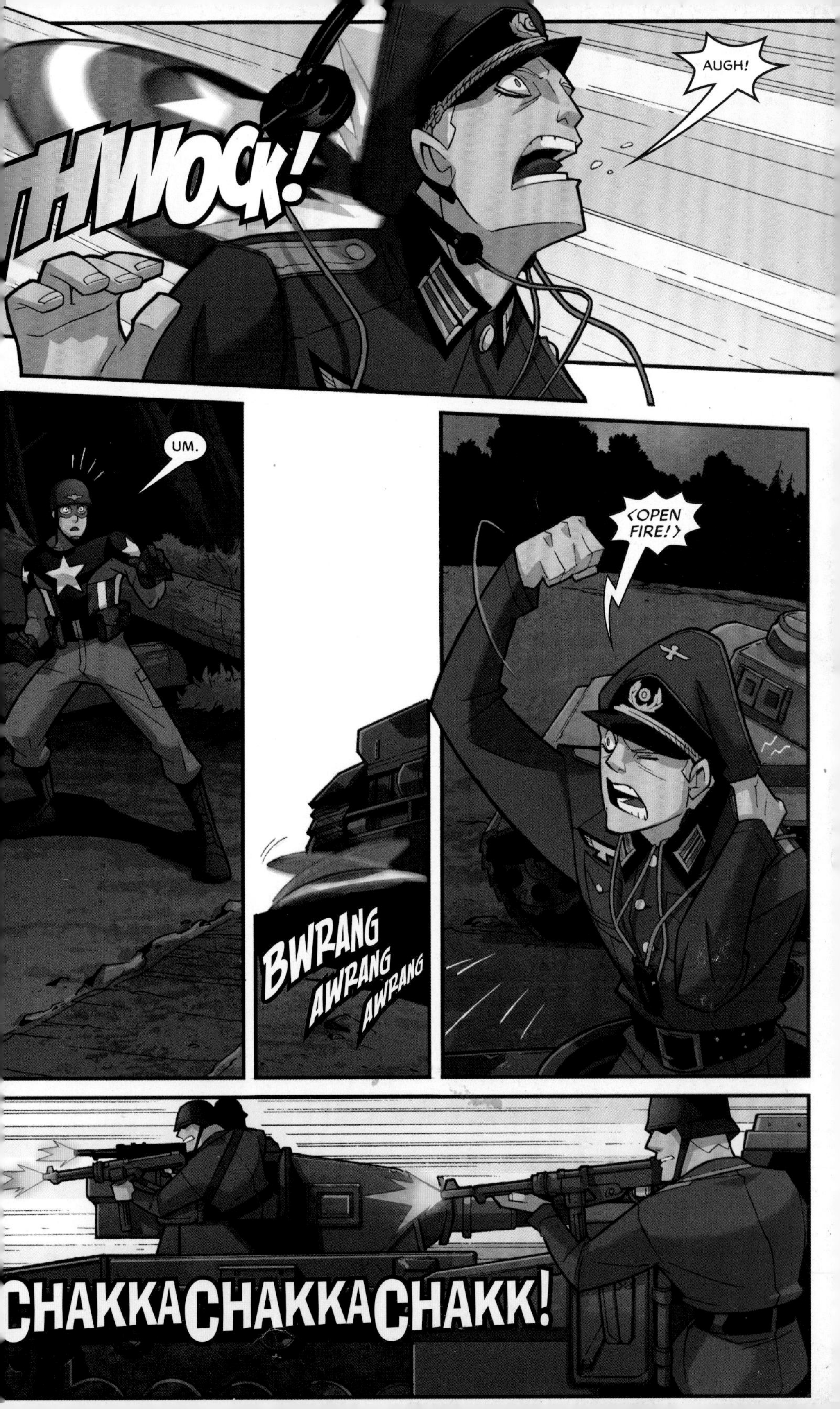
THWOCK!
AUGH!
UM.
BWRANG
AWRANG
AWRANG
<OPEN FIRE!>
CHAKKACHAKKACHAKK!

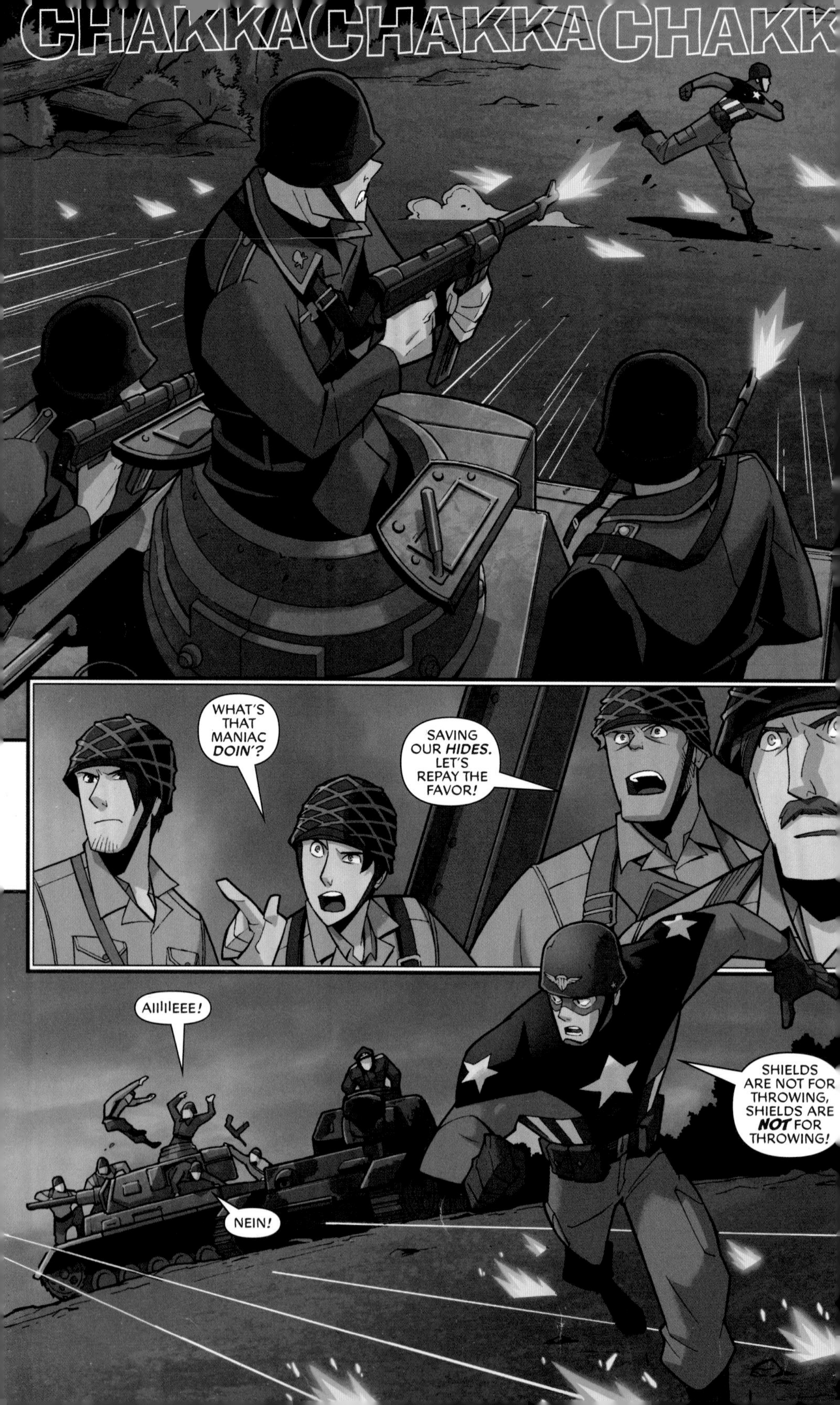
CHAKKACHAKKACHAKK
WHAT'S THAT MANIAC DOIN'?
SAVING OUR HIDES. LET'S REPAY THE FAVOR!
AIIIIIEEE!
NEIN!
SHIELDS ARE NOT FOR THROWING, SHIELDS ARE NOT FOR THROWING!

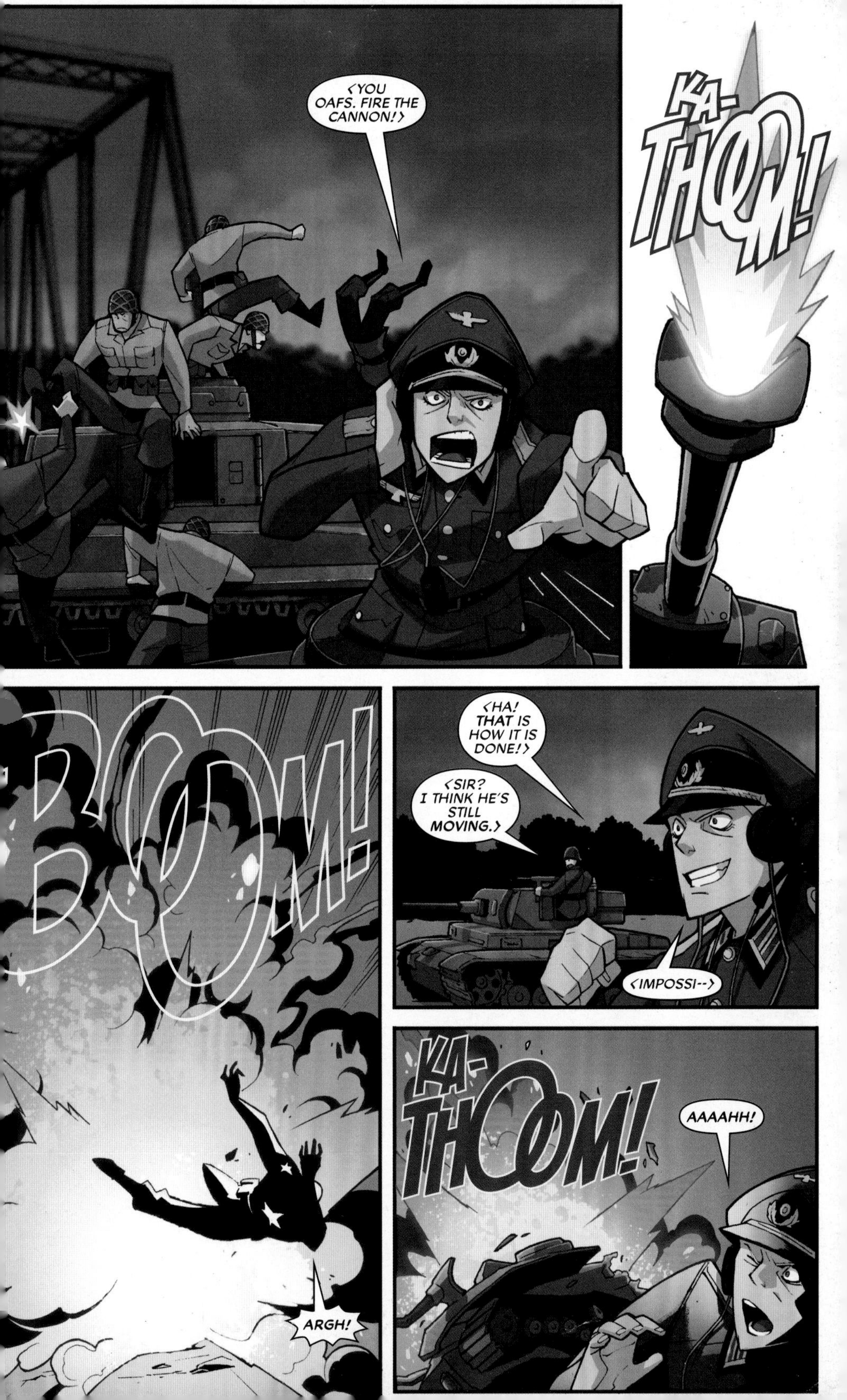

<YOU OAFS. FIRE THE CANNON!>
KA-THOOM!
BOOM!
ARGH!
<HA! THAT IS HOW IT IS DONE!>
<SIR? I THINK HE'S STILL MOVING.>
<IMPOSSI-->
KA-THOOM!
AAAAHH!

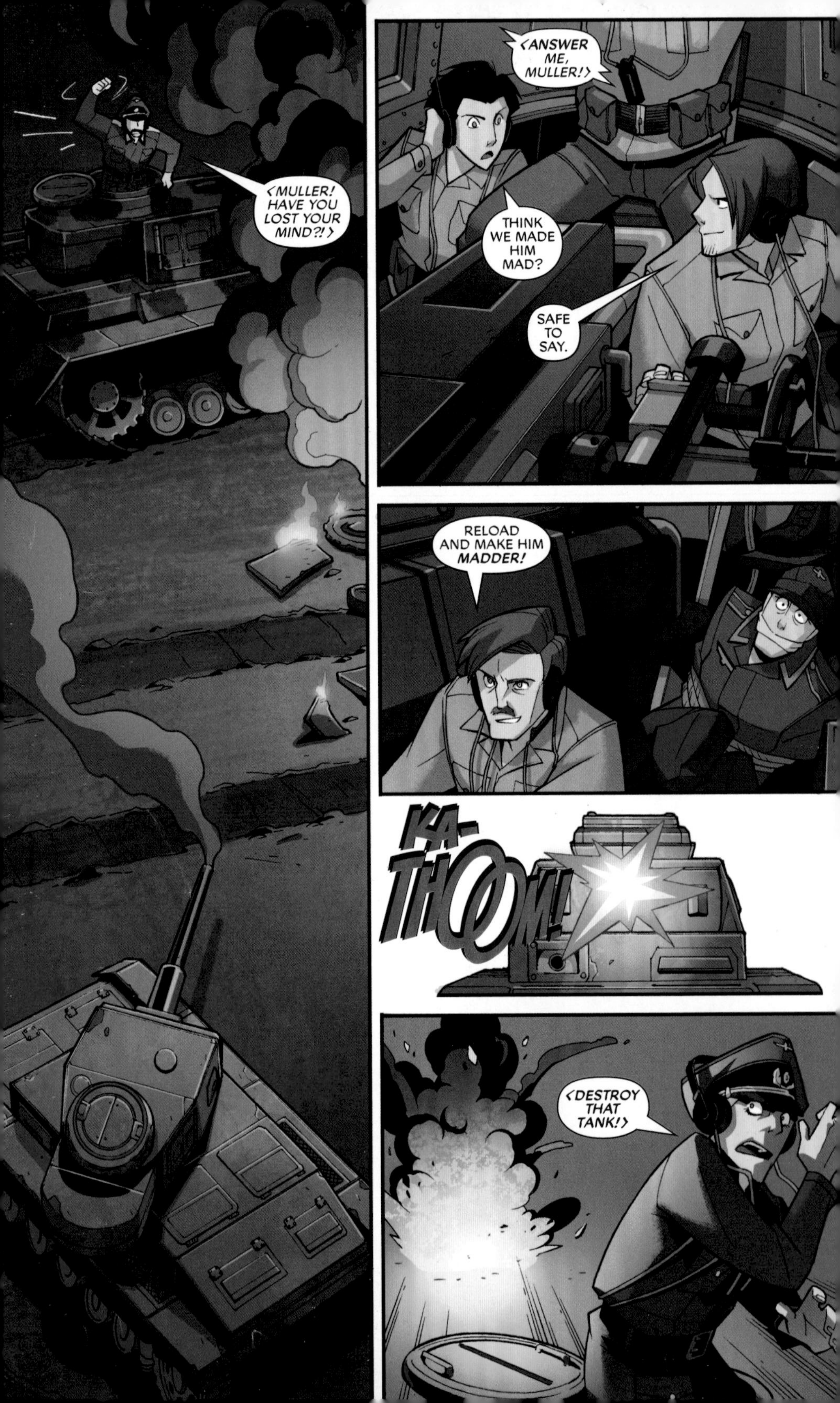

<MULLER! HAVE YOU LOST YOUR MIND?!>
<ANSWER ME, MULLER!>
THINK WE MADE HIM MAD?
SAFE TO SAY.
RELOAD AND MAKE HIM MADDER!
KA-THOOM!
<DESTROY THAT TANK!>

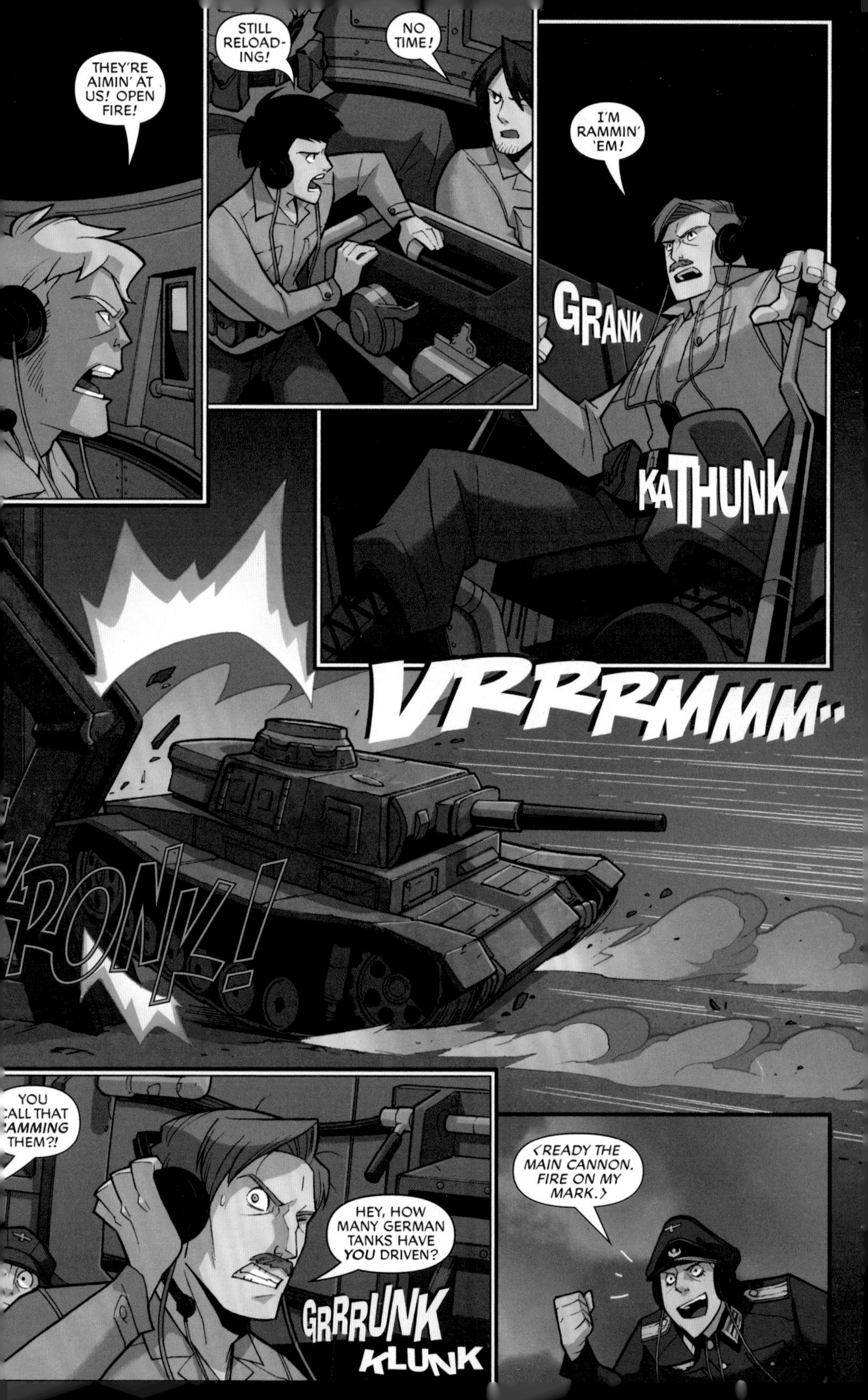
THEY'RE AIMIN' AT US! OPEN FIRE!
STILL RELOAD-ING!
NO TIME!
I'M RAMMIN' 'EM!
GRANK
KATHUNK
VRRRMMM..
KRONK!
YOU CALL THAT RAMMING THEM?!
HEY, HOW MANY GERMAN TANKS HAVE YOU DRIVEN?
GRRRUNK
KLUNK
<READY THE MAIN CANNON. FIRE ON MY MARK.>

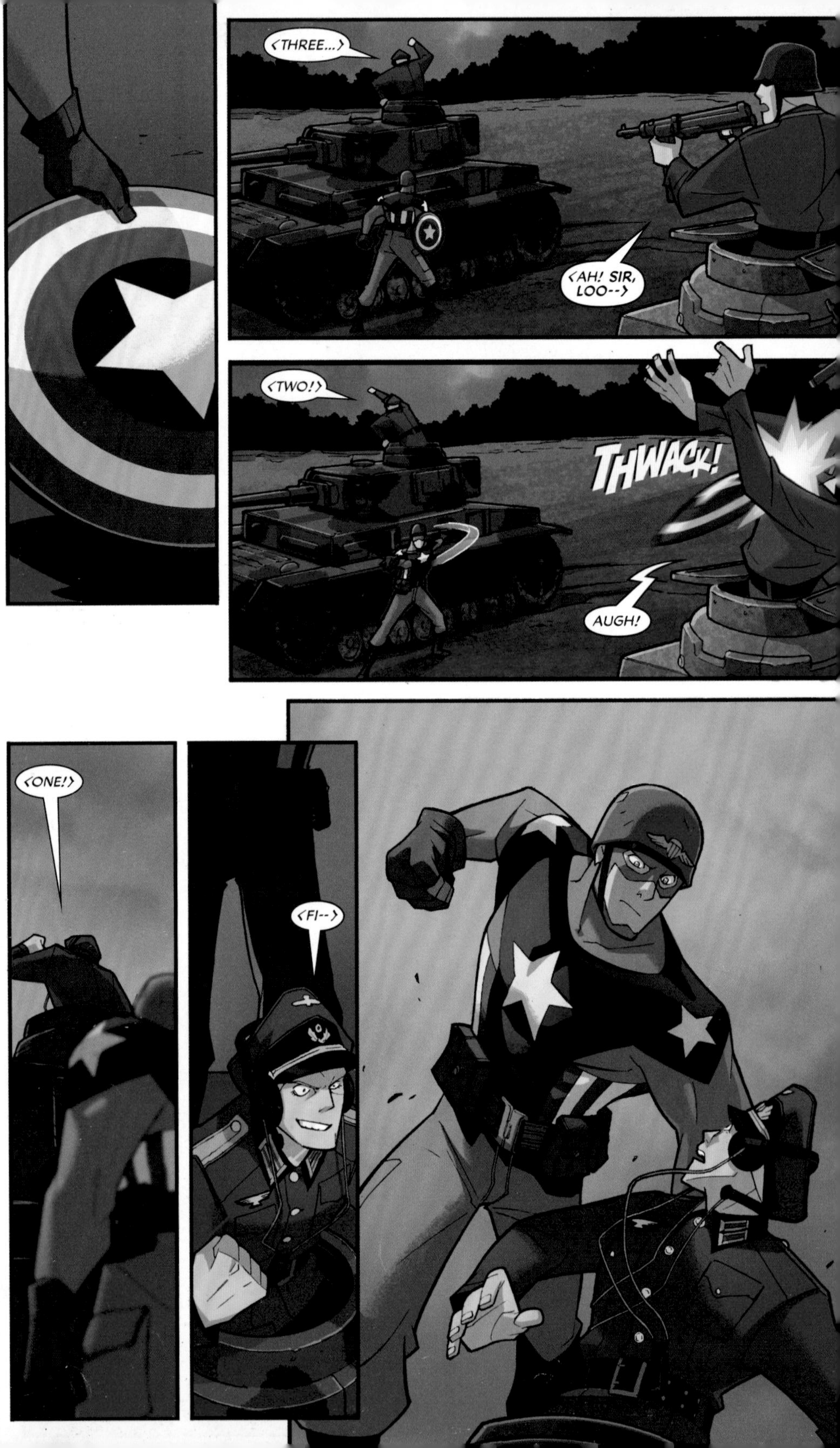

<THREE...>
<AH! SIR, LOO-->
<TWO!>
THWACK!
AUGH!
<ONE!>
<FI-->

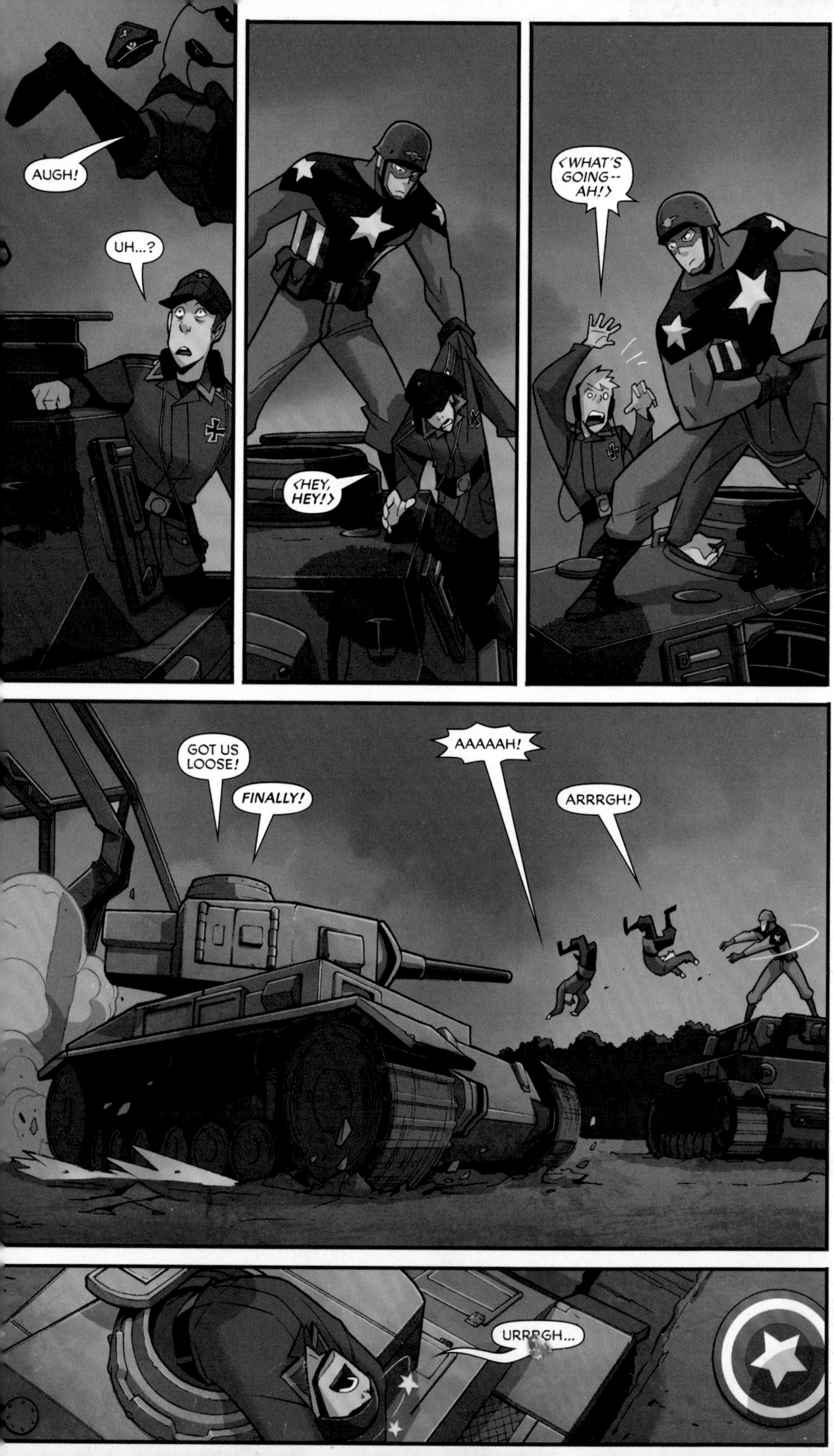
AUGH!
UH...?
<HEY, HEY!>
<WHAT'S GOING-- AH!>
GOT US LOOSE!
FINALLY!
AAAAAH!
ARRRGH!
URRRGH...

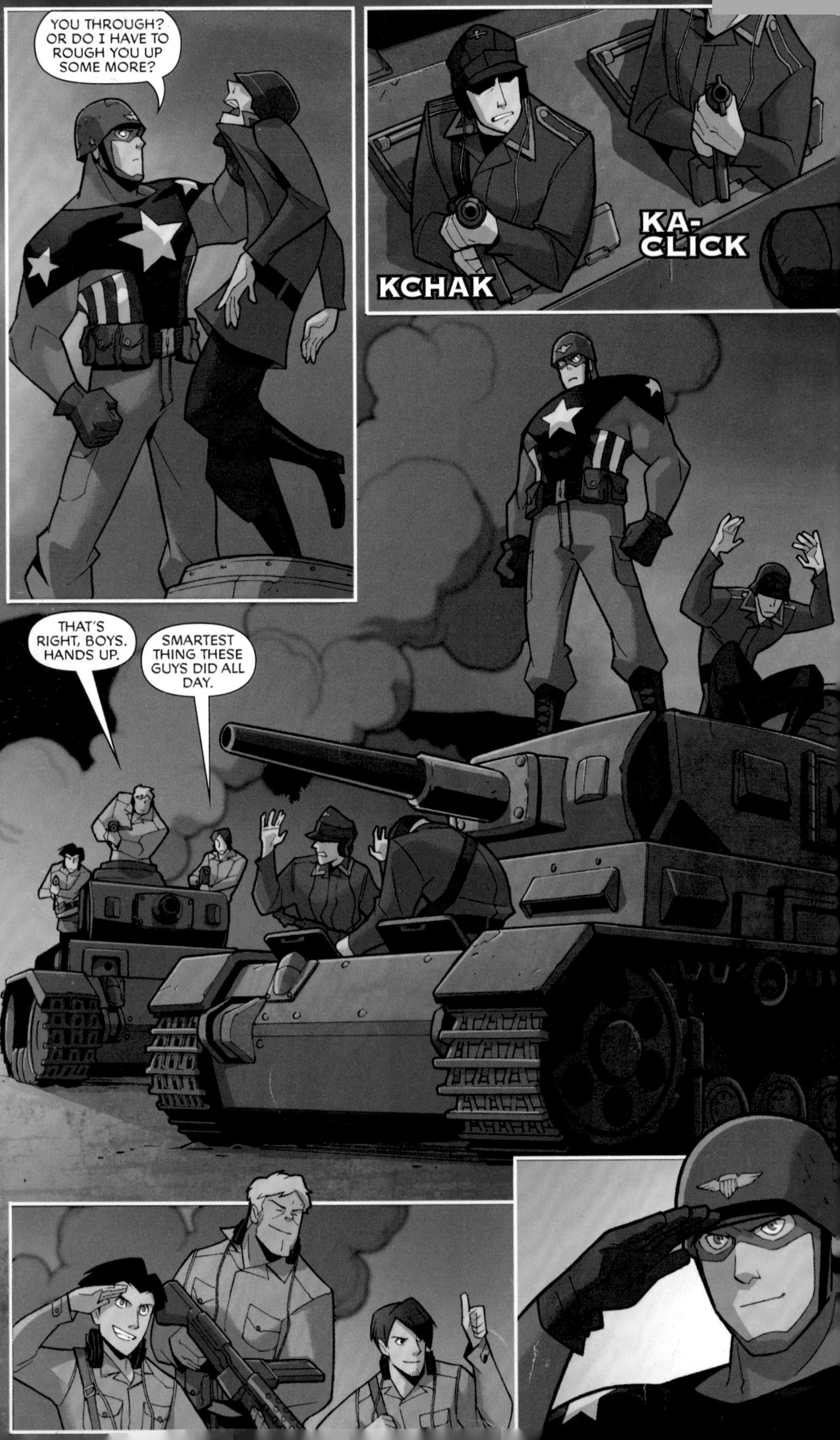
YOU THROUGH? OR DO I HAVE TO ROUGH YOU UP SOME MORE?
KCHAK
KA-CLICK
THAT'S RIGHT, BOYS. HANDS UP.
SMARTEST THING THESE GUYS DID ALL DAY.

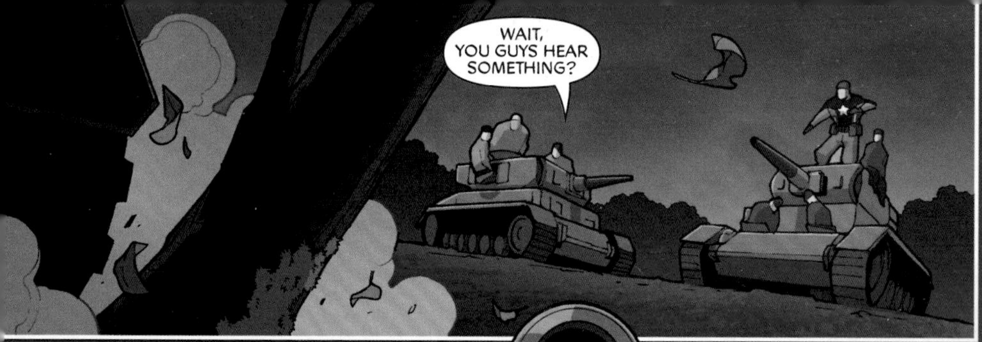
WAIT, YOU GUYS HEAR SOMETHING?

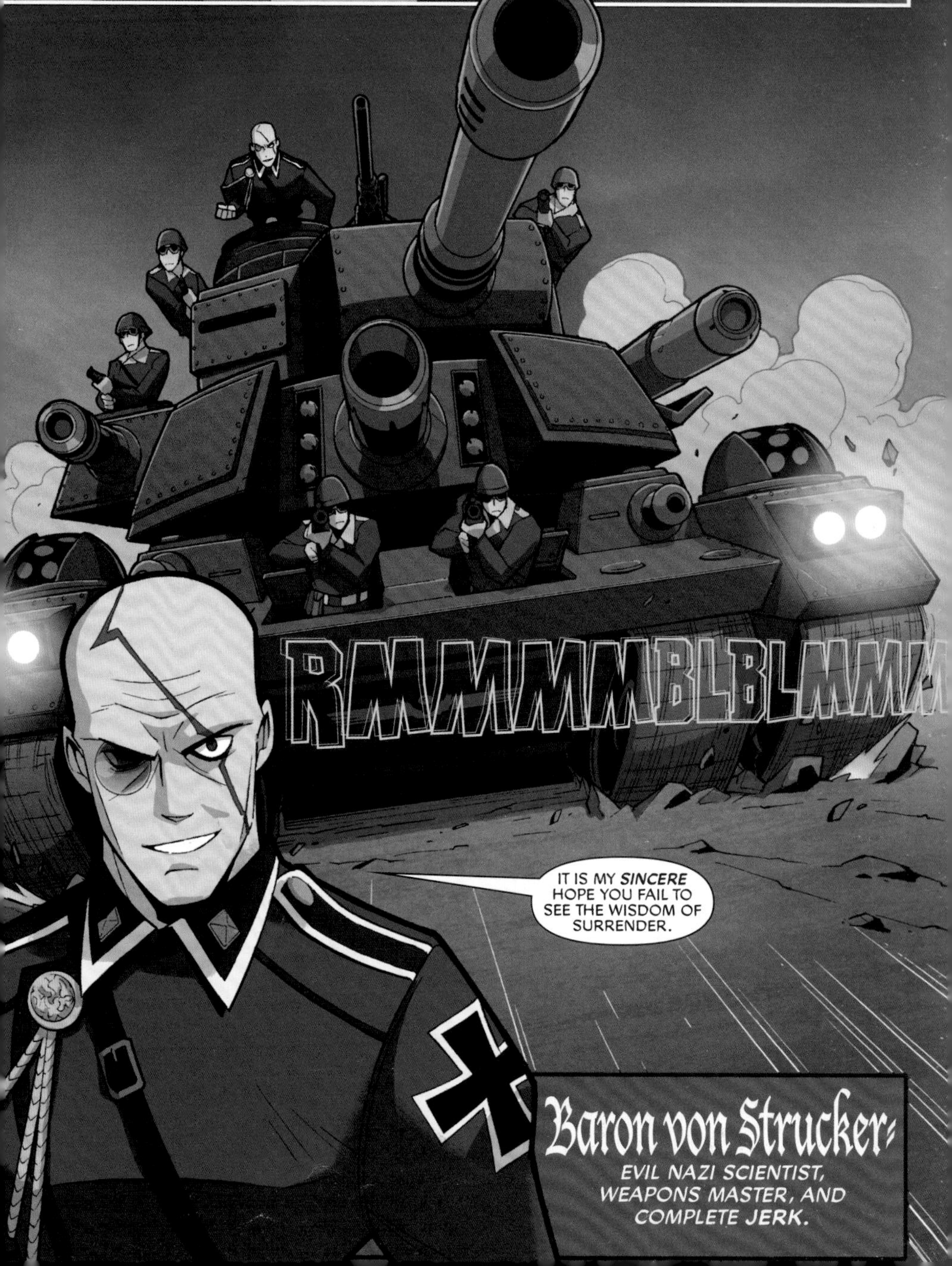
RMMMMMBLBLMMMM
IT IS MY SINCERE HOPE YOU FAIL TO SEE THE WISDOM OF SURRENDER.
Baron von Strucker:
EVIL NAZI SCIENTIST, WEAPONS MASTER, AND COMPLETE JERK.

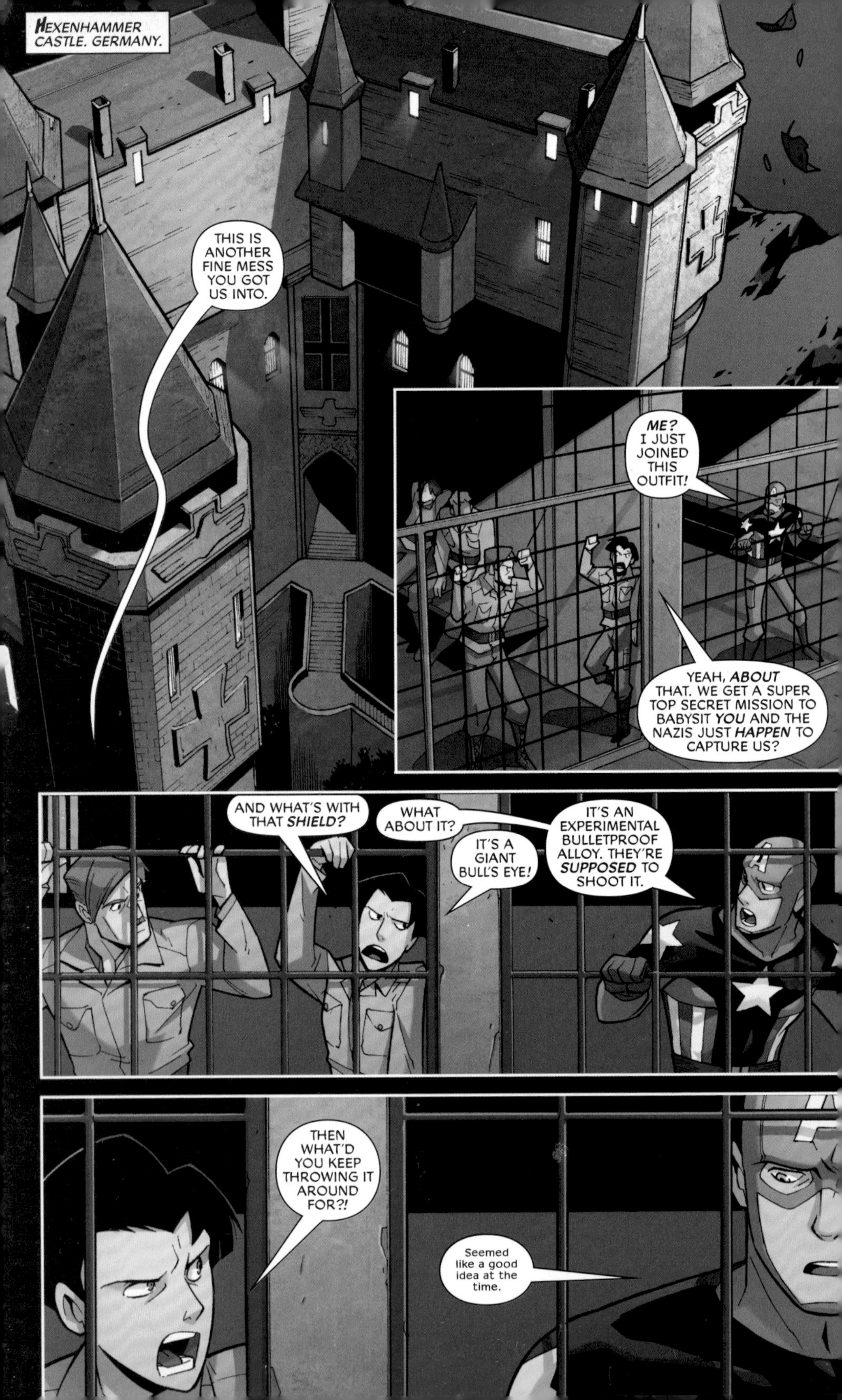
HEXENHAMMER CASTLE. GERMANY.
THIS IS ANOTHER FINE MESS YOU GOT US INTO.
ME? I JUST JOINED THIS OUTFIT!
YEAH, ABOUT THAT. WE GET A SUPER TOP SECRET MISSION TO BABYSIT YOU AND THE NAZIS JUST HAPPEN TO CAPTURE US?
AND WHAT'S WITH THAT SHIELD?
WHAT ABOUT IT?
IT'S A GIANT BULL'S EYE!
IT'S AN EXPERIMENTAL BULLETPROOF ALLOY. THEY'RE SUPPOSED TO SHOOT IT.
THEN WHAT'D YOU KEEP THROWING IT AROUND FOR?!
Seemed like a good idea at the time.

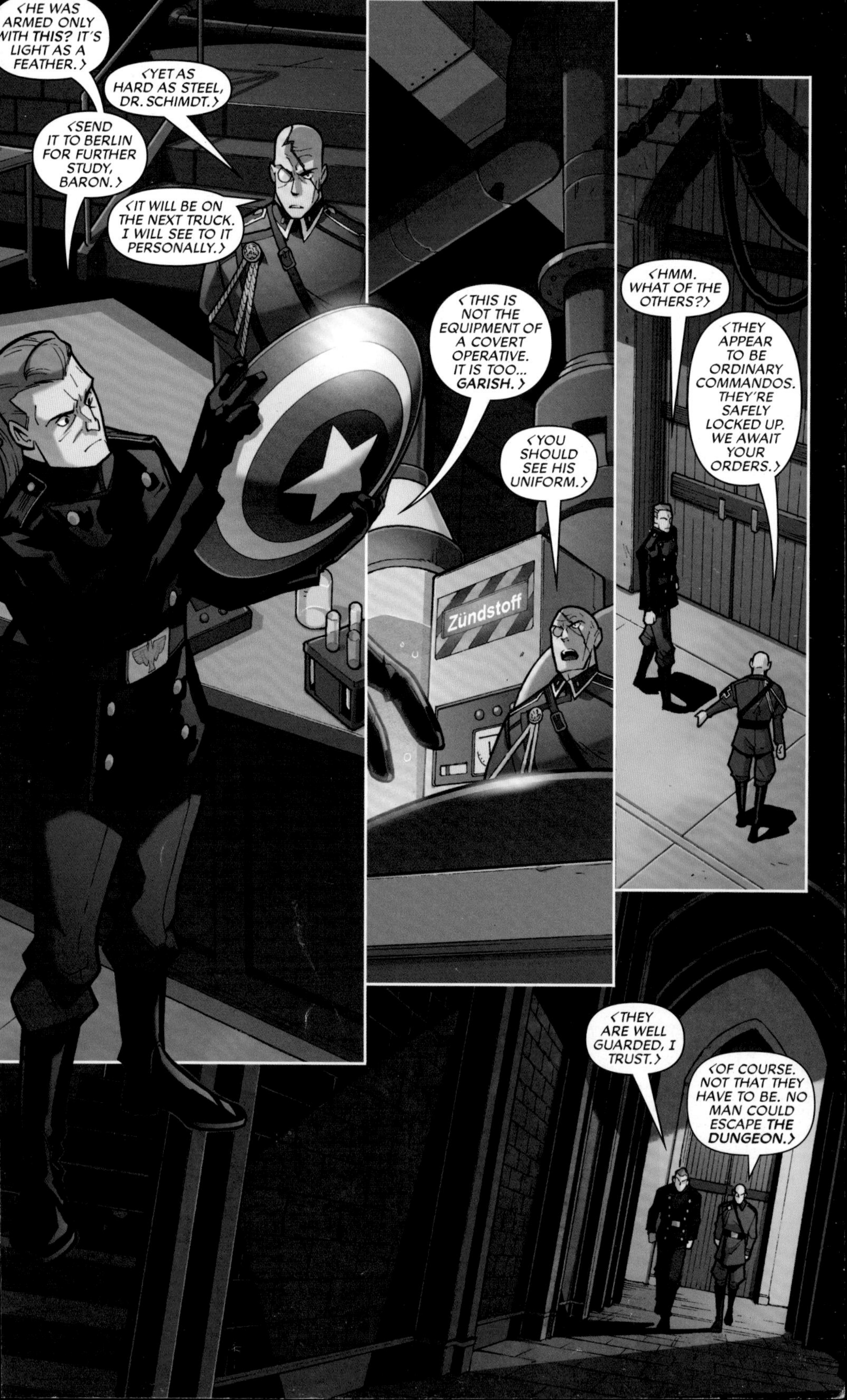

<HE WAS ARMED ONLY WITH THIS? IT'S LIGHT AS A FEATHER.>
<YET AS HARD AS STEEL, DR. SCHIMDT.>
<SEND IT TO BERLIN FOR FURTHER STUDY, BARON.>
<IT WILL BE ON THE NEXT TRUCK. I WILL SEE TO IT PERSONALLY.>
<THIS IS NOT THE EQUIPMENT OF A COVERT OPERATIVE. IT IS TOO... GARISH.>
Zündstoff
<YOU SHOULD SEE HIS UNIFORM.>
<HMM. WHAT OF THE OTHERS?>
<THEY APPEAR TO BE ORDINARY COMMANDOS. THEY'RE SAFELY LOCKED UP. WE AWAIT YOUR ORDERS.>
<THEY ARE WELL GUARDED, I TRUST.>
<OF COURSE. NOT THAT THEY HAVE TO BE. NO MAN COULD ESCAPE THE DUNGEON.>

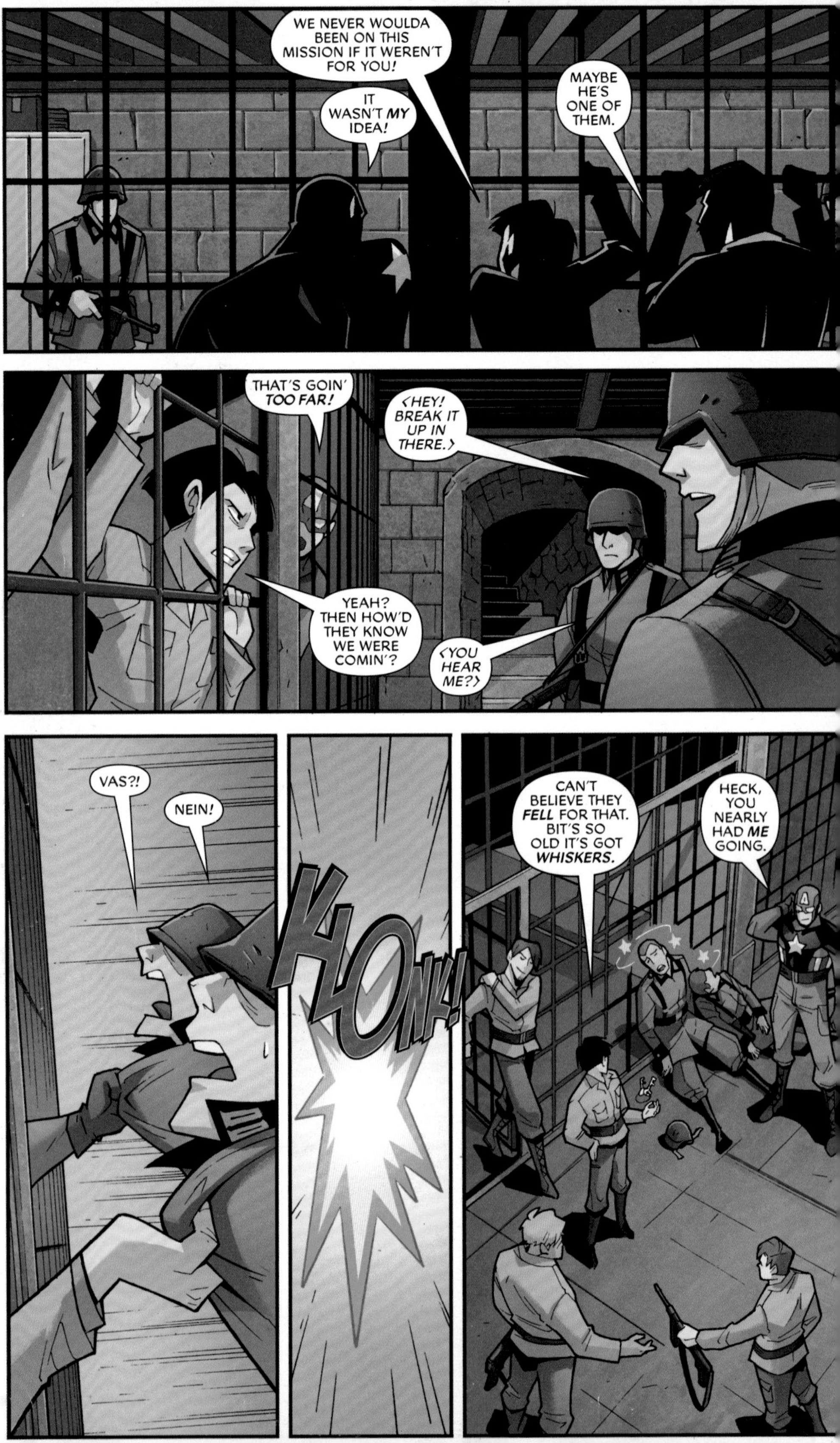

WE NEVER WOULDA BEEN ON THIS MISSION IF IT WEREN'T FOR YOU!
IT WASN'T MY IDEA!
MAYBE HE'S ONE OF THEM.
THAT'S GOIN' TOO FAR!
YEAH? THEN HOW'D THEY KNOW WE WERE COMIN'?
<HEY! BREAK IT UP IN THERE.>
<YOU HEAR ME?>
VAS?!
NEIN!
KLONK!
CAN'T BELIEVE THEY FELL FOR THAT. BIT'S SO OLD IT'S GOT WHISKERS.
HECK, YOU NEARLY HAD ME GOING.

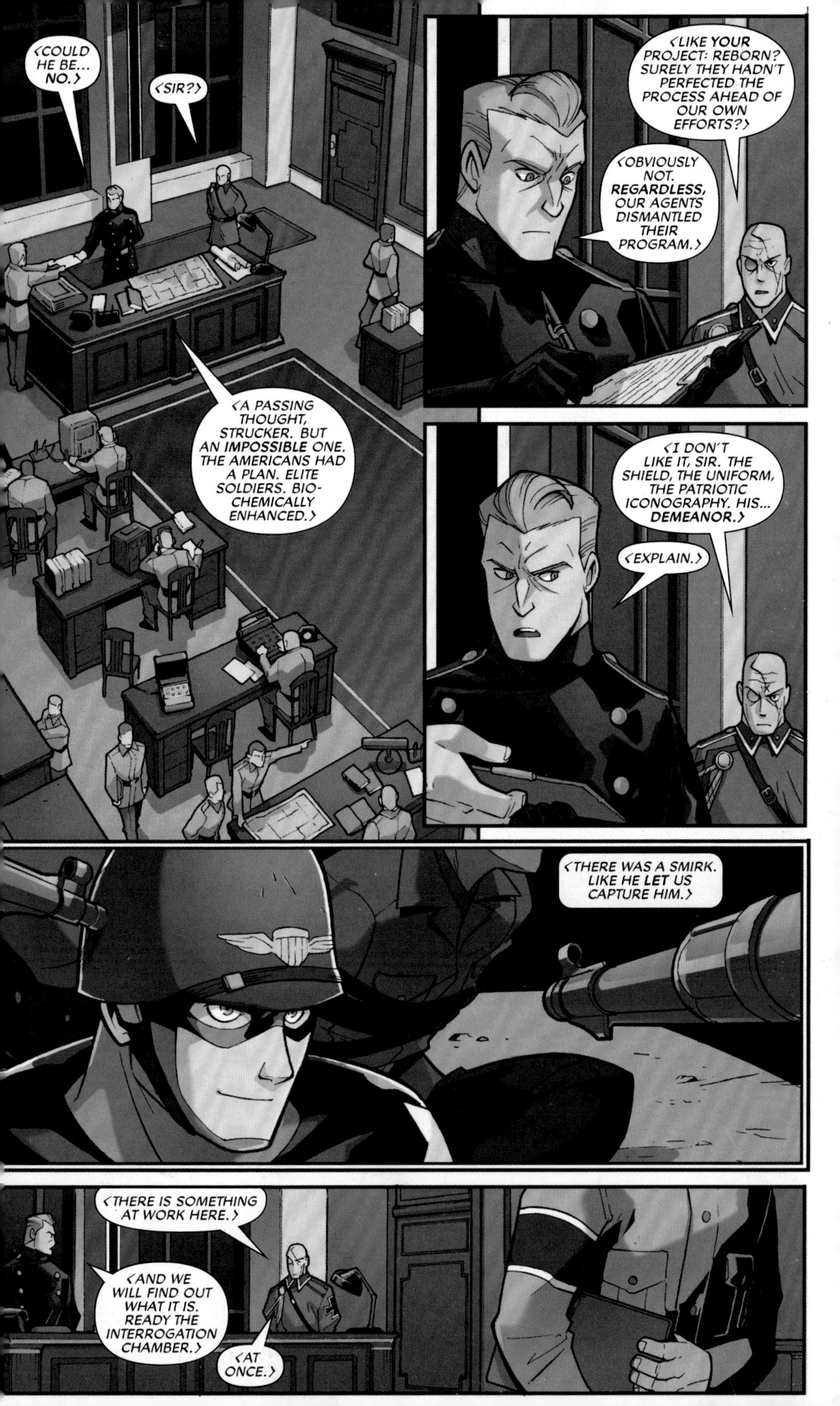

<COULD HE BE... NO.>
<SIR?>
<A PASSING THOUGHT, STRUCKER. BUT AN IMPOSSIBLE ONE. THE AMERICANS HAD A PLAN. ELITE SOLDIERS. BIO-CHEMICALLY ENHANCED.>
<LIKE YOUR PROJECT: REBORN? SURELY THEY HADN'T PERFECTED THE PROCESS AHEAD OF OUR OWN EFFORTS?>
<OBVIOUSLY NOT. REGARDLESS, OUR AGENTS DISMANTLED THEIR PROGRAM.>
<I DON'T LIKE IT, SIR. THE SHIELD, THE UNIFORM, THE PATRIOTIC ICONOGRAPHY. HIS... DEMEANOR.>
<EXPLAIN.>
<THERE WAS A SMIRK. LIKE HE LET US CAPTURE HIM.>
<THERE IS SOMETHING AT WORK HERE.>
<AND WE WILL FIND OUT WHAT IT IS. READY THE INTERROGATION CHAMBER.>
<AT ONCE.>

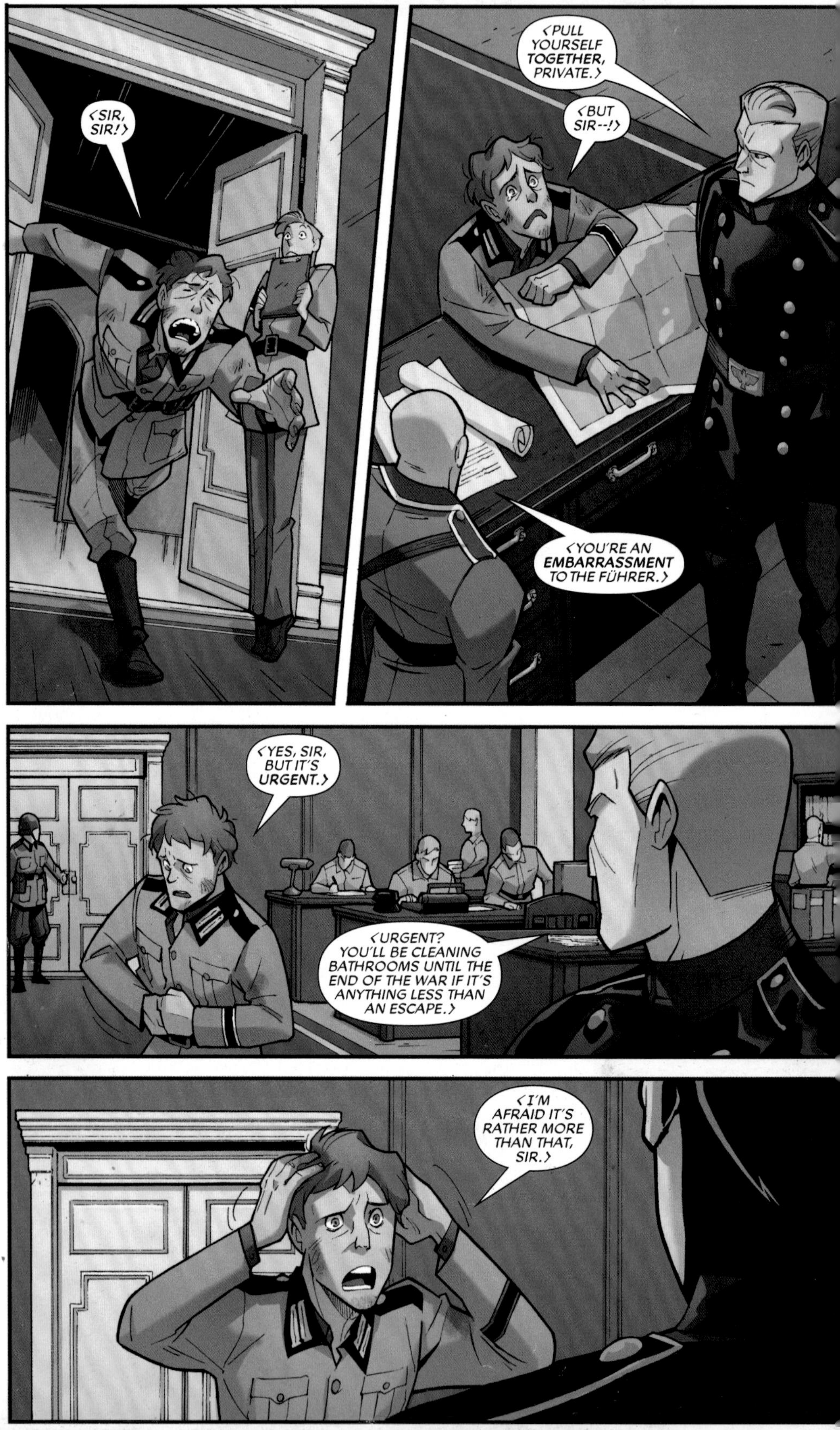

<SIR, SIR!>
<PULL YOURSELF TOGETHER, PRIVATE.>
<BUT SIR--!>
<YOU'RE AN EMBARRASSMENT TO THE FÜHRER.>
<YES, SIR, BUT IT'S URGENT.>
<URGENT? YOU'LL BE CLEANING BATHROOMS UNTIL THE END OF THE WAR IF IT'S ANYTHING LESS THAN AN ESCAPE.>
<I'M AFRAID IT'S RATHER MORE THAN THAT, SIR.>

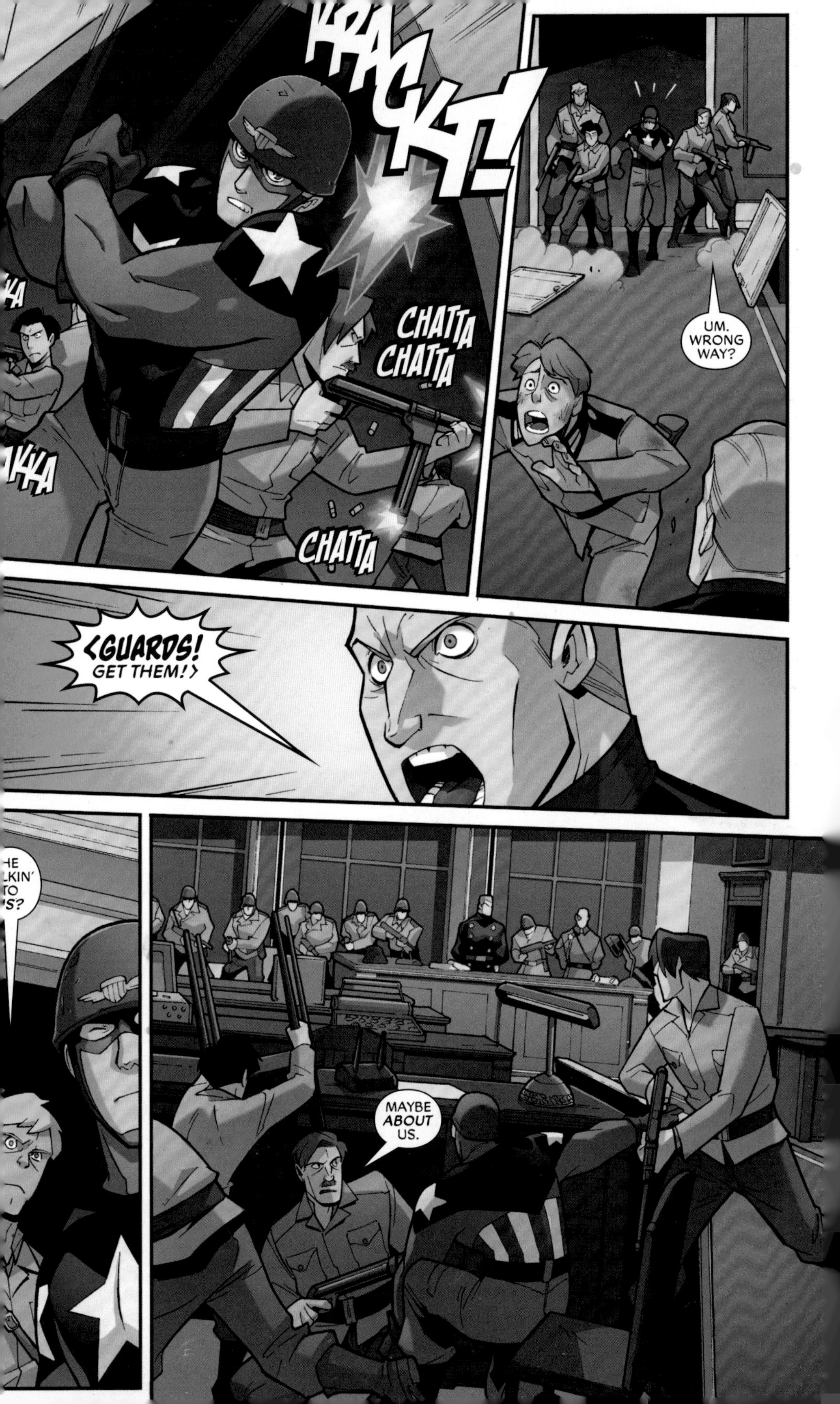

KRACK!!
CHATTA CHATTA
CHATTA
UM. WRONG WAY?
<GUARDS! GET THEM!>
MAYBE ABOUT US.

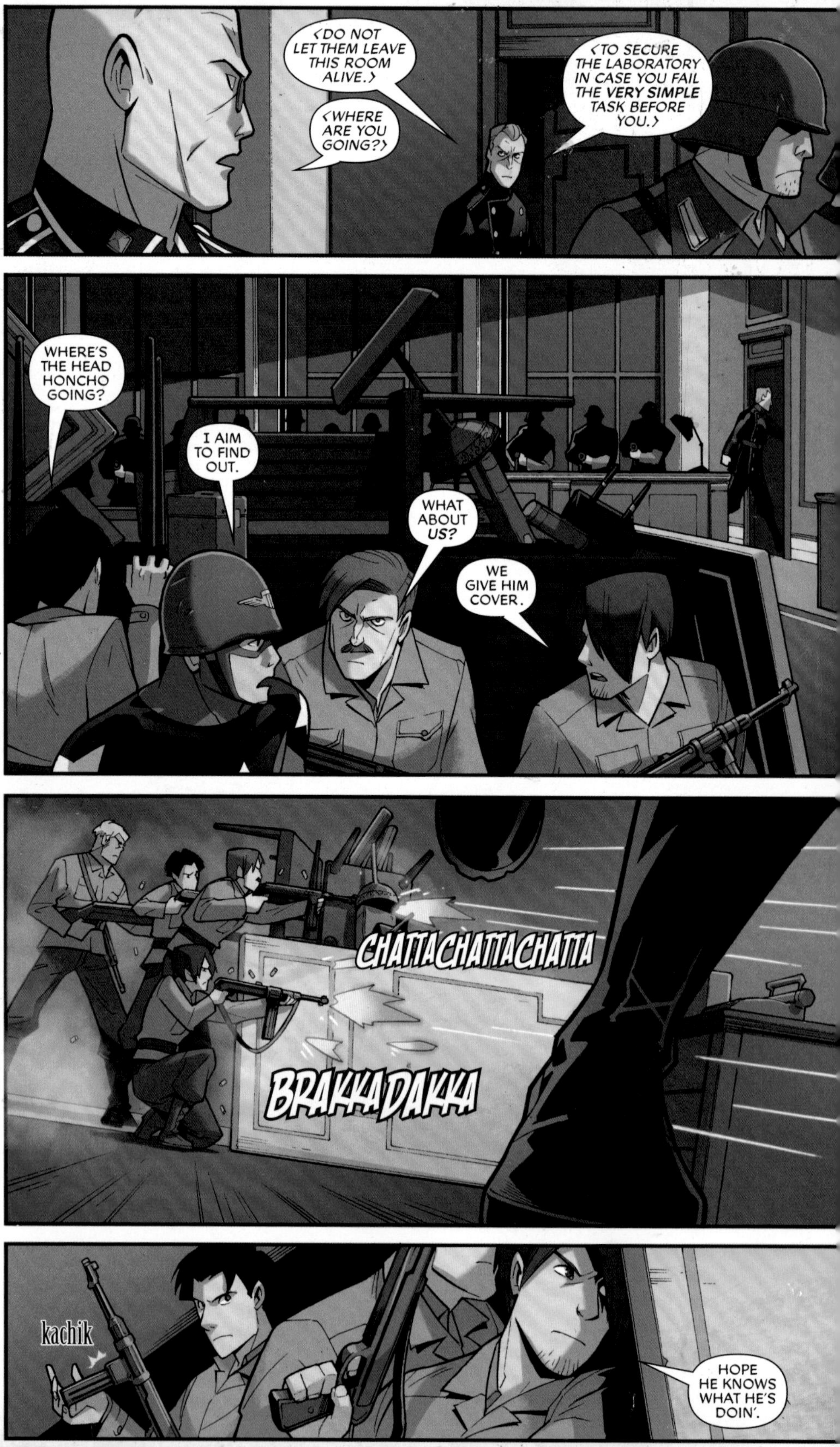

<DO NOT LET THEM LEAVE THIS ROOM ALIVE.>
<WHERE ARE YOU GOING?>
<TO SECURE THE LABORATORY IN CASE YOU FAIL THE **VERY SIMPLE** TASK BEFORE YOU.>
WHERE'S THE HEAD HONCHO GOING?
I AIM TO FIND OUT.
WHAT ABOUT *US?*
WE GIVE HIM COVER.
CHATTACHATTACHATTA
BRAKKADAKKA
kachik
HOPE HE KNOWS WHAT HE'S DOIN'.

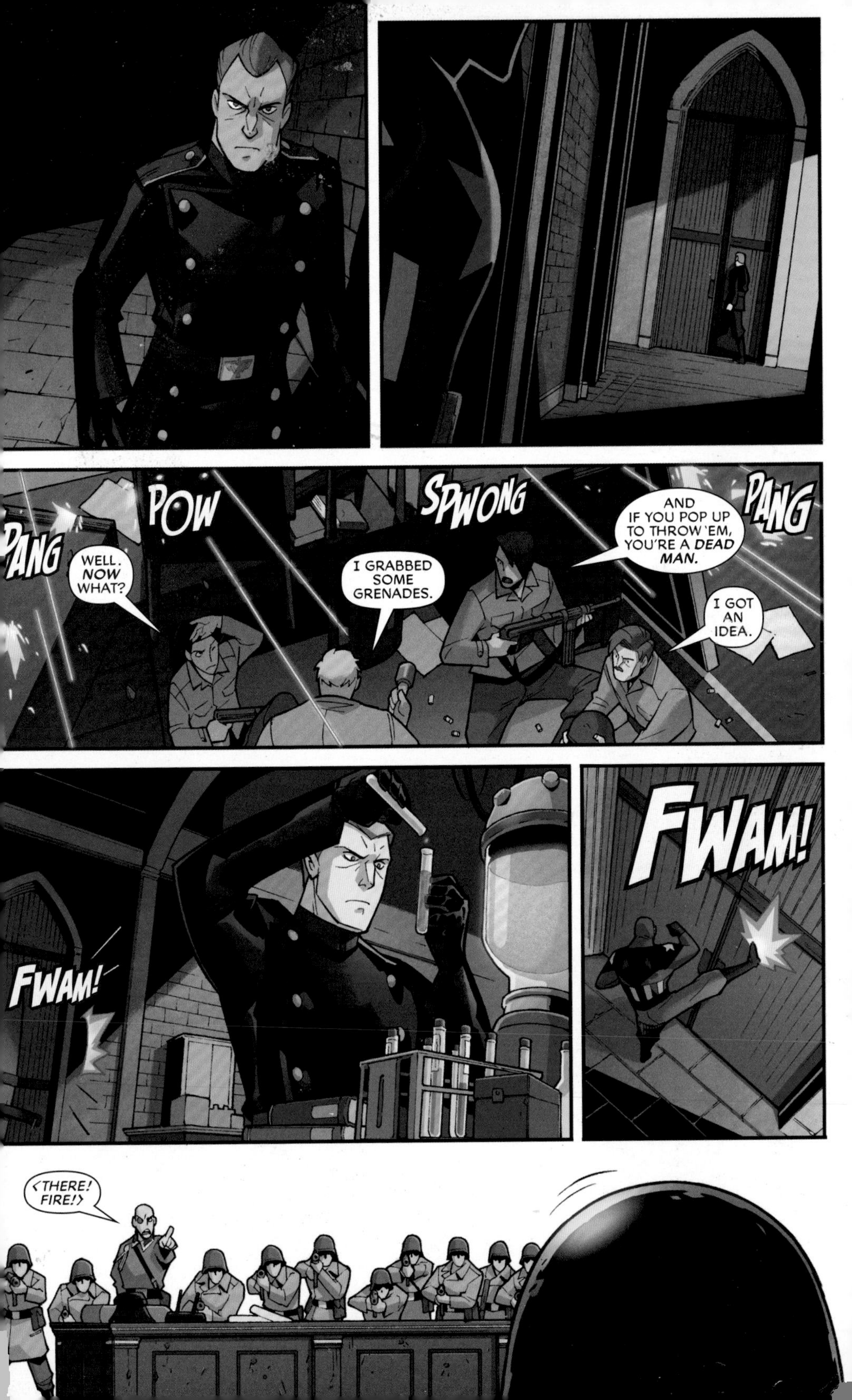
PANG
POW
SPWONG
PANG
WELL. *NOW* WHAT?
I GRABBED SOME GRENADES.
AND IF YOU POP UP TO THROW 'EM, YOU'RE A *DEAD MAN.*
I GOT AN IDEA.
FWAM!
FWAM!
‹THERE! FIRE!›

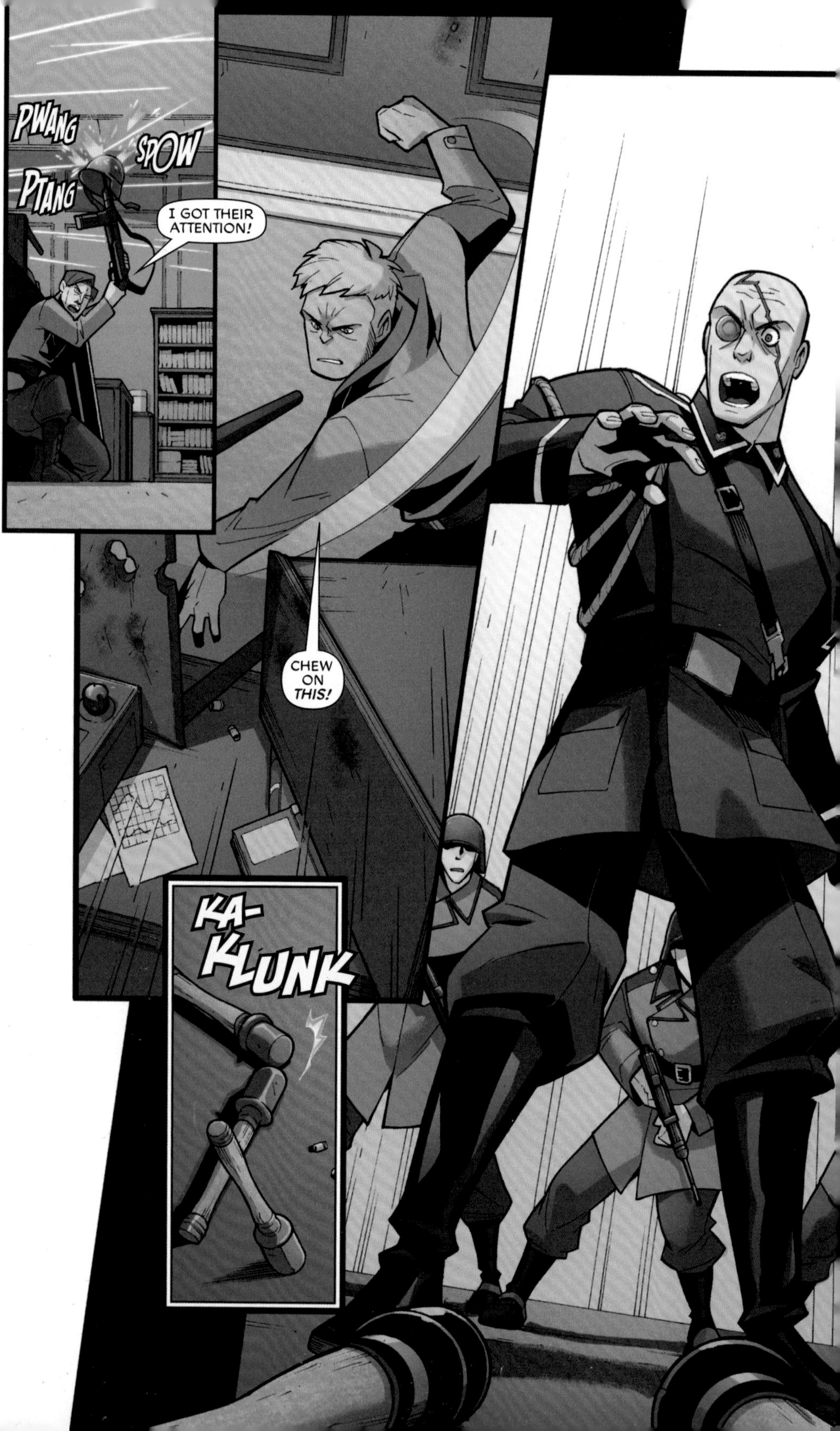
PWANG
SPOW
PTANG
I GOT THEIR ATTENTION!
CHEW ON THIS!
KA-KLUNK

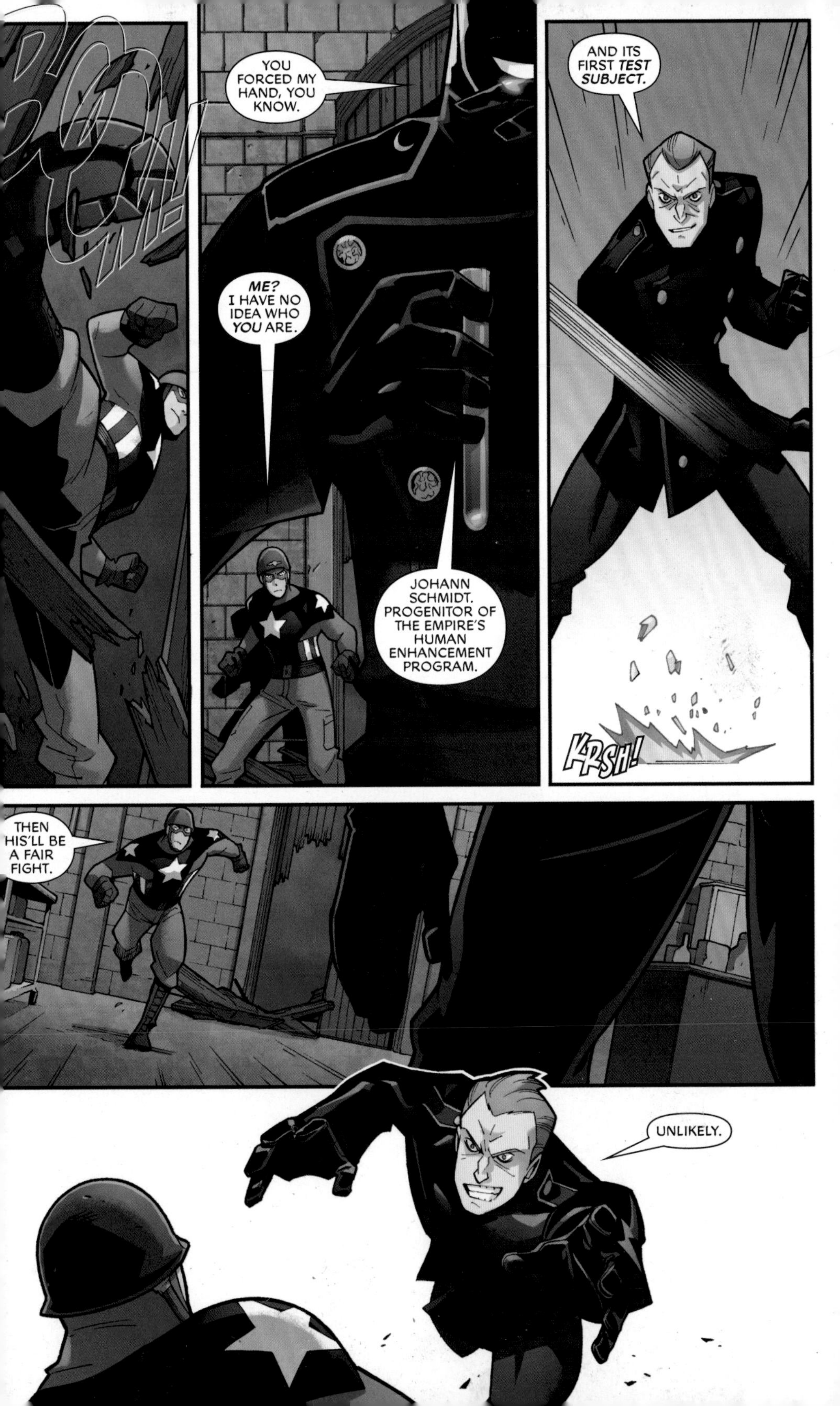
BOOM!
YOU FORCED MY HAND, YOU KNOW.
ME? I HAVE NO IDEA WHO YOU ARE.
JOHANN SCHMIDT. PROGENITOR OF THE EMPIRE'S HUMAN ENHANCEMENT PROGRAM.
AND ITS FIRST TEST SUBJECT.
KRSH!
THEN THIS'LL BE A FAIR FIGHT.
UNLIKELY.

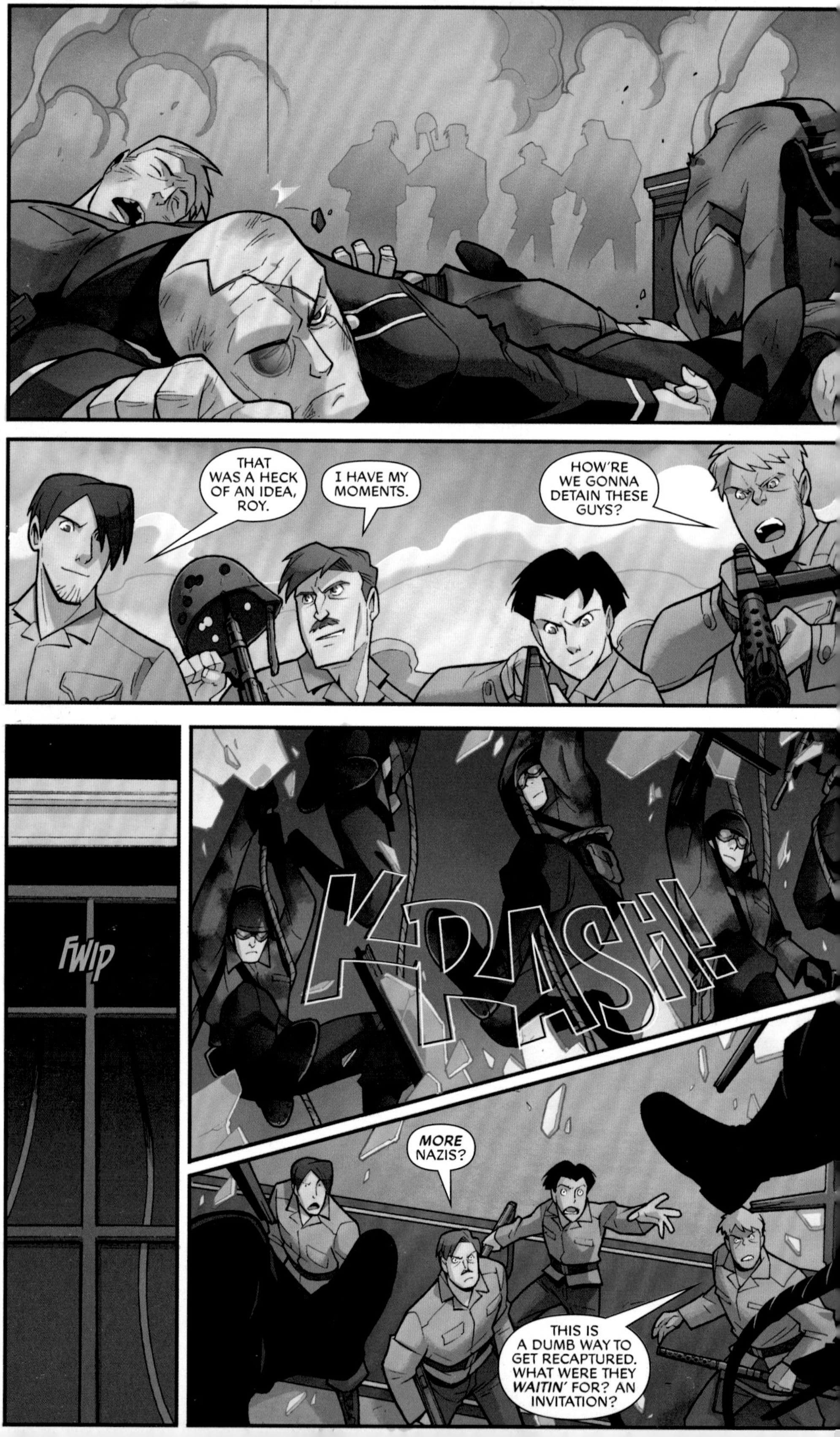
THAT WAS A HECK OF AN IDEA, ROY.
I HAVE MY MOMENTS.
HOW'RE WE GONNA DETAIN THESE GUYS?
FWIP
KRASH!
MORE NAZIS?
THIS IS A DUMB WAY TO GET RECAPTURED. WHAT WERE THEY WAITIN' FOR? AN INVITATION?

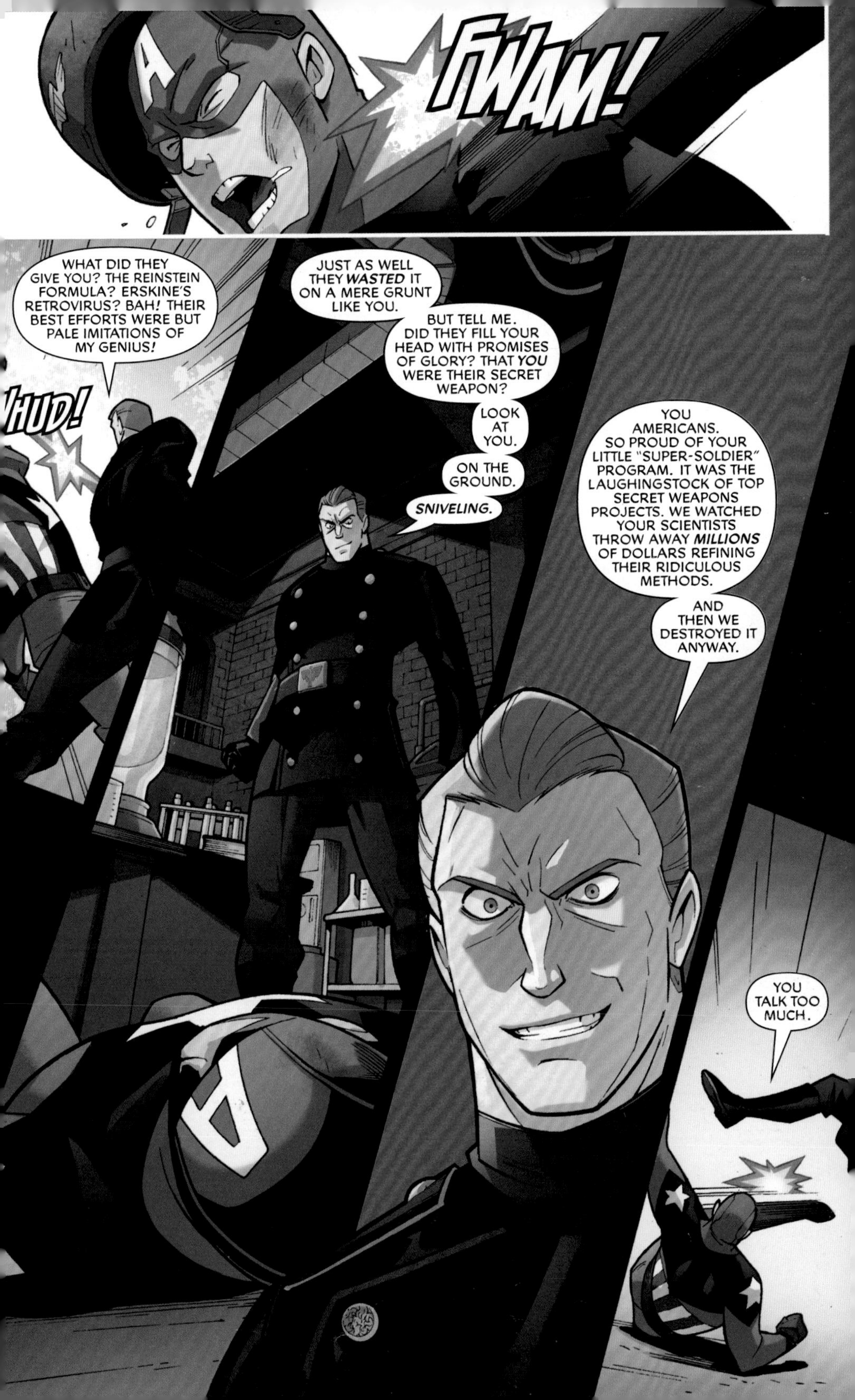
FWAM!
WHAT DID THEY GIVE YOU? THE REINSTEIN FORMULA? ERSKINE'S RETROVIRUS? BAH! THEIR BEST EFFORTS WERE BUT PALE IMITATIONS OF MY GENIUS!
HUD!
JUST AS WELL THEY WASTED IT ON A MERE GRUNT LIKE YOU.
BUT TELL ME. DID THEY FILL YOUR HEAD WITH PROMISES OF GLORY? THAT YOU WERE THEIR SECRET WEAPON?
LOOK AT YOU.
ON THE GROUND.
SNIVELING.
YOU AMERICANS. SO PROUD OF YOUR LITTLE "SUPER-SOLDIER" PROGRAM. IT WAS THE LAUGHINGSTOCK OF TOP SECRET WEAPONS PROJECTS. WE WATCHED YOUR SCIENTISTS THROW AWAY MILLIONS OF DOLLARS REFINING THEIR RIDICULOUS METHODS.
AND THEN WE DESTROYED IT ANYWAY.
YOU TALK TOO MUCH.

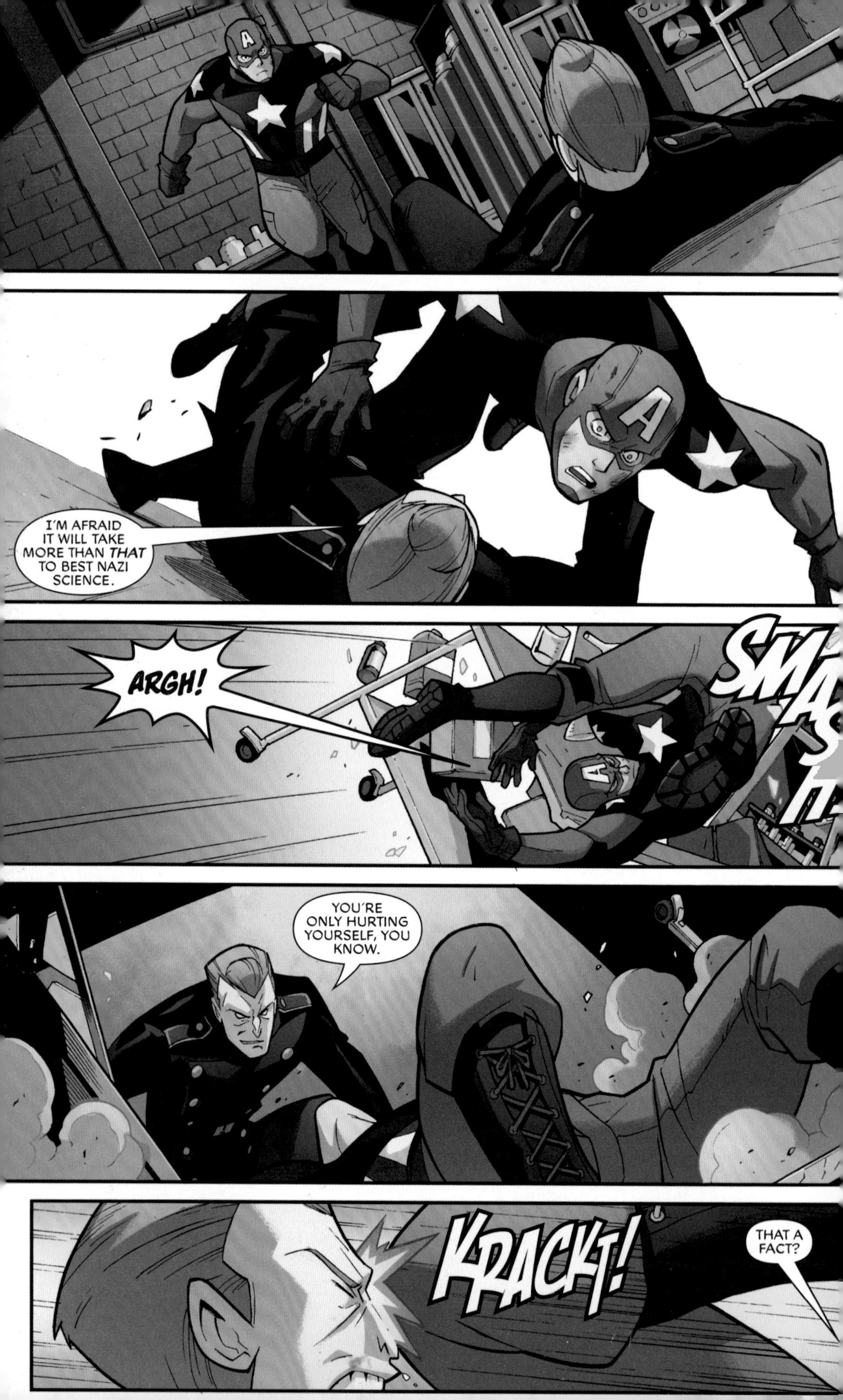
I'M AFRAID IT WILL TAKE MORE THAN *THAT* TO BEST NAZI SCIENCE.
ARGH!
YOU'RE ONLY HURTING YOURSELF, YOU KNOW.
KRACKT!
THAT A FACT?

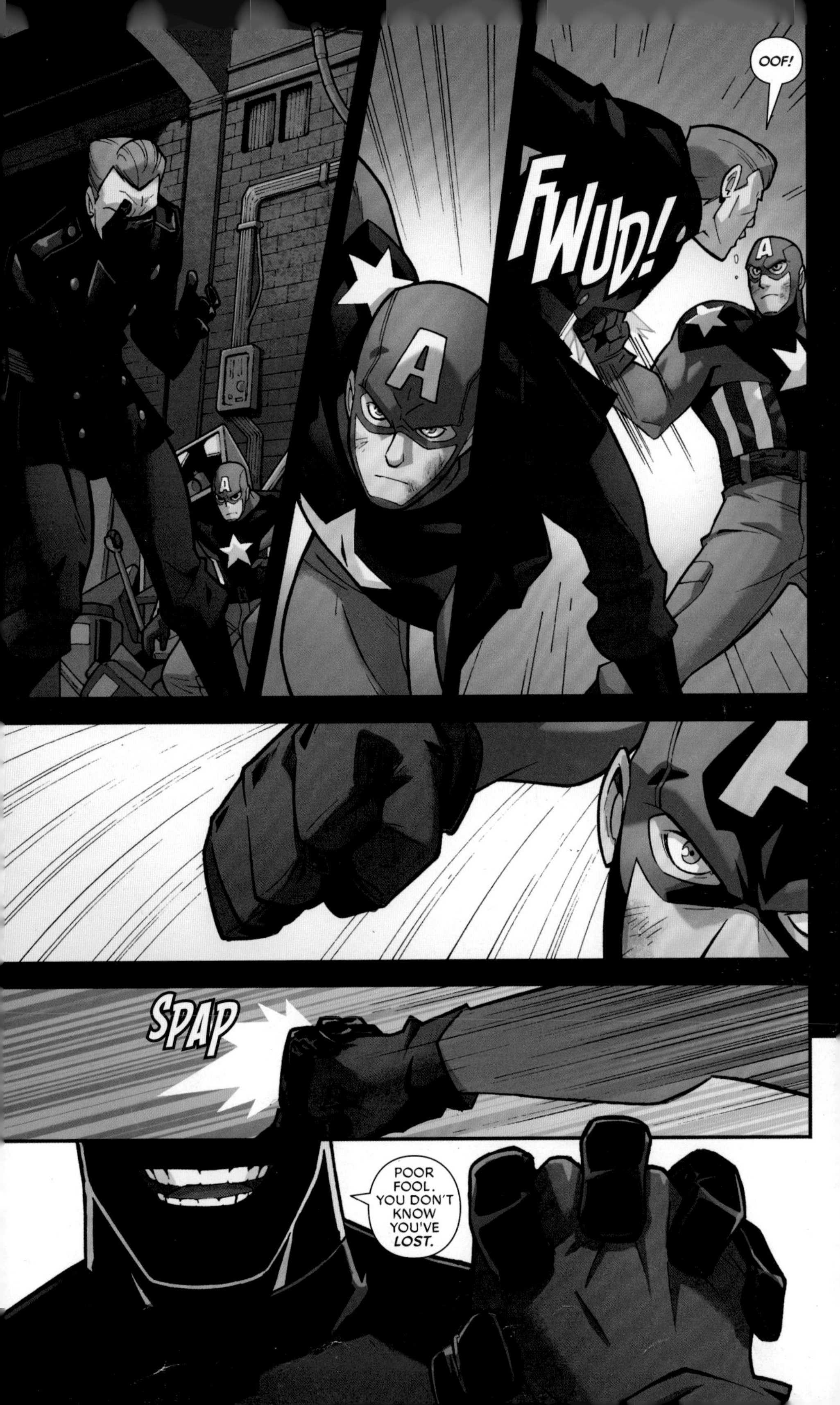
OOF!
FWUD!
SPAP
POOR FOOL. YOU DON'T KNOW YOU'VE *LOST.*

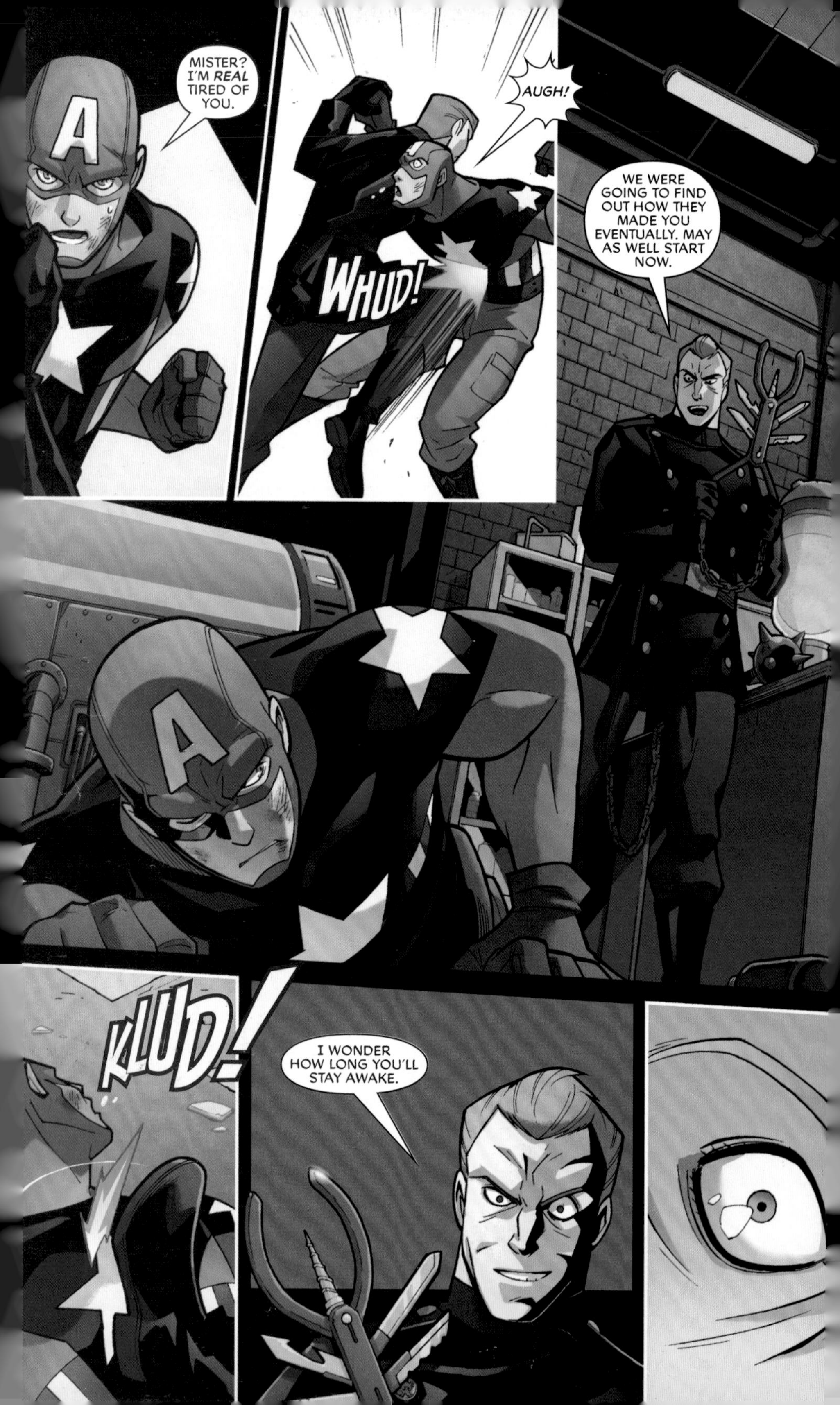
MISTER? I'M *REAL* TIRED OF YOU.
AUGH!
WHUD!
WE WERE GOING TO FIND OUT HOW THEY MADE YOU EVENTUALLY. MAY AS WELL START NOW.
KLUD!
I WONDER HOW LONG YOU'LL STAY AWAKE.

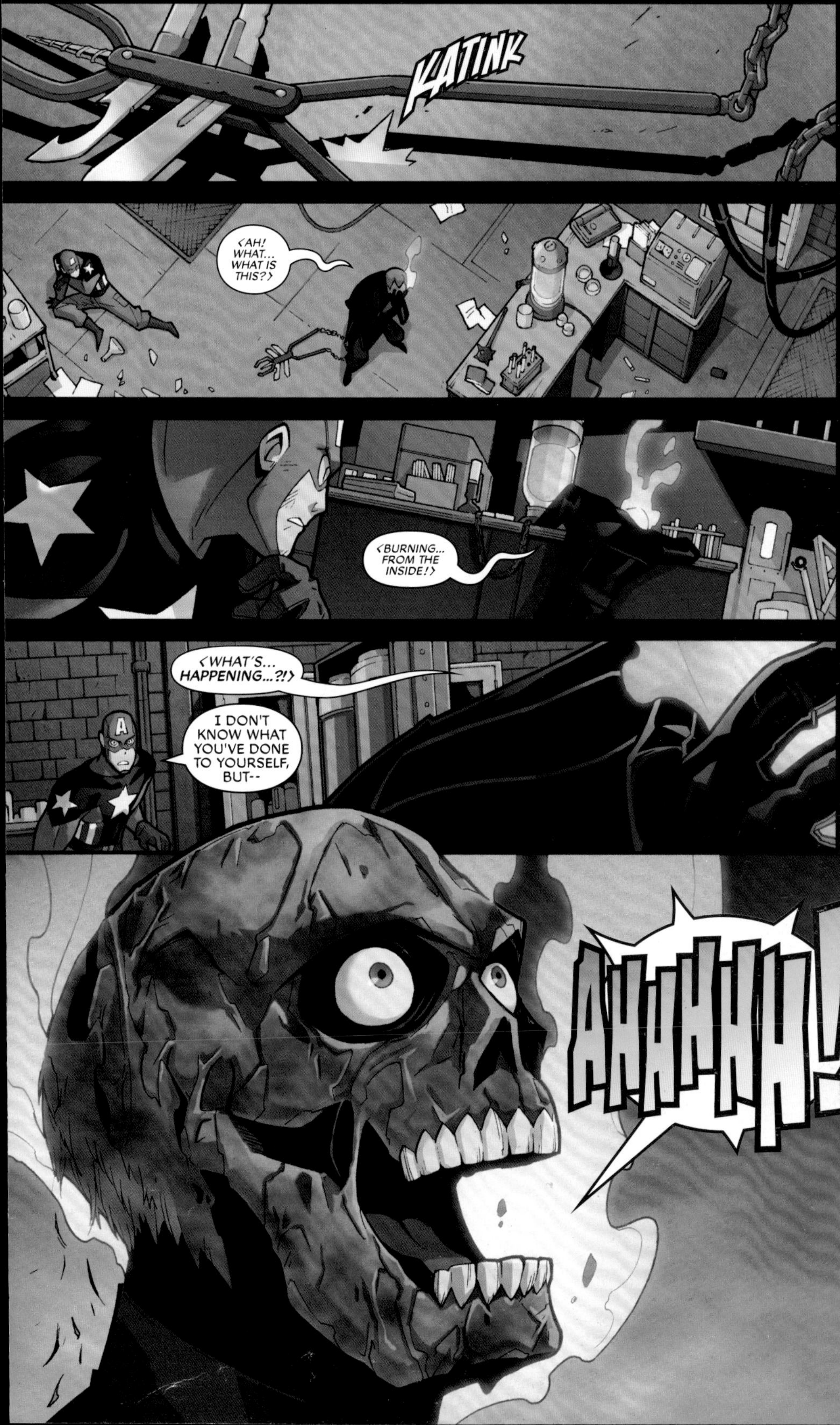
KATINK
‹AH! WHAT... WHAT IS THIS?›
‹BURNING... FROM THE INSIDE!›
‹WHAT'S... HAPPENING...?!›
I DON'T KNOW WHAT YOU'VE DONE TO YOURSELF, BUT--
AHHHHH!

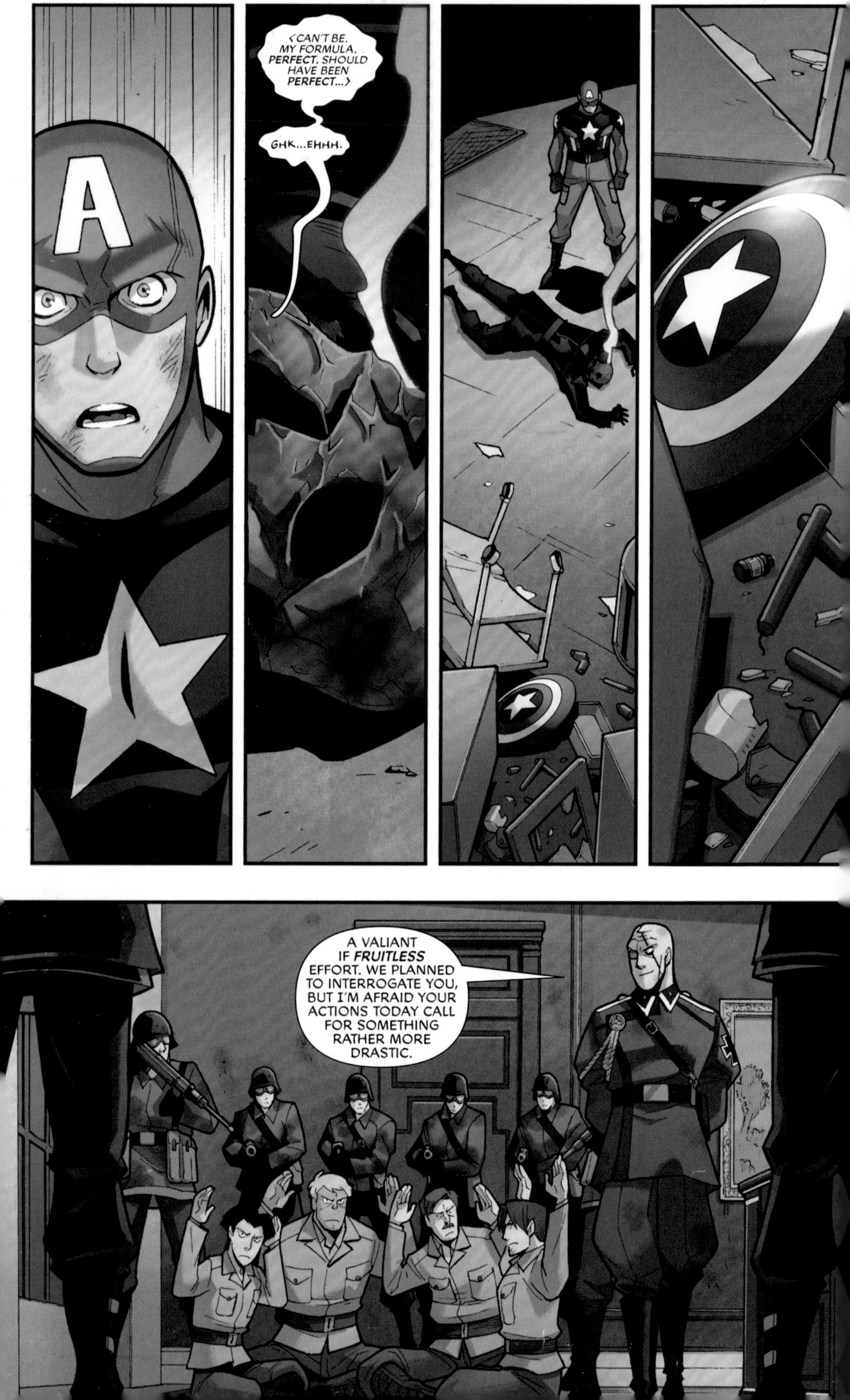
<CAN'T BE. MY FORMULA. PERFECT. SHOULD HAVE BEEN PERFECT...>
GHK...EHHH.
A VALIANT IF FRUITLESS EFFORT. WE PLANNED TO INTERROGATE YOU, BUT I'M AFRAID YOUR ACTIONS TODAY CALL FOR SOMETHING RATHER MORE DRASTIC.

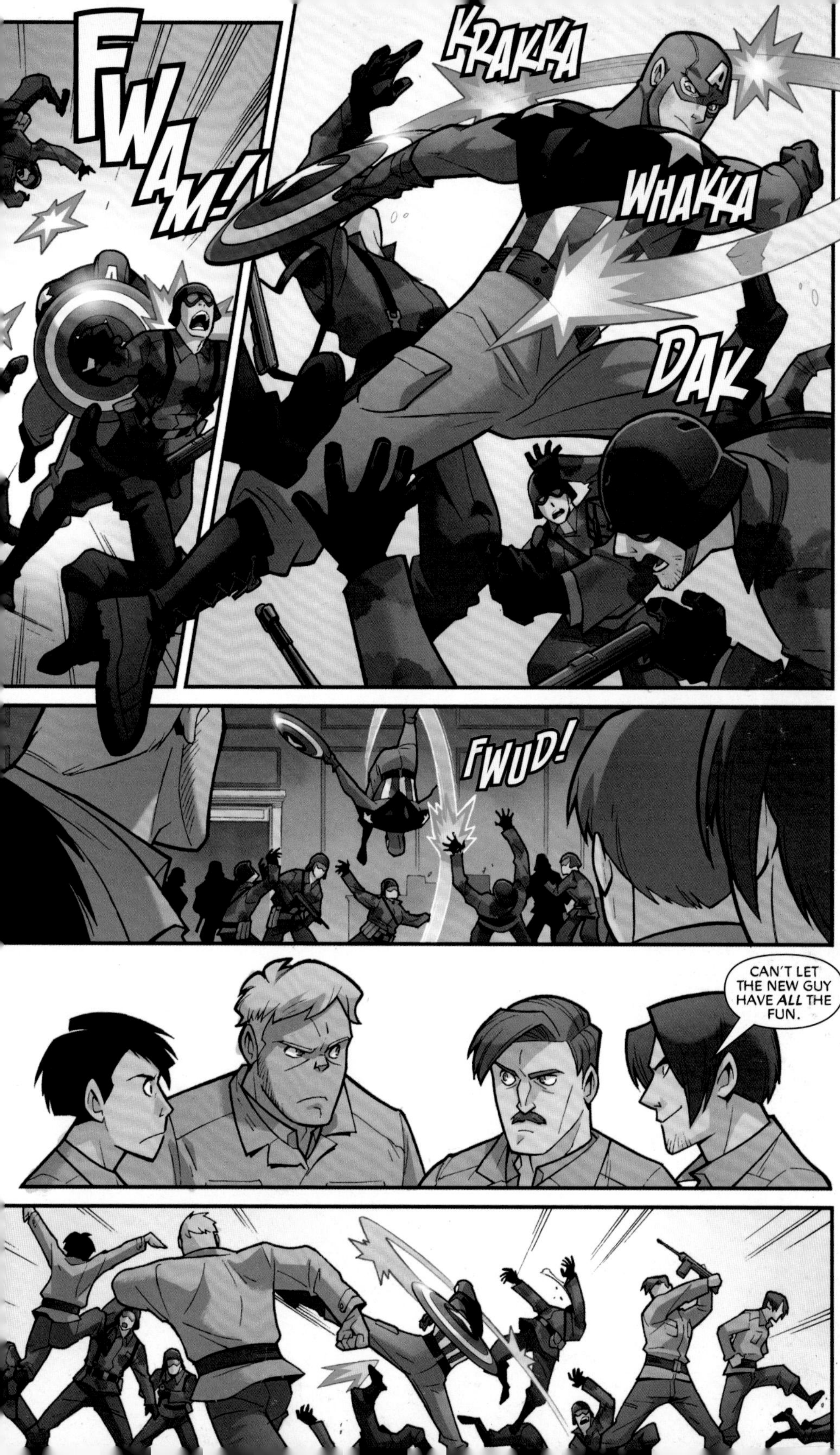
FWAM-!
KRAKKA
WHAKKA
DAK
FWUD!
CAN'T LET THE NEW GUY HAVE ALL THE FUN.

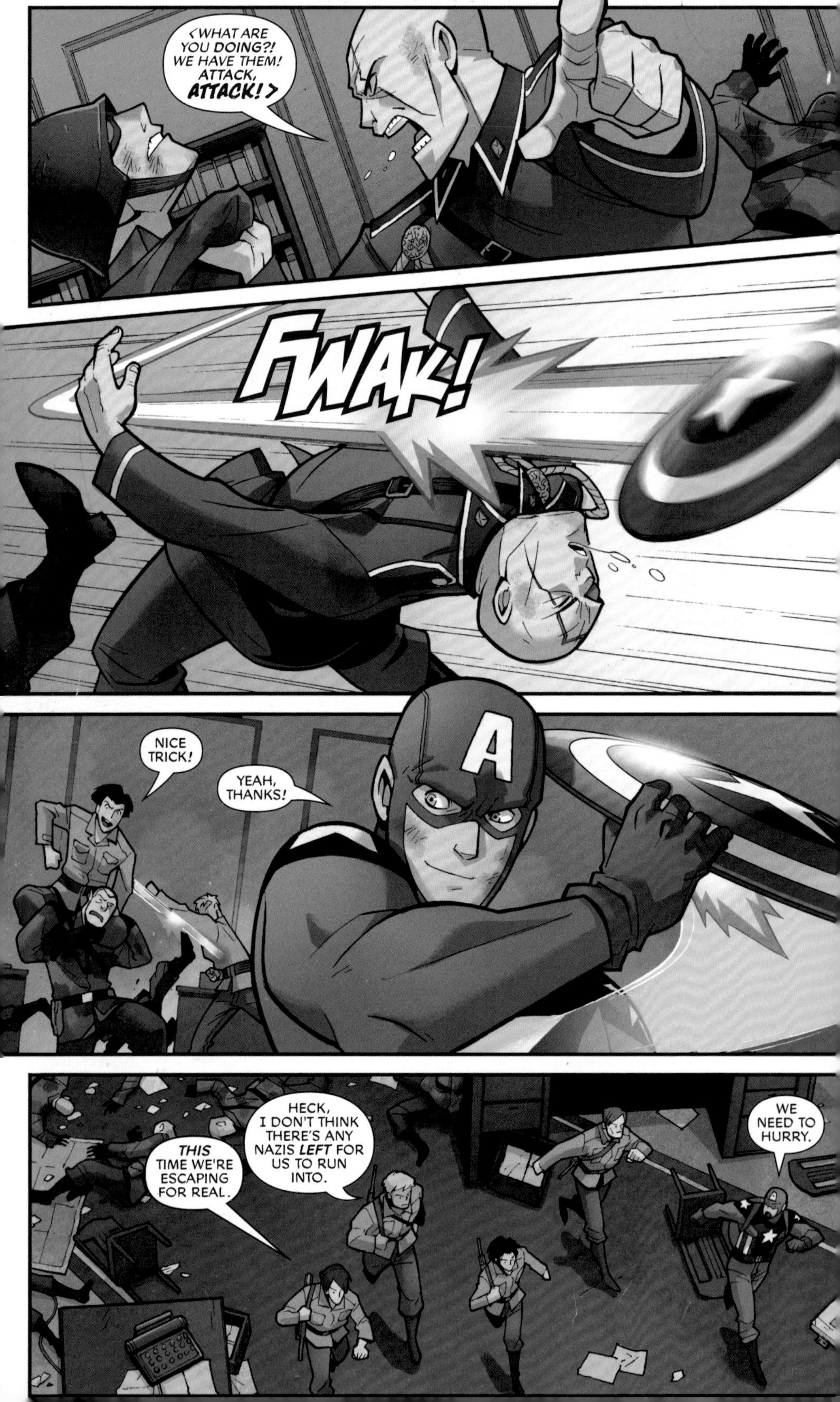
<WHAT ARE YOU DOING?! WE HAVE THEM! ATTACK, ATTACK!>
FWAK!
NICE TRICK!
YEAH, THANKS!
THIS TIME WE'RE ESCAPING FOR REAL.
HECK, I DON'T THINK THERE'S ANY NAZIS LEFT FOR US TO RUN INTO.
WE NEED TO HURRY.

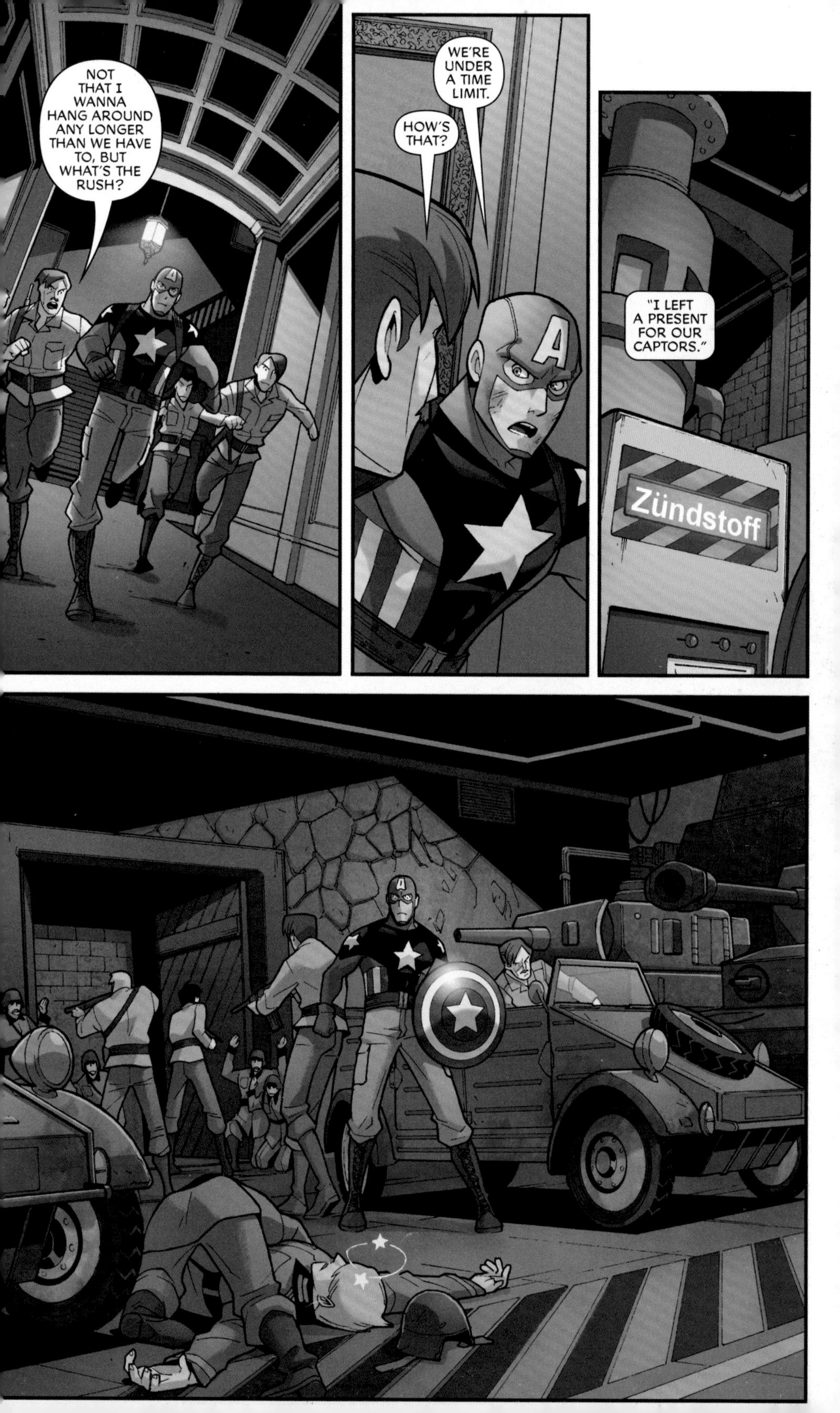
NOT THAT I WANNA HANG AROUND ANY LONGER THAN WE HAVE TO, BUT WHAT'S THE RUSH?
WE'RE UNDER A TIME LIMIT.
HOW'S THAT?
"I LEFT A PRESENT FOR OUR CAPTORS."
Zündstoff

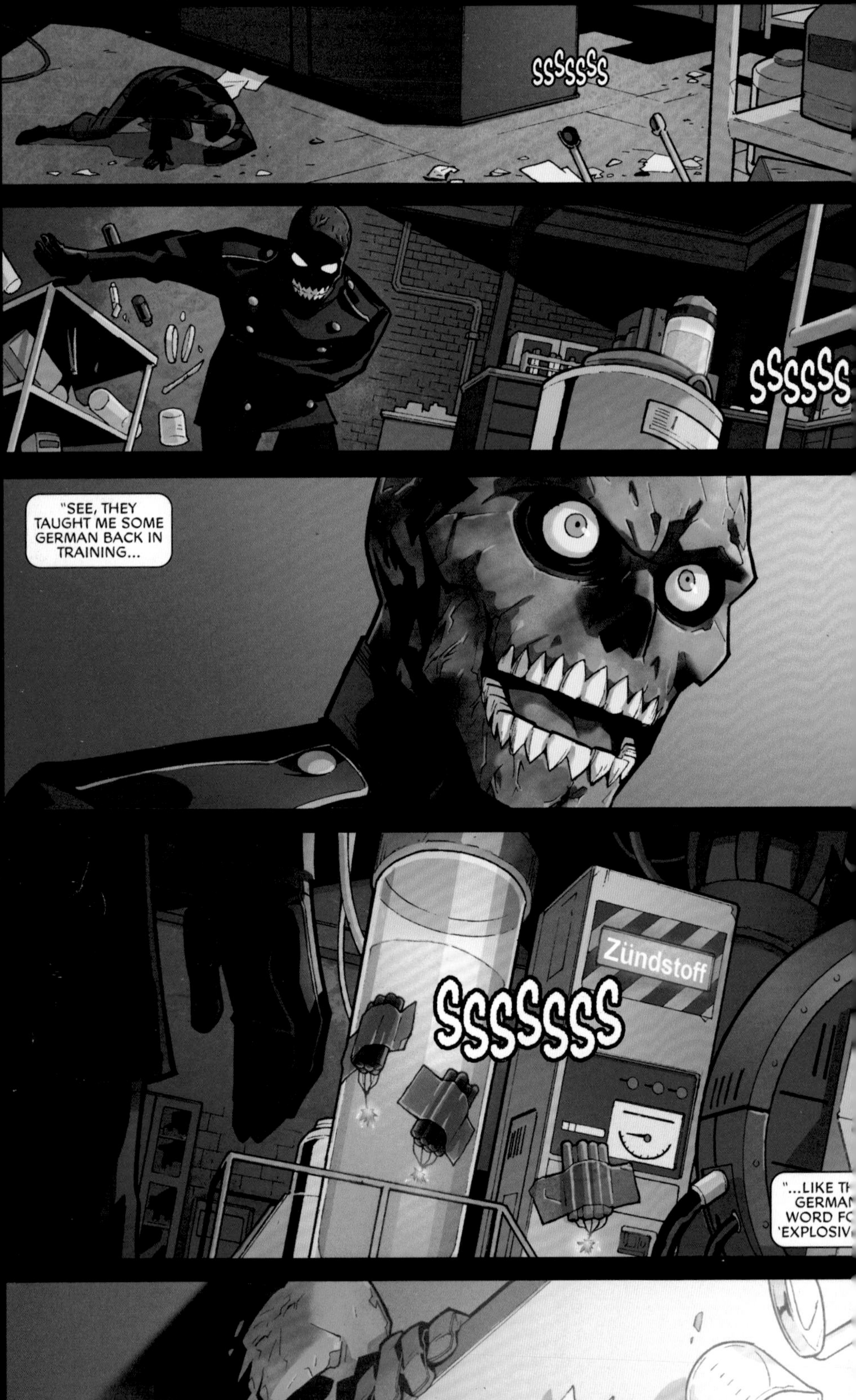
SSSSSSS
SSSSSS
"SEE, THEY TAUGHT ME SOME GERMAN BACK IN TRAINING...
Zündstoff
SSSSSSS

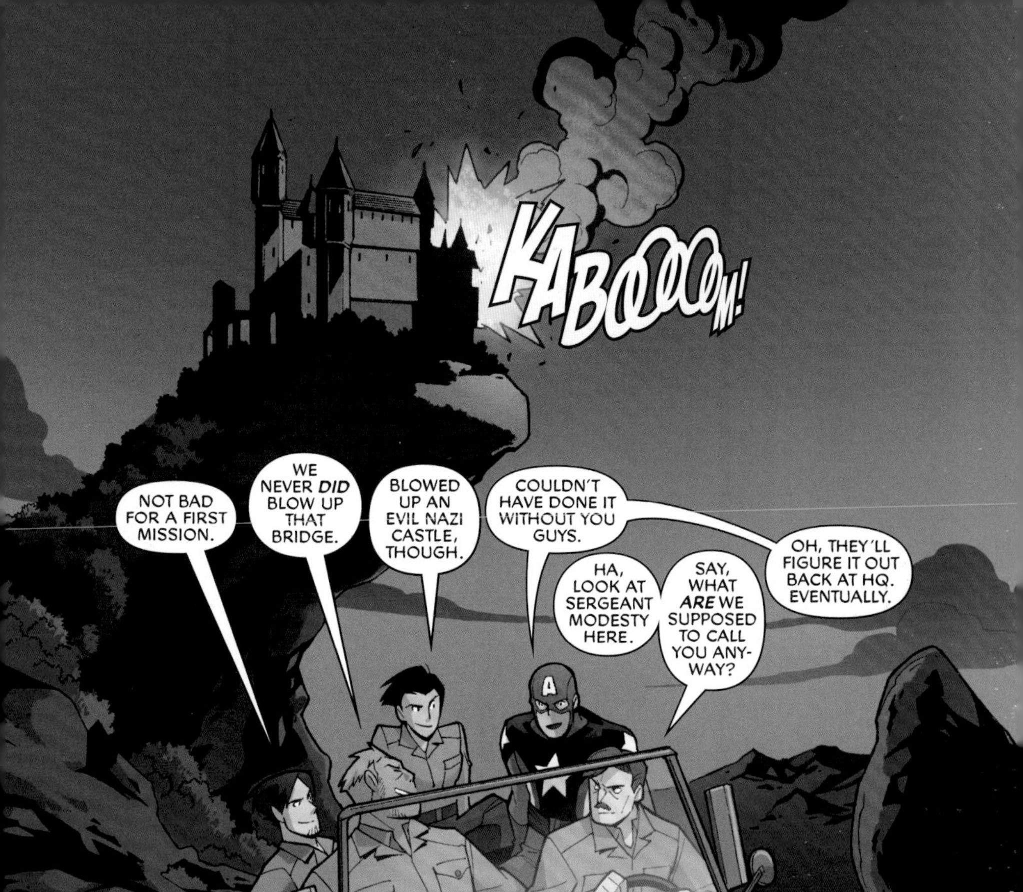
KABOOOOM!
NOT BAD FOR A FIRST MISSION.
WE NEVER DID BLOW UP THAT BRIDGE.
BLOWED UP AN EVIL NAZI CASTLE, THOUGH.
COULDN'T HAVE DONE IT WITHOUT YOU GUYS.
HA, LOOK AT SERGEANT MODESTY HERE.
SAY, WHAT ARE WE SUPPOSED TO CALL YOU ANYWAY?
OH, THEY'LL FIGURE IT OUT BACK AT HQ. EVENTUALLY.

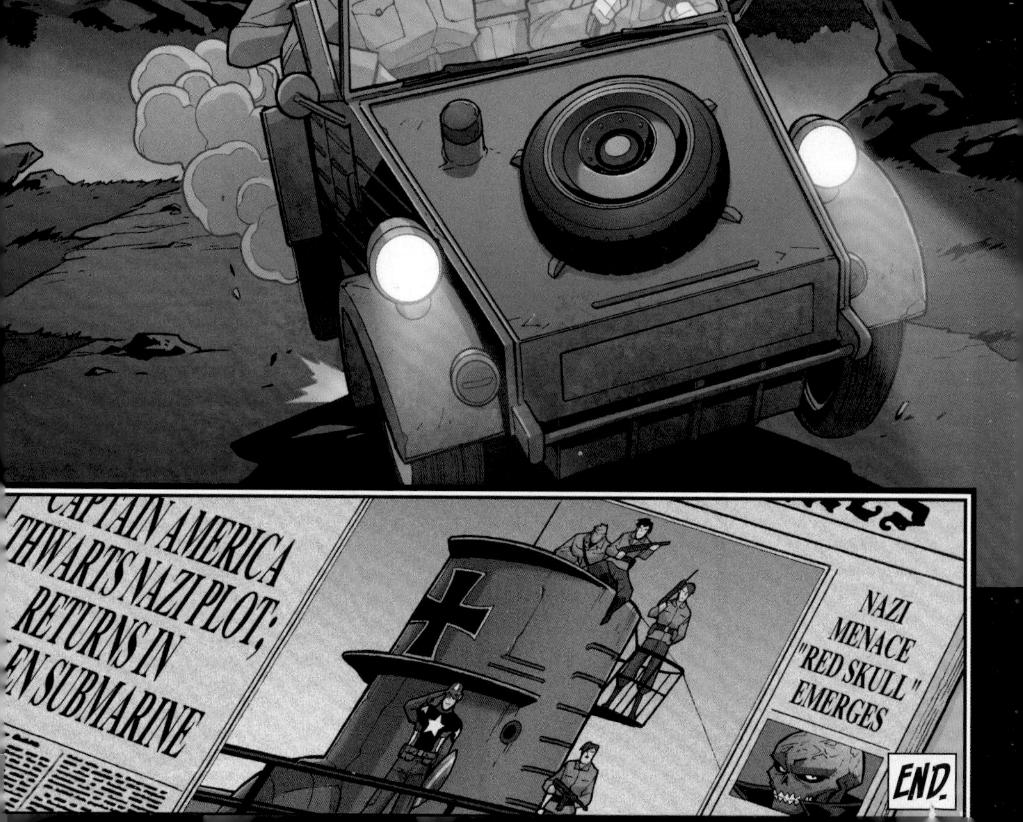
CAPTAIN AMERICA
THWARTS NAZI PLOT;
RETURNS IN
EN SUBMARINE
NAZI MENACE "RED SKULL" EMERGES
END.

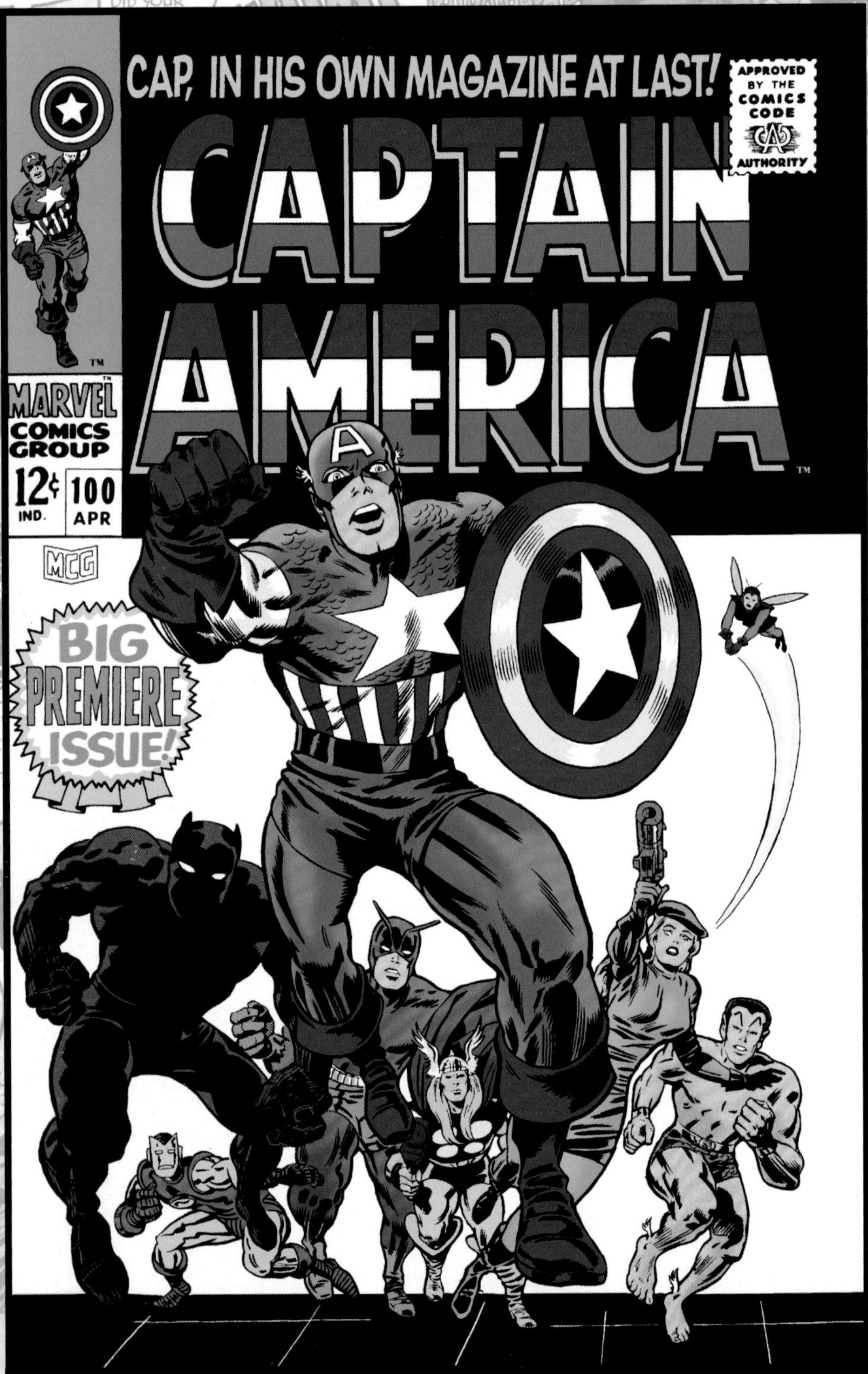
CAP, IN HIS OWN MAGAZINE AT LAST!
APPROVED BY THE COMICS CODE AUTHORITY
CAPTAIN AMERICA
MARVEL COMICS GROUP
12¢ IND.
100 APR
MCG
BIG PREMIERE ISSUE!

CAPTAIN AMERICA (1968) #100

WITH THE HELP OF BLACK PANTHER AND AGENT 13, CAPTAIN AMERICA MUST STOP BARON ZEMO BEFORE ZEMO CAN USE HIS EVIL DEATH RAY!

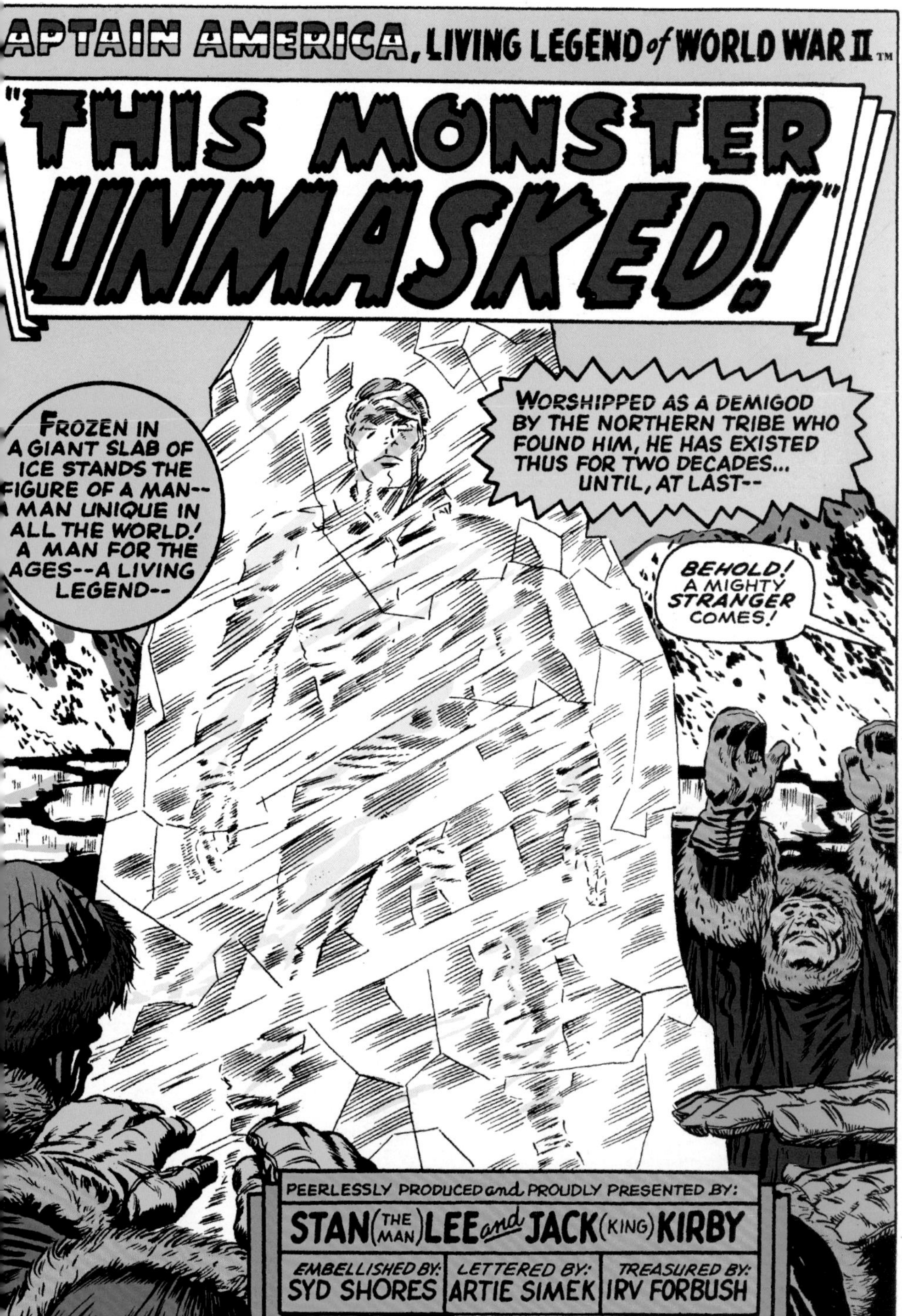

CAPTAIN AMERICA, LIVING LEGEND of WORLD WAR II™
"THIS MONSTER UNMASKED!"
FROZEN IN A GIANT SLAB OF ICE STANDS THE FIGURE OF A MAN-- MAN UNIQUE IN ALL THE WORLD! A MAN FOR THE AGES--A LIVING LEGEND--
WORSHIPPED AS A DEMIGOD BY THE NORTHERN TRIBE WHO FOUND HIM, HE HAS EXISTED THUS FOR TWO DECADES... UNTIL, AT LAST--
BEHOLD! A MIGHTY STRANGER COMES!
PEERLESSLY PRODUCED and PROUDLY PRESENTED BY:
STAN (THE MAN) LEE and JACK (KING) KIRBY
EMBELLISHED BY: SYD SHORES
LETTERED BY: ARTIE SIMEK
TREASURED BY: IRV FORBUSH
1

LET THE STRANGER *WAIT!*

O, MIGHTY LORD OF THE FROZEN ICE, HEAR OUR PRAYERS--!

THE *FOOLS!* THEY BOW TO A PETRIFIED FIGURE, FROZEN WITHIN THE ICE!

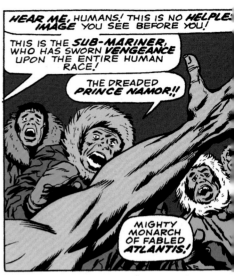

HEAR ME, HUMANS! THIS IS NO *HELPLESS IMAGE* YOU SEE BEFORE YOU!

THIS IS THE *SUB-MARINER,* WHO HAS SWORN *VENGEANCE* UPON THE ENTIRE HUMAN RACE!

THE DREADED *PRINCE NAMOR!!*

MIGHTY MONARCH OF FABLED *ATLANTIS!*

*RUN--*WEAK, HELPLESS MORTALS! *RUN!!*

FLEE IN TERROR BEFORE THE RIGHTFUL *WRATH* OF NAMOR!

THUS SHALL *ALL* ONE DAY RETREAT IN *PANIC* AT THE COMING OF THE *SUB-MARINER!*

AND TAKE YOUR ACCURSED IDOL *WITH* YOU!

LET THE WORD *RING FORTH*--

NAMOR IS RETURNED! NOW LET THE HUMAN RACE *BEWARE!!*

BUT, OUR STORY AT THIS TIME IS NOT CONCERNED WITH THE PRINCE OF THE DEEP, BUT WITH THE MYSTERIOUS *FIGURE* SILENTLY FLOATING AWAY--DRIFTING TOWARDS THE GULF STREAM--

--WHERE THE WARMER WATERS CAUSE THE ROCK-HARD ICE SHEATH TO SLOWLY *MELT*-- UNTIL--

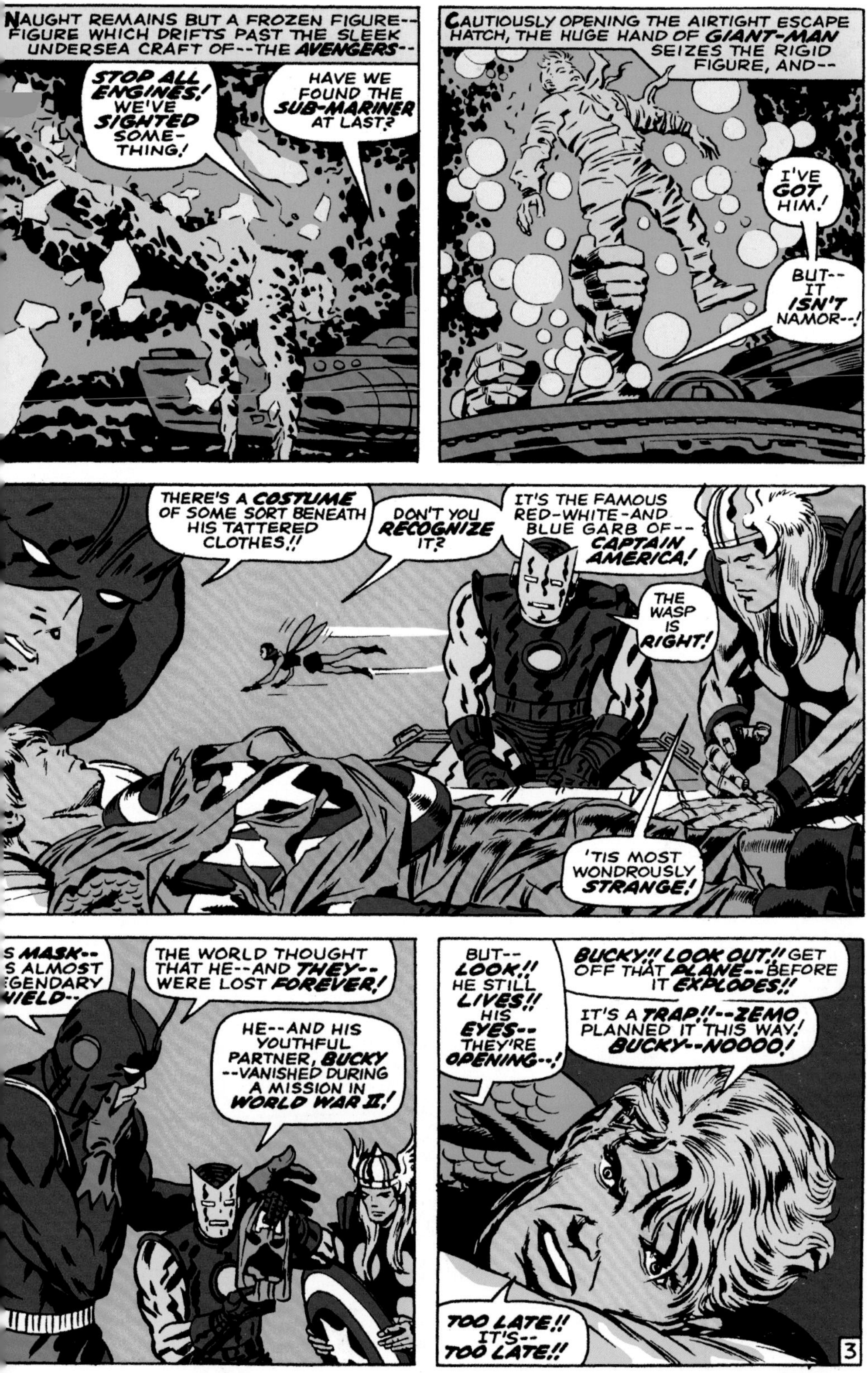
NAUGHT REMAINS BUT A FROZEN FIGURE--FIGURE WHICH DRIFTS PAST THE SLEEK UNDERSEA CRAFT OF--THE AVENGERS--
STOP ALL ENGINES! WE'VE SIGHTED SOME-THING!
HAVE WE FOUND THE SUB-MARINER AT LAST?
CAUTIOUSLY OPENING THE AIRTIGHT ESCAPE HATCH, THE HUGE HAND OF GIANT-MAN SEIZES THE RIGID FIGURE, AND--
I'VE GOT HIM!
BUT--IT ISN'T NAMOR--!
THERE'S A COSTUME OF SOME SORT BENEATH HIS TATTERED CLOTHES!!
DON'T YOU RECOGNIZE IT?
IT'S THE FAMOUS RED-WHITE-AND BLUE GARB OF--CAPTAIN AMERICA!
THE WASP IS RIGHT!
'TIS MOST WONDROUSLY STRANGE!
S MASK--S ALMOST EGENDARY HIELD--
THE WORLD THOUGHT THAT HE--AND THEY--WERE LOST FOREVER!
HE--AND HIS YOUTHFUL PARTNER, BUCKY--VANISHED DURING A MISSION IN WORLD WAR II!
BUT--LOOK!! HE STILL LIVES!! HIS EYES--THEY'RE OPENING--!
BUCKY!! LOOK OUT!! GET OFF THAT PLANE--BEFORE IT EXPLODES!!
IT'S A TRAP!!--ZEMO PLANNED IT THIS WAY! BUCKY--NOOOO!
TOO LATE!! IT'S--TOO LATE!!
3

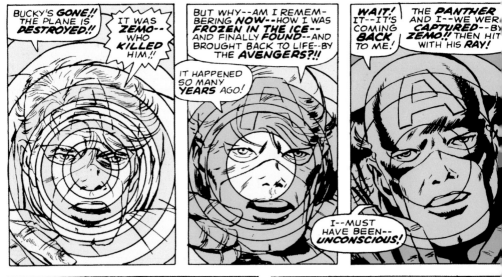

BUCKY'S **GONE!!** THE PLANE IS **DESTROYED!!**

IT WAS **ZEMO**--WHO **KILLED** HIM!!

BUT WHY--AM I REMEM-BERING **NOW**--HOW I WAS **FROZEN IN THE ICE**--AND FINALLY **FOUND**--AND BROUGHT BACK TO LIFE--BY THE **AVENGERS?!!**

IT HAPPENED SO MANY **YEARS** AGO!

WAIT! IT--IT'S COMING **BACK** TO ME!

THE **PANTHER** AND I--WE WER **CAPTURED**--BY **ZEMO!!** THEN HIT WITH HIS **RAY!**

I--MUST HAVE BEEN--**UNCONSCIOUS!**

CAP! SNAP **OUT** OF IT! YOU'VE BEEN **DELIRIOUS!**

WE'VE GOT TO **MOVE!!**

ZEMO JUST ORDERED THE GIRL--TO **SHOOT** YOU!

GIRL? **WHAT** GIRL??

BACK! YOU CANNOT **HELP** HIM!

THE **RAY**--IT'S WEARING OFF--AT LAST!

I HEAR--THE VOICE OF **ZEMO** AGAIN--ORDERING--MY **DEATH!**

YOU MUST **PROVE** YOUR LOYALTY TO ME--BY DESTROYING CAPTAIN AMERICA!

NOW! DO IT **NOW!**

I'VE GOT TO LEAP INTO ACT--**NO!** WAIT!

SHE'S **HESITATING!!** SHE DOESN'T **WANT** TO HURT ME!

WHO **IS** SHE? WHY DOES SHE **PAUSE**--

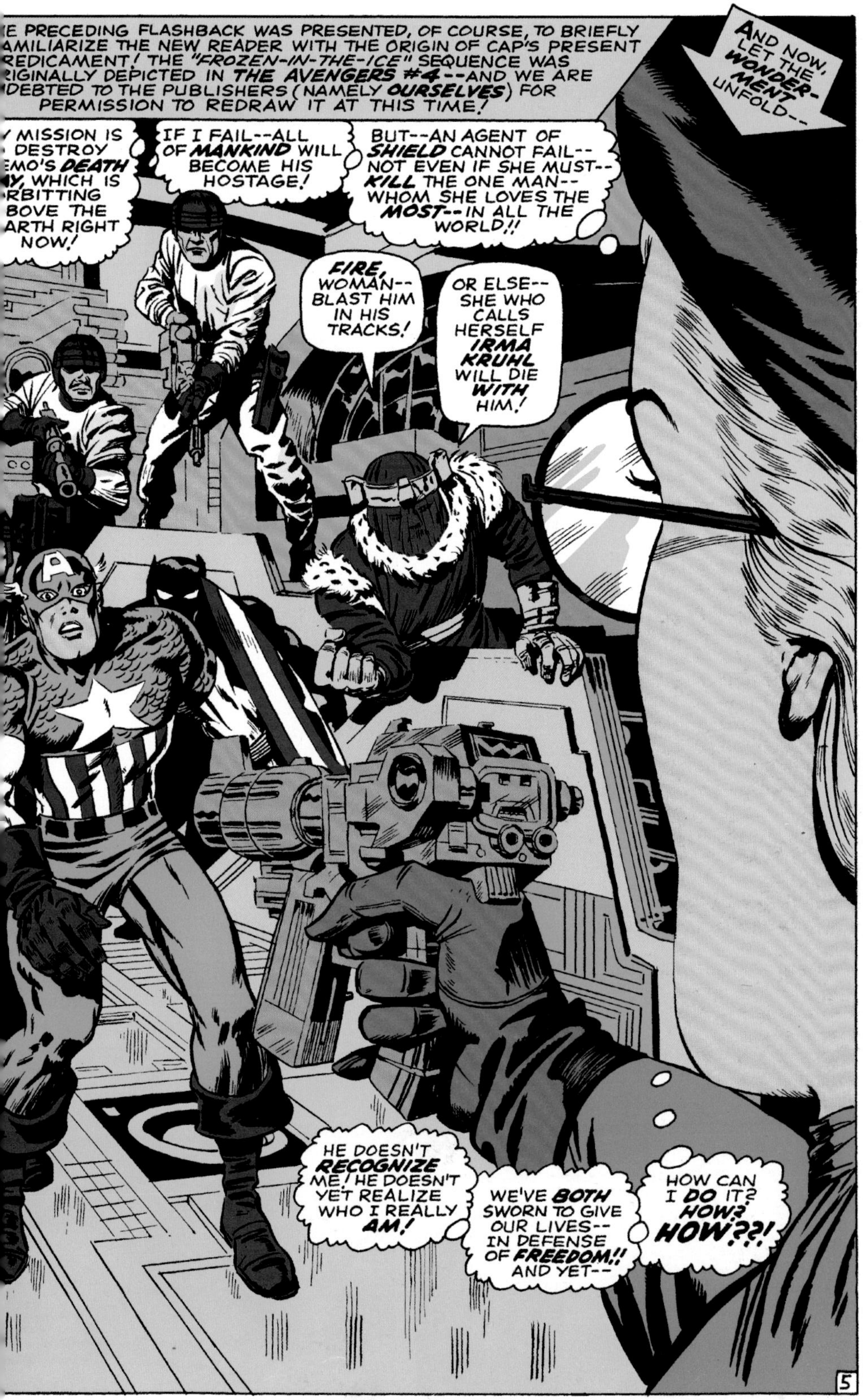

E PRECEDING FLASHBACK WAS PRESENTED, OF COURSE, TO BRIEFLY AMILIARIZE THE NEW READER WITH THE ORIGIN OF CAP'S PRESENT REDICAMENT! THE "FROZEN-IN-THE-ICE" SEQUENCE WAS RIGINALLY DEPICTED IN THE AVENGERS #4--AND WE ARE NDEBTED TO THE PUBLISHERS (NAMELY OURSELVES) FOR PERMISSION TO REDRAW IT AT THIS TIME!
AND NOW, LET THE WONDERMENT UNFOLD--
Y MISSION IS DESTROY EMO'S DEATH Y, WHICH IS RBITTING BOVE THE ARTH RIGHT NOW!
IF I FAIL--ALL OF MANKIND WILL BECOME HIS HOSTAGE!
BUT--AN AGENT OF SHIELD CANNOT FAIL--NOT EVEN IF SHE MUST--KILL THE ONE MAN--WHOM SHE LOVES THE MOST--IN ALL THE WORLD!!
FIRE, WOMAN--BLAST HIM IN HIS TRACKS!
OR ELSE--SHE WHO CALLS HERSELF IRMA KRUHL WILL DIE WITH HIM!
HE DOESN'T RECOGNIZE ME! HE DOESN'T YET REALIZE WHO I REALLY AM!
WE'VE BOTH SWORN TO GIVE OUR LIVES--IN DEFENSE OF FREEDOM!! AND YET--
HOW CAN I DO IT? HOW? HOW??!
5

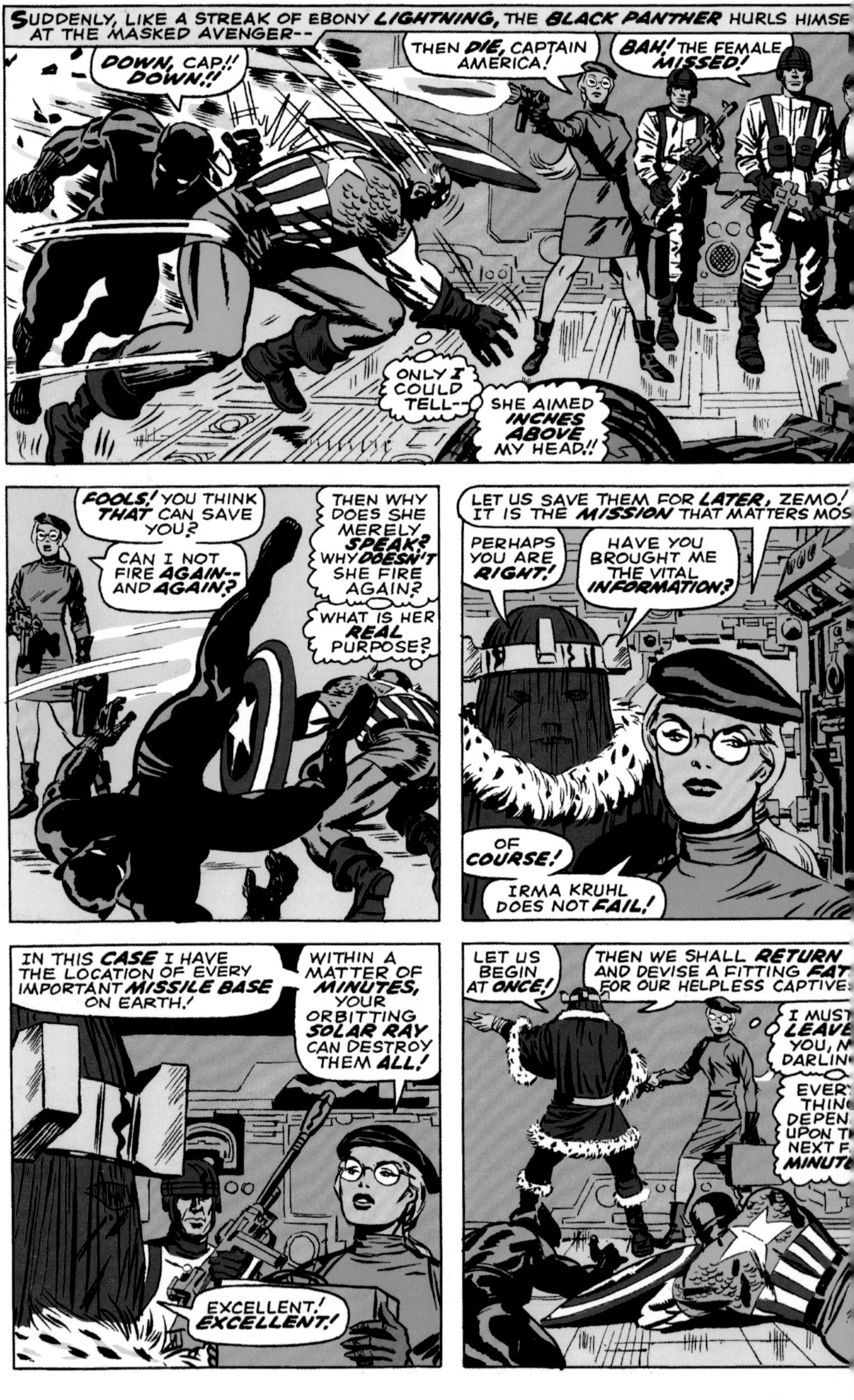
SUDDENLY, LIKE A STREAK OF EBONY LIGHTNING, THE BLACK PANTHER HURLS HIMSE AT THE MASKED AVENGER--
DOWN, CAP!! DOWN!!
THEN DIE, CAPTAIN AMERICA!
BAH! THE FEMALE MISSED!
ONLY I COULD TELL--
SHE AIMED INCHES ABOVE MY HEAD!!
FOOLS! YOU THINK THAT CAN SAVE YOU?
CAN I NOT FIRE AGAIN-- AND AGAIN?
THEN WHY DOES SHE MERELY SPEAK? WHY DOESN'T SHE FIRE AGAIN?
WHAT IS HER REAL PURPOSE?
LET US SAVE THEM FOR LATER, ZEMO! IT IS THE MISSION THAT MATTERS MOS
PERHAPS YOU ARE RIGHT!
HAVE YOU BROUGHT ME THE VITAL INFORMATION?
OF COURSE!
IRMA KRUHL DOES NOT FAIL!
IN THIS CASE I HAVE THE LOCATION OF EVERY IMPORTANT MISSILE BASE ON EARTH!
WITHIN A MATTER OF MINUTES, YOUR ORBITTING SOLAR RAY CAN DESTROY THEM ALL!
EXCELLENT! EXCELLENT!
LET US BEGIN AT ONCE!
THEN WE SHALL RETURN AND DEVISE A FITTING FAT FOR OUR HELPLESS CAPTIVE
I MUST LEAVE YOU, M DARLIN
EVER THIN DEPEN UPON T NEXT F MINUT

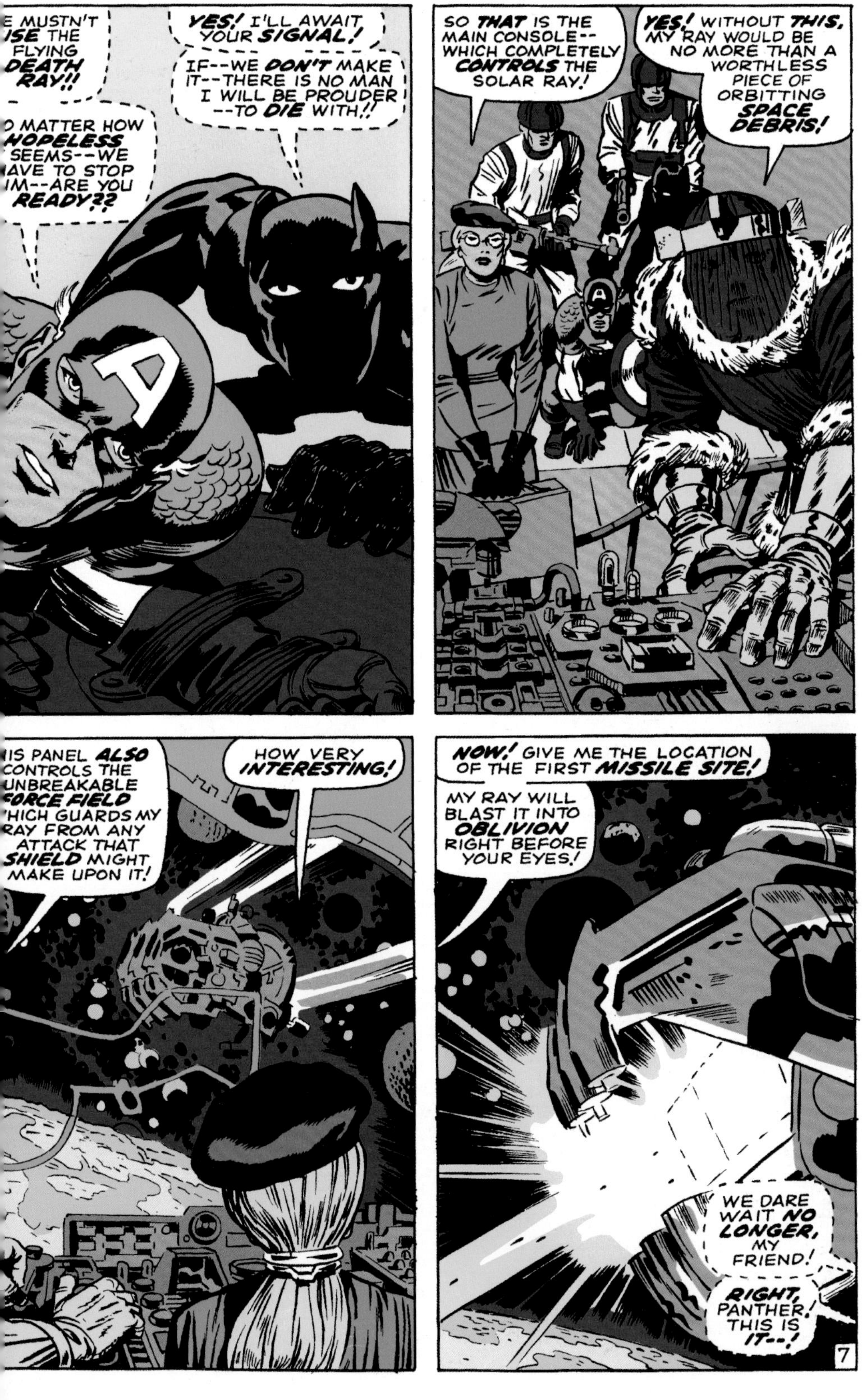

E MUSTN'T USE THE FLYING DEATH RAY!!
YES! I'LL AWAIT YOUR SIGNAL!
IF--WE DON'T MAKE IT--THERE IS NO MAN I WILL BE PROUDER --TO DIE WITH!!
O MATTER HOW HOPELESS SEEMS--WE AVE TO STOP IM--ARE YOU READY??
SO THAT IS THE MAIN CONSOLE--WHICH COMPLETELY CONTROLS THE SOLAR RAY!
YES! WITHOUT THIS, MY RAY WOULD BE NO MORE THAN A WORTHLESS PIECE OF ORBITTING SPACE DEBRIS!
IIS PANEL ALSO CONTROLS THE UNBREAKABLE FORCE FIELD HICH GUARDS MY RAY FROM ANY ATTACK THAT SHIELD MIGHT MAKE UPON IT!
HOW VERY INTERESTING!
NOW! GIVE ME THE LOCATION OF THE FIRST MISSILE SITE!
MY RAY WILL BLAST IT INTO OBLIVION RIGHT BEFORE YOUR EYES!
WE DARE WAIT NO LONGER, MY FRIEND!
RIGHT, PANTHER! THIS IS IT--!
7

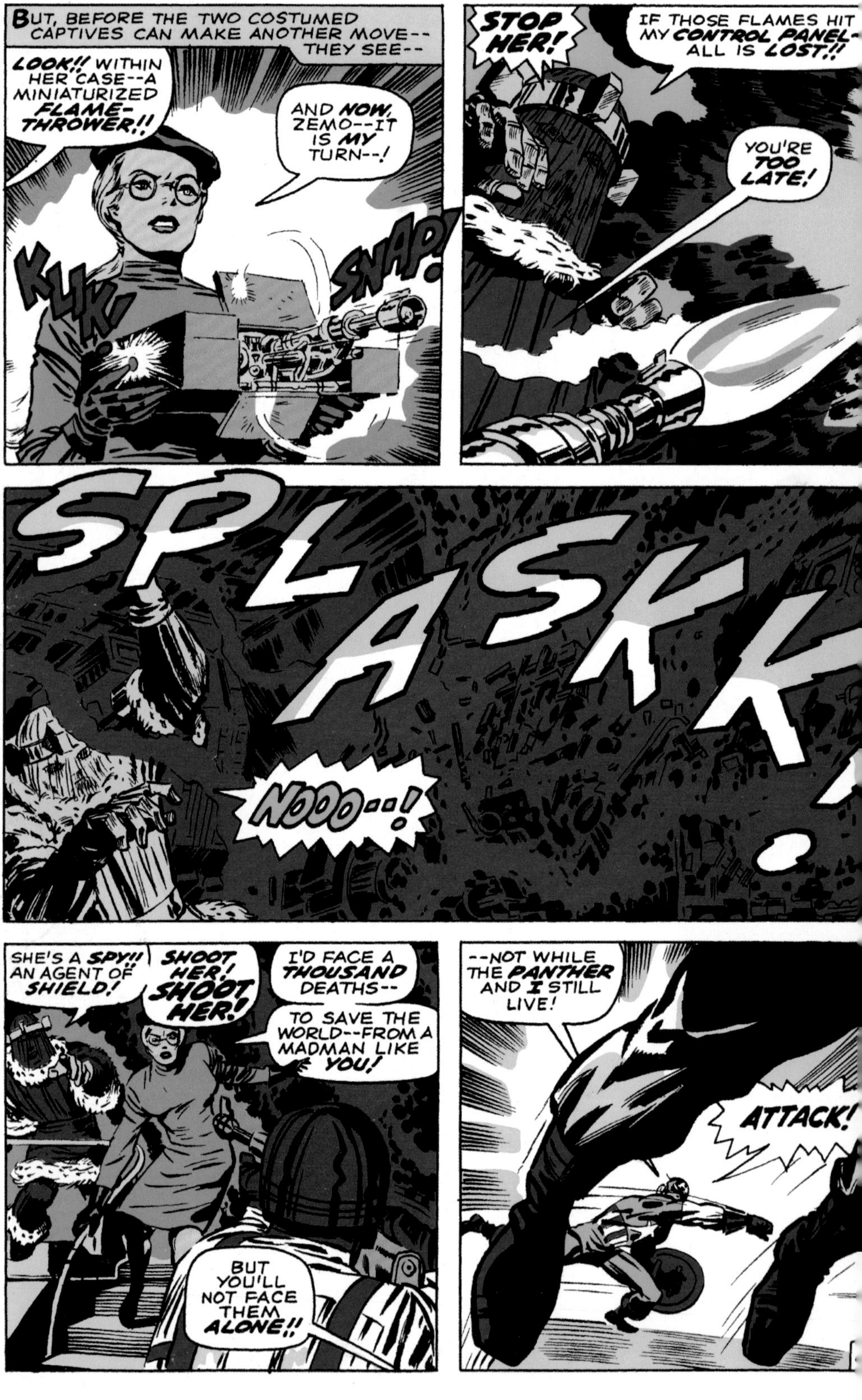

BUT, BEFORE THE TWO COSTUMED CAPTIVES CAN MAKE ANOTHER MOVE-- THEY SEE--
LOOK!! WITHIN HER CASE--A MINIATURIZED FLAME-THROWER!!
AND NOW, ZEMO--IT IS MY TURN--!
KLIK!
SNAP!
STOP HER!
IF THOSE FLAMES HIT MY CONTROL PANEL-ALL IS LOST!!
YOU'RE TOO LATE!
SPLASKK!
NOOO--!
SHE'S A SPY!! AN AGENT OF SHIELD!
SHOOT HER! SHOOT HER!
I'D FACE A THOUSAND DEATHS--
TO SAVE THE WORLD--FROM A MADMAN LIKE YOU!
BUT YOU'LL NOT FACE THEM ALONE!!
--NOT WHILE THE PANTHER AND I STILL LIVE!
ATTACK!

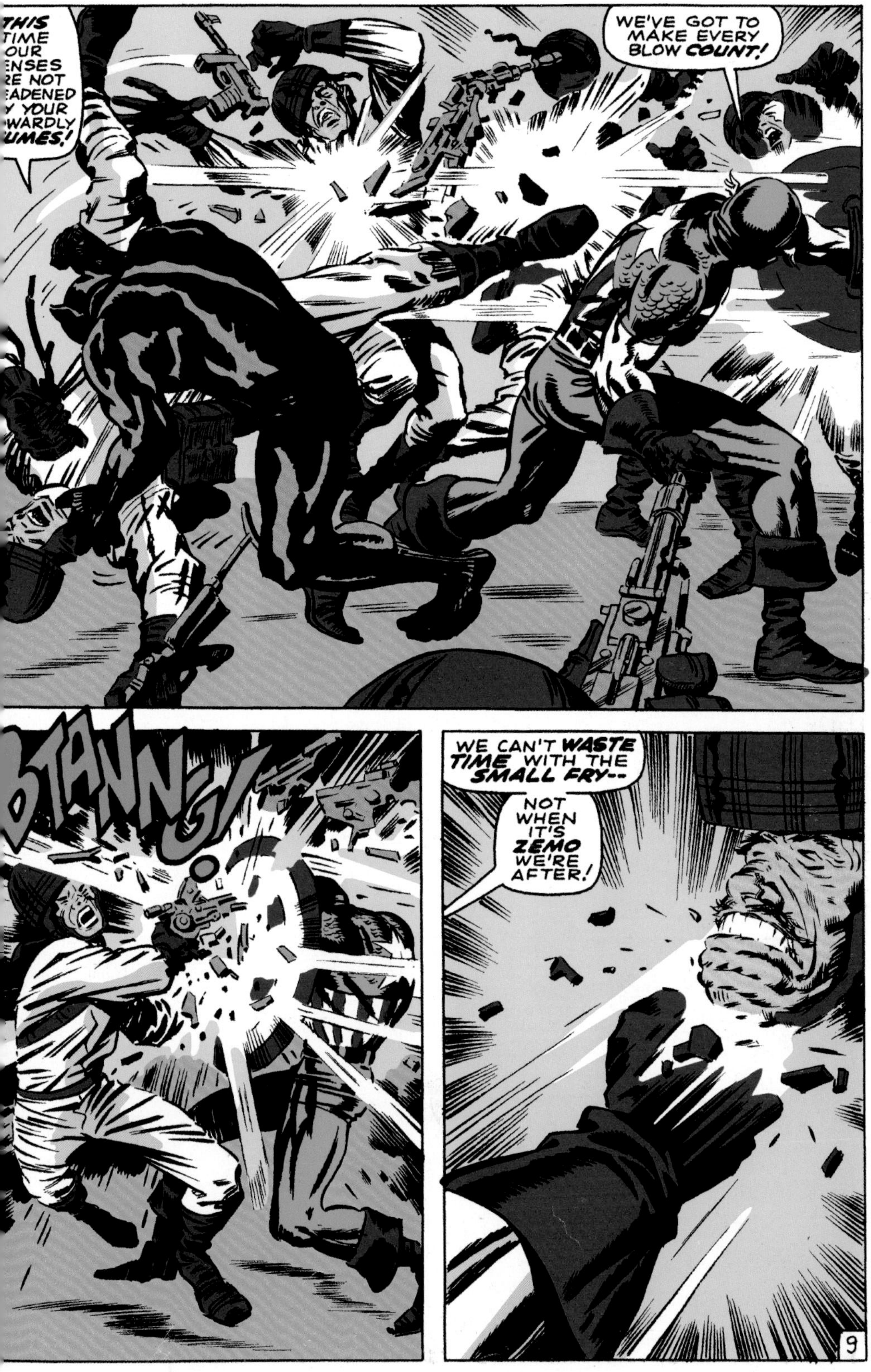
THIS TIME OUR ENSES RE NOT EADENED Y YOUR WARDLY UMES!
WE'VE GOT TO MAKE EVERY BLOW COUNT!
BTANNG!
WE CAN'T WASTE TIME WITH THE SMALL FRY--
NOT WHEN IT'S ZEMO WE'RE AFTER!

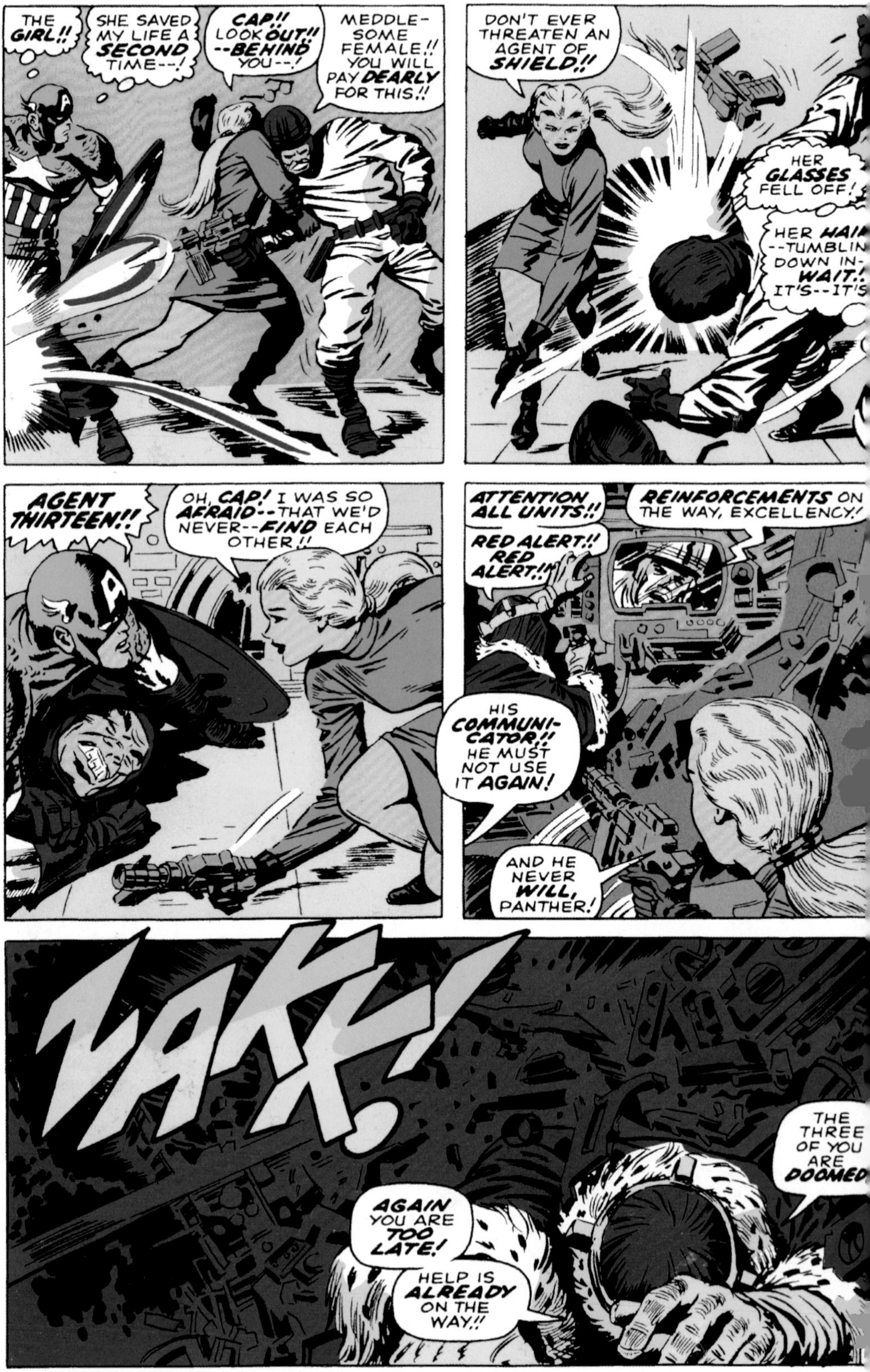

THE GIRL!!
SHE SAVED MY LIFE A SECOND TIME--!
CAP!! LOOK OUT!! --BEHIND YOU--!
MEDDLESOME FEMALE!! YOU WILL PAY DEARLY FOR THIS!!
DON'T EVER THREATEN AN AGENT OF SHIELD!!
HER GLASSES FELL OFF!
HER HAI --TUMBLIN DOWN IN- WAIT!! IT'S--IT'S
AGENT THIRTEEN!!
OH, CAP! I WAS SO AFRAID--THAT WE'D NEVER--FIND EACH OTHER!!
ATTENTION ALL UNITS!!
RED ALERT!! RED ALERT!!
REINFORCEMENTS ON THE WAY, EXCELLENCY!
HIS COMMUNICATOR!! HE MUST NOT USE IT AGAIN!
AND HE NEVER WILL, PANTHER!
ZAK-!
THE THREE OF YOU ARE DOOMED
AGAIN YOU ARE TOO LATE!
HELP IS ALREADY ON THE WAY!!

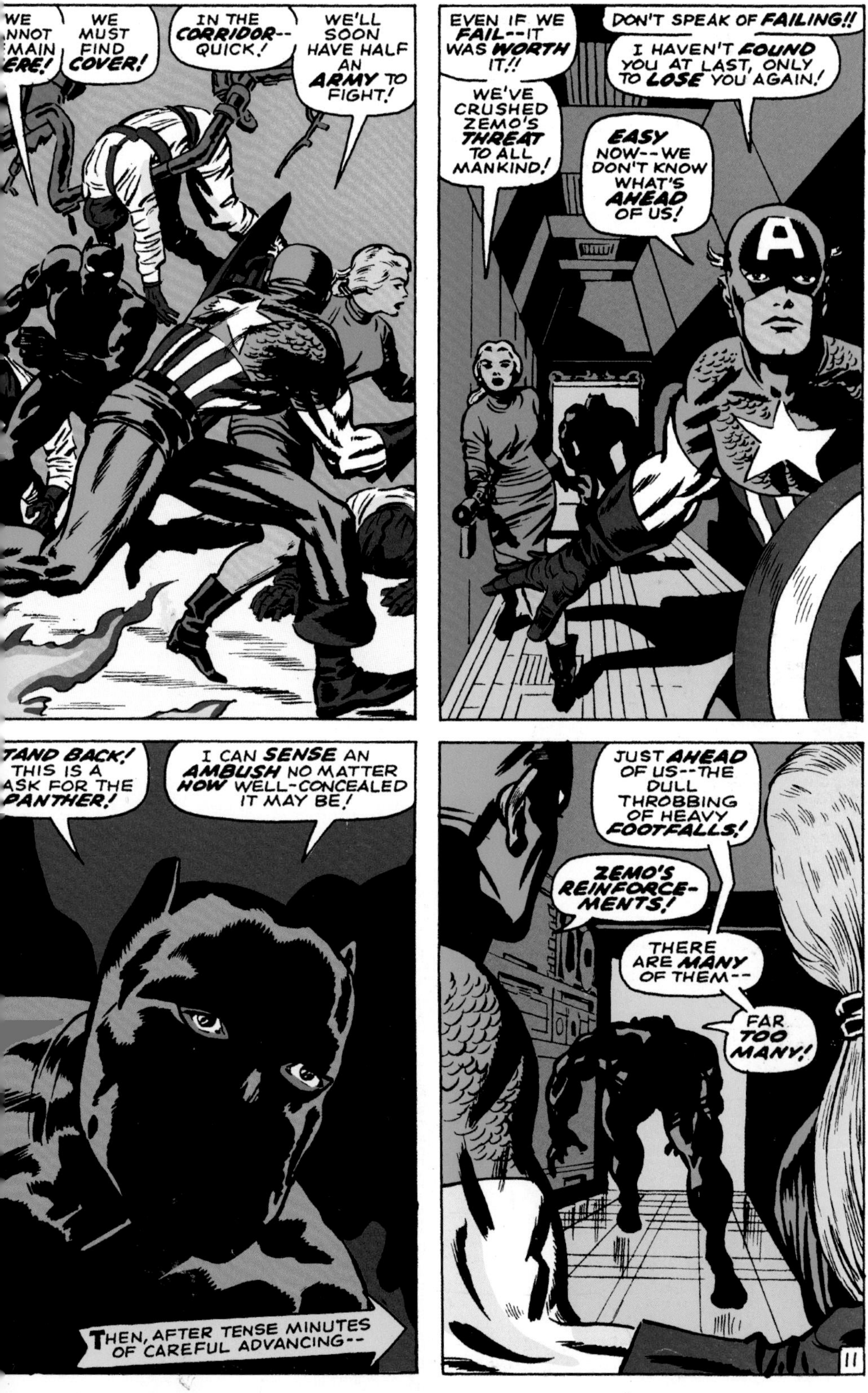

WE NNOT MAIN ERE!
WE MUST FIND COVER!
IN THE CORRIDOR-- QUICK!
WE'LL SOON HAVE HALF AN ARMY TO FIGHT!
EVEN IF WE FAIL--IT WAS WORTH IT!!
WE'VE CRUSHED ZEMO'S THREAT TO ALL MANKIND!
DON'T SPEAK OF FAILING!!
I HAVEN'T FOUND YOU AT LAST, ONLY TO LOSE YOU AGAIN!
EASY NOW--WE DON'T KNOW WHAT'S AHEAD OF US!
TAND BACK! THIS IS A ASK FOR THE PANTHER!
I CAN SENSE AN AMBUSH NO MATTER HOW WELL-CONCEALED IT MAY BE!
THEN, AFTER TENSE MINUTES OF CAREFUL ADVANCING--
JUST AHEAD OF US--THE DULL THROBBING OF HEAVY FOOTFALLS!
ZEMO'S REINFORCE-MENTS!
THERE ARE MANY OF THEM--
FAR TOO MANY!
11

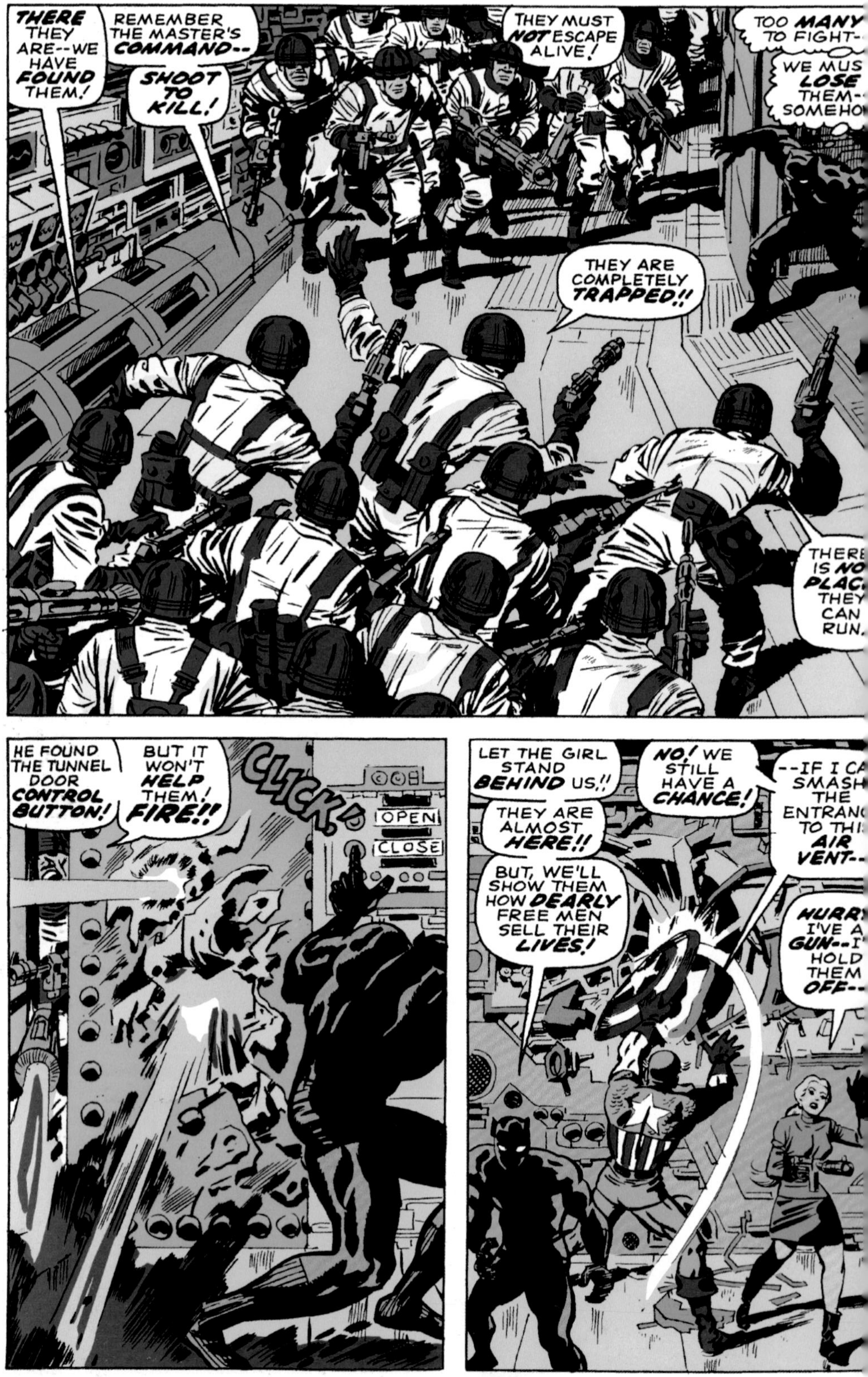
THERE THEY ARE--WE HAVE FOUND THEM!
REMEMBER THE MASTER'S COMMAND--
SHOOT TO KILL!
THEY MUST NOT ESCAPE ALIVE!
TOO MANY TO FIGHT-
WE MUS LOSE THEM- SOMEHO
THEY ARE COMPLETELY TRAPPED!!
THERE IS NO PLAC THEY CAN RUN.
HE FOUND THE TUNNEL DOOR CONTROL BUTTON!
BUT IT WON'T HELP THEM! FIRE!!
CLICK!
OPEN
CLOSE
LET THE GIRL STAND BEHIND US!!
THEY ARE ALMOST HERE!!
BUT, WE'LL SHOW THEM HOW DEARLY FREE MEN SELL THEIR LIVES!
NO! WE STILL HAVE A CHANCE!
--IF I CA SMASH THE ENTRAN TO THI AIR VENT--
HURR I'VE A GUN--I HOLD THEM OFF--

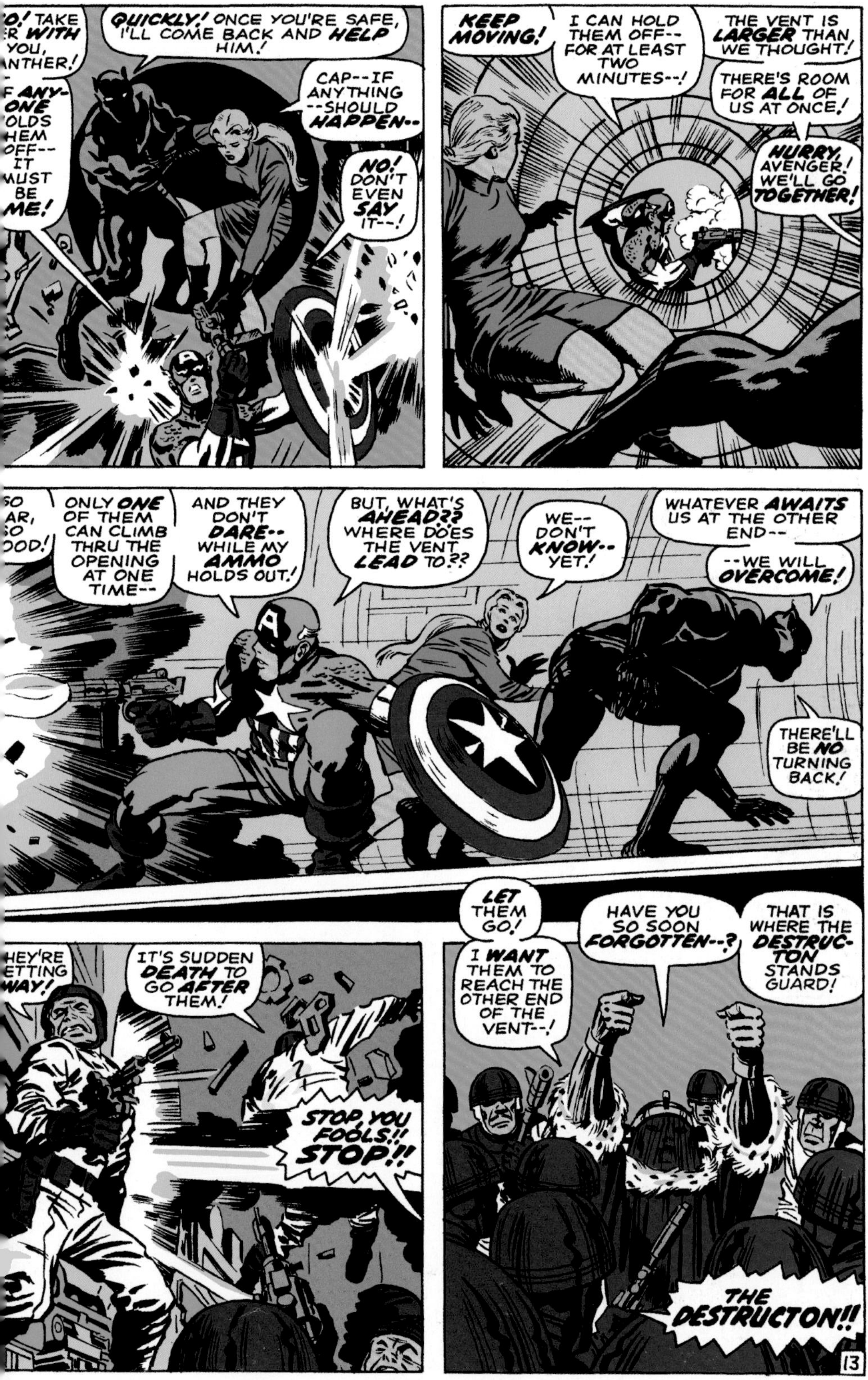

O! TAKE ER WITH YOU, ANTHER!
F ANY-ONE OLDS HEM OFF-- IT MUST BE ME!
QUICKLY! ONCE YOU'RE SAFE, I'LL COME BACK AND HELP HIM!
CAP--IF ANYTHING --SHOULD HAPPEN--
NO! DON'T EVEN SAY IT--!
KEEP MOVING!
I CAN HOLD THEM OFF-- FOR AT LEAST TWO MINUTES--!
THE VENT IS LARGER THAN WE THOUGHT!
THERE'S ROOM FOR ALL OF US AT ONCE!
HURRY, AVENGER! WE'LL GO TOGETHER!
SO AR, SO OOD!
ONLY ONE OF THEM CAN CLIMB THRU THE OPENING AT ONE TIME--
AND THEY DON'T DARE-- WHILE MY AMMO HOLDS OUT!
BUT, WHAT'S AHEAD?? WHERE DOES THE VENT LEAD TO??
WE-- DON'T KNOW-- YET!
WHATEVER AWAITS US AT THE OTHER END--
--WE WILL OVERCOME!
THERE'LL BE NO TURNING BACK!
HEY'RE ETTING WAY!
IT'S SUDDEN DEATH TO GO AFTER THEM!
STOP, YOU FOOLS!! STOP!!
LET THEM GO!
I WANT THEM TO REACH THE OTHER END OF THE VENT--!
HAVE YOU SO SOON FORGOTTEN--?
THAT IS WHERE THE DESTRUCTON STANDS GUARD!
THE DESTRUCTON!!

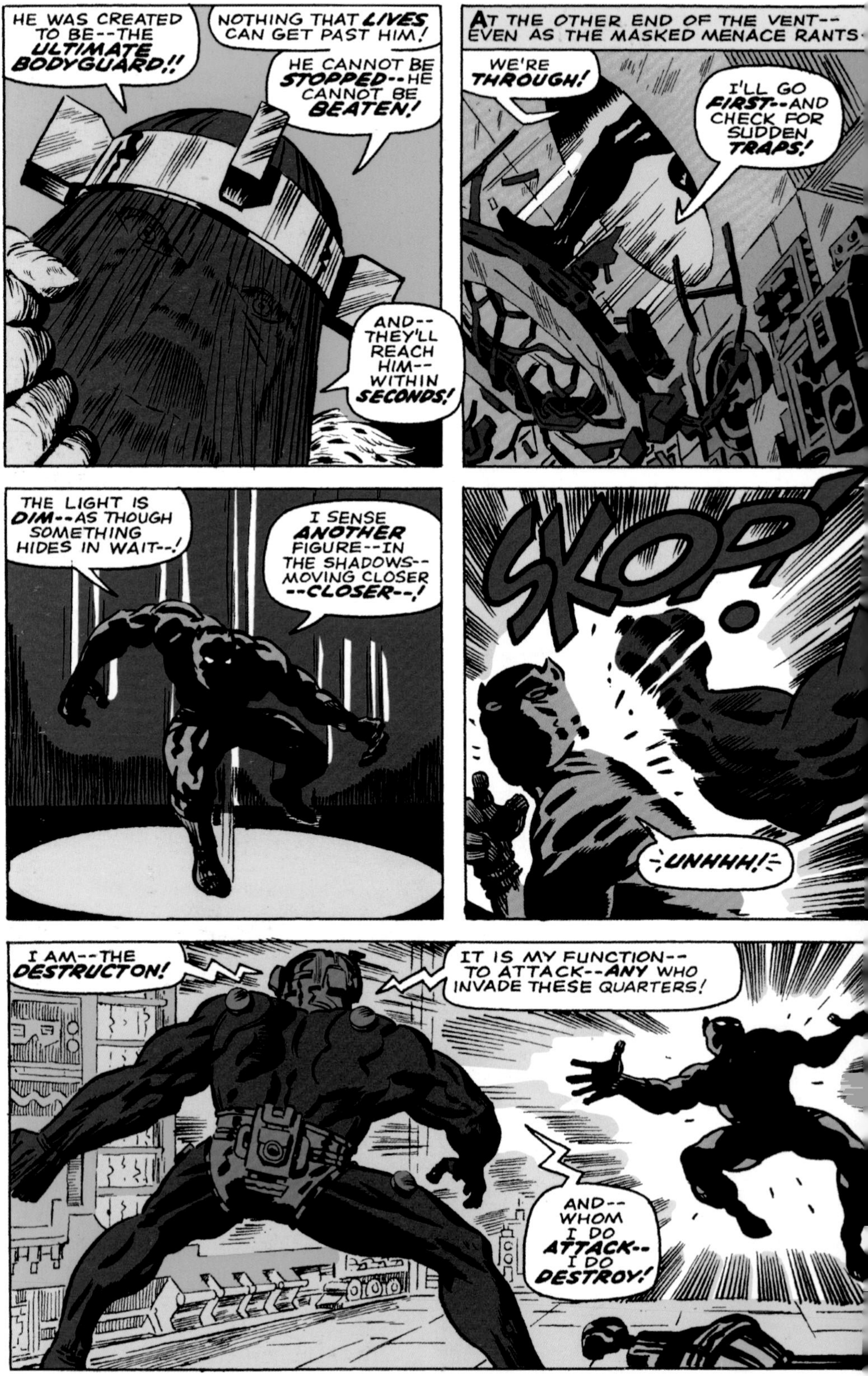
HE WAS CREATED TO BE--THE ULTIMATE BODYGUARD!!
NOTHING THAT LIVES CAN GET PAST HIM!
HE CANNOT BE STOPPED--HE CANNOT BE BEATEN!
AND--THEY'LL REACH HIM--WITHIN SECONDS!
AT THE OTHER END OF THE VENT--EVEN AS THE MASKED MENACE RANTS--
WE'RE THROUGH!
I'LL GO FIRST--AND CHECK FOR SUDDEN TRAPS!
THE LIGHT IS DIM--AS THOUGH SOMETHING HIDES IN WAIT--!
I SENSE ANOTHER FIGURE--IN THE SHADOWS--MOVING CLOSER--CLOSER--!
SKOP!
UNHHH!
I AM--THE DESTRUCTON!
IT IS MY FUNCTION--TO ATTACK--ANY WHO INVADE THESE QUARTERS!
AND--WHOM I DO ATTACK--I DO DESTROY!

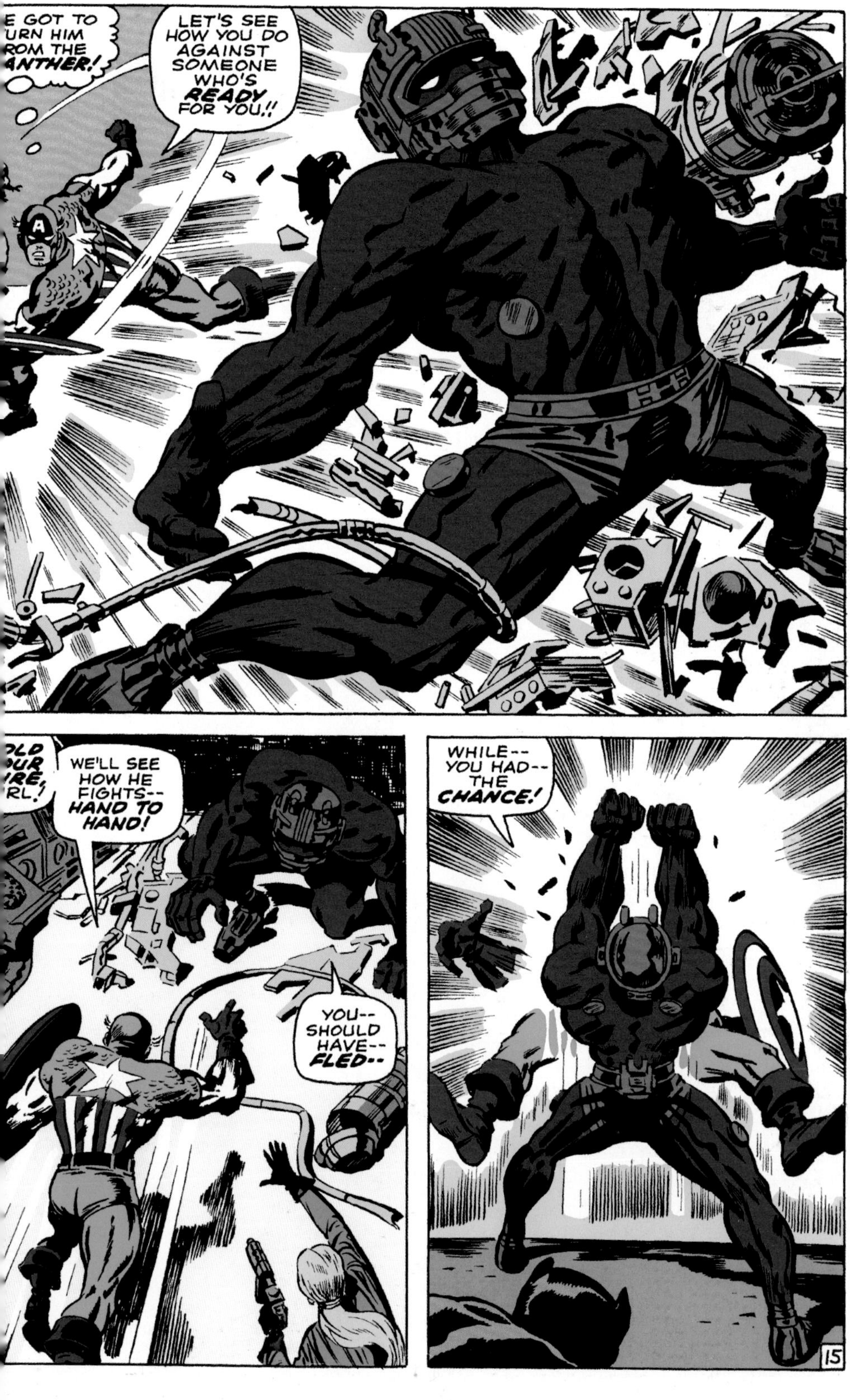
E GOT TO
URN HIM
ROM THE
ANTHER!
LET'S SEE HOW YOU DO AGAINST SOMEONE WHO'S READY FOR YOU!!
OLD
OUR
IRE,
RL.!
WE'LL SEE HOW HE FIGHTS-- HAND TO HAND!
YOU-- SHOULD HAVE-- FLED--
WHILE-- YOU HAD-- THE CHANCE!
15

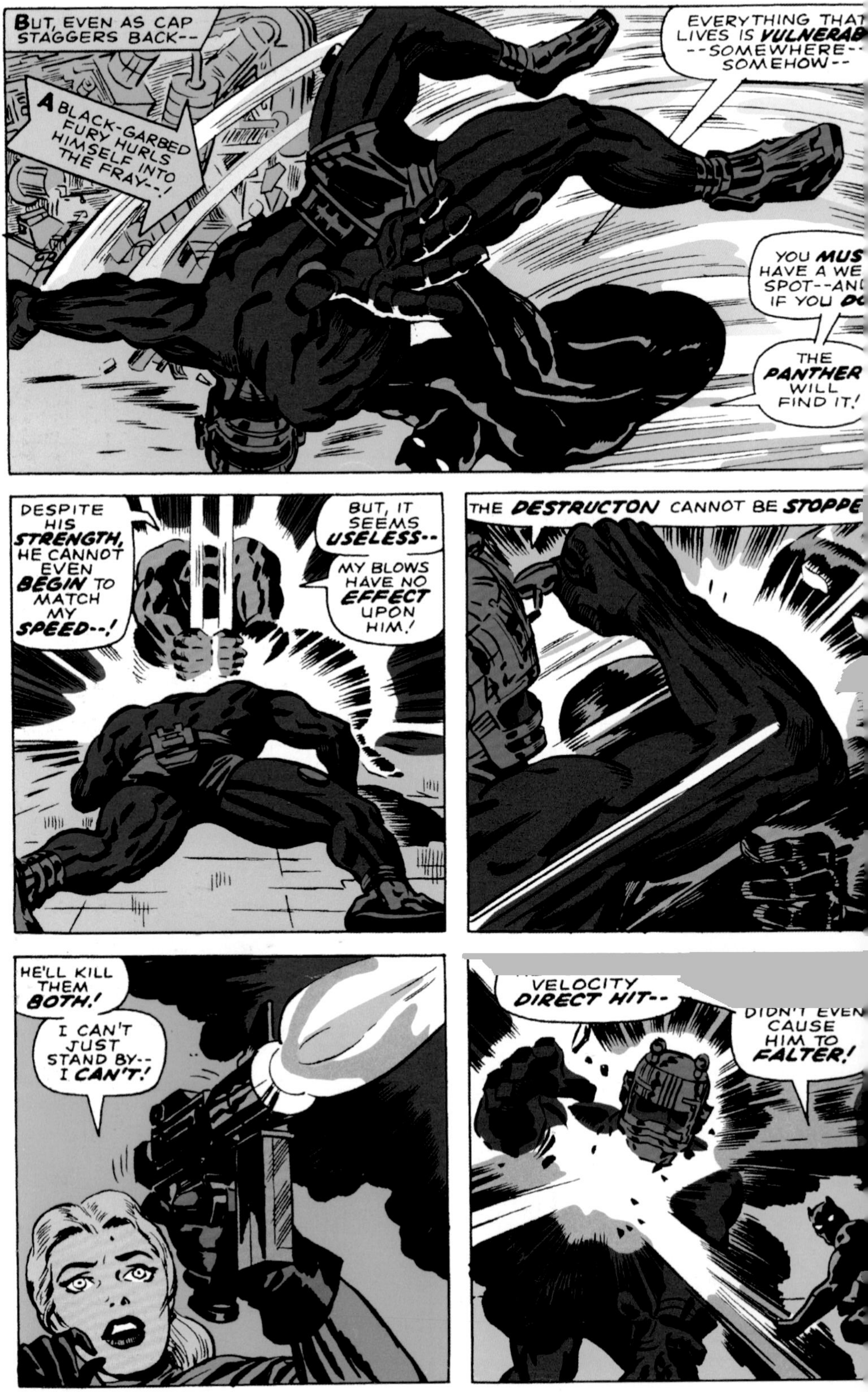
BUT, EVEN AS CAP STAGGERS BACK--
A BLACK-GARBED FURY HURLS HIMSELF INTO THE FRAY--!
EVERYTHING THAT LIVES IS VULNERAB --SOMEWHERE-- SOMEHOW--
YOU MUS HAVE A WE SPOT--AN IF YOU
THE PANTHER WILL FIND IT!
DESPITE HIS STRENGTH, HE CANNOT EVEN BEGIN TO MATCH MY SPEED--!
BUT, IT SEEMS USELESS--
MY BLOWS HAVE NO EFFECT UPON HIM!
THE DESTRUCTON CANNOT BE STOPPE
HE'LL KILL THEM BOTH!
I CAN'T JUST STAND BY-- I CAN'T!
VELOCITY DIRECT HIT--
DIDN'T EVEN CAUSE HIM TO FALTER!

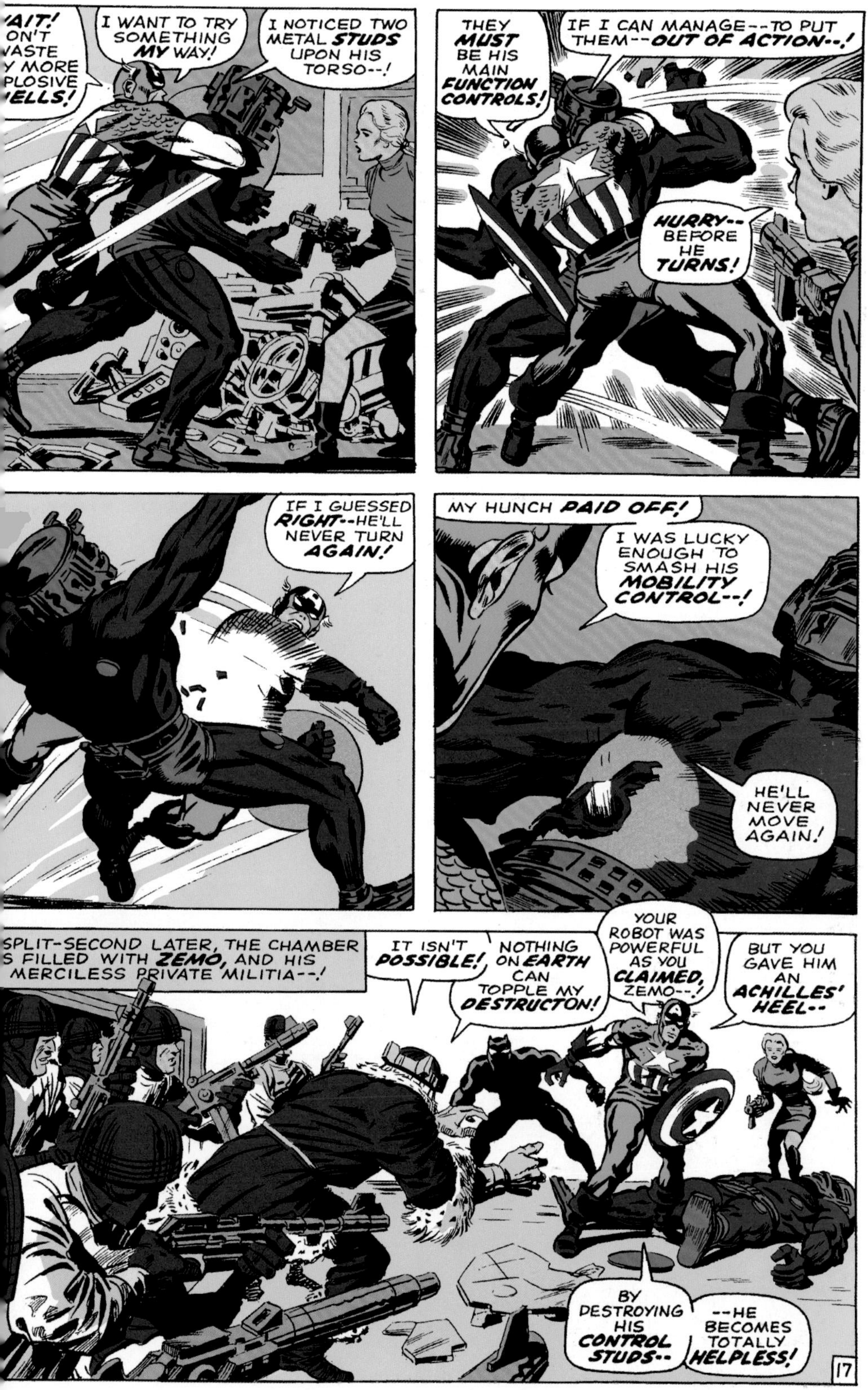

AIT! ON'T ASTE Y MORE PLOSIVE ELLS!
I WANT TO TRY SOMETHING MY WAY!
I NOTICED TWO METAL STUDS UPON HIS TORSO--!
THEY MUST BE HIS MAIN FUNCTION CONTROLS!
IF I CAN MANAGE--TO PUT THEM--OUT OF ACTION--!
HURRY--BEFORE HE TURNS!
IF I GUESSED RIGHT--HE'LL NEVER TURN AGAIN!
MY HUNCH PAID OFF!
I WAS LUCKY ENOUGH TO SMASH HIS MOBILITY CONTROL--!
HE'LL NEVER MOVE AGAIN!
SPLIT-SECOND LATER, THE CHAMBER S FILLED WITH ZEMO, AND HIS MERCILESS PRIVATE MILITIA--!
IT ISN'T POSSIBLE!
NOTHING ON EARTH CAN TOPPLE MY DESTRUCTON!
YOUR ROBOT WAS POWERFUL AS YOU CLAIMED, ZEMO--!
BUT YOU GAVE HIM AN ACHILLES' HEEL--
BY DESTROYING HIS CONTROL STUDS--
--HE BECOMES TOTALLY HELPLESS!

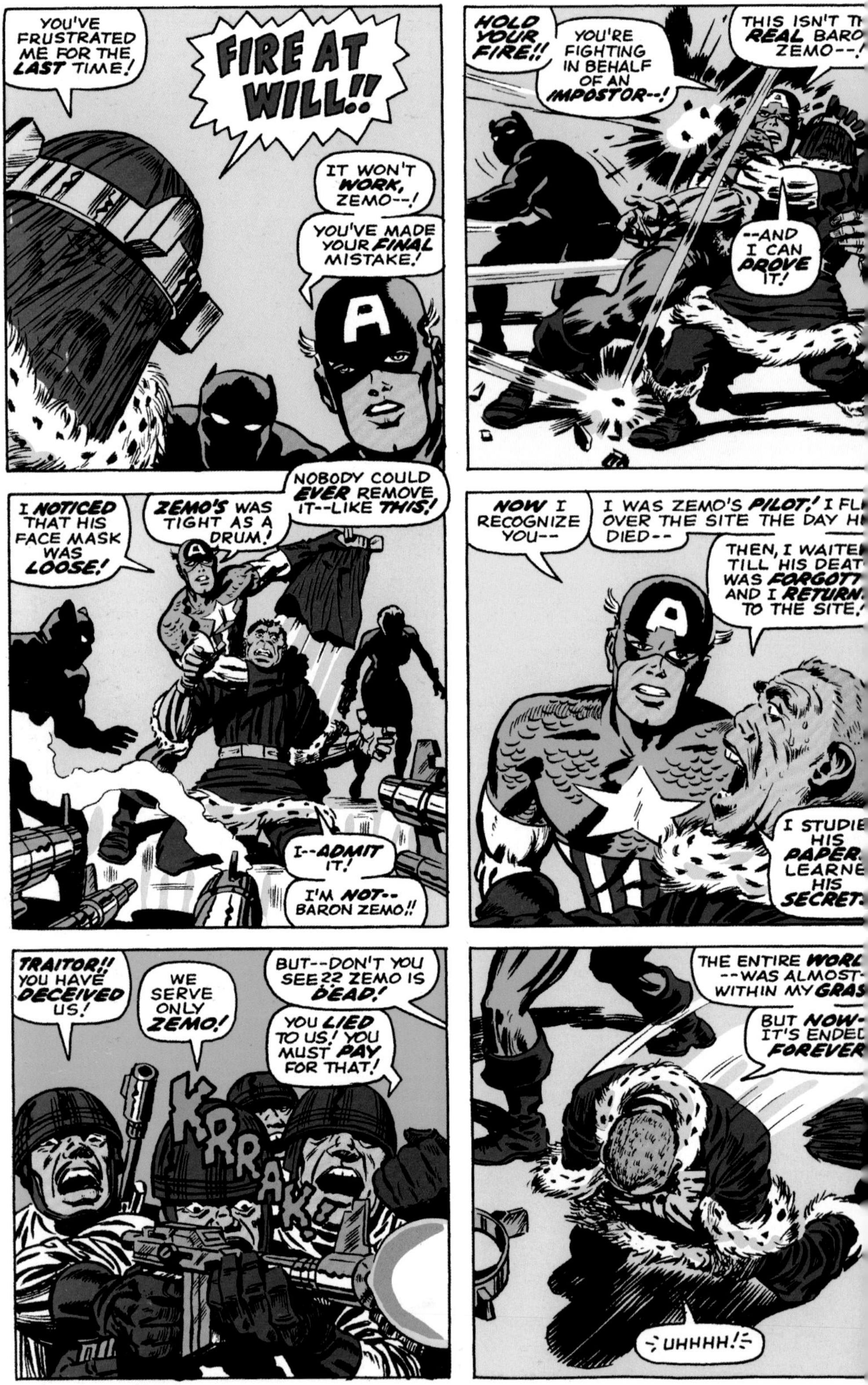

YOU'VE FRUSTRATED ME FOR THE LAST TIME!
FIRE AT WILL!!
IT WON'T WORK, ZEMO--!
YOU'VE MADE YOUR FINAL MISTAKE!
HOLD YOUR FIRE!!
YOU'RE FIGHTING IN BEHALF OF AN IMPOSTOR--!
THIS ISN'T TH REAL BARO ZEMO--!
--AND I CAN PROVE IT!
I NOTICED THAT HIS FACE MASK WAS LOOSE!
ZEMO'S WAS TIGHT AS A DRUM!
NOBODY COULD EVER REMOVE IT--LIKE THIS!
I--ADMIT IT!
I'M NOT-- BARON ZEMO!!
NOW I RECOGNIZE YOU--
I WAS ZEMO'S PILOT! I FL OVER THE SITE THE DAY H DIED--
THEN, I WAITE TILL HIS DEAT WAS FORGOTT AND I RETURN TO THE SITE!
I STUDIE HIS PAPER LEARNE HIS SECRET
TRAITOR!! YOU HAVE DECEIVED US!
WE SERVE ONLY ZEMO!
BUT--DON'T YOU SEE?? ZEMO IS DEAD!
YOU LIED TO US! YOU MUST PAY FOR THAT!
KRRAKK!
THE ENTIRE WORL --WAS ALMOST WITHIN MY GRAS
BUT NOW- IT'S ENDED FOREVER
UHHHH!

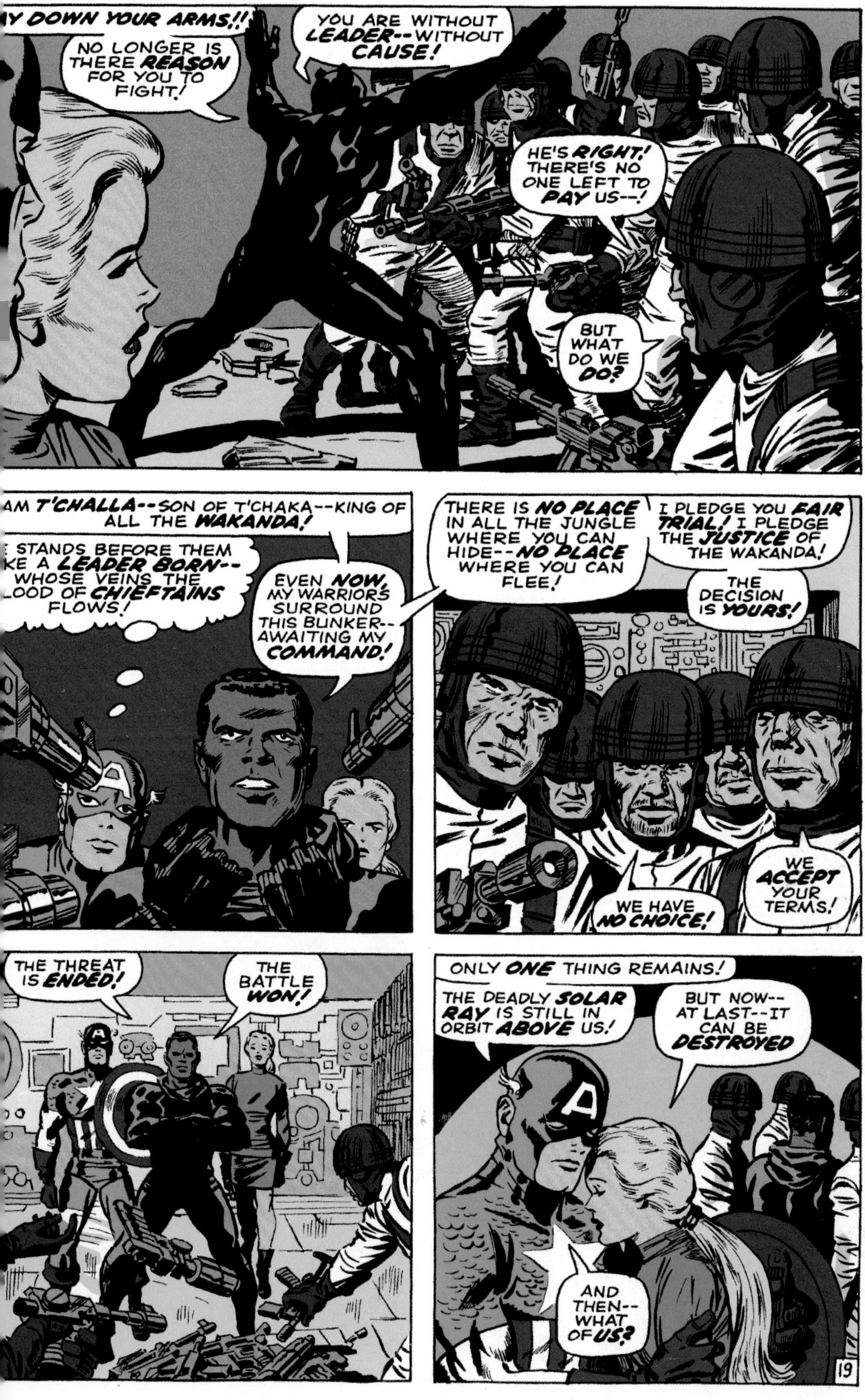

Y DOWN YOUR ARMS!!
NO LONGER IS THERE REASON FOR YOU TO FIGHT!
YOU ARE WITHOUT LEADER--WITHOUT CAUSE!
HE'S RIGHT! THERE'S NO ONE LEFT TO PAY US--!
BUT WHAT DO WE DO?
AM T'CHALLA--SON OF T'CHAKA--KING OF ALL THE WAKANDA!
STANDS BEFORE THEM KE A LEADER BORN--WHOSE VEINS THE LOOD OF CHIEFTAINS FLOWS!
EVEN NOW, MY WARRIORS SURROUND THIS BUNKER--AWAITING MY COMMAND!
THERE IS NO PLACE IN ALL THE JUNGLE WHERE YOU CAN HIDE--NO PLACE WHERE YOU CAN FLEE!
I PLEDGE YOU FAIR TRIAL! I PLEDGE THE JUSTICE OF THE WAKANDA!
THE DECISION IS YOURS!
WE HAVE NO CHOICE!
WE ACCEPT YOUR TERMS!
THE THREAT IS ENDED!
THE BATTLE WON!
ONLY ONE THING REMAINS!
THE DEADLY SOLAR RAY IS STILL IN ORBIT ABOVE US!
BUT NOW--AT LAST--IT CAN BE DESTROYED
AND THEN--WHAT OF US?
19

CAN WE EVEN DARE TO *HOPE*--THAT THERE STILL MAY BE--A LIFE FOR US--*TOGETHER?*

WE EACH HAVE OUR *DUTY*--

WHY IS *DUTY* SUCH A JEALOUS MASTER?

CAN IT NEVER SHARE THE HEART--WITH *LOVE?*

BUT, BEFORE THE VIOLINS PLAY *HEARTS AND FLOWERS*, HERE'S *COL. FURY*--

OUR ELECTRIC *SPACE PROBE* IS SENDIN' BACK *POSITIVE SIGNALS!*

THAT MEANS WE'VE *WON!* ZEMO'S *FORCE FIELD* AROUND THE SOLAR RAY IS *GONE!*

IT *FIGGERS!* --*AGENT THIRTEEN* WUZ ON THE JOB!

ATTENTION --MISSILE UNITS!

LAUNCH YER BIRDIES-- *NOW!*

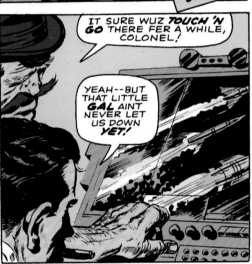

IT SURE WUZ *TOUCH 'N GO* THERE FER A WHILE, COLONEL!

YEAH--BUT THAT LITTLE *GAL* AINT NEVER LET US DOWN *YET!*

--'N NOW-- WE CAN *SCRATCH ONE DEATH RAY!*

THIS OL' PLANET'S GONNA BE *SAFE* FER A WHILE *LONGER!*

A SHORT TIME LATER, A SMALL, BUT POWERFUL PROTOTYPE JET ROCKETS SKYWARD FROM THE COAST OF AFRICA--

IT'S INDEED AN *HONOR* TO HAVE A *KING* FOR A PILOT!

DOES THIS MEAN YOU *ACCEPT* MY OFFER, T'CHALLA?

I WISH TO *CONSIDER* IT, MY FRIEND!

SINCE I AM NO LONGER ON ACTIVE DUTY WITH THE *AVENGERS*, THEY HAVE A *VACANCY* IN THEIR ROSTER--

ONE WHICH I HOPE WILL BE FILLED BY-- THE *PANTHER!!*

BUT, WHAT DOES THE FUTURE HOLD FOR *YOU?*

SO LONG AS *FREEDOM* M.. BE THREATENED--*CAPTAIN AMERICA* MUST FOLLOW HIS DESTINY--

WHEREVER IT MAY LEAD!

AND, *NEXT ISH*, IT WILL LEAD US TO THE SUPREMELY SINISTER

RED SKULL

20

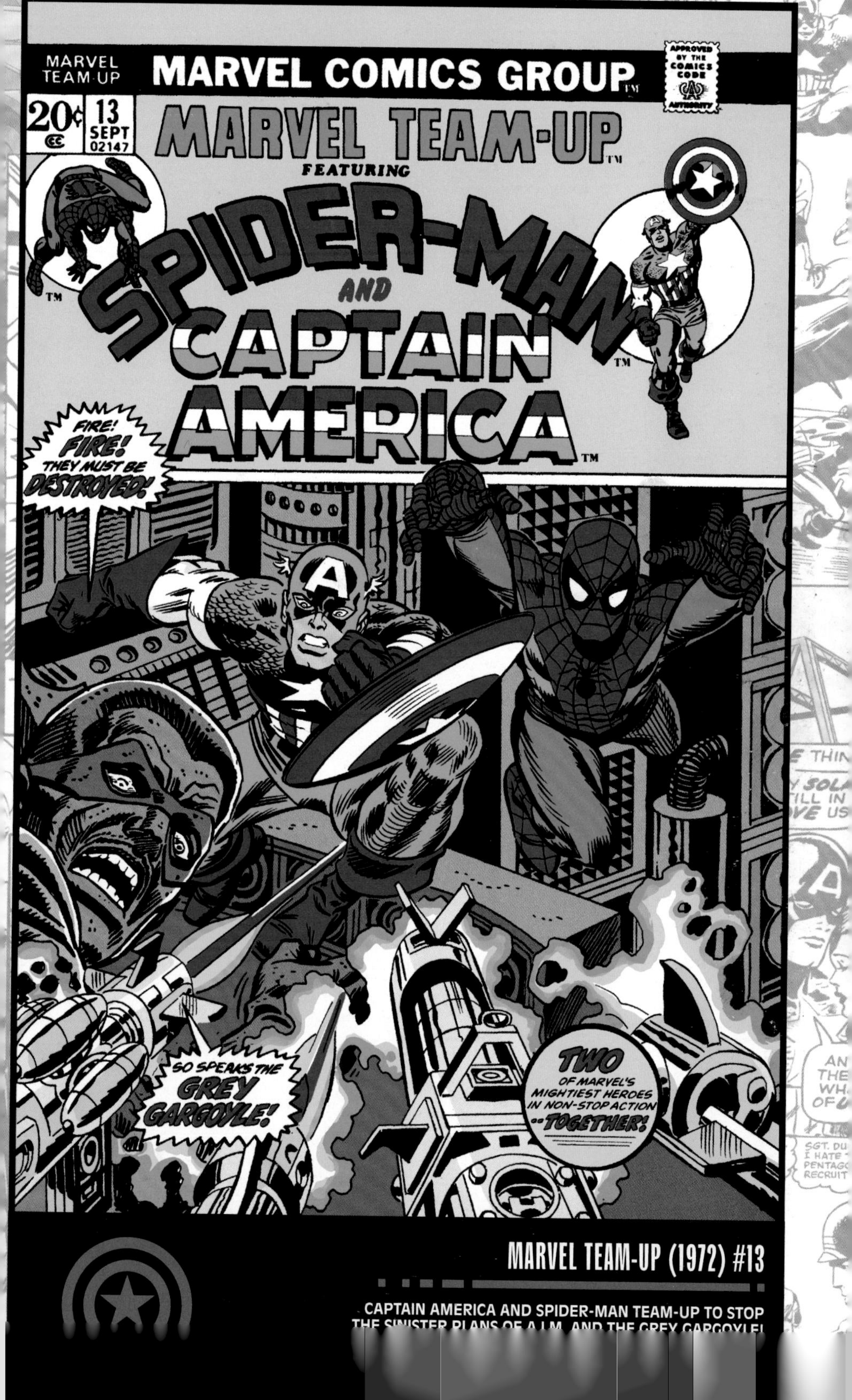
MARVEL TEAM-UP
MARVEL COMICS GROUP
APPROVED BY THE COMICS CODE AUTHORITY
20¢
13 SEPT 02147
MARVEL TEAM-UP
FEATURING
SPIDER-MAN AND CAPTAIN AMERICA
FIRE! FIRE! THEY MUST BE DESTROYED!
SO SPEAKS THE GREY GARGOYLE!
TWO OF MARVEL'S MIGHTIEST HEROES IN NON-STOP ACTION --TOGETHER!

MARVEL TEAM-UP (1972) #13

CAPTAIN AMERICA AND SPIDER-MAN TEAM-UP TO STOP THE SINISTER PLANS OF A.I.M. AND THE GREY GARGOYLE!

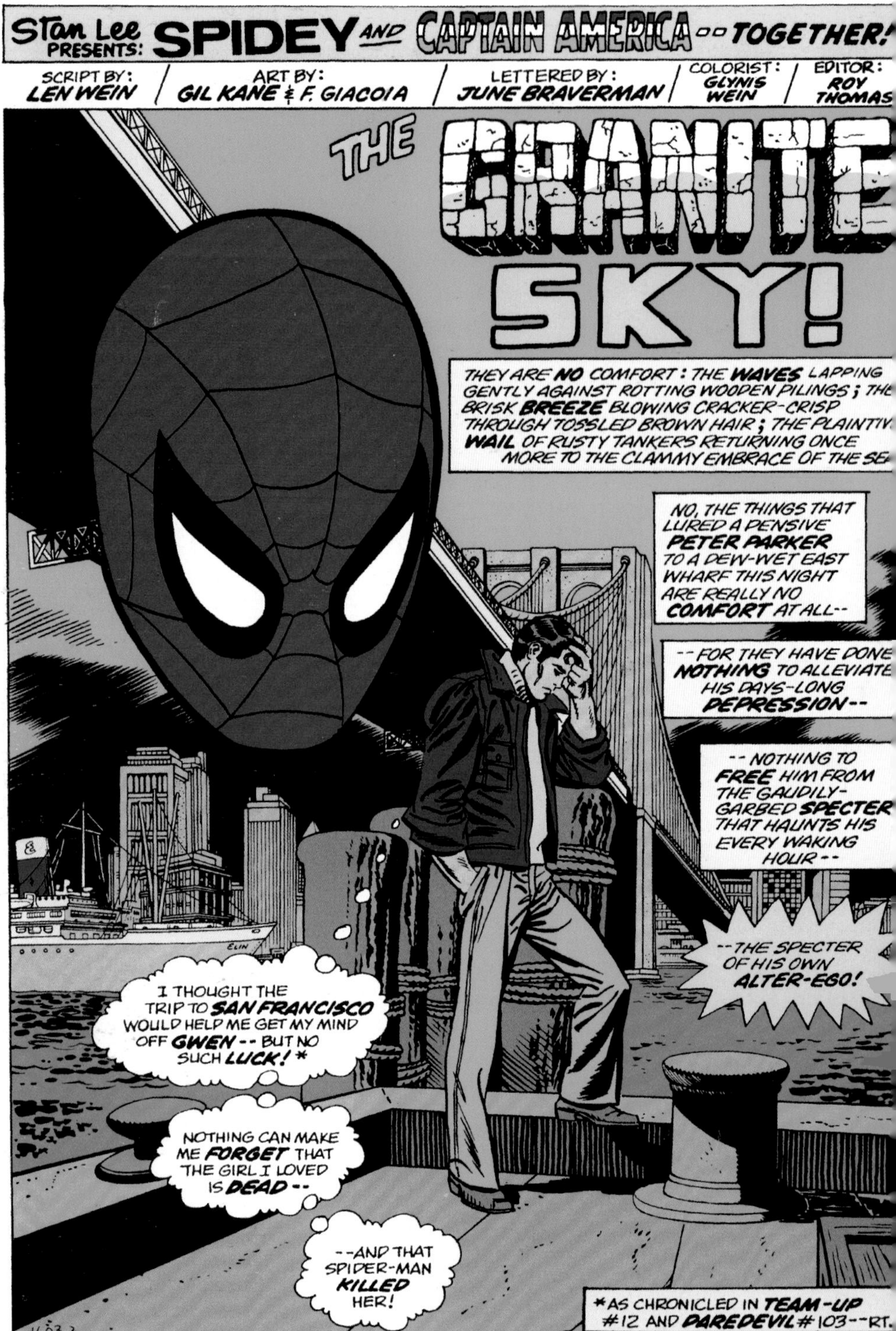

Stan Lee PRESENTS: SPIDEY AND CAPTAIN AMERICA -- TOGETHER!
SCRIPT BY: LEN WEIN
ART BY: GIL KANE & F. GIACOIA
LETTERED BY: JUNE BRAVERMAN
COLORIST: GLYNIS WEIN
EDITOR: ROY THOMAS
THE GRANITE SKY!
THEY ARE NO COMFORT: THE WAVES LAPPING GENTLY AGAINST ROTTING WOODEN PILINGS; THE BRISK BREEZE BLOWING CRACKER-CRISP THROUGH TOSSLED BROWN HAIR; THE PLAINTIVE WAIL OF RUSTY TANKERS RETURNING ONCE MORE TO THE CLAMMY EMBRACE OF THE SEA
NO, THE THINGS THAT LURED A PENSIVE PETER PARKER TO A DEW-WET EAST WHARF THIS NIGHT ARE REALLY NO COMFORT AT ALL--
--FOR THEY HAVE DONE NOTHING TO ALLEVIATE HIS DAYS-LONG DEPRESSION--
--NOTHING TO FREE HIM FROM THE GAUDILY-GARBED SPECTER THAT HAUNTS HIS EVERY WAKING HOUR--
--THE SPECTER OF HIS OWN ALTER-EGO!
I THOUGHT THE TRIP TO SAN FRANCISCO WOULD HELP ME GET MY MIND OFF GWEN -- BUT NO SUCH LUCK! *
NOTHING CAN MAKE ME FORGET THAT THE GIRL I LOVED IS DEAD --
--AND THAT SPIDER-MAN KILLED HER!
*AS CHRONICLED IN TEAM-UP #12 AND DAREDEVIL #103--RT.
16032

I MAY NOT HAVE CTUALLY **DONE** THE DEED--

--BUT IF I ASN'T **SPIDEY**, HE GREEN GOBLIN OULD **NEVER** HAVE--

'ERE NOW, LADDY--THINGS CAN'T BE AS BLACK AS ALL **THAT**!

HUH?

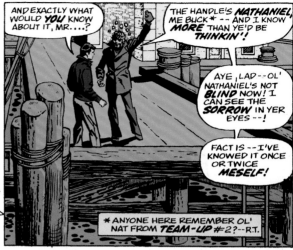

AND EXACTLY WHAT WOULD **YOU** KNOW ABOUT IT, MR....?

THE HANDLE'S **NATHANIEL**, ME BUCK* -- AND I KNOW **MORE** THAN YE'D BE **THINKIN'**!

AYE, LAD--OL' NATHANIEL'S NOT **BLIND** NOW! I CAN SEE THE **SORROW** IN YER EYES--!

FACT IS--I'VE KNOWED IT ONCE OR TWICE **MESELF**!

* ANYONE HERE REMEMBER OL' NAT FROM **TEAM-UP** #2?--R.T.

E CAN'T LET IT **GET** TO YE, LAD--!

YE GOTTA STAND UP AN' **FACE** YER HURT--

--'FORE IT GETS **HEAVY** NOUGH TO PULL YE DOWN LIKE A RUDDY **ANCHOR**!

YE GOTTA **BUCK UP**, MATE--

--TAKE THE BULL BY THE **HORNS**, SO TO SPEAK--!

JUST WHAT I **NEEDED**--A BESOTTED **PHILOSOPHER**!

THIS GUY'S GONNA KEEP **JAWWING** TILL HE **COLLAPSES**--

--AND TONIGHT I JUST HAVEN'T GOT THE PATIENCE TO **WAIT**!

AYE, LADDY--THE BEST THING FER YE TO DO IS **STAND UP** TO YER SORROWS LIKE A **MAN**!

D'YE **KNOW** WHAT I'M **SAYIN'**, LADDY?

LADDY?

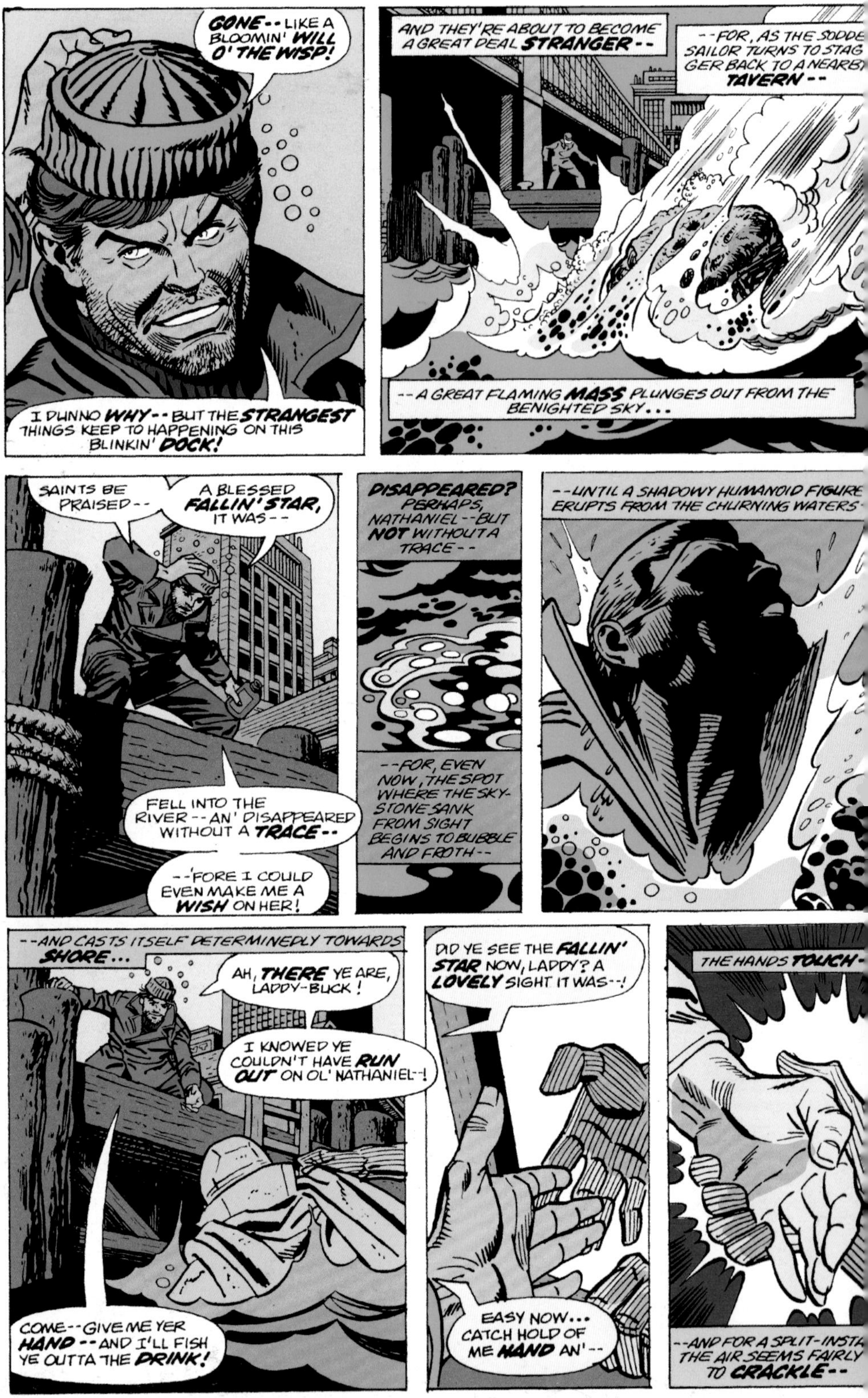
GONE--LIKE A BLOOMIN' WILL O' THE WISP!
I DUNNO WHY--BUT THE STRANGEST THINGS KEEP TO HAPPENING ON THIS BLINKIN' DOCK!
AND THEY'RE ABOUT TO BECOME A GREAT DEAL STRANGER--
--FOR, AS THE SODDE SAILOR TURNS TO STAG GER BACK TO A NEARB TAVERN--
--A GREAT FLAMING MASS PLUNGES OUT FROM THE BENIGHTED SKY...
SAINTS BE PRAISED--
A BLESSED FALLIN' STAR, IT WAS--
FELL INTO THE RIVER--AN' DISAPPEARED WITHOUT A TRACE--
--'FORE I COULD EVEN MAKE ME A WISH ON HER!
DISAPPEARED? PERHAPS, NATHANIEL--BUT NOT WITHOUT A TRACE--
--FOR, EVEN NOW, THE SPOT WHERE THE SKY-STONE SANK FROM SIGHT BEGINS TO BUBBLE AND FROTH--
--UNTIL A SHADOWY HUMANOID FIGURE ERUPTS FROM THE CHURNING WATERS-
--AND CASTS ITSELF DETERMINEDLY TOWARDS SHORE...
AH, THERE YE ARE, LADDY-BUCK!
I KNOWED YE COULDN'T HAVE RUN OUT ON OL' NATHANIEL--!
COME--GIVE ME YER HAND--AND I'LL FISH YE OUTTA THE DRINK!
DID YE SEE THE FALLIN' STAR NOW, LADDY? A LOVELY SIGHT IT WAS--!
EASY NOW... CATCH HOLD OF ME HAND AN'--
THE HANDS TOUCH-
--AND FOR A SPLIT-INSTA THE AIR SEEMS FAIRLY TO CRACKLE--

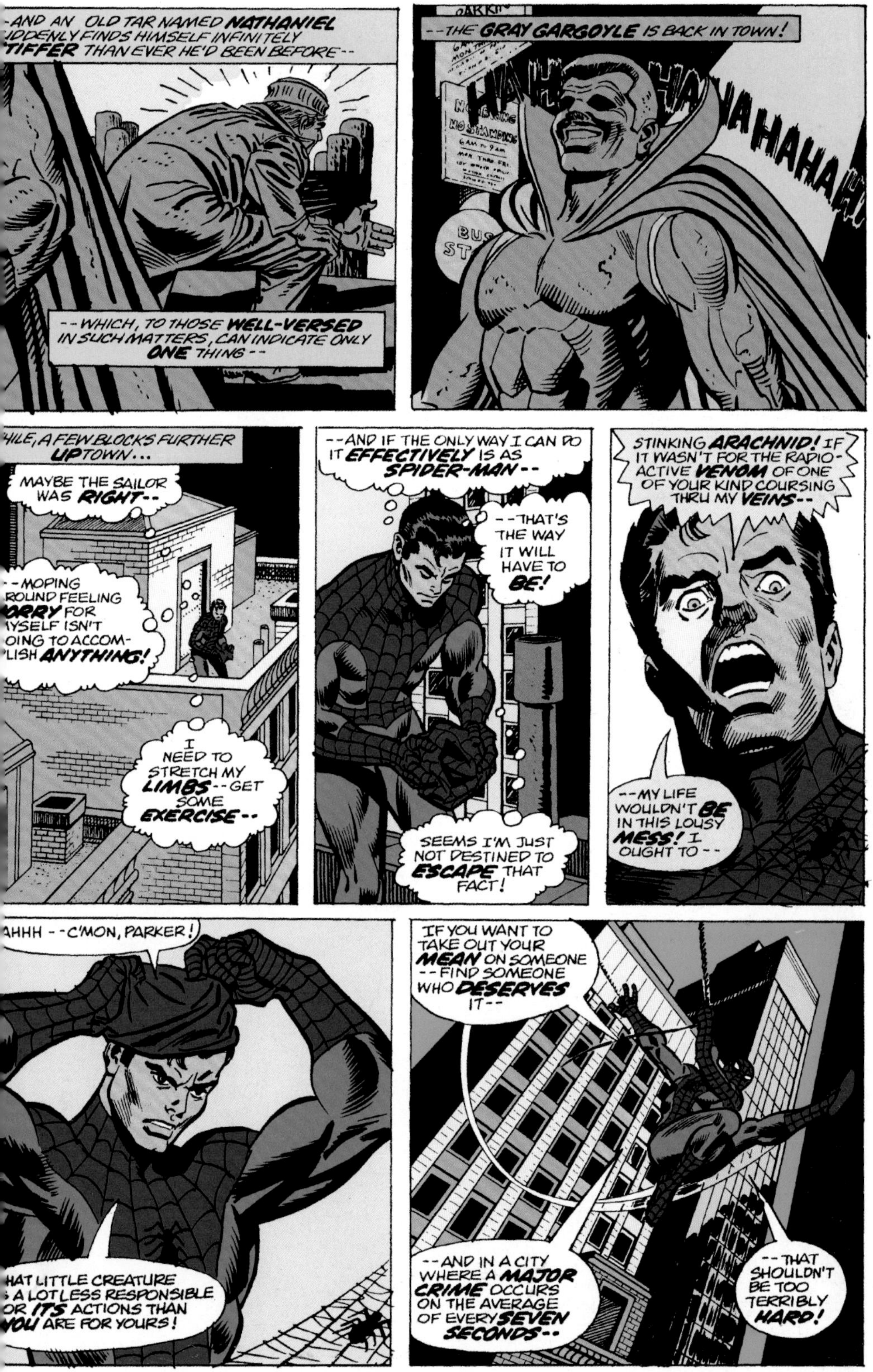
--AND AN OLD TAR NAMED NATHANIEL UDDENLY FINDS HIMSELF INFINITELY TIFFER THAN EVER HE'D BEEN BEFORE--
--WHICH, TO THOSE WELL-VERSED IN SUCH MATTERS, CAN INDICATE ONLY ONE THING--
--THE GRAY GARGOYLE IS BACK IN TOWN!
HAHAHAHAHAHAHAHAH
NO STANDING
BUS STOP
HILE, A FEW BLOCKS FURTHER UPTOWN...
MAYBE THE SAILOR WAS RIGHT--
--MOPING ROUND FEELING ORRY FOR YSELF ISN'T OING TO ACCOM-PLISH ANYTHING!
I NEED TO STRETCH MY LIMBS--GET SOME EXERCISE--
--AND IF THE ONLY WAY I CAN DO IT EFFECTIVELY IS AS SPIDER-MAN--
--THAT'S THE WAY IT WILL HAVE TO BE!
SEEMS I'M JUST NOT DESTINED TO ESCAPE THAT FACT!
STINKING ARACHNID! IF IT WASN'T FOR THE RADIO-ACTIVE VENOM OF ONE OF YOUR KIND COURSING THRU MY VEINS--
--MY LIFE WOULDN'T BE IN THIS LOUSY MESS! I OUGHT TO--
AHHH--C'MON, PARKER!
HAT LITTLE CREATURE S A LOT LESS RESPONSIBLE OR ITS ACTIONS THAN YOU ARE FOR YOURS!
IF YOU WANT TO TAKE OUT YOUR MEAN ON SOMEONE --FIND SOMEONE WHO DESERVES IT--
--AND IN A CITY WHERE A MAJOR CRIME OCCURS ON THE AVERAGE OF EVERY SEVEN SECONDS--
--THAT SHOULDN'T BE TOO TERRIBLY HARD!

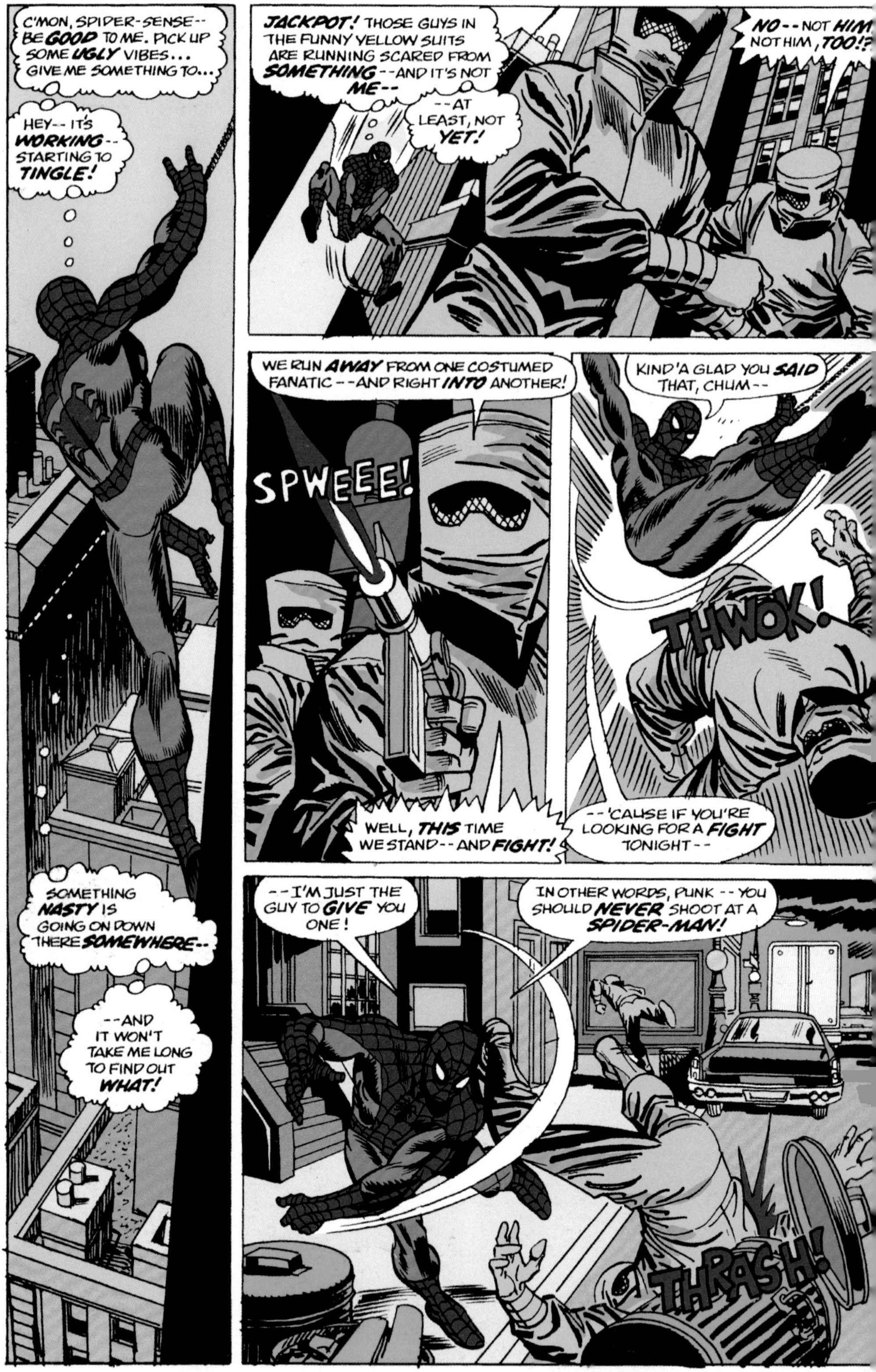
C'MON, SPIDER-SENSE-- BE GOOD TO ME. PICK UP SOME UGLY VIBES... GIVE ME SOMETHING TO...
HEY-- IT'S WORKING-- STARTING TO TINGLE!
SOMETHING NASTY IS GOING ON DOWN THERE SOMEWHERE--
--AND IT WON'T TAKE ME LONG TO FIND OUT WHAT!
JACKPOT! THOSE GUYS IN THE FUNNY YELLOW SUITS ARE RUNNING SCARED FROM SOMETHING--AND IT'S NOT ME--
--AT LEAST, NOT YET!
NO--NOT HIM NOT HIM, TOO!?
WE RUN AWAY FROM ONE COSTUMED FANATIC--AND RIGHT INTO ANOTHER!
SPWEEE!
WELL, THIS TIME WE STAND--AND FIGHT!
KIND'A GLAD YOU SAID THAT, CHUM--
THWOK!
--'CAUSE IF YOU'RE LOOKING FOR A FIGHT TONIGHT--
--I'M JUST THE GUY TO GIVE YOU ONE!
IN OTHER WORDS, PUNK--YOU SHOULD NEVER SHOOT AT A SPIDER-MAN!
THRASH!

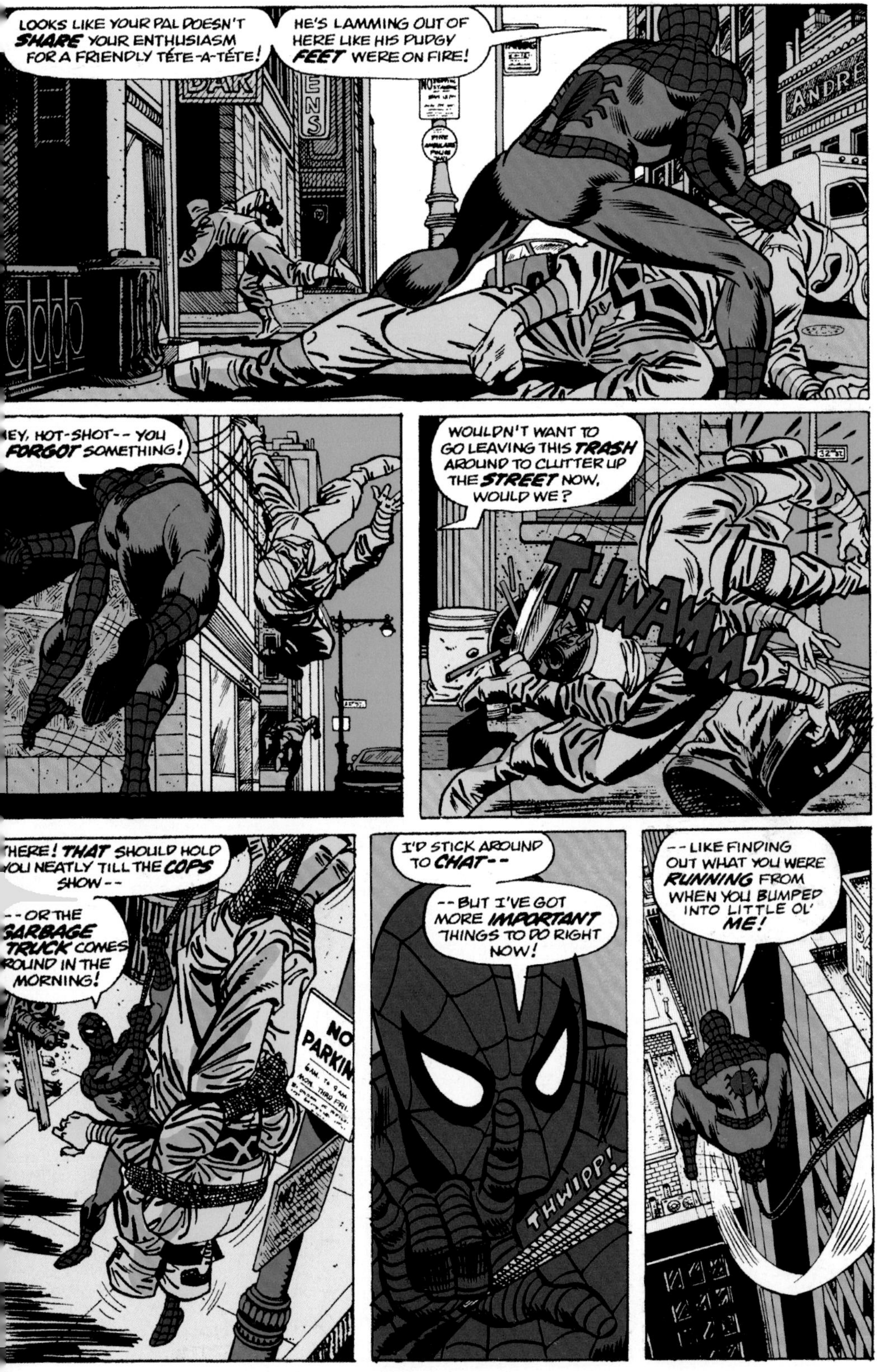

LOOKS LIKE YOUR PAL DOESN'T SHARE YOUR ENTHUSIASM FOR A FRIENDLY TÉTE-A-TÉTE!
HE'S LAMMING OUT OF HERE LIKE HIS PUDGY FEET WERE ON FIRE!
ANDRE
EY, HOT-SHOT-- YOU FORGOT SOMETHING!
WOULDN'T WANT TO GO LEAVING THIS TRASH AROUND TO CLUTTER UP THE STREET NOW, WOULD WE?
THWAMM!
HERE! THAT SHOULD HOLD YOU NEATLY TILL THE COPS SHOW--
--OR THE GARBAGE TRUCK COMES ROUND IN THE MORNING!
NO PARKIN
I'D STICK AROUND TO CHAT--
--BUT I'VE GOT MORE IMPORTANT THINGS TO DO RIGHT NOW!
THWIPP!
--LIKE FINDING OUT WHAT YOU WERE RUNNING FROM WHEN YOU BUMPED INTO LITTLE OL' ME!

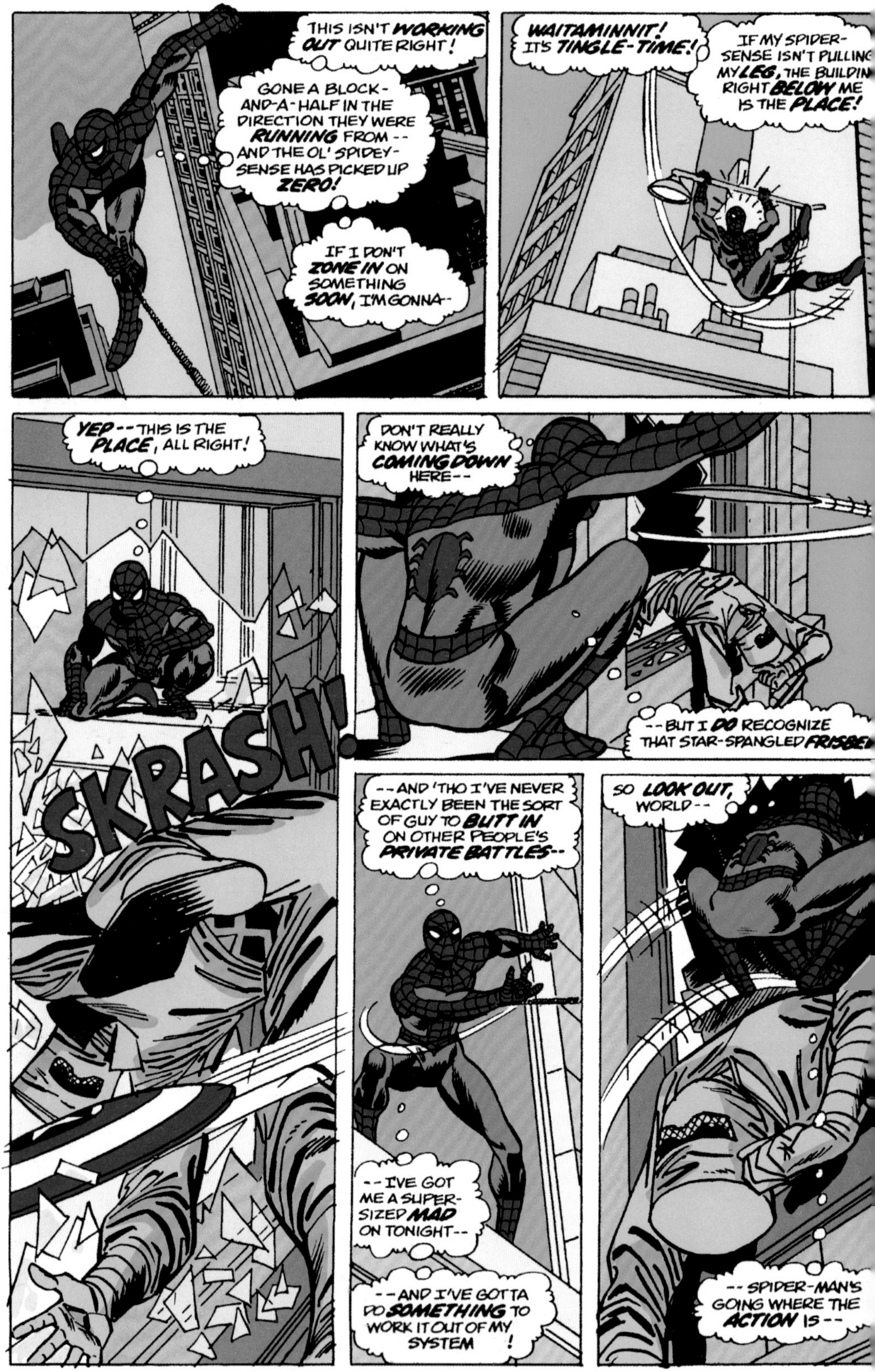
THIS ISN'T WORKING OUT QUITE RIGHT!
GONE A BLOCK-AND-A-HALF IN THE DIRECTION THEY WERE RUNNING FROM -- AND THE OL' SPIDEY-SENSE HAS PICKED UP ZERO!
IF I DON'T ZONE IN ON SOMETHING SOON, I'M GONNA--
WAITAMINNIT! IT'S TINGLE-TIME!
IF MY SPIDER-SENSE ISN'T PULLING MY LEG, THE BUILDIN RIGHT BELOW ME IS THE PLACE!
YEP -- THIS IS THE PLACE, ALL RIGHT!
SKRASH!
DON'T REALLY KNOW WHAT'S COMING DOWN HERE--
--BUT I DO RECOGNIZE THAT STAR-SPANGLED FRISBE
--AND 'THO I'VE NEVER EXACTLY BEEN THE SORT OF GUY TO BUTT IN ON OTHER PEOPLE'S PRIVATE BATTLES--
--I'VE GOT ME A SUPER-SIZED MAD ON TONIGHT--
--AND I'VE GOTTA DO SOMETHING TO WORK IT OUT OF MY SYSTEM!
SO LOOK OUT, WORLD--
--SPIDER-MAN'S GOING WHERE THE ACTION IS--

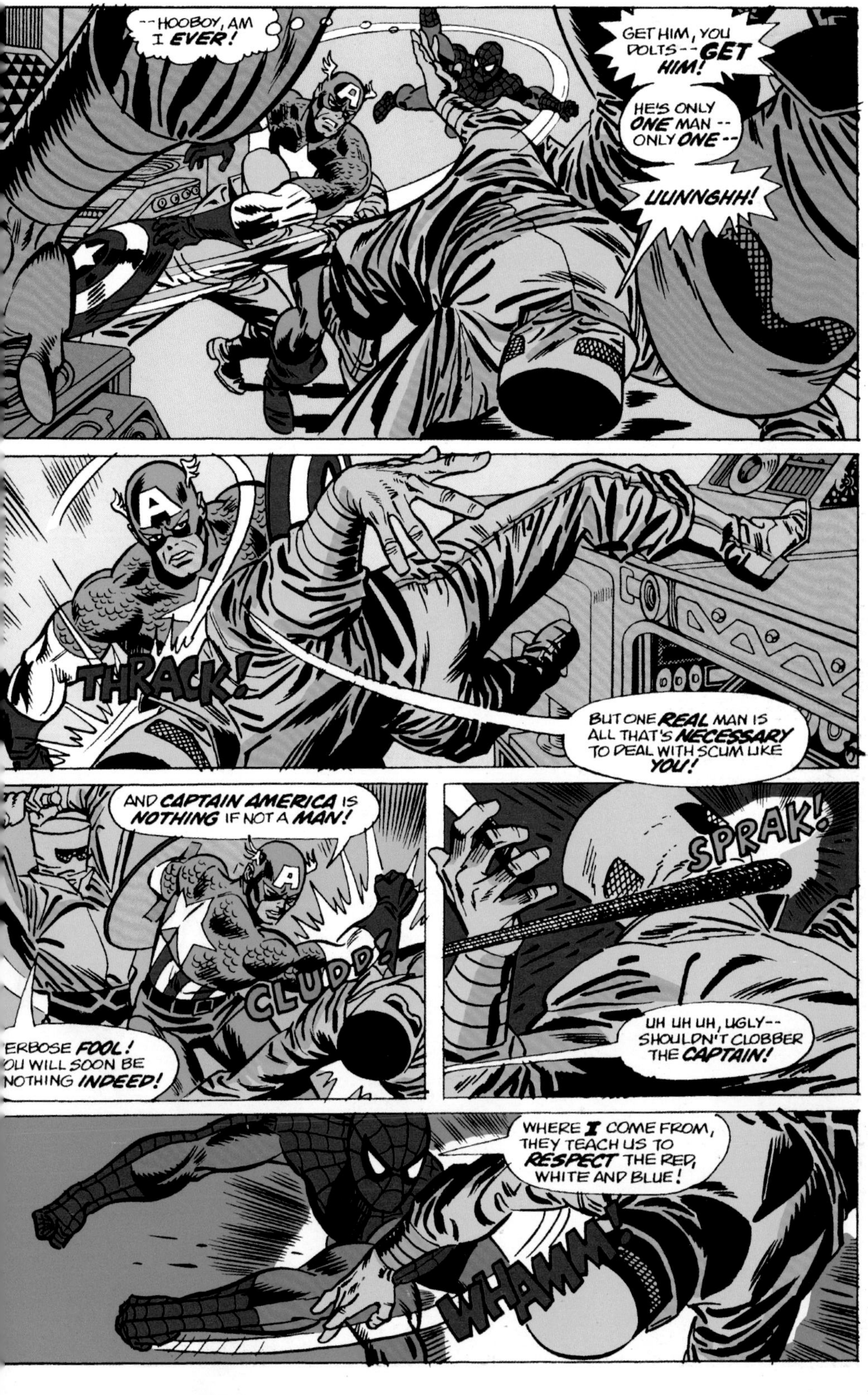
--HOOBOY, AM I EVER!
GET HIM, YOU DOLTS--GET HIM!
HE'S ONLY ONE MAN--ONLY ONE--
UUNNGHH!
THRACK!
BUT ONE REAL MAN IS ALL THAT'S NECESSARY TO DEAL WITH SCUM LIKE YOU!
AND CAPTAIN AMERICA IS NOTHING IF NOT A MAN!
CLUDD!
ERBOSE FOOL! OU WILL SOON BE NOTHING INDEED!
SPRAK!
UH UH UH, UGLY--SHOULDN'T CLOBBER THE CAPTAIN!
WHERE I COME FROM, THEY TEACH US TO RESPECT THE RED, WHITE AND BLUE!
WHAMM!

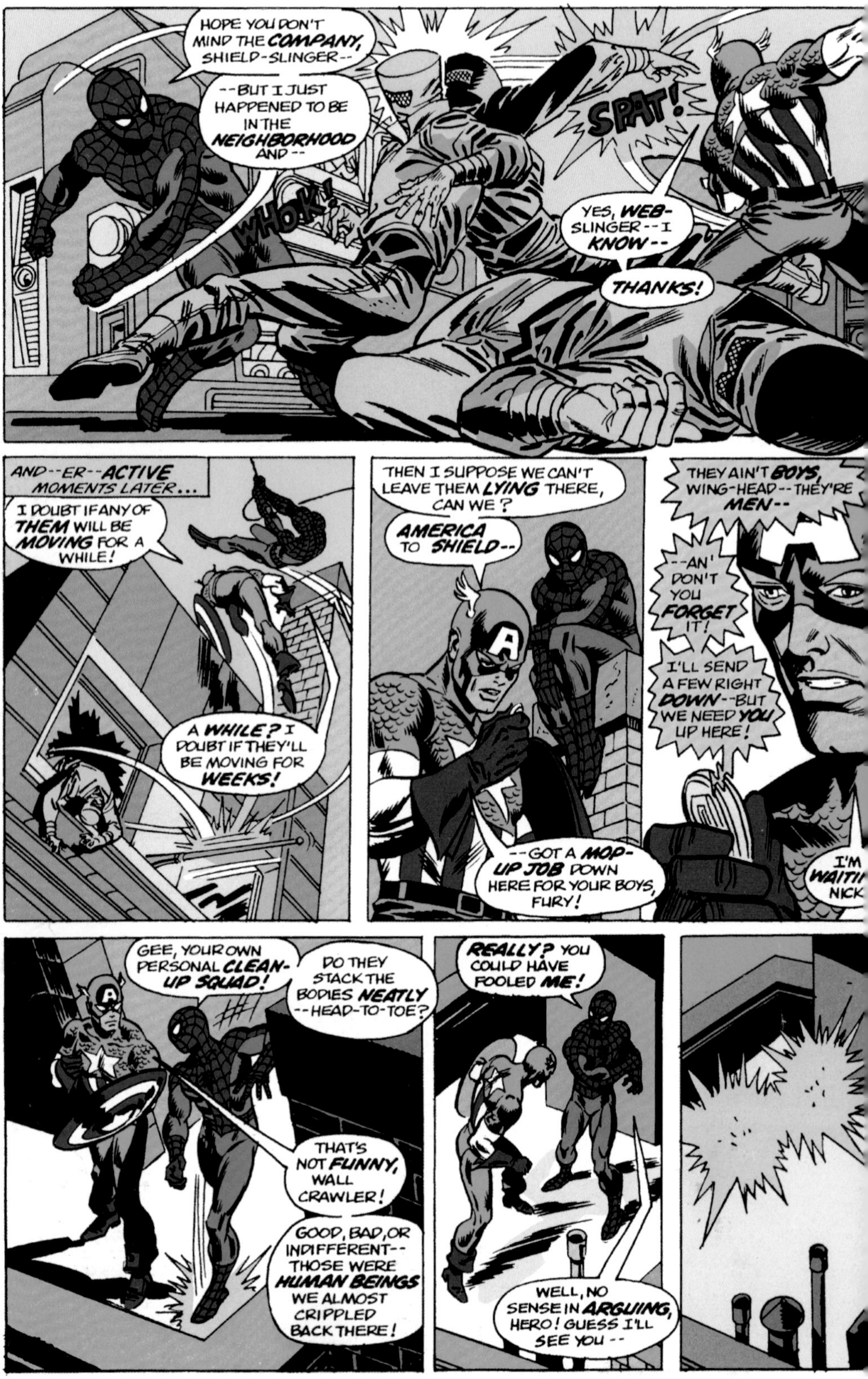
HOPE YOU DON'T MIND THE COMPANY, SHIELD-SLINGER--
--BUT I JUST HAPPENED TO BE IN THE NEIGHBORHOOD AND--
WHOK!
SPAT!
YES, WEB-SLINGER--I KNOW--
THANKS!
AND--ER--ACTIVE MOMENTS LATER...
I DOUBT IF ANY OF THEM WILL BE MOVING FOR A WHILE!
A WHILE? I DOUBT IF THEY'LL BE MOVING FOR WEEKS!
THEN I SUPPOSE WE CAN'T LEAVE THEM LYING THERE, CAN WE?
AMERICA TO SHIELD--
--GOT A MOP-UP JOB DOWN HERE FOR YOUR BOYS, FURY!
THEY AIN'T BOYS, WING-HEAD--THEY'RE MEN--
--AN' DON'T YOU FORGET IT!
I'LL SEND A FEW RIGHT DOWN--BUT WE NEED YOU UP HERE!
I'M WAITI NICK
GEE, YOUR OWN PERSONAL CLEAN-UP SQUAD!
DO THEY STACK THE BODIES NEATLY--HEAD-TO-TOE?
THAT'S NOT FUNNY, WALL CRAWLER!
GOOD, BAD, OR INDIFFERENT--THOSE WERE HUMAN BEINGS WE ALMOST CRIPPLED BACK THERE!
REALLY? YOU COULD HAVE FOOLED ME!
WELL, NO SENSE IN ARGUING, HERO! GUESS I'LL SEE YOU--

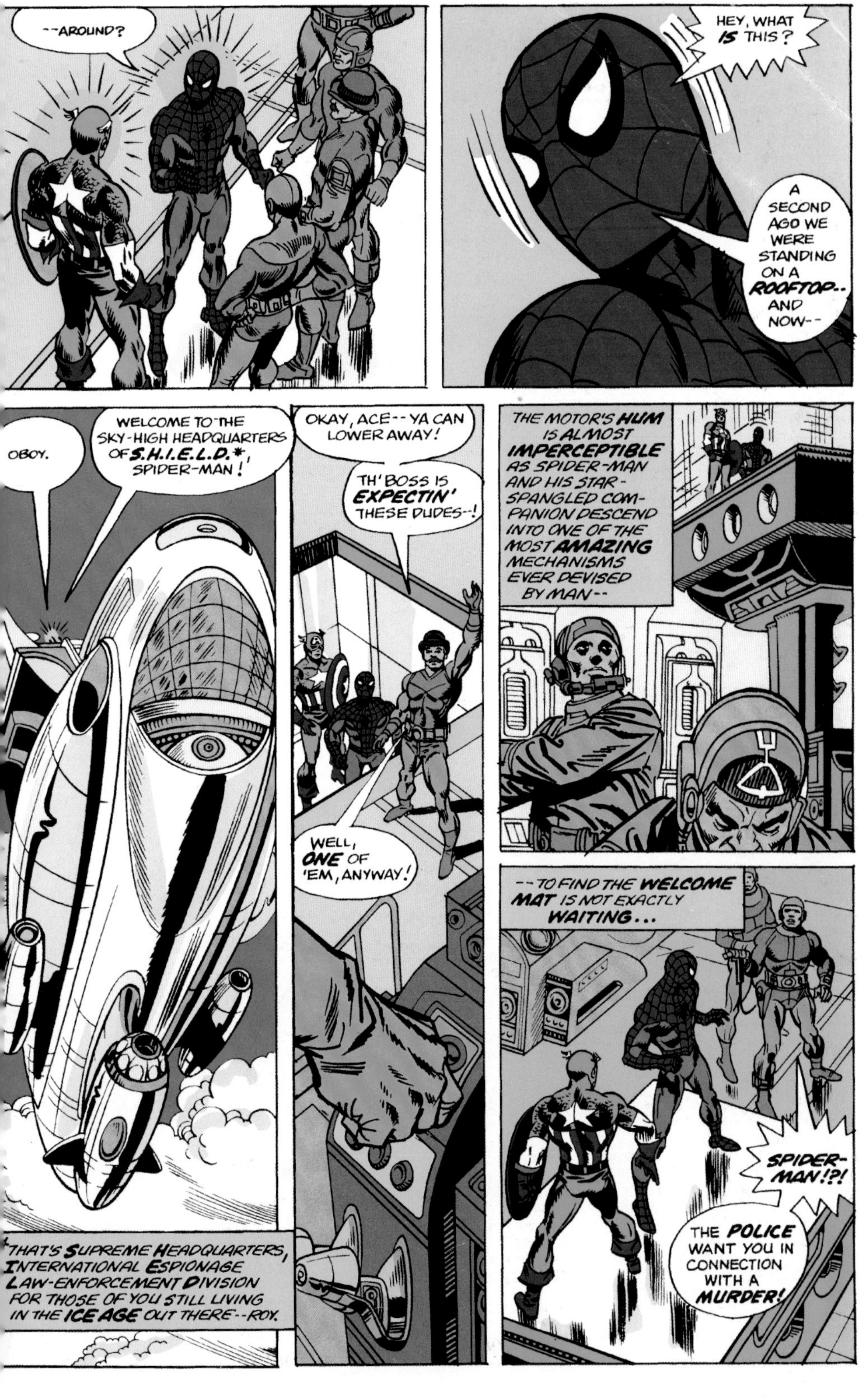

--AROUND?
HEY, WHAT IS THIS?
A SECOND AGO WE WERE STANDING ON A ROOFTOP-- AND NOW--
WELCOME TO THE SKY-HIGH HEADQUARTERS OF S.H.I.E.L.D.*, SPIDER-MAN!
OBOY.
*THAT'S SUPREME HEADQUARTERS, INTERNATIONAL ESPIONAGE LAW-ENFORCEMENT DIVISION FOR THOSE OF YOU STILL LIVING IN THE ICE AGE OUT THERE--ROY.
OKAY, ACE-- YA CAN LOWER AWAY!
TH' BOSS IS EXPECTIN' THESE DUDES--!
WELL, ONE OF 'EM, ANYWAY!
THE MOTOR'S HUM IS ALMOST IMPERCEPTIBLE AS SPIDER-MAN AND HIS STAR-SPANGLED COMPANION DESCEND INTO ONE OF THE MOST AMAZING MECHANISMS EVER DEVISED BY MAN--
--TO FIND THE WELCOME MAT IS NOT EXACTLY WAITING...
SPIDER-MAN!?!
THE POLICE WANT YOU IN CONNECTION WITH A MURDER!

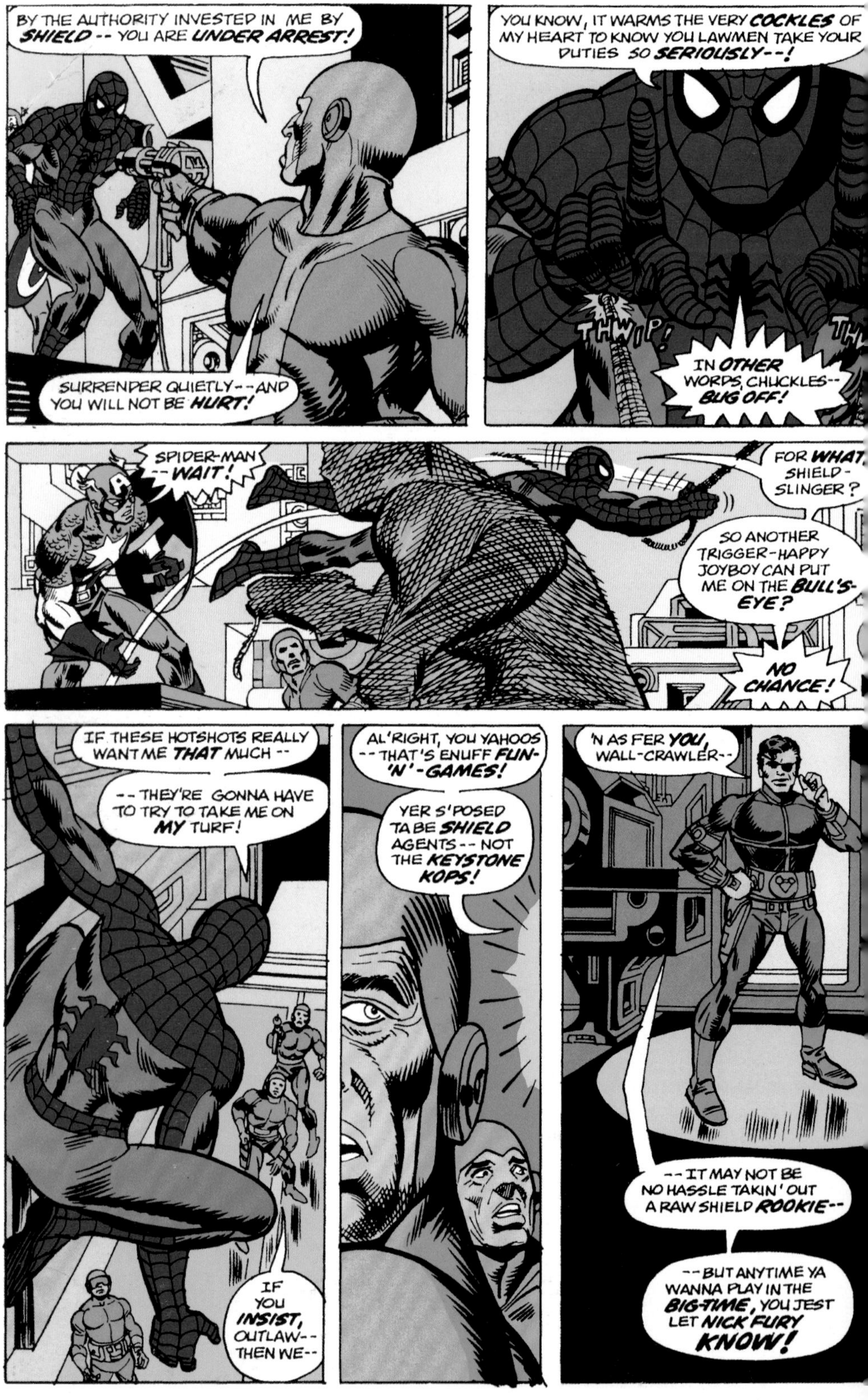
BY THE AUTHORITY INVESTED IN ME BY SHIELD -- YOU ARE UNDER ARREST!
SURRENDER QUIETLY--AND YOU WILL NOT BE HURT!
YOU KNOW, IT WARMS THE VERY COCKLES OF MY HEART TO KNOW YOU LAWMEN TAKE YOUR DUTIES SO SERIOUSLY--!
THWIP!
IN OTHER WORDS, CHUCKLES-- BUG OFF!
SPIDER-MAN --WAIT!
FOR WHAT, SHIELD-SLINGER?
SO ANOTHER TRIGGER-HAPPY JOYBOY CAN PUT ME ON THE BULL'S-EYE?
NO CHANCE!
IF THESE HOTSHOTS REALLY WANT ME THAT MUCH --
-- THEY'RE GONNA HAVE TO TRY TO TAKE ME ON MY TURF!
IF YOU INSIST, OUTLAW-- THEN WE--
AL'RIGHT, YOU YAHOOS -- THAT'S ENUFF FUN-'N'-GAMES!
YER S'POSED TA BE SHIELD AGENTS -- NOT THE KEYSTONE KOPS!
'N AS FER YOU, WALL-CRAWLER--
-- IT MAY NOT BE NO HASSLE TAKIN' OUT A RAW SHIELD ROOKIE--
--BUT ANYTIME YA WANNA PLAY IN THE BIG-TIME, YOU JEST LET NICK FURY KNOW!

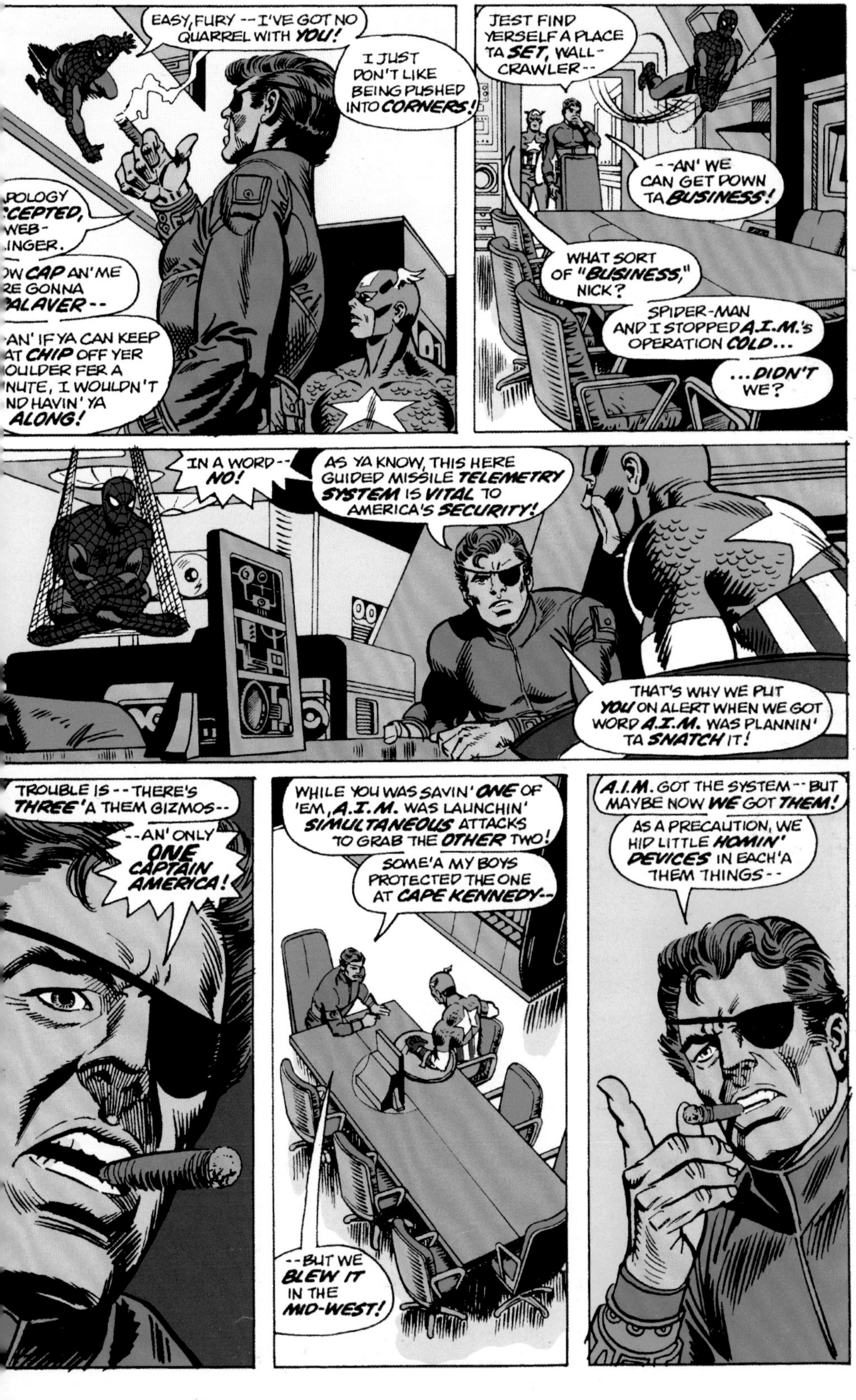
EASY, FURY -- I'VE GOT NO QUARREL WITH YOU!
I JUST DON'T LIKE BEING PUSHED INTO CORNERS!
POLOGY CEPTED, WEB- INGER.
W CAP AN' ME E GONNA ALAVER --
AN' IF YA CAN KEEP AT CHIP OFF YER OULDER FER A NUTE, I WOULDN'T ND HAVIN' YA ALONG!
JEST FIND YERSELF A PLACE TA SET, WALL-CRAWLER --
-- AN' WE CAN GET DOWN TA BUSINESS!
WHAT SORT OF "BUSINESS," NICK?
SPIDER-MAN AND I STOPPED A.I.M.'s OPERATION COLD...
...DIDN'T WE?
IN A WORD -- NO!
AS YA KNOW, THIS HERE GUIDED MISSILE TELEMETRY SYSTEM IS VITAL TO AMERICA'S SECURITY!
THAT'S WHY WE PUT YOU ON ALERT WHEN WE GOT WORD A.I.M. WAS PLANNIN' TA SNATCH IT!
TROUBLE IS -- THERE'S THREE 'A THEM GIZMOS --
-- AN' ONLY ONE CAPTAIN AMERICA!
WHILE YOU WAS SAVIN' ONE OF 'EM, A.I.M. WAS LAUNCHIN' SIMULTANEOUS ATTACKS TO GRAB THE OTHER TWO!
SOME'A MY BOYS PROTECTED THE ONE AT CAPE KENNEDY --
-- BUT WE BLEW IT IN THE MID-WEST!
A.I.M. GOT THE SYSTEM -- BUT MAYBE NOW WE GOT THEM!
AS A PRECAUTION, WE HID LITTLE HOMIN' DEVICES IN EACH'A THEM THINGS --

--AN' THE SYSTEM *A.I.M.* SWIPED IS HEADIN' STRAIGHT FER *NEW YORK*--

--*QUEENS*, TA BE EXACT!

WHICH IS WHERE *I* COME IN, RIGHT?

YOU *GUESSED* IT, CAP.

WE GOT THE GIZMO'S LOCATION *PIN-POINTED*--AN' IF YOU AN' THE WEB-SLINGER ARE *READY*, WE CAN--

WAITAMIN WHAT'S TH' "YOU AN' THE WEB SLINGER" JAZZ?

I DON'T REMEME *VOLUNTEE* FOR ANYTHIN

SORRY. I JEST SORT'A FIGURED YOU'D BE INTERESTED IN *PROTECTIN'* YER NATION'S *SECURITY*--

'COURSE-- IF YER TOO *CHICKEN*--!

LET US MERCIFULLY *TURN AWAY* FROM SPIDER-MAN'S REPLY--

--AND CAST OUR *GAZE* INSTEAD TO A QUIE CORNER OF *FLUSHING MEADOW PARK* THE BOROUGH OF QUEENS--

--WHERE, BENEATH THE AUSTER EXTERIOR OF THE OLD *SCIENCE PAVILION* LEFT OVER FROM THE *'64 WORLD'S FAIR*--

--LURKS ONE OF THE MANY HIDDEN HEADQUARTERS OF THE ORGANIZATION KNOWN AS *A.I.M.**--

--AND AT THE MOMENT, THIS PARTICULAR H.Q. BOASTS THE PRESENCE OF A MOST *UNEXPECTE* GUEST--

--THE *GREY GARGOYLE!*

*THAT'S *ADVANCED IDEA MECHANICS* FOR YOU FEW UNIN-FORMED ICE-AGERS. --*RT.*

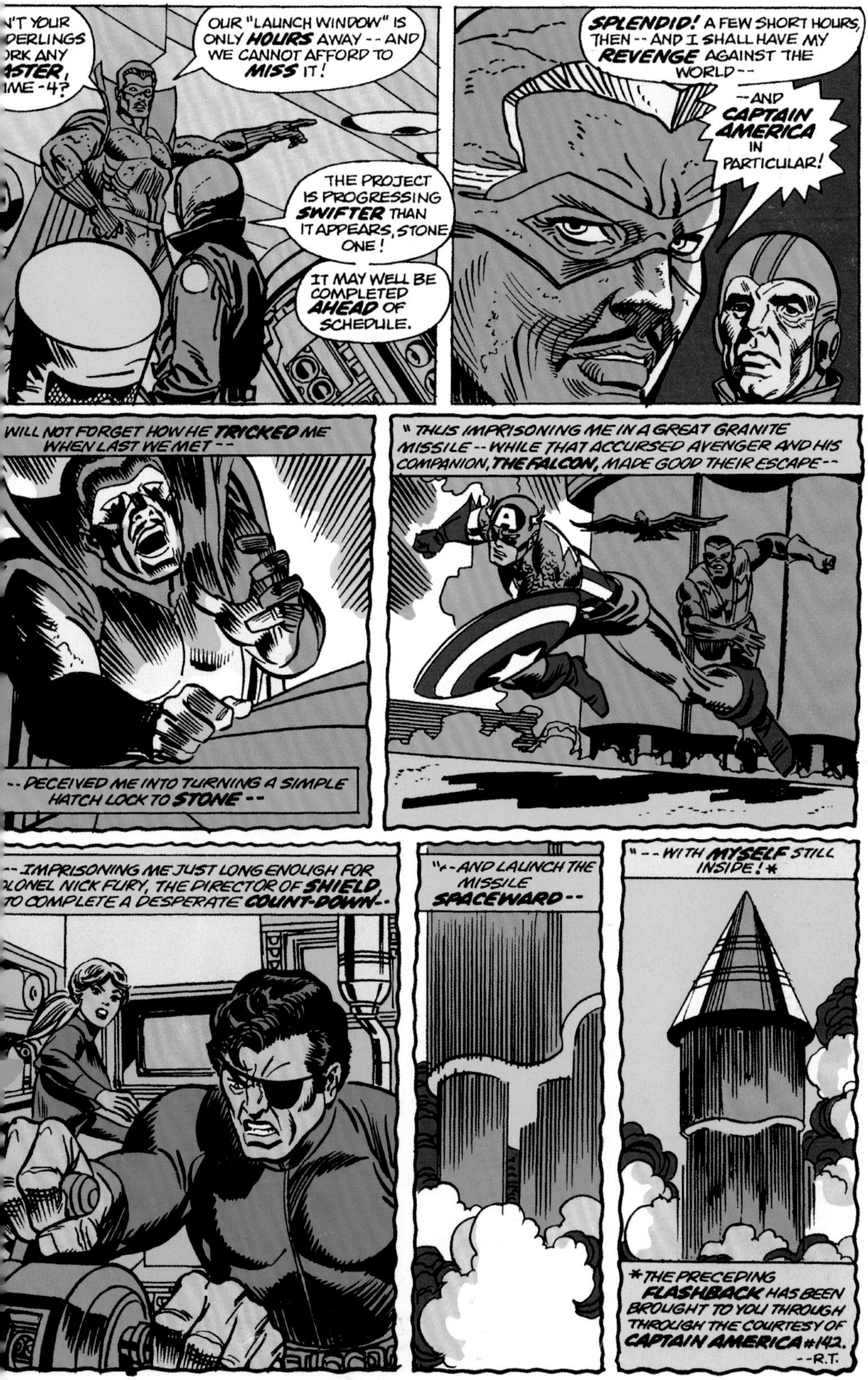

N'T YOUR
DERLINGS
ORK ANY
ASTER,
IME-4?
OUR "LAUNCH WINDOW" IS ONLY HOURS AWAY -- AND WE CANNOT AFFORD TO MISS IT!
THE PROJECT IS PROGRESSING SWIFTER THAN IT APPEARS, STONE ONE!
IT MAY WELL BE COMPLETED AHEAD OF SCHEDULE.
SPLENDID! A FEW SHORT HOURS, THEN -- AND I SHALL HAVE MY REVENGE AGAINST THE WORLD--
--AND CAPTAIN AMERICA IN PARTICULAR!
WILL NOT FORGET HOW HE TRICKED ME WHEN LAST WE MET--
-- DECEIVED ME INTO TURNING A SIMPLE HATCH LOCK TO STONE--
"THUS IMPRISONING ME IN A GREAT GRANITE MISSILE -- WHILE THAT ACCURSED AVENGER AND HIS COMPANION, THE FALCON, MADE GOOD THEIR ESCAPE--
--IMPRISONING ME JUST LONG ENOUGH FOR
OLONEL NICK FURY, THE DIRECTOR OF SHIELD,
TO COMPLETE A DESPERATE COUNT-DOWN--
"--AND LAUNCH THE MISSILE SPACEWARD--
"--WITH MYSELF STILL INSIDE!*
*THE PRECEDING FLASHBACK HAS BEEN BROUGHT TO YOU THROUGH THROUGH THE COURTESY OF CAPTAIN AMERICA #142. --R.T.

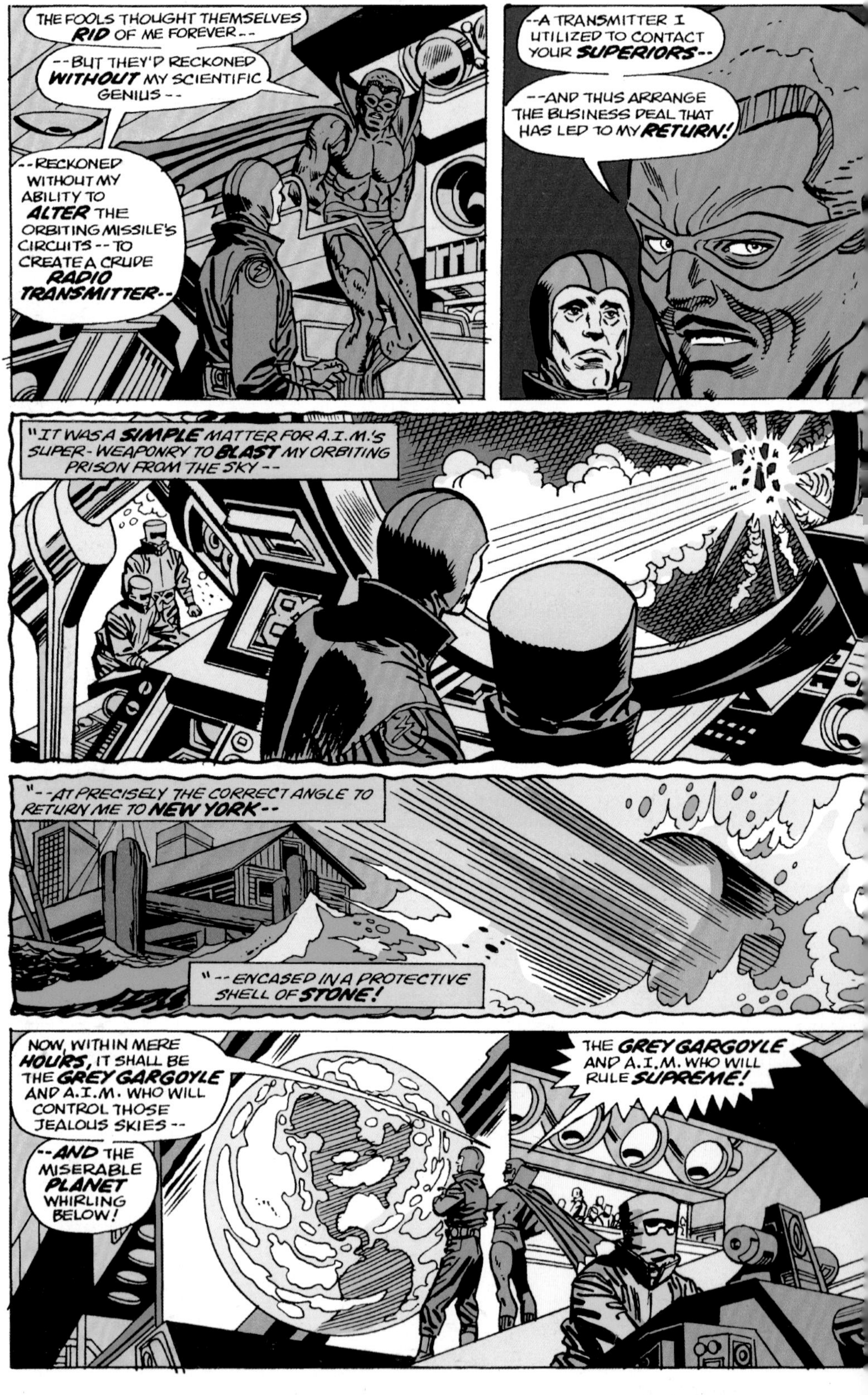
THE FOOLS THOUGHT THEMSELVES RID OF ME FOREVER--
--BUT THEY'D RECKONED WITHOUT MY SCIENTIFIC GENIUS--
--RECKONED WITHOUT MY ABILITY TO ALTER THE ORBITING MISSILE'S CIRCUITS--TO CREATE A CRUDE RADIO TRANSMITTER--
--A TRANSMITTER I UTILIZED TO CONTACT YOUR SUPERIORS--
--AND THUS ARRANGE THE BUSINESS DEAL THAT HAS LED TO MY RETURN!
"IT WAS A SIMPLE MATTER FOR A.I.M.'S SUPER-WEAPONRY TO BLAST MY ORBITING PRISON FROM THE SKY--
"--AT PRECISELY THE CORRECT ANGLE TO RETURN ME TO NEW YORK--
"--ENCASED IN A PROTECTIVE SHELL OF STONE!
NOW, WITHIN MERE HOURS, IT SHALL BE THE GREY GARGOYLE AND A.I.M. WHO WILL CONTROL THOSE JEALOUS SKIES--
--AND THE MISERABLE PLANET WHIRLING BELOW!
THE GREY GARGOYLE AND A.I.M. WHO WILL RULE SUPREME!

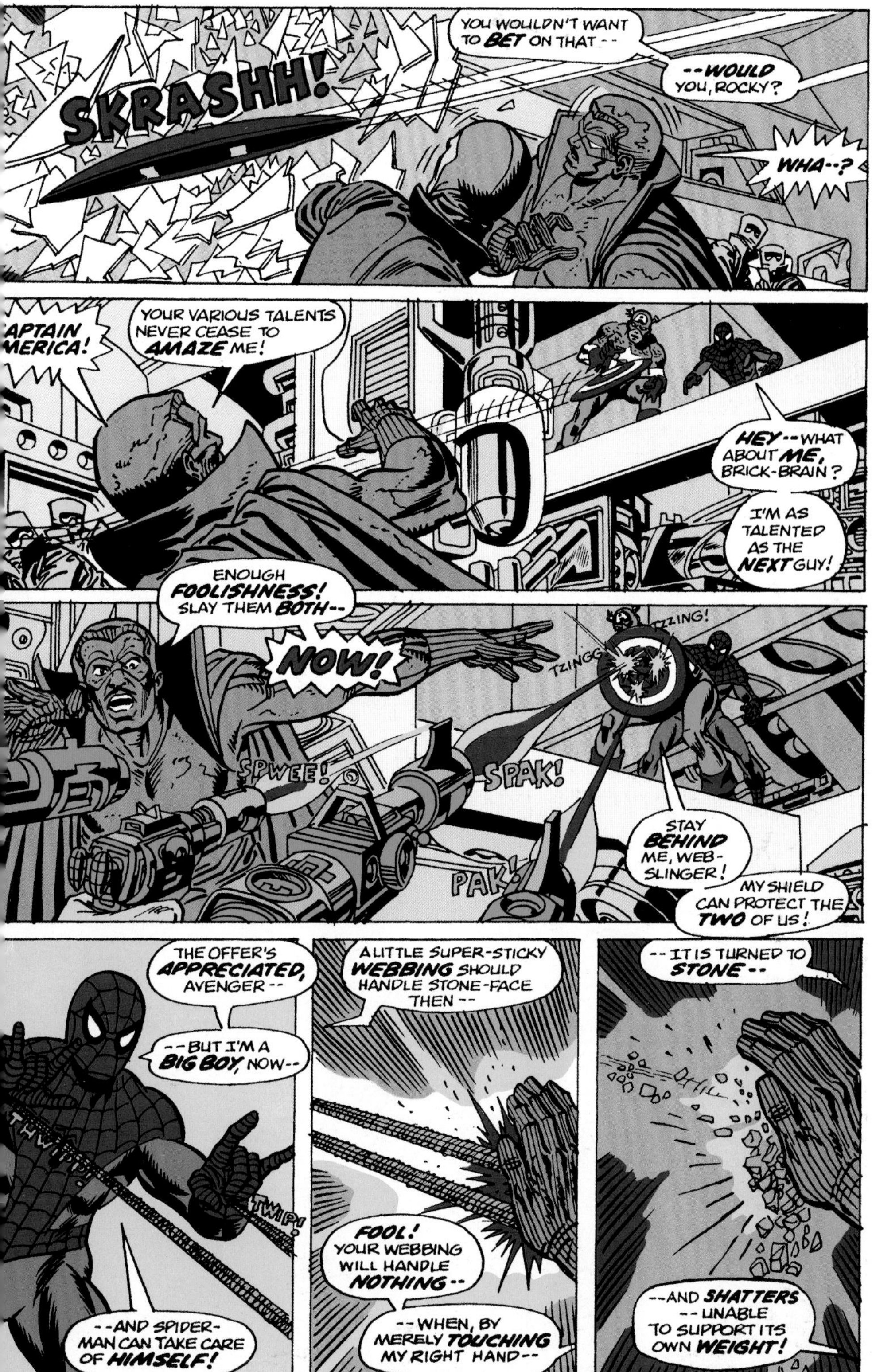
SKRASHH!
YOU WOULDN'T WANT TO BET ON THAT --
--WOULD YOU, ROCKY?
WHA--?
CAPTAIN AMERICA!
YOUR VARIOUS TALENTS NEVER CEASE TO AMAZE ME!
HEY--WHAT ABOUT ME, BRICK-BRAIN?
I'M AS TALENTED AS THE NEXT GUY!
ENOUGH FOOLISHNESS! SLAY THEM BOTH--
NOW!
TZINGG!
TZZING!
SPWEE!
SPAK!
PAK!
STAY BEHIND ME, WEB-SLINGER!
MY SHIELD CAN PROTECT THE TWO OF US!
THE OFFER'S APPRECIATED, AVENGER--
--BUT I'M A BIG BOY, NOW--
THWIP!
TWIP!
--AND SPIDER-MAN CAN TAKE CARE OF HIMSELF!
A LITTLE SUPER-STICKY WEBBING SHOULD HANDLE STONE-FACE THEN--
FOOL! YOUR WEBBING WILL HANDLE NOTHING--
--WHEN, BY MERELY TOUCHING MY RIGHT HAND--
--IT IS TURNED TO STONE--
--AND SHATTERS --UNABLE TO SUPPORT ITS OWN WEIGHT!

NICE *TRY*, WEB-HEAD -- BUT YOU'D BEST LEAVE THE *GARGOYLE* TO *ME!*

HE AND I HAVE TANGLED A TIME OR TWO *BEFORE!*

THEN BE MY *GUEST*, CAP! I WOULDN'T WANNA *DENY* A MAN HIS SIMPLE *PLEASURES!*

I'LL FIND SOMETHING *ELSE* TO KEEP ME BUSY!

ALL RIGHT, GARGOYLE -- YOU MAY HAVE ESCAPED YOUR ORBITING *PRISON* --

--BUT YOU *WON'T ESCAPE ME* --

-- NOT *THIS* TIME!

BUT I HAVE NO *INTENTION* OF ESCAPING YOU, CAPTAIN --

-- I'M PLANNING TO *DESTROY* YOU!

WITH THE TOUCH OF MY RIGHT HAND, I'LL TURN YOU TO *STONE* --

-- THEN *SHATTER* YOU TO BITS!

SO WE'LL HAVE TO MAKE CERTAIN YOU DON'T *TOUCH* ME THEN --

--*WON'T* WE?

HUH?

THRASSHH!

NO -- KICKED HIM INTO AN *EQUIPMENT BANK* --

-- *LIVE WIRES* FLYING AROUND *EVERYWHERE* --!

GOT TO LEAP O OF THEIR *PA?* OR THEY'LL --

AARRGG!

SKIZZAATT!

UH-OH -- THAT CABLE PUT CAP OUT *COLD!*

BETTER GE HIM TO *SAFE* BEFORE HE'S

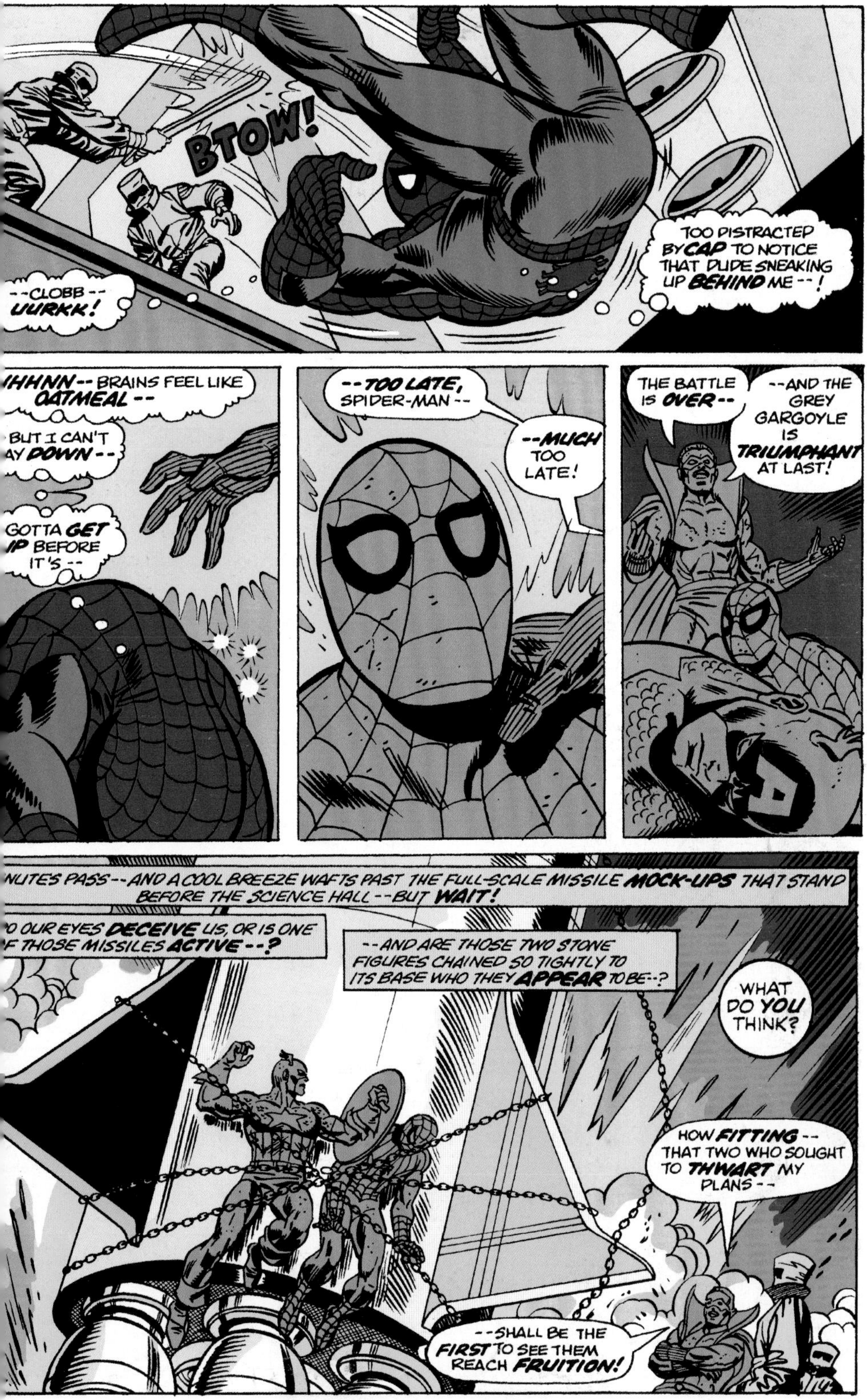
BTOW!
--CLOBB-- UURKK!
TOO DISTRACTED BY CAP TO NOTICE THAT DUDE SNEAKING UP BEHIND ME--!
HHNN-- BRAINS FEEL LIKE OATMEAL--
BUT I CAN'T AY DOWN--
GOTTA GET IP BEFORE IT'S--
--TOO LATE, SPIDER-MAN--
--MUCH TOO LATE!
THE BATTLE IS OVER--
--AND THE GREY GARGOYLE IS TRIUMPHANT AT LAST!
NUTES PASS--AND A COOL BREEZE WAFTS PAST THE FULL-SCALE MISSILE MOCK-UPS THAT STAND BEFORE THE SCIENCE HALL--BUT WAIT!
O OUR EYES DECEIVE US, OR IS ONE F THOSE MISSILES ACTIVE--?
--AND ARE THOSE TWO STONE FIGURES CHAINED SO TIGHTLY TO ITS BASE WHO THEY APPEAR TO BE--?
WHAT DO YOU THINK?
HOW FITTING-- THAT TWO WHO SOUGHT TO THWART MY PLANS--
--SHALL BE THE FIRST TO SEE THEM REACH FRUITION!

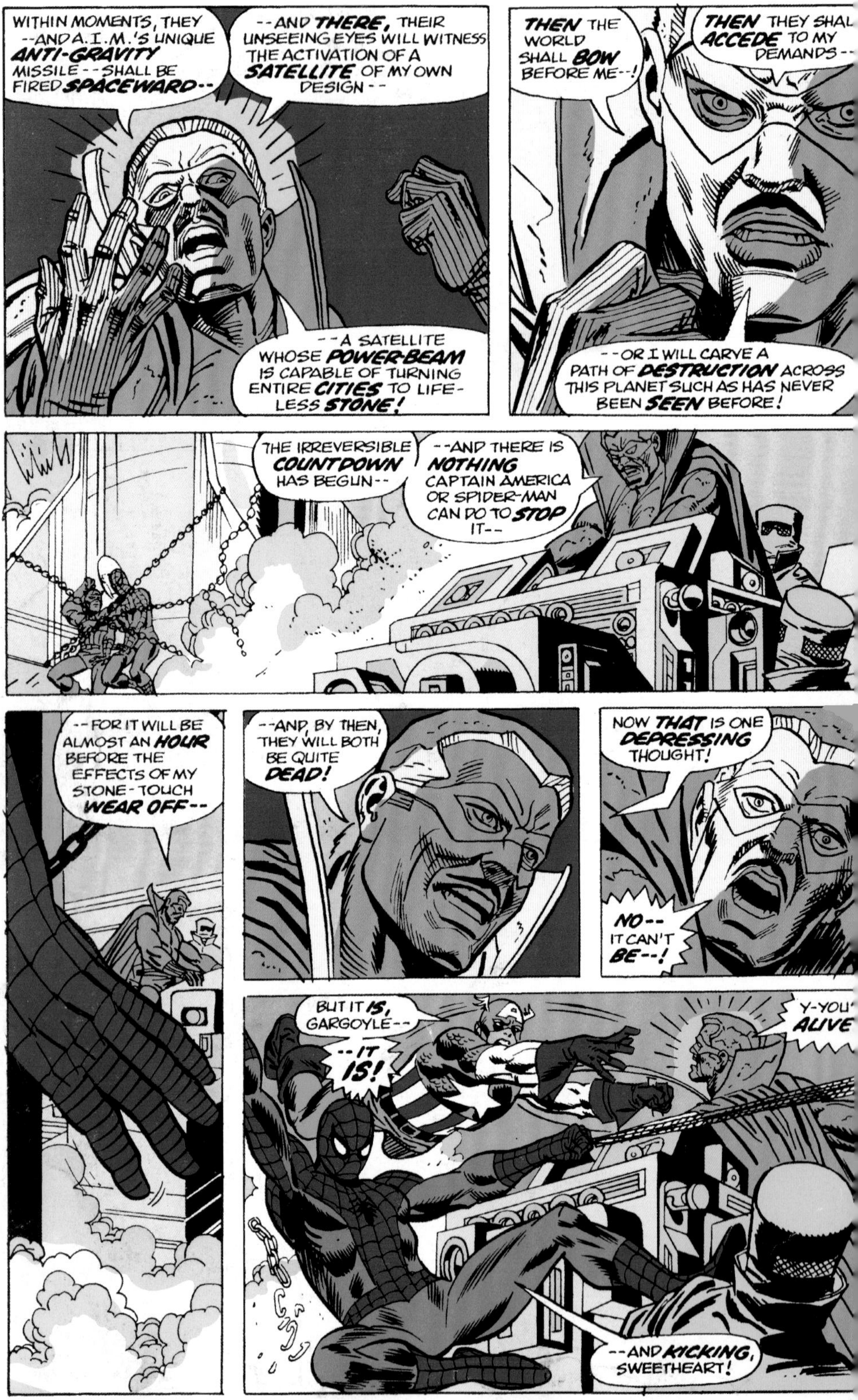
WITHIN MOMENTS, THEY --AND A.I.M.'S UNIQUE ANTI-GRAVITY MISSILE--SHALL BE FIRED SPACEWARD--
--AND THERE, THEIR UNSEEING EYES WILL WITNESS THE ACTIVATION OF A SATELLITE OF MY OWN DESIGN--
--A SATELLITE WHOSE POWER-BEAM IS CAPABLE OF TURNING ENTIRE CITIES TO LIFE-LESS STONE!
THEN THE WORLD SHALL BOW BEFORE ME--!
THEN THEY SHAL ACCEDE TO MY DEMANDS--
--OR I WILL CARVE A PATH OF DESTRUCTION ACROSS THIS PLANET SUCH AS HAS NEVER BEEN SEEN BEFORE!
THE IRREVERSIBLE COUNTDOWN HAS BEGUN--
--AND THERE IS NOTHING CAPTAIN AMERICA OR SPIDER-MAN CAN DO TO STOP IT--
--FOR IT WILL BE ALMOST AN HOUR BEFORE THE EFFECTS OF MY STONE-TOUCH WEAR OFF--
--AND, BY THEN, THEY WILL BOTH BE QUITE DEAD!
NOW THAT IS ONE DEPRESSING THOUGHT!
NO-- IT CAN'T BE--!
BUT IT IS, GARGOYLE--
--IT IS!
Y-YOU' ALIVE
--AND KICKING, SWEETHEART!

IMPOSSIBLE! MY TOUCH OF STONE HAS NEVER FAILED BEFORE!

IT DID THIS TIME! PERHAPS THE UNIQUE VENOM THE VIPER INJECTED ME WITH * HAD SOMETHING TO DO WITH IT--!

HEAVEN ONLY KNOWS WHAT SAVED SPIDER-MAN--!

AS SEEN IN CAPTAIN AMERICA 157, TRUE BELIEVER. THAT'S WHAT GAVE CAP HIS NEW-FOUND SUPER-STRENGTH.-- RT.

STILL, I DON'T HAVE TIME RIGHT NOW TO PUZZLE OUT THE ANSWERS FOR CERTAIN!

GOT TO GET THE GARGOYLE AWAY FROM THE CONTROL PANEL--OR ELSE!

STAR-SPANGLED FOOL! SUCH A SIMPLE FALL CANNOT HARM A BEING MADE OF RAW STONE!

THRAMM!

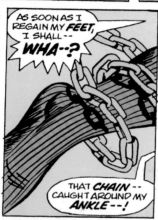

AS SOON AS I REGAIN MY FEET, I SHALL--

WHA--?

THAT CHAIN -- CAUGHT AROUND MY ANKLE--!

STOP THE COUNTDOWN!

IN PITY'S NAME -- STOP THE COUNTDOWN!!

THEN, THE GROUND SHUDDERS-- SHAKES -- AS A GREAT, STEAMING SPIRE ERUPTS SKYWARD--

--ITS SAVAGE ROAR DROWNING OUT THE SCREAMS OF A ROUGH-HEWN GREY FIGURE WHO VANISHES WITH IT INTO THE VOID...

THE GARGOYLE IS GONE -- VICTIM OF THE FATE HE INTENDED FOR US!

AND IT COULDN'T HAVE HAPPENED TO A NICER GUY!

WELL, CAP, IT'S GETTING LATE -- AND EVEN A SPIDER NEEDS HIS REST!

KEEP YOUR SHIELD SHINY, HERO! I'LL SEE YOU AROUND!

NEXT: THE SAVAGE SUB-MARINER!

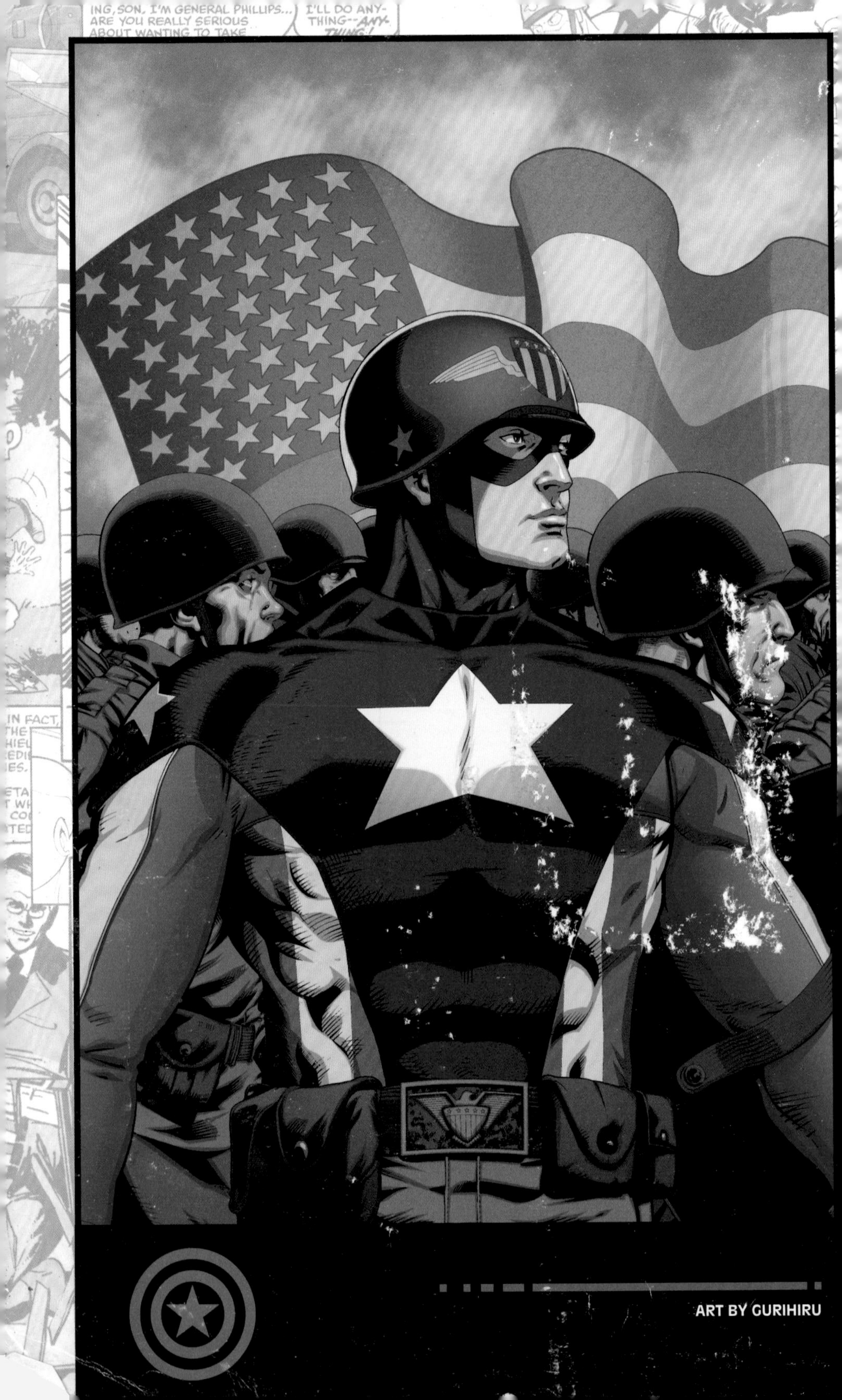
ING, SON, I'M GENERAL PHILLIPS... ARE YOU REALLY SERIOUS ABOUT WANTING TO TAKE
I'LL DO ANY-THING--ANY-THING!

ART BY GURIHIRU